THE
THROWAWAY

THE
THROWAWAY

MICHAEL MORECI

A TOM DOHERTY ASSOCIATES BOOK · NEW YORK

THE THROWAWAY

A Forge Book
Published by Tom Doherty Associates
175 Fifth Avenue
New York, NY 10010

www.tor-forge.com

Forge® is a registered trademark of Macmillan Publishing Group, LLC.

The Library of Congress Cataloging-in-Publication Data is available upon request.

ISBN 978-1-250-06501-8 (hardcover)
ISBN 978-1-4668-7150-2 (ebook)

Our books may be purchased in bulk for promotional, educational, or business use. Please contact your local bookseller or the Macmillan Corporate and Premium Sales Department at 1-800-221-7945, extension 5442, or by email at MacmillanSpecialMarkets@macmillan.com.

First Edition: June 2018

Printed in the United States of America

0 9 8 7 6 5 4 3 2 1

PART ONE

1

Gregori watched as the American disembarked the plane onto the tarmac, wondering if the handcuffs were necessary. Ultimately, it didn't matter. He took a long drag of his unfiltered cigarette and watched the man walk with a hobbled gait that was almost like an affectation.

Then, the American stopped. He was lined up in a neat row alongside the other two captives—trained FSB spies. A searchlight lit up the area, revealing specks of fluttering dust hovering throughout the beam's circumference. There were two sides: Americans holding Russians on one side, Russians holding Americans on the other. No one spoke. The Russian and American intelligence officers mirrored one another, men and women who had devoted their lives to warfare of the mind. Information gathering, identity assimilation, normalized paranoia—all part of the game. As one of Russia's oldest still-active handlers of intelligence assets, Gregori knew it all quite well.

With a subtle nod from the old spy, a trio of young and eager Russian SVR officers marched their American prisoners a few steps forward. Two spies: one female, one male. They were well kept, clean, healthy. These weren't the old days, Gregori acknowledged, where wrecking the psyche of a captured spy and sending home his husk was expected. Friends are enemies, enemies friends, and delicate politics held sway. Russia and America maintained a cautious relationship, though it was a relationship poised on the edge of a razor. Spying on your allies was more vital than ever, Gregori realized. That's just how things were.

A voice called out from the other side, in English. "Bring our operatives out to the center, and we will meet you there for the exchange."

Gregori hesitated. He remembered similar trades in the dead of cold, dark nights, over the Wall. He remembered the palpable unease of never knowing what to expect, what could happen. Sabotage. Brainwashing. Spies killing their own handlers. He remembered the fear and still saw its echoes everywhere around him. The young men and women in his field, they thought him paranoid and out-of-touch. But the experienced handler knew, no matter what, in this game you can never harbor too much suspicion.

"Send out the girl," Gregori called. "She and I will speak first."

There was silence from the other side. Then he heard murmurs before catching the elongated shadow of the lone female agent as she strode forward.

Ania. Young and attractive, purposefully so. She was meant to be a distraction, and she had performed her duty as expected. Gregori didn't know her well; they had only met a few times before she was sent to the States. He observed her often, in training, knowing that she compartmentalized him as just another leering old man, like the rest.

Gregori greeted her tersely in their native tongue; he could feel the sniper's sights set on him. "How is the American?" he asked.

"What do you mean?"

"Did they get to him? If he's been made to work against us, I need to know."

Ania glanced over her shoulder, at the other side. She turned back. "He hardly knows where he is or what's happening. He got aggressive on the plane, physical, and had to be . . . restrained." Gregori caught the flash of regret on her face. "Is he the kind of threat that you mean? No, I don't think so."

"Don't 'think'?"

Ania inhaled deep, inflating her confidence. "He's not a threat."

"And you? Did you get comfortable living in the United States?"

"I remain true to my service and my country."

Gregori nodded, ending the conversation. Ania was left to stand by the aging handler's side as he took his time making his next move. After a long silence that was finally broken by a grumbling in Gregori's throat, he spoke. Only it wasn't to her; it was to the other side.

"We will make the exchange now," he declared.

The SVR officers brought the two captured American spies forward, their PP-19s trained on them both. The remaining Russian captives from the other side began their walk over, but the American fought.

The handcuffed prisoner, the centerpiece of this exchange, resisted. It took three men in dark suits to half push, half haul the man forward. It surprised Gregori to see so much fight in the American. After all, there was no one here to convince of his innocence, no one of consequence who could deliver him back into his life as Mark Strain, Washington, D.C., lobbyist. And should he escape, he'd be a known traitor—a terrorist—trapped in a foreign country without so much as a library card. It was futile, all his struggling, yet Gregori admired his tenacity.

The SVR officers shoved their prisoners forward, and the Americans did the same. When he got close enough, the SVR officers took hold of the handcuffed American and Gregori got a good look at him as he passed. His face was absolute hell—manic, disheveled, disoriented. It would be hard to get him to understand the importance of his cooperation while in this frenzied state. His people should have taken better care of him on the flight over, soothed him, but now it was Gregori's burden to get him cleaned up. He was never good at playing the role of the comforting ally; he liked his interrogations to be straightforward, clean. Illustrate the two options available—talk or be forced to talk— and allow the prisoner to choose one.

The American had an impressive physique. He was using his physicality, now, to fight back with everything he had as the suits passed him over to the three SVR officers. With only steps to go before boarding the Russian luxury jet, Gregori imagined that the reality of the American's situation was starting to truly sink in.

"Hey!" the American yelled, addressing Gregori. "Hey! You—tell them! Tell them I don't belong here, tell them this is a mistake!"

The American wiggled an arm free, enough to deliver an elbow to the lower abdomen of one of the SVR officers. In that quick moment, with the officer doubled over, the American frantically grabbed his weapon and pried it from his hands. He trained the gun, immediately, on Gregori. *Smart,* the handler thought. *He knows who's in charge.*

"Let. Me. Go." The American, panting with rage, spoke through bared teeth, ignoring the screams from the other two SVR officers who were ready to shoot him. The handler wondered what the CIA agents watching this scene must think. Would they suspect?

"You won't shoot," Gregori said.

"Like hell I won't," the American hissed.

"You won't shoot because after you fire the first bullet, we'll fire the second, and it will be aimed directly at you. And the third? The third goes directly into *her.*"

The American turned just as one of the officers trained his gun directly on Ania's head. Though to the American, she wasn't

Ania; she was Alice, the woman he thought of as his friend. She was frozen in place, terrified. As betrayed as the American must have felt, as angry and confused, he couldn't want the girl to die, nor would he want to be responsible for her death. But the American was smart—smart enough to call Gregori's bluff.

"Go ahead," the American taunted. "Do it. In fact, kill her now. I couldn't care less."

Gregori revealed a devilish smile. "No loyalty between comrades? Fine. Then what about the woman you call your wife? What if we paid Sarah a visit?"

The American's face went flush with rage.

"Oh, we won't kill her. But we will make her life very . . . difficult."

The American's breathing eased; he was coming to his senses. Gregori knew he wanted to shoot, but the American was smarter than that. He knew it would only make things worse.

The American lowered his gun; the second his elbows slackened, the butt of an automatic rifle cracked the back of his head. He fell to the ground but was still conscious; two SVR officers hoisted him beneath his shoulders and dragged him toward the plane. "Now, let's see how long it takes you to learn how to avoid such discomfort in the future," Gregori said as he watched the American get shuttled up the jet's gangway. There was no resistance, not anymore.

Inside the jet, the returning Russian spies—Ania and her counterpart, Viktor—toasted vodka to their completed mission. The mission itself was a failure, but that was the point—something Gregori had to remind himself of. Always the bigger picture, that's what mattered. Some spies couldn't learn that, though. Spies like Viktor. Gregori watched him toss one shot of liquor into his mouth, then another; he noticed the white-knuckle grip he

had on the vodka bottle. If he clenched any tighter, Gregori esti-
mated, the bottle would smash in his fist. Too much emotion, not
enough control. It was a combination that never boded well for
people who were supposed to be equipped to lose themselves in
their assignments. To not question orders. To not, under any circumstance, take things personally.

Reconditioning was in order, and Gregori wondered if
he'd misplaced his trust in Viktor and the plans he had in mind
for him.

The handler's thoughts on Viktor were cut short by the sound
of SVR officers shouting and pointing their machine guns at the
American. The stubborn fool had apparently regained his vigor
and was trying to fight his way to the front of the plane. Gregori
wasn't surprised by his motivation for doing so.

"You lied to me!" the American yelled. "We were friends, and
you were lying the entire time!"

Ania, next to Gregori, hung her head and looked away from
the American. Her eyes glistened. Was this entire generation of
agents completely unequipped to divorce themselves from their
missions? Gregori wondered, disdainfully.

The American continued his verbal thrashing, but with a trio
of automatic rifles pointed at his chest, he kept control of his
outburst.

"Idiots," Gregori rumbled at the guards as he stepped between
them and the American, shoving their gun barrels down. "Go,
have a drink. Leave this one to me."

Gregori was exhausted by the amateurs he was surrounded
by, and that was before the American had shoved his way past
him and stormed the front of the plane. He thought the American was smarter than this; apparently, he misjudged him. Before
Gregori could turn to prevent the American from accosting an
FSB spy, he heard him cough out a choking gasp.

With a suffocating grip around his neck, Viktor had the

American lifted three inches off the ground. Desperately, the American tried to wrench free of Viktor's grasp, but the muscular Russian spy was impossible to overpower.

"I wasted two years of my *life* for *you*," Viktor snarled as beads of sweat rolled off his bald scalp. "You've served your purpose— time to die."

"Viktor, no!" Ania shouted, pulling at Viktor's arm.

Contesting Viktor physically—who was a head taller than Gregori with broad shoulders that framed his physique—was futile. Instead, Gregori relieved an SVR agent of his rifle and poked its barrel into Viktor's back.

"His life is not in your hands," Gregori coolly explained. "Let him go. Immediately."

"I should have been performing real service for my country," Viktor growled. "Instead, I was nothing but a decoy. And for *what*?"

The American's face began to turn blue.

"You've been given an order. Disobey me and I will shoot." Gregori dug the barrel into Viktor's back.

Viktor gazed back at Gregori, then shifted his focus back to the American. He snarled something in Russian, then loosened his grip on the man's throat. The American dropped to the floor, gasping for air.

"I'm owed for this assignment. I hope you and the Kremlin have taken careful note."

"You're owed *nothing*," Gregori said, shoving Viktor out of his way as he walked toward the American. "Don't make me question your loyalty or your motivations."

Gregori tried helping the American to his feet, but he proved more resilient than expected; by the time Gregori laid a hand on him, the American was rocketing back up, throwing his momentum at Viktor. He landed a right across against Viktor's cheek, sending him tumbling backward.

"Never . . ." the American huffed, "never touch me again."

Gregori held a stiff arm toward Viktor, holding him back. "Don't," he ordered and, this time, the burly Russian obeyed. Then, Gregori turned to the American, staring him down, until the other man finally shuffled to the back of the plane and sat heavily in his seat.

"What am I doing here?" the American asked once Gregori was standing above him. "What do you *want*?"

So many questions. It was to be expected. Gregori breathed deep, then turned back to look at the celebration that was getting started at the front of the plane. Viktor was rubbing his jaw, but the vodka filled his mouth all the same; he wouldn't be a problem. Alone, Gregori turned his attention back to the American, whose resolve was softening. He was disoriented, dazed. He'd seen that look in the faces of tortured prisoners. It repulsed him.

Gregori took the seat opposite the American. He pulled a bottle of whiskey from an old canvas bag and poured two glasses, passing one to the American. "You are not a spy, we both know this. But, you are also not important to us. Not in the way you might think. You are just . . . incidental."

"Are you going to kill me?"

The whiskey was warm going down Gregori's throat. It felt good, that small indulgence he allowed himself, just enough to satisfy his need to occasionally feel at ease. "We need you. The public thinks, and must always think, that you are a loyalist, a true Russian hero. We require that you not betray their trust."

"No," the American said. "I won't. You can't expect me to just forget my life, to abandon who I am. I have to get back home. My wife—"

"Yes, your wife. And your unborn child. If you want to keep them safe, comply."

The American looked away, wincing at Gregori's words. He needed to understand there was real punishment for anything less than complete obedience, and it was good that the American was starting to see that.

"So what happens? You get what you want and I just . . . what, hope that one day you reunite me with my family? That's not much of a deal."

Gregori rubbed his hand over his face. If only this arrogant young American knew, given the other possible outcomes, how fortunate he was. He leaned back in his chair and looked away, swirling his drink.

"Many years ago, when I was a young man like yourself, I, too, was captive somewhere I did not want to be. I was a young intelligence officer then, still very much active in the field. We were at war with Chechnya, winning at the time. We had taken Grozny, but still there were many rebels who opposed our occupation.

"Now, let me tell you something about the word 'rebel.' You hear it and you think of some sort of organized militia, strong men with guns who can fight. No. Most of the time, rebels . . . rebels are prisoners fighting for their freedom. Poor people with no leaders or training. Just desperation."

Gregori paused to finish his whiskey, then poured another. He motioned for the American, who hadn't moved, to drink up. Reluctantly, the man took a sip, which led to a longer drink.

"The rebels were many in the early days. So many that I couldn't get out of the city safely. So I had to wait—and, you see, I had to be of use as well. These were the Soviet days, and the military insisted on everyone contributing their share. I had to acquire information. But this was a war zone, and the military's tactics were . . . different than my own. They gave me a bag of rusty tools. Pliers. A screwdriver. A hammer. When rebels were captured, they were brought to me.

"This bag," Gregori said, motioning to the canvas one beneath his feet, "has stayed with me a long time. Always reminding me of how . . . *dark* things can get. The days were so long, and brutal, and relentless. But I did what was required of me, and I am still alive because of it."

"That story—it's supposed to make me trust you?"

"The Americans discarded you. Your government deported you without due process, believing you to be an enemy combatant. Now," Gregori said as he reached into his bag and pulled out a passport, "you have two choices. You can take this passport and act as if you've never seen it before—act like a stranger in the place you are going. Or, you accept it as your identification being returned to you upon completion of your dutiful service."

The American looked at the passport. The name, printed in heavy black typewriter ink, read "Pyotr Dvanisch." He blinked, and the words began to blur. Gregori could tell the drug that laced his glass was beginning to kick in.

The American slumped forward. Gregori put out a hand, preventing him from falling off his chair.

"Things can get dark for you, too. In ways that you do not want to experience. Make the right choice."

Gregori rested the American back, not knowing if his words had sunk in or not.

When the American awoke, he spotted Red Square outside his window, lit brilliantly in the night sky. Its magnificence dazzled him, but it also made him tremble. Because, looking at it, Mark Strain realized something:

He might never go home again.

2

Mark knew it was wrong to snoop on what his wife was looking at on the internet. But it was right there in front of him.

He was awake early, preparing for a run before he left for work; his shoes, keys, and gloves were all in the living room, scattered from one end to the next. As he reached across a dozing Sarah—who couldn't have been home for more than a half hour from her overnight shift at the hospital—he spotted her laptop screen out of the corner of his eye, glowing in the room's predawn darkness. Tabs were lined up in a neat row, a half dozen of them, their header text revealing addresses of properties on various real estate sites.

"Mmmm . . . ," Sarah murmured, starting to stir. "What are you doing?"

Mark took a quiet step back, having retrieved his gloves. "Shhhh, I'm just grabbing something. Go back to sleep."

"I wasn't sleeping," Sarah said, opening her eyes. "Just resting for a minute before I went to the bedroom. Are you going for a run?"

"Yeah," Mark said. "I couldn't sleep, so I figured I'd at least try to do something productive."

Sarah rose from the couch and greeted Mark with a peck on his cheek before looking right into his eyes. "You're worried about today."

"No, no. Not at all. I . . ." Mark got flustered, tripping over himself in a very uncommon fashion. His business was words, controlling conversations, convincing people to come to his side. Sarah was the only one, with her uncanny knack for understanding everything he was thinking and feeling—sometimes better than even Mark did—who could put him on his heels.

"And you saw my computer."

Mark opened his mouth. Nothing came out.

"Relax, I'm just looking. You don't need to have that panicked look on your face, even though—might I remind you—buying a house is a *good* thing. For both of us."

"I know, I know. It's just hard right now. I—" Mark paused, interrupted by his phone vibrating in his pocket. He quickly hit IGNORE. "With everything going on at work, moving out of D.C. is tough. I'm almost there. You know if I can just get this big one squared away, having a little separation won't matter as much. We can go to Virginia, the suburbs, whatever."

Mark moved in for a deeper kiss, but Sarah spun away toward the kitchen to get herself a glass of water. "You say that and I know—I *know*—you believe it. But this isn't the first deal you've made a promise on, Mr. Politician."

Mark gulped theatrically at being called the dreaded "P-word"—he was a lobbyist, a job with honor, not a pol spreading their legs for anyone with a slush fund. But it did actually sting, because he knew Sarah was right. He had promised for years to get them out of the apartment they'd outgrown two lease renewals ago and the neighborhood that had become noticeably younger and hipper than both of them. They passionately shared the dream of owning a home with a yard, a garage, a big kitchen, and room to grow. A place to raise a family. But being away from the center of the universe, not being able to get to K Street or the Capitol in five minutes, sitting in traffic on the

Beltway while some other gunner stole his lunch kept Mark up at night.

It was a crazy fear; he recognized that. Mark's colleagues often pointed out—with just a dash of irritation and heap of jealousy—how quickly Mark had ascended in his still-nascent career. But he wasn't satisfied. He wanted to believe the next deal was the *one*, but he knew he was barely fooling himself, let alone Sarah. Still, this particular deal was so high-profile in all the right areas—military, security—that he should be able to write his own ticket if he could bring it home. Maybe he really would be able to give the swamp a rest after that and give Sarah everything she'd been asking for.

"I really mean it this time, Sarah. But I thought we agreed to wait until you got off night shifts again anyway—"

Mark's phone buzzed again and, again, he ignored it. Two calls this early made him begin to feel a little uneasy.

"I was looking, that's all. I came home and needed to wind down, so I started poking around. Go for your run, we can talk later."

Sarah closed her laptop and shuffled off to the bedroom, clasping the back of her neck as she went. She was weary, physically drained from a long shift at George Washington, but Mark couldn't help but dig a little deeper. Never let an opening go by, the lawyer in him said. Even with your wife.

Especially with your wife.

As Sarah was entering the bedroom, he asked, "But why? Of all the things to do to unwind, why shop for real estate? That's what they made *Candy Crush* for."

Sarah laughed. "Right, like I don't see enough addicts at work." She gave Mark a wide, sunny smile. "I know you're not going to let this go, so for my own sake—and for the possibility of getting any rest today—I'll tell you why."

She took Mark's hand and pressed it to her belly. "You're really on the clock now, mister."

Mark felt everything inside him drop. "Wait . . ." His hand on Sarah's skin, he thought he sensed movement. Mark knew it was impossible, but still, touching Sarah's belly, knowing that his baby was in there—it was electric.

"Holy shit. You're pregnant? How?"

Sarah gently brought her hand to Mark's cheek and gave him a look of pitying mockery. "Oh, sweetie, you and your poor Catholic schooling. See, you take a man, then you take a woman—"

"Ha ha, hilarious. No, I mean, I thought we were being careful and . . . you know what, doesn't matter. You're pregnant!" Mark swooped Sarah off her feet and they kissed, smiling. He then put her down, as gently as a Fabergé egg, and took a big step back. "Whoa—sorry. Was that too much? Are you okay?"

Sarah playfully sighed. "You're *really* going to need to read the books."

Mark nodded, then he began to pace. "Wait, do your parents know? Do my parents know? We have so many people to call. And your job! You shouldn't be on your feet so much, not—"

Sarah grabbed hold of Mark, giving him the pause he needed. "Whoa, whoa, just slow down. Okay? Breathe. First, before we tell *anyone*, we need to get an ultrasound and make sure that, you know, everything is okay with the baby. I was waiting to tell you until I could get an appointment."

"What wouldn't be okay? What could be wrong?"

"Mark, breathing, remember? Right now, everything is fine. It's great. I've already talked to the doctor about my diet, about work, everything. We'll go see her next week."

Mark felt strange. He didn't know whether to laugh or to cry, but he knew his body was capable of either, or both at the same time. What mattered most, though, was how alive he felt. From the tips of his fingers to the tips of his toes, he could feel endorphins cycling through his body and lighting a fire to his spirit. It was the same feeling he got after pushing through a long run or closing a deal, only amplified to the umpteenth degree. Him—Mark Strain—a father. He was already loving the idea, even though it was still a little abstract.

Bolstered by excitement, fear, and joy, he felt ready for anything, yet completely unprepared for what came next.

"I can't believe this," Mark said. "This is . . . Sarah, I can't imagine being happier about anything. I love you, and I'm going to be here. I'll make some changes at work, I'll—"

Sarah laughed. "One thing at a time, we still have a long road ahead. For now, I have to get some rest. They aren't kidding when they say the first trimester wipes you out."

As they embraced, Mark knew he wasn't just going to win the day, he was going to slay whatever—and whoever—stood in his path. There was no stopping him, not now.

He kissed his wife all over her face and neck, even as she pushed him out of the bedroom. When the door shut, he closed his eyes, drinking in the moment. "A dad. A *dad*." He looked down at his phone: four missed calls, two voice mail messages, three emails.

It was 5:36 in the morning and his day had started running without him.

3

The District was still coming to life as Mark pushed through the light mist that glistened as it softly sprayed from the sky before smearing across his windshield. He raced toward his office, using every shortcut and side street he knew of in order to avoid the Beltway. He instructed Jenna, the office assistant, to do the same. It was still early but, with D.C.'s penchant for random traffic chaos, Mark sided with caution.

Jenna was waiting at the front door, without an umbrella, by the time Mark arrived. She was huddled so deep into the shelter of her fur-lined hood that Mark barely recognized her. Just her eyes and the tip of her nose were visible in the cave she'd withdrawn into. It was barely past 6 A.M., though. Nobody else was dedicated—or crazy—enough to stand in the rain and wait for Mark to arrive.

"I *hate* the rain," she said.

"What? It's the stuff of life," Mark said as he unlocked the front doors of their building, a modern-design edifice that looked like a cube made of glass. "It feeds our crops and nourishes our farms and all that."

Jenna groaned. "What are you so chipper about?"

"Huh?" Mark said, fumbling his keys out from the lock. "Nothing. Nothing at all."

Past the front door was a small security kiosk that was unattended until 7:00. While employees could hang out in the lobby and the atrium before that time, entering the building's individual offices, which were secured by an alarm, was a clear violation. Only building security, management, and top executives knew the code and protocol, and Mark's position didn't fall under any of these three categories. Nonetheless, he walked straight to the security kiosk and started entering in the code to disable the alarm.

"Ummmm," Jenna began, nervously. "Are you supposed to do that?"

Mark looked up, an expression of cavalier indifference on his face. "Do what?"

Mark led them to the elevator bank at a brisk pace, hurrying to their office on the fifteenth floor. Jenna was right there with him, and Mark took notice of her dedication. He liked Jenna, she had spunk and a whole lot of motivation. People in her position came and went all the time—their job was hard, thankless, and the pay was no solace for the amount of grief they had to deal with. Most assistants ended up back home with their parents within a year. It was rare to find one who saw the long game and its benefits; Jenna was one of those gems and, after this day was done, Mark would help her take the next step.

"So," Jenna asked. "How you holding up?"

Mark shrugged. "Well, I always knew Terrance was a slimy little shit. Now he's a slimy little shit that I'm going to choke out."

"I called you as soon as I found out. I have a friend at *The Post* who is obsessed with security contracts. When she heard that the Lockhorn Group had a meeting yesterday with General Hodges, she thought it was something I might like to know."

"You did great, and tell your friend I owe her lunch. Now, just so I'm absolutely clear: You don't know anything about the meeting, what was said, who exactly was there, or if any decisions were made?"

The elevator doors opened and Mark held out a hand to let

Jenna exit first before he motored past her in the hallway, almost sprinting to their door.

"Nothing, and I really pressed her. All she has is grapevine stuff. At most, Hodges apparently left the meeting looking very satisfied." Jenna took a breath, feeling almost winded by the pace. "Why don't you talk to Terrance, try to feel him out?"

Mark stopped at the door, contemplating for a moment. Everything he did was chess—moves, countermoves, and positioning for what would happen over the next five turns. Mark once read how Bobby Fischer would play matches that lasted ten, fifteen hours with hardly a break. Though Mark hated chess, he admired that kind of focus and intensity. He needed it now more than ever. Terrance had Mark in check—but Terrance was nothing if not supremely arrogant, and Mark knew he'd mistake his position for mate. It was crucial he kept thinking that.

"Can't do that," Mark said. "By now, he might suspect that we know. Maybe. But if I show my hand, it'll be way easier for him to plan his next move. I want him resting on his laurels."

"It's what he does best."

"Listen," Mark said, his wheels spinning. "Are they still firing that one girl . . . Sheila? Sharon? The one who talks like she's singing a show tune."

"*Linda?*"

"Sure. They still getting rid of her?"

Jenna raised an eyebrow, an involuntary reaction to the oddity that was Linda. "She's a train wreck. Last week, I caught her streaming old episodes of *Keeping Up with the Kardashians* in a bathroom stall. While eating a Kit Kat. Which . . . gross. Anyway, yeah, I'd say she's not long for this place. Why?"

"Carrie Jones, she works at Lockhorn under Terrance. From what I understand, she's very, very unsatisfied right now; she got passed up for a promotion or something. I'm going to offer her Linda's job."

"Is that . . . is that yours to offer?"

Mark pushed his way into the office, flipping on the lights. "The Janitor." That's what they all called him behind his back, a nickname affixed to him because of his penchant for being the last one to leave the office every night. Let them laugh—he wore his sobriquet with pride. Yeah, he was the first one in and the last one out. But he'd also be the first one to retire to an estate in the Hamptons, so they could all choke on his dust. "Maybe. Could be. But she doesn't know that, and dangling it in front of her in exchange for some information isn't a binding contract."

"Mark, that's kind of shitty."

Mark was unmoved. But he was glad that Jenna still retained her own sense of ethics and was bold enough to speak her mind. That's what made her valuable. And maybe dangerous down the road.

"Just get in touch with her using an outside line," he ordered, walking toward his private office. "Don't call from here—use your cell. Set up a meet for the Starbucks on F Street at eight fifteen."

Deep breath. One piece in motion. He knew salvaging this deal would require more than pooling his resources, calling in favors, and convincing people to come back to his side. Things had changed, and whatever drove this sudden change had to be, at the very least, unethical and maybe worse. This was a new ball game now, and if Terrance wanted to be bush league, then Mark had no other choice but to react in equal measure.

8:22 A.M.

"I want a twenty percent raise, my own office, and an extra week vacation. And if I come in to the office late from time to time, as long as my work is getting done, I don't want to hear shit about it."

Mark smiled a smile that said, "Well, okay then," before taking a long sip of his coffee, using the time to collect his thoughts.
Carrie Jones's brashness, at first, made him think she was a plant
for Terrance, that he knew Mark would go after her and had pre-
arranged this entire charade. But as Mark looked at her from
across the small circular table, he didn't see someone playing
a role; he saw a no-nonsense determined woman who knew exactly what she had, what it was worth, and what she expected to
get in return for it. Carrie awaited Mark's reply with an air of indifference, conveying to Mark that this was not a negotiation. He
could take what she was offering and get what he wanted in the
process or hit the bricks. She had nothing to lose—she was young,
smart, and possessed an understanding of the Beltway game that
far exceeded her rank of an assistant. Climbing the ranks wasn't
an "if" for Carrie—it was a "when."

She and Jenna would be at each other's throats.

"All right, you have a deal—pending some, well, I'll call them
'interview questions.'"

"You can ask whatever questions you want as soon as I have a
contract in hand."

Now she was pushing it. Mark slowly lowered his coffee to the
table and let out a perturbed laugh. The shop was bustling with
morning activity, mainly young gophers fetching morning joe for
their bosses, just as Mark had done many years ago. He remembered asking his first boss, Teddy Galt, for a guarantee that he'd
transition from an intern to an assistant once he wrapped his
few remaining courses. Without looking up from his computer
monitor—Teddy may have looked directly at Mark twice in the
ten weeks he interned for him—Teddy said: "Mark, marriage is a
sacred union presided over by the Almighty and over half of them
end in divorce. You're my intern, so take your guarantee and get
the fuck out of my office."

Mark didn't have it in him to treat anyone as bad as Teddy had treated him. Yet he had to contain himself from crossing that line with Carrie—maybe it was his vitriol for Terrance coming out or his life going into overdrive as the stakes rose way above his head, when not six hours ago they were at chest level. All around him people went about their business, interns fetching coffees, parents trying to appease fussy kids with apple juice, baristas slinging drinks, not one of them knowing the pressure Mark was under to justify the past eleven years of his life by securing a deal that he so thoroughly deserved. And the person sitting across from him had the nerve to ask about a contract.

"Yeah, I'll send it right over," Mark said. "Keep an eye out for the envelope with my family seal pressed in wax on it."

"I don't remember saying 'knock knock' in front of what I just said."

Most people would start to lose their cool by now, but this is what separated Mark from most people. He fed on high-pressure situations, absorbing intensity and stress and turning them into focus and determination.

"Listen," Mark said, speaking slowly and carefully so Carrie would know he was choosing his words precisely, "you know what I need is time sensitive. You're leveraging that against me, and that's fine—I would lose respect for you if you didn't. But if you deliberately screw me on this with unreasonable expectations, I'll redirect all my focus from closing this deal to ensuring you spend your political career asking the clumsy interns you see all around you if they want their coffee grande or vente. Our deal is contingent on you giving me what I want right here, right now. Take it or leave it."

Carrie didn't miss a beat—she knew where the line was, had tested it for the sake of testing it, and now she knew to pull back. "All right, we have a deal. Now what do you want to know?"

"Just one simple thing: How the *hell* did this happen? You know as well as I do that I had this deal in the bag. How could Terrance undo all my work, and change so many minds, over the course of a night?"

Carrie smiled—Mark knew by her expression that things were about to get juicy. "Terrance didn't. You know him, Mark, so you know his power of persuasion—he couldn't get laid in a women's prison with a fistful of pardons."

"So how then?"

Carrie leaned close for effect. It was all a little dramatic for Mark's tastes, but he leaned in as well to keep things going. "How do you think?"

Mark's and Carrie's eyes locked, and she raised her eyebrows leading him to the obviousness of it all. And as soon as Mark figured out the missing piece to the puzzle he'd been staring at all damn morning, he understood just how obvious it had been all along. He couldn't believe he missed it.

"Son of a bitch," Mark said, dropping back in his chair. He couldn't do anything but throw his hands up in frustration. "Terrance brought in daddy."

"Yuuuup."

"But who in our deal—"

"Dudek. He and Terrance's father have a history. Terrance went to daddy, daddy went to his senator pal, and your deal went up in smoke."

As Mark sat processing, his fist clenched so tight that his fingernails were about to pierce the skin of his palm, Carrie got up to leave. "I should get back. If I'm gone any longer—"

"No, you should go. I'll be in touch next week, and you'll get exactly what we agreed on."

Carrie took a few steps away from Mark, then turned back. "For what it's worth, I'm sorry this happened. I've always respected you and . . . what Terrance did, what he *does*, it's not okay."

"But nothing's been signed, though, right?" Mark asked.

"No, but—"

"Then don't be sorry," Mark said. "This is far from over."

With no paperwork signed, that meant General Hodges was still a free agent. While Mark already had a strategy for getting to Senator Dudek, reaching the general again without tipping Terrance off would be far more challenging. But without his commitment, Mark had nothing. Dudek had likely already brought Hodges to his side, and they were just waiting for deal documentation to make things official. Mark could bring Dudek back to his fold, but that didn't mean Hodges would follow. He was considering options for convincing the general when *The Post*'s Health and Science section dropped on his table. The folded newsprint was soggy and landed with a splat, breaking Mark's momentary reverie.

"You see," the voice behind him said. "This is what I'm reduced to when you play truant."

Alice dropped in the seat across from him, the one previously occupied by Carrie. "I waited until almost seven before giving up, and by the time I got home to steal the paper from my neighbor, it was already soaked."

Mark smiled, though it was a little forced. He was happy to have Alice surprise him, but her timing wasn't ideal. Still, she was, after all, a friend? An acquaintance? Someone, regardless of the label, he didn't dare tell Sarah about—the last thing she'd want to discover is the twenty-something med student Mark met at Starbucks after each of his runs. It was totally harmless, he knew that without question; he ran early and Alice got done with her shift at Georgetown around the same time. Their relationship was a house built on circumstance. Not that he'd even call what he had with Alice a relationship. There was nothing, as far as he was concerned, to discuss with Sarah, and he especially didn't want to be probed on the matter with questions like "Is she attractive?" But Mark would never, baby coming or not, compromise his relationship with Sarah. He thought of this like it was an alternate universe; Alice didn't exist in Mark's real world, so why mention her?

"You know," Mark said, "you can always just buy a paper from somewhere like, say, the very place you're in right now."

"I don't need a newspaper, Mark. I need the Health and Science section, which is one-eighth of a newspaper. If the good people of Starbucks are willing to sell that to me for one-eighth of the price, I'd be happy to give them my money. Besides, I have you to give me the section every morning—except today, when I really, really needed it. Where were you?"

"No rest for the wicked. I was at the office early—criminally early—so my run, and therefore my morning trip to Starbucks, were canceled."

"Ahhh," Alice said. "This for that Earth-shattering contract thing you're working on?"

Mark paused, running through what he'd told her before. He ran a tight ship, personally and professionally, and that meant loose lips were a no-no. But for some reason, just once, he ran his mouth to Alice about the security deal and regretted it even as the words were tumbling out of his mouth. He blamed the doofus boy in him, the one that wanted to impress the good-looking girl for no reason other than to seem cool. It was a professional blunder, a mistake worse than one a rookie would make. Washington had eyes and ears everywhere, and there was no telling who people were *really* working for. Maybe Mark was being paranoid, but this wasn't the first time Alice had asked about this particular contract; she'd nudged him on it before, always in casual ways that were intended to rib Mark for being a hotshot. But Mark knew that strategy all too well—establish a rapport, make the person comfortable, give a leading prompt, then sit back and let them do the talking.

It was either that, Mark thought, or he'd been playing the game for way too long and, soon enough, he'd be seeing secret codes in the daily crossword.

"Not so much," Mark replied, trying to redirect the conversation. "The bosses have put that one on ice for now. What about you? Your residency has to be ending soon, right?"

"Not soon enough. I think I'm going to go right from residency to retirement. That's a reasonable goal, right?"

As Alice spoke, Mark's phone vibrated in his pocket. It was Jenna, which reminded him that today was no day for small talk.

"Sure, sure," Mark said, distracted by his racing train of thought. "I mean, provided you have a sizable trust waiting for you in a Swedish bank."

Alice looked up at him with a sly grin. "That project's on ice, huh? Go on, get out of here, Mr. Big Time. I'll see you tomorrow."

Mark smiled and let her remark go—he'd figure out if Alice was a plant some other time.

Mark couldn't hear it as he exited the Starbucks, but electronic camera shutters were snapping furiously, taking dozens of photos of him. And anyone he was with. The cameras were held by two men in a plain car across the street. They had been watching Mark for months now, and they were especially interested in his regular trips to this exact Starbucks, at regular times, where he met with a woman who called herself Alice. But there was no Alice, not to these two men. Only Ania, a known Russian spy.

They snapped another photo of Mark as he hurried off, and they wondered what sensitive information the two had passed between each other today.

4

The laces felt good in Mark's hands and afforded him a sense of calm. He tossed the football in the air, a nice twirling spiral as it flew up and came back down, while he paced his office. He knew every inch of this ball—its grooves and texture; the spot where dirt was ground so deep into its rawhide that it would never come out, and Mark didn't want it to. This was his one game ball, earned his senior year at Duke when he caught eight passes for 102 yards and one touchdown—a leaping grab that proved to be the game-winner—for a stunning upset victory over Ohio State.

Mark wasn't even supposed to be on the active roster, but a dozen players getting hit with academic suspensions for cheating on exams had forced him into a starting role. For over three years, Mark rode the pine and was stuck on the practice roster, enduring the tedium of endlessly perfecting plays and the punishment of the defense's frustrations, but never the glory of game day. But the practice squad was what kept his athletic scholarship going, and without that, he'd have been on the first train to state school.

Mark was never bitter about his role. Despite having great hands, he was undersized—not tall enough to be a wideout, not bulky enough to be a tight end. But Mark fought. His intensity was second to no one on the team, even though he was, at best, preparing for a game he'd watch from the sidelines. Most of his teammates and coaches didn't notice Mark's tenacity, but Mark didn't care. Football was a means to an end: getting his degree, going to law school, and being ready for whatever came after that. Mark understood his lot in life at that time—he wasn't born to wealthy parents and his physique wasn't elite. So he used what he had, and what he had was dogged determination. Relentlessness in getting what he wanted.

The ball came down in Mark's hands; he felt the dirt spot, which he liked to think was made when he hit the ground with the winning catch.

He knew what he had to do.

"Jenna," Mark said, peeking his head out of his office door. "Call Chuck in Senator Dudek's office, find out where he's having lunch today. If he gives you any shit, tell him there's a set of Nationals tickets in it for him. If he still doesn't budge, remind him that I still know about Dudek's charity event last year. I'd hate to see a charitable-giving scandal show up in *The Post*."

"You want me to threaten a sitting senator?"

"No, no, no, not threaten. *Remind*. Memory is a great motivator. Just make the call and text me the directions."

Mark strode out of the office holding an unmarked manila envelope. He wasn't enthusiastic about deploying its contents, but circumstances forced his hand. Not all victories were had by making a leaping end-zone grab in front of forty thousand fans. Most of life's accomplishments were a modicum of glory and a buffet of agonizing sacrifice; it's just that people rarely saw the latter. Mark knew that he'd be giving up a little part of himself by using the contents of the envelope, but he'd worry about the moral toll of doing what had to be done after his son or daughter graduated from college without a drop of student loan debt to his or her name. In the meantime, all that mattered was the win. All that mattered was taking steps forward. There was no stasis in Mark's field, so if you weren't moving ahead, you were going in the opposite direction. Mark refused to leave Senator Dudek's lunch table with his feet sliding out beneath him.

The country club's chandeliers sprinkled golden light onto the lobby floor, making it glow like the welcoming aura of the elysian fields. The spotless marble that led to the restaurant's entrance shone with impeccable brilliance as the chandelier's many prisms caught the sun's rays and splintered them into mesmerizing pieces. It was, indeed, a veritable paradise that drew you in—but then changed its mind when you tried to enter, depending on who you were.

The maître d' sourly greeted Mark, delivering the absolute minimum acknowledgment as required by his position. He knew Mark wasn't a member of the Fairbanks Country Club, a century-old social haven for D.C.'s moneyed elite and, apparently, he had only just enough kindness in him to service proper members. Not a drop more.

Mark scanned the room, ignoring the snooty maître d'. Inside, the lunchtime crowd was filled with mega-lobbyists, congressmen, and members of families who'd been so rich for so long no one even remembered where the money had come from. Some Mark knew well, some only by reputation. There was no one in that room he'd call a friend. They were powerful beyond most anyone's wildest dreams, and they were all just sitting at their tables, enjoying inexcusably expensive lunches while putting decisions and plans into motion that would affect countless lives. And it was all just business as usual.

Mark spotted Dudek, to his relief, dining alone in the back corner. Other people at his table meant Mark would need to choose his words carefully and talk in code; alone, he could go after Dudek's jugular, which is exactly what he planned on doing.

"May I help you, *sir*?" the maître d' asked after his terse greeting, infusing his words with the perfect amount of tacit condescension.

"I'm good," Mark said. "Just a little late for lunch with Senator Dudek."

The maître d' took his eyes off Mark and acted like he was checking the club's reservations. He was saying, "I don't think the senator informed us of any guests," when Mark scooted past his stand. He was in the thick of the restaurant by the time he heard, faintly, the maître d' say something about what Mark couldn't do.

Archibald Dudek was an eight-time-elected GOP senator, hailing from Dallas, Texas. He was a rock in the Republican Party—adored by his constituents, admired by his peers, and loathed by the left. No real candidate had even run against him in the past election, knowing how fruitless an endeavor it would be. Dudek stuck to the GOP's script and wasn't one of the young radicals within the party—who Dudek kept a wary eye on—who did more to scare off swing votes than anything else. In Dudek's mind, crazy was conditional. It might get you elected some times, in some places, but you couldn't ride crazy to lasting success. And lasting success—and legacy—was all Dudek cared about.

Mark first met Dudek when he was still just an intern, serving for Dale Dale, a Wisconsin senator who would become his lifelong mentor. Dale and Dudek were both on a subcommittee on assault rifle regulation, and Dudek made no secret about bought-and-paid-for loyalties. From their limited interactions, Mark knew that even though Dudek saw the value in regulating some assault rifles, his financial supporters felt otherwise. That gave Dudek reason to sit back and watch every regulation proposal die on the vine. Every day, Mark—along with Dale, who aggressively fought for Dudek's vote—had to endure the senator's public lip service to gun safety and protecting American lives even though he had no intention of pushing for a single gun-policy change. He played all sides beautifully.

A decade later, Mark was confronting the man who had given him his first encounter with true political doublespeak, where you don't even pretend to deliver on your promises. He wondered how much smoke-blowing he was willing to endure before he tossed the contents of the envelope on Dudek's lap.

Mark confidently leaned over Dudek's table, hoping to catch him off guard. But it took more than popping up at lunch unannounced to get a jolt out of the old senator. Dudek didn't skip a beat; he rose to greet Mark, smiling, and gestured for him to take a seat. It was too perfect—Dudek knew why he was there. And now he was trying to distract Mark, and diminish his anger, with kindness. It was his way to try to control the conversation.

"Mark Strain, to what do I owe the pleasure" Dudek asked as he sat back down. "Care for a drink?"

"No," Mark said, sliding into the seat across from Dudek. "I'm just passing through. Thanks, though."

"My father used to tell me how important it was to enjoy a good drink. 'That's what men do,'" Dudek said, aping his father's Texas twang as he looked around the room. His eyes seemed to stop on each of the women in the crowd, as if to point out their presence. "But this isn't the boys club of his generation, not anymore. He wouldn't allow someone to sit at his table without a drink. Things certainly have changed around here."

"I wouldn't know," Mark said, his attention drawn to one of the floor-to-ceiling windows that looked out onto the glistening expanse of an impeccably green golf course. "My family wasn't around a place like this in the old days. Or the new ones, for that matter."

Dudek took a pull of his drink, a whiskey of some kind as far as Mark could tell. "So," he said, "you want to talk about who gets the contract to provide the Pentagon with its security software, correct? That's the reason you're hijacking my lunch."

"Well, it's a little more complicated of a contract than that, but that's the gist. Specifically, I want to know what the hell is going on. Bidding has been underway for months, and no other party has come close to matching my client's proposal to provide the best, most comprehensive protection against hackers and foreign agents compromising the defense mainframe of our country. Verge has done everything right in these proceedings, and they have an impeccable record for combatting this kind of warfare."

Dudek cut a chunk off the steak he was eating and, before he popped it in his mouth, said, "Son, I've heard the spiel. Verge is a strong American company, there's no questioning that. So, what's the problem?"

Mark had to allow himself a pause before attacking Dudek's cavalier reply. A heated confrontation would get him nowhere.

"The problem is that now, even though Verge has the best offer on the table, Terrance Wilson and the Lockhorn Group seem to be closing in on this contract."

"Hmpf. You've got some good eyes and ears out there, son."

"Look, Senator, your committee will determine who this contract goes to, and you know Verge is the deserving bidder. I've worked my ass off for months to prove that, and I'm not going to lose this deal now, especially not like this."

"That's your first mistake, Mark. This deal isn't yours to lose— these things aren't personal. Besides, we encourage open bidding and competition; that's how our economy thrives. You ever think, maybe the company Terrance represents has the better offer? Terrance's daddy and I go way back, and he assured me this company can deliver on the potential they've shown in their proposal."

"And you're considering awarding a security contract based on a firm's 'potential'? You're being serious with me right now?"

Mark watched as Dudek sat back in his chair and flashed an arrogant smile. He kept the anger from his face, because he knew the old man didn't owe Mark, or anyone, any explanation. Whoever the senator declared the winner for the contract would stand based on his word alone. He was an arrogant prick, one who always acted like he had the upper hand, but that was because he usually did.

Not today, though, Mark thought with grim satisfaction. Not today.

"Every future prospect is potential, Mark. Past performance is never an indication of future success. Take a look at yourself, right here and now. Your past success isn't getting you all that far, is it?"

"Funny you should mention the past, Senator," Mark said, pulling the envelope from his inside coat pocket. "It may not be able to predict performance, but that doesn't mean it can't be used in other ways."

Mark was ready to fling the envelope in Dudek's face and then start eating the rest of his steak. As tempting as that was, he wanted Dudek to actually open the envelope and read its contents. Tossing it in his face was a sure way to invite that Texas temper to kick in and get Mark tossed out on his behind. So, he simply slid the envelope across the table and waited for Dudek to respond. For a moment, there was nothing. Dudek sat silently, looking at Mark, ignoring the envelope. His eyes stayed trained on Mark even as he meticulously wiped the corners of his mouth with his napkin, reached out for the envelope, and opened it. In the final moment of their standoff, Mark half expected the senator to tear up its contents, not caring what it was. Instead, his eyes finally dropped down to the four sheets of paper in his hand, and he started to read.

Dudek nodded his head to the rhythm of his reading, though

it seemed more like skimming to Mark. It was evident that he wasn't at all surprised by the envelope's contents—he knew exactly what he was guilty of, and it was most certainly, Mark assumed, not his first transgression. He folded the papers three times, then gently nestled them beneath the lip of his plate, like they were a napkin. Mark could tell that he was trying his best to be calm and, as accustomed, in control. But he could sense the rage simmering beneath Dudek's skin.

"Let me ask you one question, Mark," Dudek said. "Do you want a job or a career? Because if you want the latter, then you need to take this information, burn it, and forget everything you've seen."

Mark leaned in closer to Dudek—he was in the driver's seat now, and he'd be the one to control the tempo.

"What I want is what I rightfully deserve."

That got a laugh out of Dudek. "This is D.C., son. No one gets what they deserve by virtue. Do you think you're the first person to get muscled out of a deal for all the wrong reasons? Get over it, go get the next one."

"Do you think you're the first person I've done this to? Like you said, I've got good eyes and ears, and I know how to get information. Like, for instance, a senator's penchant for shuffling around funds until they suddenly disappear. That's an easy one. What's more difficult," Mark said, leaning in even closer to Dudek, locking eyes with him, "is tracing the path that reveals how those funds were used."

Dudek bared his teeth as he spat out his words in a controlled but rage-filled hush. "You slimy little son of a bi—"

"You're not exactly in a position to be issuing judgments, *Senator*. Now what's it going to be?"

Dudek leaned back and looked outside, processing his rage. "You get to pull something like this maybe once in your career.

You really want to empty your chamber so soon? Never mind my stake in this—think about Terrance's daddy. He's a very powerful man, and he doesn't take kindly to not getting what he wants."

"Yeah, people who always get their way tend to get all pissy when they don't. But they should get over it, go get the next one," Mark said, twisting the knife into Dudek for no other reason than his own satisfaction. He felt comfortable; Mark read Dudek's body language, and he knew the senator was only trying to maintain some dignity in his surrender. He just had to lean a little bit more, and the ordeal would be over. "Now let me ask you a question: What will you survive—the wrath of Terrance's daddy, or the fallout from your South American escapades being made public?"

The senator flashed a quick, close-lipped smile, then he went back to cutting his steak. "You've gone and made yourself some enemies today, boy. You better hope this deal is worth it."

Mark stepped out the front doors, shoving them open, and found his car parked right out front. It had been waiting for him.

The valet, a square-headed Eastern-European kid, flipped Mark his keys. "I'd never be part of a club that would have me as a member, anyway," Mark said.

He smiled as he drove away, but Jenna's words about threatening a senator floated back to him. It was a dangerous move, but it was the only play he had left to him, and he'd be damned if he'd be made into the bad guy for fighting to keep what was his. As the awareness of his success with Dudek sunk in, Mark felt the same rush of adrenaline he'd felt that morning wash over him, reminding him of the real news of the day.

Traveling at the speed of "do whatever it takes to cement your career," Mark never slowed his mind long enough to let the future sink in. He had to repeat it to himself, aloud, a few times for it to stop seeming like an abstract concept.

"I'm going to be a dad. I'm going to be a dad. I'm going to be a dad."

He'd heard that men lost a lot of testosterone once they became fathers, how that explained the existence of minivans and fanny packs and all that. Yes, there were going to be diapers and feedings for the baby and sleep deprivation for the adults. This was real, he was going to be a dad.

Mark never felt more joyful in his life.

Senator Dudek stepped outside after finishing his lunch and downing two more old-fashioneds. He lit a cigar in the hopes that its aroma and rich body flavor—it was Cuban, after all—would cool his still-flaring temper. He'd feed Mark to Terrance's old man, Dodd, there was no doubting that. If Mark wanted to tussle with the big dogs, Dudek would be happy to oblige. But that wasn't enough. Dudek needed to find some way to satisfy his craven desire for payback. He'd serve that dish nice and cold, and anonymously, but derive the revenge he required nonetheless. His mind wandered to possible scenarios for inflicting existential suffering of the first order on Mark Strain when two men in black suits came up from behind him, jolting him from his reverie. He dropped his cigar and was convinced the universe was out to get him today.

"Senator Dudek," the man on his right said. "We need you to come with us and answer a few questions."

Four old-fashioneds in, and the senator's mind wasn't processing his surroundings as it normally would. It took a moment for him to realize that there were not one but two men standing beside him, and the one on his left had gently grabbed his elbow.

"I'm sorry, do I know you, son?" Dudek asked, looking over

his shoulder at the young, serious man standing behind him. The man didn't answer, though the other man, on his left, began pulling Dudek forward. "Hey now, what's the meaning of—"

A black sedan, Dudek couldn't tell the model, pulled up to the valet stand. The man on his right opened the door and helped usher Dudek into the back seat. It was like he was floating, being guided directly into this strange car before he could even grasp what was happening. Not until the last moment, when he began to offer some resistance.

"What is this?" he asked, his voice growing louder. "God damn it, do you know who I am? What do you think you're doing? Answer me!"

Neither man spoke, and once Dudek was in the car, it pulled away swiftly and left no trace. It was like he had never been there.

The valet pulled up with Dudek's car, a mint Escalade, but the vestibule was empty. The senator wouldn't retrieve his car until two days later, offering no explanation where he went after his meal or what he had done.

5

After a long call with his contacts at Verge, assuring them, in specific detail, that their deal was safe—and being certain to stress the magic he had pulled to make it safe—Mark decided to call it a day.

He left the office before 6:00 P.M. once every never, but he was feeling good enough to convince himself that he'd earned it. Mark peered outside his window, down Thirteenth Street. His immediate sight captured the modern glass edifices that housed lobbyist firms, think tanks, legal practices, and all the other industries that could only exist in a place as contentious as D.C. But beyond those buildings, the district soon gave way to a different kind of architecture and culture. Beyond where Mark could see rested colonial and Victorian row houses, squat federal homes, and Tudor estates. Just the thought of those buildings always managed to fill Mark with a sense of patriotism. Many of these homes belonged to pioneers who had conquered adversity and built new lives for themselves and their families. That spirit of reinvention is what defined the American experience, at least to Mark it did. The settlers, and even their ancestors, were stuck as one people who lived in one place until they decided to be someone, and somewhere, else.

Mark relied on that reinvention narrative to see him through his darkest times, when he thought he'd never break free of the lower-middle-class rut he was born into. He dreamed of getting out, of having the means to support his mom—who raised Mark on her own—and living a life free of the anxiety and desperation that his upbringing had bred into him. Through luck and determination, Mark had clawed his way out, and there was no way he—and now, his family—would ever turn back. Maybe he'd buy one of those colonial homes one day; he'd get Sarah the home she'd always wanted and, in the process, have a constant reminder of that American spirit of reinvention.

Mark stepped out of his office feeling, for the first time in what seemed like ages, calm. "Jenna," Mark said, "I'm heading out for the day."

Jenna looked up at him, a blank expression on her face. "Oh my God," she said after a brief pause. "You lost the contract and now we're all fired."

"What? Jenna, no—"

"I can't believe this," Jenna continued, not listening to Mark. "I'm going to have to spend time in the wasteland known as LinkedIn. I just . . . I knew this would happen, Mark. You shouldn't have gone after Dudek. You messed with Texas, and here we are. That's why they have that saying, to let people know not to fuck with Texas. But you went and did it anyway."

"Jenna, listen," Mark said, trying to interject, but it was no use, she was on a roll.

"Now I have to start from scratch as an assistant, all the way at the bottom. And you know what? I'm too old for that shit. Mark, you told me this deal was ironclad and made promises about my career that—"

"Jenna!" Mark said, clapping his hands twice. "We did not lose the contract. You are not fired. In fact, you can consider me leaving early a cause for celebration. Okay?"

Jenna was silent, letting the news really sink in. "I see," she said, and Mark could tell she was trying to rewind the tape that would put everything she'd just said back into her mouth. "You know, all those things I just said . . ."

"Forget it," Mark replied. "We've all been wound super tight. Take the night off, but keep your cell on you in case of an emergency. Okay?"

Jenna was grabbing her things before Mark had even finished speaking. "No objection from me—see you later!" she said, then practically sprinted to the elevators.

Mark headed to the elevator as well, slowly, letting his victory sink in. His colleagues watched as he went by, noticing the time. *That's right*, Mark thought, *The Janitor is leaving early because his work here is done.*

It was date night with Sarah, but instead of sitting in bed half asleep streaming Netflix, they had plans for the evening. Mark had made dinner reservations, weeks ago, for a new fusion restaurant on L Street. Granted, Mark made reservations for them all the time, at least twice a month. But this time, they were actually going and there would be no interruptions. Tonight, they were celebrating.

Mark had two hours to spare before Sarah's alarm went off, so he decided to stop and grab a coffee, read *The Post*, and get acquainted with the world beyond K Street.

No sooner had Mark stretched out his legs as he eased into a stiff Starbucks armchair than he started to get the feeling that he was being watched. He tried focusing on the newspaper spread in front of his face; after reading the same sentence six times and still not understanding what it said, he tried losing himself in the bland pop music crackling through the speakers. That didn't work, either. Mark could not shake the feeling that something was slowly closing in on him.

As casually as he could, Mark looked over both sides of the

newspaper, trying to see if his feelings of being watched were at all founded. On his right, he spotted the usual throng of customers, like the solo mom trying to wrangle her kid long enough to get her caffeine fix and the pretentious grad student looking for a place to work on that novel of his. On his left was more of the same, though something stood out in the background—a grim man in a black suit, alone, who didn't seem to belong anywhere other than the inside of a casket. He sat at a table, no beverage in sight. Whenever Mark looked at him, the man's eyes jumped sideways, like he'd just been caught in the act.

Mark nervously tapped his right hand on the chair's slightly worn armrest—worn for character, not from actual usage, Mark was sure. He couldn't help feeling paranoid. He knew Dudek would be trying to get back at him, if only for pride's sake. And he couldn't discount Dodd Wilson either, who was, as far as Mark could tell, one of those D.C. ghosts who officially did nothing but was involved in everything. The man in black could be working for either, or both.

Or maybe Mark was making a boogeyman out of his own anxiety. Weirdos hung out in Starbucks all the time. It's just where they seemed to go. In any case, Mark thought, it was time to be on his way.

Flowers were in order for Sarah, that was a given. But was Mark supposed to get her something more significant, more memorable and lasting? He knew about the push gift, but was there a gift for kicking off a pregnancy? It hadn't dawned on Mark until now, when he was too short on time to act on a tradition he wasn't even sure existed.

The flower shop's door chimed as Mark entered, and an older man, the florist, shuffled out from behind a set of cooling units. He had gray hair that fell behind his ears in curls and a small hump in his back. His steps were slow and careful, and he kept a polite distance from Mark, seemingly giving him space to come to him when he needed help. Mark walked slowly through the shop, unsure of what he was even looking for. The hushed stillness and mingling of innumerable flower scents made Mark think of a funeral home, which is one reason why he was never thrilled about the idea of bringing flowers to Sarah. Funeral homes also made Mark think of caskets, which brought his mind back to the man who'd been watching him—*maybe* watching him—at Starbucks. Suddenly, Mark didn't feel much like getting flowers at all.

"May I help you find something?" the florist quietly asked, perhaps picking up on Mark's consternation. He was in his late sixties, Mark assumed, with large hands that were impossible not to notice. They were the hands of a laborer or carpenter, not a florist, Mark thought, and he wondered what his occupation was before he started arranging flowers.

"What do you get when your wife tells you she's pregnant?" Mark asked.

"Well," the florist replied, "in nine months, you get a baby." Mark smiled and nodded, knowing he had walked right into that one. "But," he continued, "as for what flower to get her, you don't get her any."

"You're quite the salesman."

"Just a man who's done this a few times myself," the florist said, patting Mark on the shoulder and leading him away from the flowers. "What you want is a plant. Something that will grow and endure. Flowers, they wither in a few days. They go bad— you don't want your wife thinking of that. You want her thinking of life and . . ."

The florist continued talking, but Mark lost his focus. The florist was showing him a potted plant when Mark spotted a black-and-white shape in his periphery. As casually as possible, Mark pulled out his phone and set his camera to selfie mode, using it as a makeshift rearview mirror. Through the shop's picture window, he spotted a man in a black suit standing across the street. Casket Man. He had a newspaper in his hand, acting like he was reading it, but Mark could see him look up every few seconds.

"Excuse me," Mark said, cutting the florist off. "Do you have a back exit?"

Mark walked briskly toward the coolers from where the florist had emerged. "A what? Why?" the florist asked, perplexed.

"Another way out. Anything." Mark looked through the picture window—the man in the suit was gone. Presumably knowing what Mark was doing. Mark cursed himself; he shouldn't have made such a sudden movement for the back of the store. Now the guy was likely heading to cut Mark off.

"There's a back door, but that's just for deliveries. Customers aren't allowed—"

Mark took out his wallet and handed the man three twenties. "I just need to leave. Please."

The florist led Mark at a brisk pace—as brisk as he was capable of—to the back of the property. There, he unlocked the delivery door's dead bolt and pushed the solid metal door open, allowing a burst of sunlight to rush in. The back of the florist shop spilled out onto a cobblestone alleyway that connected to the east and west and opened up midway through for a T that headed south. The shortest distance from the front of the building to the rear was from the east, so Mark headed west.

He walked swiftly, but also tried to not seem like he was in a panic. No one else was around, but should Casket Man pop up again, he didn't want it to look like he was fleeing—he just casually left the florist through the rear exit without buying anything because that was a thing he liked to do, he'd tell the judge.

His hard-soled shoes sounded like high heels on the cobblestones, heightening Mark's anxiety level with each step he took. His brow was moist with sweat, his breathing labored. Every five steps, he turned to look over his shoulder, scanning. Mark pictured the man running down the alley, gun in hand, ordering Mark to stop. Mark didn't know if he'd do as he was told or if he'd run and try to escape. Where would running get him, after all?

"This is ridiculous," Mark said, even as he quickened his pace. As Mark approached the T, he convinced himself this was all just a delusion. He was sleep-deprived, stressed about work, and feeling all kinds of things about Sarah's pregnancy. And in this heightened state, he had conjured a boogeyman following him through the city. He felt silly for a moment, then relieved. But the moment was short-lived.

At the western end of the alley, a man in a black suit—a different man, this one taller and bald—emerged.

Mark didn't waste a moment, there was no hesitation in thought or action. He simply ran. Mark turned down the T and bolted as fast as he could through the alley, unsure of what to do or where to go. His shoes slapped the cobblestones with surprising resonance, and his panting deafened him to any other sound. He panted not out of any physical exhaustion, but out of fear. Mark was terrified.

He looked back over his shoulder, but there was no one there. No men pursuing him, no sound of bullets whizzing past him. Distracted, Mark didn't see the metal door swing open right in front of him, and he ran straight into it. The blow knocked him clear off his feet, sending him to the ground; the back of his skull cracked on the cobbles, and Mark saw stars. Out of breath and woozy, Mark struggled to get back on his feet. He rolled onto his stomach and tried to push himself up, but his arms felt like rubber. All he could do was lie there and wait for the person standing above him to pick him up and drag him away—or worse.

"Hey man, you okay?" a voice, distant and muffled, said. "You hearing me?"

Mark's eyes blinked open. He was still alive, still lying on the alley floor. Slowly, despite his aching body's pleas to not be moved, he turned to look at the person standing above him. It was a teenage kid in a solid white chef's coat, not a federal agent or mercenary contractor. Just a kid with a joint in his hand, looking to duck out from, presumably, his dishwashing gig to get a little high.

Mark struggled to get up, shaking off the cobwebs. "You see anyone out here?"

"I see you," the kid replied.

Mark groaned. "Anyone *else*?"

"No, dude, just you. Why? Cops looking for your ass?"

Mark paused. No, of course no one was chasing him. And all he got from his paranoia was a ruined suit and, quite possibly, a concussion. "No . . . no. Just forget I said anything. Listen, mind if I cut through your restaurant to get to the street?"

The kid looked back at the restaurant with a look of uncertainty on his face. Mark was certain he was suspicious of being ratted on, for the door, the joint, or both. "I don't know, man. Boss doesn't like us letting people in from here, you know?"

"Look, kid, whatever you do out here, I don't give a shit about. Just let me pass through, and I'll be out of your life forever. Deal?"

After a long sigh, the kid agreed, and Mark was on his way. But before he left, he took one last look down the alleyway and saw that no one was there.

The moment Mark left, the kid lit up his joint and took a deep puff. Through the cloud of smoke, he saw two men, both in black suits, step out from either side of the alley's mouth. Terrified, the kid threw away his joint and rushed back inside, slamming the door shut behind him.

6

Mark had forgotten about the fund-raiser.

It was some meet-and-greet event for a young hotshot senator from Pennsylvania, Laney Griffin, who was billed as the next rock star in the Democratic Party. He was strong on cultural equality and inclusion and, surprisingly, very candid about his strong military policy ideas. That was the kicker—a Democrat who was aggressive on national defense. If Mark could win Griffin's good graces before his ascension to the top of the party, he could be looking at easy contracts for his firm—or better yet, the firm he would start—for a long time.

Sarah exited the bedroom in a tight-fitting dress that accentuated her toned body. It was Mark's favorite. He loved seeing Sarah, even after eight years of being together, embrace her sexiness, even though she was usually shy about doing so. Her wearing this dress was a sign, Mark knew, of how excited she was for this evening. It was special to her, and she wanted it to be special and memorable to Mark as well. Mark also knew he wouldn't be seeing this dress for a good long time, and it killed him to take all the steam out of their evening—out of their celebration—by asking Sarah to change their plans. It was like dumping a bucket of ice water on a burgeoning fire. But he had to do it. Wrapping up the contract today was nice—great, even. But Mark's world was one that hinged on a simple question: "But what have you done for me lately?" He knew that finishing one deal only meant that you had to get started on the next one.

"You look incredible," Mark said, standing opposite Sarah, holding her shoulders gently. "I've never seen you more beautiful than you are right now."

Sarah smiled. "I actually believe that you mean that, but I also know it means you need something."

"Just remember: You're pregnant, and you wouldn't want to upset the baby by hurting his father."

"What's this 'his' talk? And the baby has no ears at this point, so we don't have to worry about what we say or do."

"How about, instead of a nice, romantic dinner, we go to a fund-raiser for a hundred people?" He watched her face turn to stone. "It's just . . . I know, okay? I don't want to do it, I truly, truly don't. But I've got to try and grease a few wheels. Future prospects—that's where my head's at now. I need to secure the future, for all of us," Mark said, putting his hands on Sarah's belly.

Sarah promptly slapped his hands away, playfully. "Don't you even think about it. You don't get to play the pregnancy card before I do."

"Yeah, that makes sense," Mark said, smiling. "Okay, how about we make a deal—if we go, for just thirty minutes, I'll let you have a girl."

Sarah shook her head with playful exasperation. "You're such an asshole," she said, then sucked in a deep breath. "Okay, we'll go. But thirty minutes."

"Thirty minutes."

"I'm not kidding. Anything longer, and I act drunk and make a scene. A *weird* one."

"Your definition of weird scares me, I'm not going to lie."

"Then don't force my hand, Mark."

Mark embraced Sarah and, as he often did, realized how fortunate he was.

"You know," Mark said, lingering in their embrace, "we don't have to go anywhere . . ."

"I didn't put this dress on just for you, sweetie. Now let's move."

The fund-raiser was located on the rooftop of a D.C. cultural center, and the space was filled with two types of people. First, there were the scenesters, people who wanted to be seen at important places for the sake of being seen. They were mainly young and idealistic, at least by Mark's standards, and always stuck out at these events for their lack of proper attire. Those words, "proper attire," always played in Mark's head like they were being said by an aging British butler. But it was no less true. These were the interns, office assistants, and other lower-level employees in important places who stumbled upon an invitation when someone from their office bowed out at the last minute and offered up their space. On days like today, Mark remembered those eager and far more innocent days with especial fondness.

The second type were the movers and shakers, those who came bloodthirsty with a specific agenda in mind. Mark could practically see their fangs sticking out from beneath their lips. Although Mark was technically like them, he was far from being one of them. K Street was all about roots and how deeply—and richly—they penetrated the Earth. And Mark? Mark's roots were still fighting to absorb water from the top of the soil; his competition—and his peers, at times—drew their water from deep underground, so deep most people didn't even know the roots were there. That's why Mark had to fight so hard against the Terrance Wilsons of the world; there was no telling what amount of power people like him could rally with just a few phone calls.

Mark had no golden parachute to gently lower him to the ground if he failed. The way Mark graduated from eighth grade to high school was the way these people graduated from adolescence to lives of immense power and influence. Should Mark stumble, a flood would wash his roots right out, like he'd never even been there at all.

The party was what Mark expected, a healthy mixture of these two groups, with an unusually high showing for the first due to Griffin's traction with young audiences. Waiters in jeans and loose ties served tomato soup and grilled-cheese appetizers, tying into the senator's middle-class, "regular Joe" brand. From the rooftop, Mark caught sight of the Washington Monument shimmering in the distance, like an eye in the sky watching them all.

The moment they walked in, Sarah set the alarm on her phone for thirty minutes. She smiled and waved at people she knew in the crowd while whispering to Mark, "That's the second time I put you on the clock today—let's not make this a habit."

Mark, shaking hands with a Democratic Party strategist, mouthed back, "I love you so much," and was off to work the room in record time.

The rooftop was lit by strands of naked bulbs strung along the perimeter, making the center of the room a little difficult to read as Mark scoured the crowd for essential people to bump into. Despite being a head taller than most, Mark had a hard time spotting the key personnel he was looking for. But that just meant he had to put a little extra pep in his step.

He recognized most of the faces. These were the people who attended every event, jockeying for position the same as Mark. He nodded to them with a smile, and they did the same in return, even though they both knew, deep down, they'd each feed the other one to the wolves for a moment of Griffin's time. Mark shook hands in passing with a house representative, a federal judge who had trouble hiding her disdain, and a *Post* reporter who, on more than one occasion, tried to bait Mark into becoming an unwitting source for a story. Then in the center of the room, Mark spotted the prize: Griffin, the Thanksgiving turkey of the evening.

Mark wanted to, at least, introduce himself. At the moment, Griffin was engaged in a conversation he clearly had no interest in. The signs were all there: that bored expression, the disinterested nods of agreement, those eyes that couldn't help but dart around the room looking for something, anything, that would allow him to break away. The last resort would be checking his phone and acting like an important message had come through. Mark wanted, desperately, to avoid that step; once Griffin pulled out his phone, his handlers would pick up on it and shuttle him to the next important person to speak with. And Mark wasn't on the handlers' list.

Zig-zagging his way through the crowed, Mark had to hurry. Griffin seemed ready to fire off his flare—i.e., flash his phone—at any given moment. And Mark was just about there, he was nearly close enough to touch the man of the hour when a firm hand grasped his shoulder and pulled him back.

Men in black suits flashed in Mark's mind, and he shivered. His hands balled into fists, but when he turned around he wasn't greeted by his ghastly stalker. Instead, Mark found himself standing face to face with Dale Schmidt, his mentor. And Dale didn't seem at all happy.

"Mark," he said, already sounding perturbed. "What the hell do you think you're doing?"

Mark inhaled sharply—he knew he had some explaining to do.

Not only was Dale Mark's mentor, he had been the first person to recognize Mark's skill and perseverance and put them both to use. Mark had completed three other government internships without making much of an impression; he tended to get lost beneath more polished interns who worked their roles like they were already seasoned pros. Where his classmates already had accepted lucrative job offers by the start of their senior year, Mark was interning with Dale during his winter quarter and had another internship lined up for the spring. Dale, a former athlete who had played some pro ball with half the teams in the NFL, understood Mark's brand of tenacity and, more importantly, he knew how to put it to use. For that, Mark was, and always would be, grateful. The fact that many people went their entire lives without having their strengths recognized was not lost on Mark, especially since, even at a young age, that fear had already begun creeping into his life. Mark had spent many nights lying awake in his ramshackle college apartment, choking down no small amount of fear as he trembled at the idea of what he was going to do once he threw his mortarboard in the air. It felt like everyone around him knew exactly where theirs were going to land while Mark's just spun in the air. Not going up or down—it was just stuck.

Now, ten years later, Mark still looked up to Dale. That's why being caught in the crosshairs of his role model's anger filled him with an unnerving sense of dread.

"What do you mean?" Mark asked, knowing full well what Dale meant. Word traveled fast through the Beltway; Dale had undoubtedly heard about his lunch with Dudek by now.

Dale led Mark away from the throng at the party, and away from Griffin. Mark looked back to see him getting lost in the crowd and felt Sarah's ticking clock wasting away.

"What did I tell you about making enemies? I think, if I taught you anything, I was pretty clear on this point."

"You said, above all else, be careful who you become enemies with."

Dale pursed his lips, shooting Mark a disapproving look. "No, Mark. That's not what I said. What I said was that enemies are like bacteria. Some are good for you. Others, like, say, dysentery, will make you shit out your organs. Don't make enemies with dysentery. And what did you do today?"

Mark paused and took in a deep breath. There was no speeding this up—he was stuck spending what little precious time he had on getting lectured. "I made enemies with dysentery."

"You're damn right you did," Dale barbed. After a long breath, he softened, transitioning from Mark's superior to his father figure, and a concerned father figure at that. "Mark . . . what were you thinking? Confronting him in his own club? As ridiculous as Dudek can be, he's a guy you don't want gunning for you. And, believe me, he's going to be gunning for you."

Mark turned to lean over the side of the building. For the first time, he took a step back and let what he'd done sink in. Dudek was a real person with real power, and Mark had extorted him. This time, there'd be a reckoning for his boldness. And it would be much, much worse than paranoid delusions of men in black suits chasing after him.

"It was a high-risk play, and I know that I'm going to catch hell for it. But—"

"But you couldn't let Terrance win. I know you, Mark, and I know your Achilles heel is people getting things they haven't earned. You can't stand it. But that's the way of the world, for better or worse. Terrance wouldn't have deserved that software contract, there's no question. But you have to think about the big picture. Had he won, everyone would know why, and there'd be no recourse for you. But now, Mark, you're starting to garner a reputation, and it isn't a good one. Losing a contract goes away—bad reputations, playing dirty, those things stick."

Mark lowered his head and looked down at the street. Just beyond the bars and restaurants was a neighborhood crowded with those beautiful colonial homes that were rich with history and character; they had yards and lawns, they were surrounded by terrific schools, and they provided any modern comfort imaginable. Mark coveted that life and the security it represented for him and his family. His ambitions, even when they got the best of him, were still true and good. And that's why he couldn't bring himself to feel any shame about how he had played Dudek. Not after what he and Terrance had tried to do to him. Not after how dramatically his life's stakes had risen that very morning.

"Sarah's pregnant," Mark told Dale, looking out to the city. "She told me this morning."

"Jesus," Dale said, joining Mark on the rooftop's ledge. "You're in even more trouble than I thought." After a short pause, Dale clasped Mark on the shoulder and looked at him. "I don't know anything about being a dad, but I'd venture to guess that, if I was in your shoes, I would have done the same damn thing. You've got a family to think about now."

"Some job I'm doing if my rep—and my future—is as deep in the toilet as you're saying."

Dale waved Mark off with a casual swipe of his hand. "Eh, Dudek is corrupt as hell and everyone knows it. I'll do some counter-programming on your behalf and plant the seed about how things really went down. You won over General Hodges fair and square and all the sound and fury from the Dudek camp is just sour grapes."

Mark breathed a sigh of relief and pushed away from the ledge. "Thank you, Dale. That means a lot."

"Consider it your first baby gift. Now go find that beautiful wife of yours and celebrate. There'll be plenty more opportunities on the horizon for you to kiss Griffin's ass, trust me."

Sarah was tapping her wrist at the spot where a watch would be when Mark found her by the exit, waiting.

"Thirty-two minutes. You lose, Strain."

"I didn't know we were wagering anything."

"You didn't? Well, keep in mind that every minute you waste is a minute off your window to get laid. Because a few months from now, you're going cold turkey."

While the news did catch Mark in the gut, he made it a point to oversell his reaction. "My God. Cancel dinner, get an Uber! We're going straight home."

Mark tried to pull Sarah out the door, but she stayed put. "No, no, no. I don't think so. We don't get to skip what I want from this evening so we can go hop in the sack."

"Oh, and you don't want sex?"

Sarah shrugged her shoulder. "Meh. Not as much as I want the pork belly from Redbird."

Mark drew Sarah close and kissed her. Whatever his day brought, he knew he'd be rescued by these moments with his wife. Small moments that brought him more joy than closing any deal. "You're the worst, you know that?"

Sarah was about to respond when they both heard a voice calling from behind them.

"Look at these little lovebirds! Get a room, you two!"

Mark knew who it was before he even turned around: Aaron Cutter, Pentagon IT something-or-other, Sarah's college flame, and a general pain in Mark's ass.

"Aaron," Sarah said, forcing a pleasant response. "What a nice surprise to see you."

Aaron grabbed both of Sarah's hands and pulled her arms away from her body, scanning her from head to toe. A minute into their encounter and Mark already wanted to toss Aaron over the side of the building. He was half a foot shorter than Mark and had the physical composition of a waterbed.

"Check you out!" Aaron said, crass and loud. "You're looking *hot* tonight!"

"Hey Aaron," Mark said, forcing Aaron's hand off Sarah by

way of a firm—maybe too firm—handshake. "We were just on our way out."

"Of course, of course," Aaron said, agreeing but not going away. "I just wanted to say what's up, see how you're holding up."

"We're good," Sarah said, trying to speed the conversation along. "How are you?"

"I'm good, thanks for asking. Just gearing up for this big security upgrade I've been hearing about. Believe me, it's looooong overdue."

Aaron was about to jump into another topic when Mark cut him off. "Wait," he said. "Why are you asking how we're holding up? You say that to people after something bad has happened."

Aaron's face dropped, though Mark knew it was for intentional dramatic effect. He relished these moments, and Mark knew it.

"Well, you lost out on that contract," Aaron said as he ran his fingers through the wild black curls that grew like weeds on his head. "Before I left the office, I'd heard that General Hodges was sending paperwork over to what's his name's client?"

"Terrance Wilson."

"Yeah, that dude."

"No, no," Mark said, feeling a slight bit of panic grow within him. "I straightened this all out just today, this afternoon. The contract is going to my client."

"Oh, shit. Mark, man, I honestly didn't mean to rain on your parade. I thought you knew—as far as I know, all this just went down a few hours ago."

Mark's stomach dropped, but he'd been in plenty of tight spots before. He knew not to let panic get the best of him; instead, he'd let the scorn he harbored for Terrance Wilson take the driver's seat. He couldn't allow this to happen. After everything he'd endured, he couldn't lose that damn contract.

He looked at Sarah, who knew immediately. "Go," she said.

She was doubtless disappointed, and Mark swore a silent vow to make it up to her.

"I'm sorry," Mark said, searching for words that wouldn't come. "I just—I have to."

With nothing left to say, nothing that could assuage Sarah's hurt, Mark kissed her on the cheek and bolted out the door. He sprinted down the street, hailing a taxi.

"The Pentagon," Mark told the driver. "And hurry."

7

"You need to take a leak? *That's* your cover for gaining entry? This isn't a McDonald's, Mark. It's the Pentagon."

Private First Class Danny Rand had been working the Pentagon overnight security shift for over a year. He and Mark met at the retirement party for some Marine general the previous winter; Mark sent him a pair of courtside Wizards tickets the next week, saying he'd gotten them last minute and couldn't use them. Mark sold it as one fan connecting another—after all, what kind of travesty would it be if such great seats went to waste? But, in reality, Mark figured it was never a bad thing to have an inside man at the Pentagon. And now, here he was.

"Listen, Danny, you know me."

"Actually, I kinda don't."

"Well, you know me enough to know that I'm not a threat in any sense of the word. Okay? I just . . . look. You give me a visitor's pass, I'll get you off the night shift. I'll move heaven and Earth to get you off this night shift. I promise you that."

Danny folded his arms over his chest and cocked an eyebrow. "And?"

"Seriously? Fine—*and* I'll get you more courtside seats."

Danny stepped to the side and unlocked the security door, letting Mark pass. As Mark hustled through the metal detector, Danny delivered a final warning with no indication of humor in his tone. "You have thirty minutes. Not thirty-one, not forty-two. Thirty. And if you're not back here, I'll come find you, knock your ass out, and feed you to Homeland Security. Understood?"

Years from now, Mark figured he'd look back on this day and call it "pizza delivery day." Thirty minutes or less with everything. Right now, though, he didn't find much humor in having an impossible clock to race against. He was just annoyed.

But, he couldn't let that show. So instead, Mark turned, walking backward to keep moving, and shot Danny a mock salute. "I'll be back in twenty-nine, sir. You just worry about which lady friend of yours you'll be impressing courtside, all right?"

The mail room was still bustling with a skeleton crew prepping the day's outgoing mail for tomorrow's release. The room itself was cold and gray, lit by unflattering overhead fluorescent lights that cast the entire operation in a milky gossamer sheen. And for all Mark knew, the lights probably came equipped with security cameras, adding to the Kafka-esque feel this place was trying hard to sell.

There was no doubt that he shouldn't have been there. Mark knew it. During daytime hours, the mail room would be closed off so no random wanderer—like, for instance, Mark—could infiltrate its workings and introduce who knows what to the fast-moving system of ingress and egress. Anthrax? A letter bomb? The wrong Netflix disc? Mark had no idea, and he really wasn't concerned about security issues, especially as he was guilty of at least two security breaches just by being there. And he was plotting a third—mail fraud. He had to get his hands on a piece of General Hodges's mail and extract his office location from it. In an operation this robust, the odds of snagging such a specific piece of mail, Mark knew, were not in his favor.

One of the best lessons Mark had ever learned is that when

you don't belong or don't know what you're doing, fake it. In fact, do more than fake it: Act like you're somehow in charge. Even the vaguest sense of authority tended to keep people from questioning things too deeply, at least for a little while. Mark's job was to understand people, and he was especially skilled at understanding what they wanted. If you could take what one person desired and satisfy it with what another person had, and vice versa, then you got the deal done. In the mania of brokering deals, what people wanted most was to know the plan. They craved feeling like they were in strong, capable hands, and that meant someone had to step up and be the leader. Someone had to take control. And when you did that, people tended to get in line and follow. In fact, they'd wanted to follow all along. With that in mind, if Mark was going to make it to Hodges through the mail room, he wasn't going to get there through kindness and sincerity; he needed to bullshit his way through by acting like a person who was in charge.

In the middle of the room, Mark spotted a tall older man with a clipboard directing traffic. He ordered one worker to a stack of packages over here, another to a row of boxes over there. Then he checked his watch, released a long sigh, and looked up to the heavens as if praying that it would all be over soon. Mark pegged him both as the supervisor and a man who wanted, above all, to be left alone. That made him perfect. People who couldn't tolerate being bothered were always the most desperate to remove the source of bother.

Mark approached him hastily, giving the impression that there was no time to waste. "Excuse me, excuse me. Sir? You're in charge? They told me to look for you."

"God damn it," the supervisor replied. "Whose Amazon package got stolen this time?"

"What's your name?" Mark asked, intoning his words to sound more official. "And are you or are you not in charge?"

"Yeah, yeah. I supervise the night shift. Name's Randall. Look, just tell me who's missing their package, and I'll tell you what hands it passed through. That'll narrow down the culprit in no time."

"There's no culprit, Randall. Well, except for somebody's negligence."

"I don't follow."

Mark walked Randall over to what he assumed to be an outgoing bin of mail. He picked up a few letters, casually thumbed through them, then tossed them back onto the pile. "General Hodges sent an outgoing package down here earlier today. We've sent three requests and have been waiting four hours for someone to retrieve it. Do you think the general should come down here himself and get his package back? Is that what you all think? Maybe while he's busy doing that, you can strategize how to win our next war."

"Wait, wait . . . ," Randall said, rubbing his temples. "I didn't get any request to intercept a package. Are you sure—"

"Am I sure we asked more than once to get the general's package back to him? Are *you* sure that's the question you want to be asking right now?"

Mark saw Randall feeling the pinch. A little bit of perspiration appeared on his forehead and his breathing got a little deeper. His rheumy eyes started to narrow. "Okay, okay. Look, I'll track the package myself and have it sent up immediately. If you can tell me General Hodges's office location code, I'll have it taken—"

"All hands on deck, Randall! I want everyone here, including you, to rummage through this disaster of a mail room until you find it. I'll wait."

Randall threw up his arms, then called in his team. As he delivered instructions on finding Hodges's parcel, Mark looked at the people surrounding him and realized how much he was counting on these total strangers. They had to not only materialize a piece of mail Mark wasn't even sure existed, but that letter, package, whatever, had to include Hodges's return address, complete with his office location.

Mark waited, each moment stretching on endlessly. He couldn't believe so much—his career, his future, his reputation—was going to be decided in the Pentagon's mail room. Succeed and his sins would, largely, be forgiven. Fail and he might as well tie a red cape around his neck and wait to be gored by a pack of stampeding bulls.

Randall walked over to Mark, arms folded over his chest. "Who did you say you were again?"

Mark was taken aback by Randall's temerity. "William Lowe," Mark said.

"Where's your ID?" Randall asked, pointing to the identification card clipped to his belt.

Mark looked at Randall—this wasn't small talk. Mark was being vetted, and he had nothing to say in response. Claiming he left it in his office wouldn't cut it; any follow-up question would take a wrecking ball to his house of cards. No, he didn't know where his office was. No, he couldn't go get it. The tables turned on Mark, and now he was the one sweating. But then, as if to undermine Mark's steadfast belief that the universe was a cold and indifferent place, he heard the two words that salvaged his day:

"Got it!" someone yelled from behind one of the shelves.

And out came a middle-aged woman who walked with a slight limp and a voice so raspy she had to smoke no less than a carton a day. "Was with the next batch to go out, so you got here just in time."

Mark grabbed the package greedily and inspected the return address. The coveted information was there—Mark already knew what to do, and now he knew where to go. He thanked the chain-smoking lady and hurried toward the exit. Randall tried to intercept his stride, asking clumsily about Mark's ID, but Mark wasn't about to allow even a starving puma to get in his way. A burned-out overnight mail room supervisor had zero chance.

"You just be glad no one lost their job tonight," Mark said, then shoved the exit door open. He had only eighteen minutes to go.

The door to Hodges's office was monochrome gray, like every other door up and down the hall. Except behind this door was Mark's future. Mark took a moment to collect his thoughts. He heard Hodges inside, shuffling around, maybe pouring himself a drink, judging by the sound of clinking glass. Mark had his facts, his case was solid, his conviction on behalf of his client was real. All he had to do now was execute. And that started with a knock on General Hodges's door.

Mark had never met Hodges, even while trying to secure the contract. Mark knew two things about the decorated general: first, he was a celebrated war hero who had the rare distinction of being respected by the many people below him and the few above. Second, Hodges was known to be a guarded and private individual. He had no family, no life that anyone knew of outside the U.S. military, which made him difficult to reach on a personal level. That was worrisome. Commonalities helped drive connections. Mark made his clients and partners feel like friends, not commodities, and he used his authenticity to compensate for any shortcomings in negotiations to get deals closed. General Hodges, Mark knew, required a different strategy.

The voice calling for Mark to enter the office was softer than he expected. Though Mark had watched Hodges in press conferences over the years, he expected him to sound, away from the camera, like a man who'd endured war and combat—Mark expected him to sound hard, abrasive even. But the "come in" that came from the other side of the door could have come from anyone at all.

Mark did as he was told. He opened the door and was greeted by Hodges, who looked back over his shoulder at Mark, drink in hand. The room was sparsely decorated. A simple, tidy desk was positioned on Mark's right and behind it stood an American flag perfectly upright on a pole. It—the flag—reminded Mark of his days as a Cub Scout. Next to Hodges was a drink cart with a decanter of whiskey resting on it. Hodges didn't recognize Mark, but wasn't alarmed by his presence, either; Mark was certain the general had already pinpointed a half dozen ways to kill him before he could so much as pantomime a gun out of his thumb and finger.

"Can I help you? Is there something wrong with the package?"

Mark looked down at the package gripped in his hands, having forgotten about it completely. "No . . . no, sir. I'm actually here to talk to you about something different. My name's Mark. Mark Strain."

"Ahhh," Hodges said, heading over to his drink cart. "The lobbyist. How'd you get in here?"

Mark entered the office with hesitant, careful steps. He didn't want to seem brash or inconsiderate of Hodges's space. "That's a long story, sir. But I think it's safe to say that I used all of my skills to make it here to you."

The general smiled. "Okay, you're here. What do you want?"

"Well, sir," Mark said, placing the package on Hodges's desk, "I'm just going to be honest with you—I think giving the contract to Lockhorn is a huge mistake. With all due respect. Sir." Keying everything to being humble and respectful was a gamble, but it felt like the right play.

Hodges paused, his poker face unreadable. Authority figures—especially military authority figures—didn't typically enjoy being defied, so Mark was ready for anything. Anything except Hodges being patient and kind.

"I see," Hodges said after his contemplative moment. "Would you care for a drink, Mark?"

"Ummm, well, I would typically say no. But after the day I've had . . . yes. I would love a drink."

Hodges poured Mark a healthy glass of bourbon, neat, and handed it to him. "I hope you're driven by more than winning a contract," Hodges said. "Cyber warfare . . . it's a big deal these days. We've got terrorists trying to breach our servers round the clock, the Russians messing with our elections, and who knows what else. So, before we go any further, I want you to ask yourself if this is about a personal win, or is it about something greater."

Mark moved to the window to capture the moon's glow over D.C. He loved the D.C. skyline at night. After a moment of soaking in the district he so adored, Mark took a long drink, and the whiskey made his eyes burst open. He was grateful his back was to Hodges.

"General, I'm in a pretty good place, professionally. I've worked my way to the top of my firm, and that affords me certain . . . licenses. One of which is being selective about who I take on as clients. If I don't believe in what I'm selling, I don't sell it. Not anymore. So, if you're asking if I believe in Verge, the answer, without a doubt, is yes. Yes I do."

Hodges eyed Mark, contemplating. "That's a better response than what I got from the other guys, I can tell you that."

"Verge knows what they're doing, sir. They have an impeccable record, and they've proven, time and time again, to be on the cutting edge of cyber defense. I know this is a delicate time, and this contract is more important than most people realize. But Verge is the firm who will keep the Pentagon protected."

"But Verge hasn't secured a contract this large in its history," Hodges countered. "How do you know they can handle it?"

Yes. A crack. Asking for details meant more time to negotiate. Time to push.

Mark took a long, cleansing breath as he steadied himself to make his closing argument. "General, this morning—which, to be honest, feels about ten years ago—my wife told me she was pregnant. I can't even wrap my head around what that means, being a dad. It's so . . . immense. The point, salient to you and me, is that even in this very, very brief window of time I've entertained the idea of being a father, I've felt the stakes of the world get a lot higher. And that's why, if someone's going to be on the frontline of this battle, I'll sleep better at night knowing it's Verge."

Hodges poured another glass of whiskey, took a drink, and walked to his desk. He leaned back, hands behind his head. "Okay," he said.

"Okay?" Mark asked.

"Okay, Verge gets the contract. You sold me."

Mark, feeling like he just got an elephant off his chest, was speechless.

"I had a feeling I was making this decision for the wrong reasons. My gut has always told me to go with Verge, and that's what I'm going to do."

Mark wanted to leap into Hodges's arms, embrace him tight, but restrained himself. "General, truly, thank you. I appreciate your open mind and—"

"Good night, Mark," Hodges replied. "You have a pregnant wife. Go home to her."

Mark nodded and left.

He'd won. He felt the laces hit his hands, making that game-winning grab against Ohio State. Victory was a high, and Mark was cruising on it. He'd been down, out, manipulated, and cheated. But here he was, still, on top.

There was no better feeling.

8

And there was no worse feeling than coming home to an angry wife.

Mark knew he'd messed up. He didn't even know where to start cataloging his sins. Abandoned wife at party. Broke date night. Broke date night on the same day Sarah told him she was pregnant. And those were just the things that had happened *today*. Mark wasn't proud of any of his transgressions and shortcomings, and though he knew that his reasons for doing them were for a greater good—especially now—he'd given Sarah the same excuses for so long that they no longer meant anything to either of them. They were just words that tumbled out of his mouth. There was going to be hell to pay, and all Mark could do was pull out his wallet.

Only hell wasn't looking to settle its debt, not tonight. And that only made things worse.

Sarah wasn't angry. She wasn't hurt. She was worried.

By the time Mark got home, she was already in her pajamas and curled up on the couch, streaming *Stranger Things* for the umpteenth time on her iPad. The living room windows were open, ushering in a cool breeze and the ambient sounds of D.C. at night. Mark could almost identify and pick out each bit of chatter: the distant sounds of interns partying deep into the night; the political junkies conversing over the Beltway news of the day; the soft tread of tires on the streets as hustlers, like Mark, kept chasing their next meal.

"This has to stop," Sarah said. Nothing further was needed; they both knew what "this" was and why it had to stop.

"I know," Mark said, sidling up to her as she tossed her iPad onto the chair. "But some things, they can't just end midsentence. That deal had to be closed, other deals will need to be closed. It's my job."

"It's not your job, Mark. It's your *life*. You do this twenty-four seven and despite promises to slow down, to get better organized, to get help from your firm, it never happens. Every other problem takes precedence over *our* problems." Sarah took Mark's hand and placed it on her belly. She met his gaze, and Mark could feel her deep concern. "What's going to happen in nine months?"

Mark knew it was crazy, but he felt something in Sarah's belly. Not a kick or anything like that, but an energy. Something inside of her was alive, and it was the most amazing thing in the world. It made him feel immediately remorseful, like he'd already become the father he never wanted to be.

Mark let out a deep breath. "Sarah, when I was a kid—"

"Don't," Sarah said, stopping Mark cold. "Don't try to game me with some sentimental nugget from your youth. I'm not a client."

"Fine, you want the truth?" Mark asked, pulling back on his blatant attempt to play on Sarah's emotions. "My days are filled with relentless fear. I'm constantly afraid that if I fail, if I stumble, I'll lose everything. *We* will lose everything. And I have nothing to fall back on. These other guys who do what I do, they have a margin for error. They have powerful people in their lives who can scrub their record, and if that doesn't work they have trust funds to rely on. If I slip up—"

"I'll be there to catch you," Sarah said. "That is what this *is*,

Mark. Me. You. We are together, and when one of us falls we pick each other back up again."

Mark smiled, getting emotional. "I know that, and it's taken me a long time to realize that if you weren't here, I'd fall forever. I need you more than anything else in the world, and I will become the man you need me to be. The man our baby needs me to be. I promise."

Sarah embraced Mark. "I don't want you to change," she said. "You already *are* the man I want. I just want you to be *here*."

Mark stood up, holding Sarah's hand and raising her up with him. "Come on, let's go get some sleep. It's late."

Sarah shot Mark a sly smile. "Sleep? Are you saying date night is over?"

"Well, we'll sleep eventually."

6:07 A.M.

Mark heard something.

He was startled from sleep by a muffled and unusual sound. His phone could vibrate all night, and it often did, but he could snooze through it. But this sound, whatever it was, was an intrusion on Mark's rest; its foreignness trickled into his mind and sounded an unconscious alarm. He rolled over on his back, looking up at the ceiling as the memory of the noise played and replayed in his head. Maybe it came from outside; maybe it was the thud of newspapers landing on a neighboring stoop; maybe it was an animal rooting through a garbage can.

None of the speculations gave Mark enough peace of mind to close his eyes and enjoy the fifty precious minutes he had left before his alarm went off. He looked over at Sarah, who was still sleeping. The morning light bathed her in a soft glow. She looked peaceful. Mark knew he was likely being paranoid, but he couldn't help but think about the safety of Sarah and the baby inside her, and he wondered if this was how his life was going to be for the next eighteen years. Quietly, Mark eased out of bed.

Stepping over the three creaky floorboards between his bed and the door, Mark slipped out of the room. He tiptoed down the stairs to the living room where he found the windows still open. The curtains gently billowed with the entry of crisp morning air. Mark was struck by the strangeness of seeing the windows open, like he was walking in a dream. He never left them open, just like he never left a door unlocked or a key hidden in a fake rock on the porch. He was strict about safety, but between getting carried away with Sarah and his sheer exhaustion, he forgave himself for the lapse. It was a comfort, in fact, to have an unmistakable source for the sound that still nagged at his mind. Something must have happened outside and the noise carried right into the house. Mark closed the windows, and as he did, he spotted two vans parked across the street. A matching pair of all-black utility vans with no one in them. He didn't think much of it, other than acknowledging that a utility van on his residential street at this time of the morning felt somehow strange.

As Mark turned around, windows now closed, he heard the sound again. It was clearer this time. Something like footsteps.

Before Mark could even turn to peek out the windows to see if something was happening outside, he heard the crashing of the front door as it exploded off its hinges.

He only got a glimpse of the men dressed in black tactical gear as they charged into his home. Mark raced toward his bedroom the moment he heard the sound; he had no idea who these people were or why they were there. It didn't even cross his mind. He had only one thought:

Protect Sarah.

A man's voice roared from behind, ordering Mark to stop. It

was loud, but the man's voice sounded muffled to Mark, like his head had been submerged in water. Adrenaline, fear, and the instinct to protect his wife and unborn child overwhelmed Mark's entire system, drowning out the world around him. He was being carried away by primal impulses—there was no stopping his body even if he wanted to.

Mark reached the hallway and spotted Sarah standing in the doorway, wide awake and terrified. She screamed, but Mark couldn't hear her through the pounding in his ears. She wanted him to stop, or maybe move, Mark wasn't sure. He hardly had a moment to react when, suddenly, he was blasted by the debilitating charge of 50,000 volts erupting into his back. Mark's body crashed to the ground and he began to twitch uncontrollably. No matter how hard he tried, no amount of determination would grant him control over his body. He was locked in a state of convulsive paralysis and could merely watch as Sarah tried to rush to him only to be cut off by two of the intruders. They grabbed her and dragged her back, and that's when the sound rushed back to his ears. She screamed for them to let her go, to leave Mark alone. But all he could do was lay there and helplessly watch.

He willed his mouth to produce sound. *"Preeee,"* he said, nearly inaudible. Sarah continued to thrash against the men, screaming to be let go, but they didn't relent. *"Preegggnnaa,"* Mark mumbled. He pushed to get off the floor, feeling the effects of the Taser blast wear off just enough for him to fight his way up.

A nearby intruder, though, didn't like Mark's fight.

As Mark rose, the intruder yanked Mark up to his feet and threw him against the wall. Mark could feel the plaster shatter at his back, and he would have collapsed back to the ground had the same man not held him up. He wrapped his hands around Mark's throat and began to squeeze.

"We could end this right now, quick and easy," the man said, and Mark could see cold fury behind his eyes. "The traitor resisted; the traitor had to be neutralized."

Mark was suffocating; he could feel his windpipe on the verge of shattering.

"Banks!" a voice called from behind. "Damn it, Banks, let him go! That's an order!"

The man, Banks, shot an icy look at Mark. "You'll get it. Soon, you'll get it." He released his grip, and Mark dropped to the floor. He held his throat and used what little oxygen he had to squeeze out one word:

"Pregnant," he gasped inaudibly. Then again, this time louder: "Pregnant." Still, no one paid him any mind. Mark huffed in a deep breath, ignoring the pain it caused his damaged throat, and yelled, "PREGNANT!"

The room grew quiet, and Sarah stopped resisting. The men understood what Mark was conveying, and it caused them to pause—this gave Mark hope. These men weren't here to kill them. Or, at least they weren't there to kill Sarah.

But his optimism was short-lived. Banks and another man grabbed Mark beneath his shoulders and lifted him up. They turned Mark around and he found himself facing a man in a gray suit with a pockmarked face, intense blue eyes, and a discomforting grin. He cocked his head to the side and looked at Mark, examining. His expression turned to sardonic pity.

"Mark, Mark, Mark," the man said. "This is *some* trouble you've made for yourself."

Mark's mind began to clear, and he started running through scenarios of who this man might be working for. Senator Dudek? Terrance's dad? Someone else? What had he done—who had he pissed off—to warrant this kind of extreme action?

"My name is Agent Richard O'Neal," the man continued.

"And you're under arrest for conspiracy to commit espionage against the United States."

Mark opened his mouth to speak, but no words came out. Everything this O'Neal had said—conspiracy, espionage—made absolutely no sense, and Mark didn't even know where his response should begin.

He had no time to consider his words, though. O'Neal continued to smile as he nodded to one of the men at Mark's side. The agent's grin was the last thing Mark saw before a hood was thrown over his head and the world went dark. He heard Sarah yelling that O'Neal had made a mistake, that this was impossible, but soon her voice drifted away.

Two men dragged Mark forward, his toes scraping across the hardwood floor all the way to the front door. Before leaving the building, someone slapped a set of handcuffs, hard, on his wrists. Mark cringed, but didn't bother to protest. He was too shocked. The men continued their forward march with Mark in tow, and just as he heard his building's front door squeak open he felt a rush of brisk autumn air turn the sweat on his body frigid. Mark began to tremble, from the cold and from the fear. The men quickened their pace once they got outside, and Mark heard O'Neal tell someone, "Get the doors."

The men carrying Mark stopped. Mark assumed he was in the street, judging by the cold, gravelly texture beneath his feet. He tried to plead, desperately.

"This, this . . ." Shivering uncontrollably, Mark struggled to get his words out. "A mistake. I'm not . . . I didn't do anything wr-wrong."

Mark felt a hand on his shoulder—O'Neal's. Mark could practically hear a smile on his face through his satisfied tone. "Strain—we're well beyond that point," he said. Then, after a pause: "Toss him."

Mark was shoved forward, and he landed with a hollow thud on a corrugated, metallic surface. The utility van he'd seen earlier, most likely. Mark's head cracked against the floor, inducing a nauseating feeling of vertigo. By the time he lifted himself up, he heard the van doors slam shut. There was no time to yell in protest, no time to scream for someone to help.

As the van pulled away, Mark felt something warm trickling down his face. Blood. Coming from his head and flowing in a steady stream. Mark had no idea where he was being taken. And he had no clue why. The blood, the vertigo, the growing claustrophobia—Mark's final thought before passing out was that this was all just a dream.

Soon, he'd be back home.

9

When the van finally stopped, Mark was yanked out of the back and forced to his feet, which were still bare. He didn't resist. He was too tired and too afraid that any act of aggression might be grounds for a bullet, and he had no interest in committing suicide by stupidity. When a voice behind him told him to walk, that's exactly what he did.

Once inside wherever they were, Mark felt cold concrete beneath his feet, but not like the concrete from outside. This was like the kind of sterile cold floor found in a warehouse. He could see it was painted a flat bluish gray through the bottom edge of the hood, but that gave him no indication as to where he was. It might have been a Costco warehouse for all Mark could tell. He only knew to keep quiet and obedient as he was nudged down a small corridor, unsure what lined either side of him. He could sense something was there, though. Maybe it was warehouse pallets or stacked freight; or, maybe it was the armory of a terrorist operation, and this was all much worse than he had even imagined. Mark tried to convince himself that if his captors wanted to kill him, he'd be dead by now. But there was no palliative for the incessant thought that he was going to die an anonymous, violent death in this place, whatever it was.

A voice told Mark to stop, and he did. Ahead of him, just a few paces away, he heard a heavy door get pulled open. Mark was shoved past the doorway's threshold and pushed down on a cold, metallic chair. First his feet were cuffed to the legs, then his hands were briefly uncuffed then cuffed again behind the back of the chair. The hood was pulled off his head and, even though the room's light was a muted fluorescent, the shock to his eyes made him recoil. Mark turned to catch a glimpse of the men who'd been moving him along, but all his eyes captured were two blurry figures in all black just as they were leaving the room. The reinforced door was pushed shut, and Mark was alone.

All he could do was stare at the floor, and that helped straighten and focus his mind. He could think a little clearer. Mark knew where he was—sort of. He'd heard about this kind of place before. Clandestine holding centers operated by federal agencies for people who weren't going to be entered into the system. They were never charged with a crime, they never saw the inside of a courtroom. They went to these centers and then, a day or two later, went somewhere else.

Mark shivered at the idea of where somewhere else might be.

If his captors were trying to disorient him, they'd done an exceptional job. Mark had no idea where he was or whether it was day or night. When he'd come to, the van was still driving, and it kept going for what seemed like hours. He could be in South Carolina for all he knew, or he could be ten minutes from his house, and they'd just gone in circles to confuse and destabilize Mark's sense of time and place. It was a common interrogation tactic, keeping the subject afraid and disoriented; in this weakened state, detainees were more likely to comply with questioning and, ultimately, surrender useful intel. Mark knew the textbook. You had to when dealing with military contracts. He just never dreamt, not in a million years, that those tactics would be used on him.

Mark's room had no character. Gray walls, gray floors, a single fluorescent tube light hanging from the ceiling. A metal chair directly across from him. There was no two-way mirror common to interrogation rooms, no camera perched in the corner. No one would watch what would happen, no one would record it.

Mark startled at the sound of the door opening. He looked up to see O'Neal enter. The cocksure agent sauntered across the room and sat in the chair opposite Mark. But the satisfied smile he'd been wearing earlier was absent; now, he just look exhausted. Weary, even.

"Hello, Mark," he said. "I'm really sorry to break it to you, but the game's over."

"I want a lawyer," Mark said, as confidently as possible.

O'Neal grunted.

"Mark, Mark," he said, composing himself. "Do you really think you're in a place that welcomes lawyers? You're caught. Your entire ring is in our custody. It's over."

"Who put you up to this? Who? Was it Dudek? Is this his twisted way of getting back at me?"

"You mean Senator Dudek, the man you blackmailed to help your client secure a lucrative security contract? Don't worry, Mark, we've spoken to the senator. And we are in the process of thoroughly investigating Verge and getting to the bottom of what they were planning to do with this contract."

Mark shook his head. The more O'Neal spoke, the less he understood. This was real. Mark understood that, clearly. Whatever was happening, whatever all this was, it was *real*.

"I want to talk to my wife. Let me talk to Sarah. She can help explain, she can—"

O'Neal interrupted. "You have no wife. No life. You're a spy, an enemy agent of a foreign power. Everything you had, your wife, your job, your home—it's gone. It never was."

For a moment, Mark felt like he was going to laugh. That was all he could do in the face of this epic farce, after all. Laugh, and uncontrollably at that. But as quickly as the urge arose, Mark felt it disappear. The room began to spin. Words began to echo in his mind. Spy. Enemy. In a way, O'Neal was right—Mark did have a life that wasn't his, only the grizzled agent had it backward. Whatever this spy thing was, Mark knew, obviously, that it was all a lie—but based on everything he'd been through today and the look on O'Neal's face, this wasn't a joke. For the first time in as long as he could remember, Mark couldn't think of a way to talk himself out of a situation. His words, his greatest asset, wouldn't be enough to save him. The realization terrified him more than anything else that'd happened through the entire ordeal.

"I—no. No!" Mark yelled, lunging forward in his chair. The handcuffs scraped against his wrists, tearing away layers of skin. "Spy? Spy?! Listen to me. Listen! This is a mistake. You've made a mistake. Just, please, let me talk to Sarah. I can fix this!"

O'Neal's face remained impassive. He got out of his chair and grasped Mark's shoulder as he spoke directly in his ear: "Mark, or whatever your real name is, you can drop the act. Everyone else did. The only thing you're getting is a one-way ticket out of here."

"Ticket? Ticket to where?" Mark thrashed in his chair, causing the abrasions in his wrist to deepen. He turned to O'Neal, catching him just as he was about to leave the room. "Tell me where you're sending me!"

O'Neal turned to look back one last time. "Home, of course. Agent transfer. We're sending you back to Russia."

Mark screamed. He fought against his restraints, tensing every muscle in his body as he pulled with all his strength, desperately trying to break himself free. In his mind, he was tearing the bolts that held his chair down right out of the floor. But that didn't happen. He screamed and thrashed, deepening the wounds in his wrists and causing fresh lacerations around his ankles. And he was so lost in his resistance that he didn't even notice the two guards enter the room from the door behind him. Mark only realized their presence when he was shocked by a Taser for the second time. His muscle control fled his body just like before, leaving Mark paralyzed in the chair. The fight he'd put up, however futile it was, was over.

The black hood came down again, and for the second time Mark's world went black.

PART TWO

PART TWO

10

Sarah stood by the windows, feeling numb to everything around her. The world she saw with her eyes and could touch with her hands seemed immaterial; as she stared impassively at the curtains that covered her living room windows, Sarah found herself nearly convinced that if she reached out her hand and disturbed the maroon fabric that hung from the garishly ornate rod and nearly to the floor, reality as she knew it would simply fall away. The world around her would then reflect how she felt: like she was falling through a depthless, black abyss, screaming without sound as she plunged down, down, down. Sarah reached out more than once and, with a stuttered breath, stopped short of making contact with her surroundings for fear that it might all come undone—even more than it already had.

But Sarah knew that was impossible. Despite the shock of the past twenty-four hours, she still had her pragmatic brain, which was working overtime to keep her sane. Sarah knew, despite the sheer lunacy of it all, what was real and what was not. Mark was her husband. Mark was a D.C. lobbyist.

Mark was *not* a Russian spy.

Sarah also knew that if she tugged on the curtains that opened to her postage stamp–sized front lawn, the only thing she'd see was the outside world. Same as it was yesterday, same as it'd be tomorrow. The problem was that Sarah wanted nothing to do with the thing that'd somehow come to be known as *reality*. Because in reality, she'd shove aside her curtains and be exposed to a world where pitch-black helicopters roamed the skies over-head; where police barricades stood resolutely at each end of her block; where police officers, hands holding the butts of their guns, patrolled up and down the street. It made her feel like she was living in some kind of dystopian military state. Even more un-nerving were the bloodsuckers that were camped out in front of her building waiting for a drop of blood—in the form of a glimpse of Sarah—to splash into their water. Sarah spotted only a slice of the esteemed press corps in the narrow slit between two of her curtains, but it was enough. Reporters and their film crews lazed about the front lawn, cameras and microphones at the ready, though Sarah could hardly fathom what they were hoping for. A picture of her? What would that prove or add to their story? Judg-ing by what she'd seen on the news so far, not a single outlet was interested in that pesky little matter of the truth. If any of these so-called reporters bothered doing the slightest bit of research, they'd see what a sham the allegations against Mark were. In-stead, they were wasting time on her lawn, chomping for their chance to harass the wife of an alleged American traitor. The truth would just have to wait, apparently.

Not for Sarah, though. While it still made her head spin to re-call the events of the past day, she couldn't help herself from playing them over and over in her mind, trying to remember an overlooked detail that would shed light on what was *actually* hap-pening or puzzle together what she knew into a more coherent whole.

First, Sarah recalled, came the federal goons in black suits who interrogated her for hours. Were they CIA? NSA? In all the time they took asking Sarah questions they seemed to already know the answers to, they never identified themselves. Did Sarah know Mark was a Russian spy? Did she know the other members of his espionage ring? Did she notice anything suspicious about his behavior? Did he have any unusual technology in their house, any items he tried to keep hidden from her? No. No. No. No. They asked her the same questions over and over, varying the sequence, changing the delivery, modifying a word or two. If their aim was to disorient her, they didn't need to try so hard; their colleagues had violently ripped her husband out of their home, draping a black hood over his head while physically restraining her. They violated her sense of security and, even more traumatizing, tried to confuse her into accepting a reality she knew was a complete fiction. But who's weaving this narrative? Sarah wondered as the goons pressed their questions. Sarah knew Mark had enemies—all lobbyists do—but was there one out there powerful and vindictive enough to have Mark declared an enemy of the state? Just the idea of such a bitter vendetta made Sarah tremble; after all, if Mark did have this kind of enemy out there, who knew what else he or she was capable of—or if this was the culmination of their plans, or just the beginning.

By the time the nameless goons finished their circuitous questioning, dusk was falling; Sarah looked out her windows and saw the golden sunset hovering over the bare branches that stretched from the poplar in front of her home. She noticed that the front door, which was bashed off its hinges when the raid began, had been neatly replaced. Like nothing had happened. Like armed men hadn't erupted into her life and stolen her husband as she helplessly watched. Sarah unlocked and locked the door at least ten times, trying to will herself to believe that the dead bolt mattered. That she could feel safe within her own home. It was an unconvincing exercise.

The news of Mark's abduction—Sarah couldn't stomach the term "arrest" to properly describe what happened—broke at nightfall. At the time, Sarah was sitting on her couch in the living room, gripping her phone in one hand and the bat she used in her summer softball leagues in the other. She hadn't spoken to anyone about what had happened; she didn't even know how. What would she tell her parents? That her husband, their son-in-law, had been ripped from their home on allegations of being a Russian spy? It didn't even make sense. She didn't know where Mark was, didn't know if what the goons or that agent O'Neal had said was even true. And while she tried her hardest to push the thought from her mind, she didn't even know if Mark was alive. More than once she considered the possibility that what she'd been told were lies—well, she knew they were lies, and that Mark's captors also knew they were lies—and this was all an elaborate cover for something *else*. Sarah considered calling the D.C. police, but even that seemed futile; there was no one to trust, no one who could make sense of this living nightmare. As much as Sarah considered the worst outcome of what had happened, she also envisioned the best—that someone would realize the hideous mistake that'd been made, and Mark would walk through their front door, worse for the wear but with a hell of a story to tell at dinner parties.

Those hopes were dashed the moment her phone began to vibrate in her grasp. Sarah jolted upright on the couch at the intrusive alert. Up to that point, she had been ensconced in a bubble of silence. The TV was off and she hadn't received a single call or text all day. Then, suddenly, her phone was thrown into a fit of spasms without end. Her text and email tones—the nauseating stock chime that she perpetually vowed to change—hardly had time to fully ding before another alert came rushing in. Dozens of messages all asking the same two questions: What happened to Mark? Are you okay? In that order—first the dirt, then the concern. Chime after chime after chime. And when Sarah ignored the messages—many of them coming from people she hardly spoke to, hadn't spoken to in years, or flat out didn't even know— the phone started to ring. Sarah ignored every call. Her boss, her brother, even her best friend. She wasn't prepared to talk about what had happened, not without bursting into a screaming rage or collapsing into a fit of tears. There was no time for either; Mark was out there, somewhere, and she had to hold her shit together in case he needed her. Wherever he was, whatever she needed to do to get him back home to her, Sarah was ready to do it.

The only text Sarah sent was to her parents. Sarah knew how crippled with fear and anxiety they'd be, and she didn't want them to be distraught on her account. To assuage their nerves, Sarah told them it was all a misunderstanding, that it would be worked out soon. And she urged them to keep her message to themselves. Sarah was aware of their love of forwarding messages, however banal, factual, or relevant, to their entire contact lists. For the time being, Sarah preferred, profoundly, to keep this situation close to the chest—which was impossible, considering.

As the barrage of texts, emails, and calls continued unabated, Sarah finally worked up the nerve to flip on her TV, cringing as she did, to find out what was being said about Mark. News of his arrest, and his role as a saboteur, had to be what sparked all the attention Sarah was now the victim of. It relieved her, in a way. At least Mark hitting the news cycle gave credibility to everything that had happened.

Even though she knew it was all but impossible, Sarah tried to filter her news to weed out partisan propaganda. She wasn't a news junkie like Mark, so her investment in the networks warring over which claimed the truth most accurately didn't mean that much to her, but in this case, she needed information that was, she truly hoped, as accurate as possible. But as she turned on the station she trusted most, it quickly became evident that they were guilty of being just another avenue for pumping out whatever information was fed to them without even blinking an eye—or, better yet, verifying the validity of what they'd been told. Because what she saw and heard painted Mark as an enemy combatant determined to dismantle the very structure of American democracy. They spoke of him like he'd not only been accused, but also tried and convicted.

In the first segment Sarah caught, an unreasonably sexy anchor lobbed softball questions to an intelligence "expert"—his credentials were never made clear—who explained how domestic spies—sleeper agents, he said, again and again—were so prevalent on American soil that it was almost commonplace. The reason Mark's case was so shocking, apparently, was because he was an American-born citizen who had abandoned his allegiance to the United States in favor of Mother Russia. Sarah's heart, which had been tumbling around her chest since turning on the TV, sunk down into the pit of her stomach when this expert speculated that Mark's turn came during a semester abroad in Russia while in college—an excursion Sarah *knew* never happened. They'd been friends since their sophomore year, when they were neighbors in a dingy apartment complex on the south end of Duke's campus; while they didn't get involved romantically until after graduation, Sarah was acquainted with Mark's life enough to know he had never gone to Russia. Mark studied, he played football, and he worked on a loading dock near his house every summer. That was it. This excursion to Russia was an absolute fabrication that was being passed off as truth to millions of people. It made Sarah sick.

Reality never felt so tenuous, and Sarah had to pinch the corners of her eyes to keep her head from spinning. Who was filling Mark's life with fiction? And *why*?

Sarah was snapped back to the present by the sound of a growing clamor outside her window. She separated the curtains enough to see that the reporters' attention was no longer affixed to her window; instead, the bloodsuckers were flocking to her front staircase, mobbing someone who was trying to walk up her stairs. The tight swarm of paparazzi blocked her view, so she couldn't see who was trying to make their way into her building. The person had to be determined, though, and a touch crazy to fully expose themselves to the media vultures just to get to her front door. The doorbell rang, a shrill buzzing that sounded like an air raid siren. Sarah was startled by the noise even though she knew to expect it. Her nerves were beyond shot.

Though just a few steps separated Sarah from her front door, it seemed so much farther. Her paces slow and calculated, she stalked forward like a hunter angling in on a deer. The grip on her baseball bat couldn't have been tighter. In her mind, the door was just waiting to crack open again. Its permeability was her new normal, and she couldn't imagine that changing for a long, long time.

Choking down her fear, Sarah willed herself close enough to the door so she could reach the adjacent intercom. She pressed the talk button—"Who is it?" she calmly asked, but when the reply came in, all she could hear was the cacophonous chatter of one reporter after another shouting questions at whoever was at the door. Sarah's instincts screamed for her to ignore whoever was looking to enter her home. But the idea of having someone to talk to, someone who could help make sense of the madness engulfing her, was hard to resist. And after all, whoever this person was, they obviously weren't there in an official capacity; they weren't there to question, harass, or arrest her. If they had been, Sarah learned, they wouldn't buzz. They'd just enter.

Steeling herself with a deep breath, Sarah jammed her finger into the buzzer and opened the complex's door. After flipping over the dead bolt, Sarah took a half-dozen steps back and raised the bat in a slugging position. She gripped its handle and mentally prepared herself to attack if whoever came through her front door, whoever entered *her* home, was someone she didn't like.

The doorknob clicked, and Sarah twisted her fingers around the bat's worn rubber; she was ready.

Every muscle in her body relaxed, though, when Aaron entered. He recoiled at the sight of Sarah, falling back against the closed door. After all, Sarah was standing just a few feet away, ready to crack his skull open with an aluminum baseball bat. "Jesus!" he yelled.

"Oh, thank God," Sarah said as she lowered the bat. She realized she must have looked like a maniac; not only because of the bat she wielded, but also the wide-eyed stare that'd been locked on her face.

"What the *hell* is going on, Sarah?" Aaron asked, confusion and shock lacing his words.

Sarah dropped the bat onto the couch. She gripped the back as she tried to decide where to even start. "I have no idea," she said. "It isn't true. *None* of it is true."

"I know, I know," Aaron said, and he started to rub Sarah's back. She recoiled at the contact, and Aaron immediately pulled his hand away. "Sorry—sorry," he said, and Sarah could tell he meant it. Mark hated Aaron, but he didn't know him the way Sarah did. Sure, he could be loud and obnoxious, but it was all a front that masked his deep insecurities and anxiety. And, truth be told, he sometimes acted even crasser than normal just to piss Mark off. Still, despite all of it, Sarah knew Aaron was a good person, and a good friend. If anyone had to be with her right now, she was glad it was him. "I'm going to go and get you a cup of tea or something." Aaron continued, "You're a *little* on edge. When I get back, you can start at the beginning."

Sarah nodded, and Aaron disappeared into the kitchen. She then flopped down on the couch, and released a deep breath. It felt like her entire body was exhaling, and she let her eyelids close. She blinked once, twice, and was sound asleep.

* * *

When Sarah woke up it was still nighttime. Aaron was facing the curtains, entranced by the spectacle right outside her door.

"I'm guessing they haven't left yet," she said as she used the back of her hand to wipe off the little bit of drool that had slid down the side of her mouth while she was asleep.

"There was a shift change, but that's it," Aaron replied.

He turned away from the view and sat on the armchair opposite Sarah. She was used to Mark sitting in that chair, and when he did, he filled it out. His muscular frame, wide hips, and broad shoulders covered the chair's lavender fabric backing, whereas Aaron's frame allowed for the light purple coloring to poke out on both sides. Mark also sat differently; he opened up on the chair, spreading his legs and pushing his back into the fabric like he was demanding the seat to accommodate him; Aaron, on the other hand, folded one leg over another, and he sat with a bit of a hunch in his posture, like he was cold and needed to huddle for warmth. While Sarah was thankful Aaron was there and she appreciated him exposing himself to the media—she could see the footage of him pushing into her house in her mind, accompanied by a tawdry headline, "Enemy Sympathizer?" or something of the sort—his presence, and the way it screamed how unlike Mark he was, only made her miss her husband even more.

"So, this is all pretty crazy. Do you want to talk about it?" Aaron asked after a silent lull.

"No," Sarah replied. "Yes. I mean . . . I don't even know where to start."

"Start by telling me if Putin's cool or what," Aaron said, and he cracked a kind smile, really selling his humor. Sarah furrowed her brow, but she couldn't stop a laugh from escaping her mouth.

"This is so insane!" she said, pulling at the frayed strands of her hair. "I mean, I don't even know how to feel. Sometimes I feel like it's a hoax or a mistake or . . . who knows. It's so crazy I can't even understand it."

"Look, Mark and I might not be buds, but I know him enough to know this whole thing is bullshit. So, tell me about it. Maybe a fresh set of eyes can make sense of this whole . . . whatever it is."

Sarah took a long, deep breath and started at the beginning: Mark's abduction, then her interrogation, the bullshit news she saw on TV, all the while weaving a twisting and turning path through every theory she'd mentally catalogued. Aaron listened without interruption, letting Sarah get it all out of her system.

"That . . . ," Aaron said once Sarah had exhausted herself talking. "That's horrifying, what happened. I'm sorry you had to go through it."

Sarah sighed. "Don't be sorry for me. Be sorry for Mark—he's the one who's been falsely accused of spying and is being shipped to Moscow. He doesn't even speak a word of Russian."

"Well, 'vodka.' And 'nyet,' I'm sure he knows."

Sarah shot Aaron a cold look.

"Right," he said. "Sorry."

Sarah shot up from her seat and started to pace. She wanted to climb the walls; while she couldn't even begin to understand what Mark was enduring, she couldn't stop herself from feeling like a prisoner. She was trapped where she was, afraid to go anywhere or do anything. Before Aaron arrived, she had glimpsed at the news headlines on her phone, one of which mentioned that the president was going to address the press on Mark's arrest and what he was apparently calling "the enemy within." That quote alone made Sarah shiver, and it gave her little doubt that the president was going to do what he typically did—spout a bunch of nonsense and stir people into a frenzy through wild declarations and no shortage of reminders that they should be in a state of constant fear. Would she become a target for some fanatic looking to boast of their patriotism? Would she be picked up off the street by a nameless, faceless intelligence agency and detained over a vague concern that she, too, was a spy?

"I just don't know what to do," she said. "Where do I go? How do I keep myself safe?"

"You and the baby," Aaron said.

Sarah stopped dead in her tracks. She screwed her head toward Aaron, and she could feel him recoil at her glare.

"Oh, shiiiiiit," he said in slow motion. "You don't know."

"Know *what*?" Sarah growled through gritted teeth. Though she'd only been a mother, and an expectant one at that, for a few days, she already felt her primal protection instinct kicking in. A threshold had been crossed from threatening Sarah to threatening her unborn child, and she felt all the fear that'd been bottling up inside of her transform into rage. No one would hurt her baby, not before it was born, not after, not when it was a thirty-year-old with children of his or her own. *No one.*

"You should probably see for yourself," Aaron said as he took hold of the remote control and turned the TV on. He flipped to Fox News. A panel of guests were tiled on the screen, like the opening credits to *The Brady Bunch*, engaged in a heated debate. Sarah couldn't discern the topic based on the brief snippets each panelist allowed one another before shouting over whoever was trying to get their voice heard. But then it became clear—words like "legitimacy," "forfeited citizenship," and "rightful place," clued her into the conversation.

They were talking about shipping her baby to Russia.

"You've got to be fucking kidding me!" she bellowed, then she marched to where the TV was hanging on the wall and slapped its side control panel four times, until it finally turned off.

"Mark is not a traitor," Sarah said, spinning on her heels to face Aaron. "He doesn't belong in Russia, and my baby sure as *hell* doesn't belong in that damn country."

"I know, I know," Aaron said, holding out his arm to urge Sarah to calm down. "Let's think this through, okay? Mark had to be set up—by who? Who has he made enemies with?"

Sarah huffed. "Get comfortable," she said.

"No, I mean *real* enemies. People who not only had the nerve to orchestrate something as crazy as this, but also the power."

"There's that senator," Sarah said, trying to slow her racing mind so she could remember the things Mark had said about him. "Dudek was his name."

Aaron whistled. "Yeah, that's a scary dude to have on your bad side. But, I don't know. For as rotten and crooked as he can be, he's had a long career free of any real wrongdoing. Doing something as risky as this seems out of character."

"I—I don't know. I mean, there's plenty of people Mark has rubbed the wrong way. It's the competitive nature of his job. But we'll see these same guys at a bar or something, and we'll all have a drink and everything's fine. They get over their losses, same as Mark gets over it when he loses."

"Somebody has to be behind this, we know that," Aaron said, stroking his chin. "Someone had to tip the Feds, someone has to be feeding this information, the lies and the truth, to the media. I guess the other question, other than who is doing this, is why. Why Russia? Maybe if we can figure out why that became Mark's destination, we can understand who put him there—they'd have to have ties to the Kremlin, right? I mean, this has to be a two-way street. Did Mark ever mention anyone who had that kind of association?"

Sarah jabbed her palms into her forehead. She loved listening to Mark talk—he had the gift of gab, and there was hardly any other quality so quintessential to who he was. But that meant he told her *a lot* of things. A lot of names, a lot of stories, a lot of details about whatever deal he was in the middle of. And that made it difficult to shuffle through the Rolodex of her memory and pull out such a specific detail. She groaned at her own shortcoming, because if she couldn't save Mark, who could? Suddenly, Sarah was choked by the realization that she might never see her husband again.

And that premise, she refused to abide.

"I'll go to Russia," she said, almost simultaneously to the thought being born in her mind.

"*What?*" Aaron asked, an expression of utter horror on his face.

"I won't do it, Aaron. I won't live without my husband; I won't raise my baby—*our* baby—without him. And, judging by what the news said, the U.S. doesn't want me and my baby here anyway."

"Okay, okay," Aaron said, his patronizing tone digging beneath Sarah's skin. "You're in shock right now. I know this all . . . it's crazy, but, Sarah, if you leave this country now, you'll *never* get back in."

"I'd rather be with my husband in the worst place on Earth than alone in the best place."

Aaron shrugged his shoulders. "Fine. But what if you can't get to Mark? What then? What happens to you, and the baby, if you're marooned in Russia?"

Sarah stopped pacing and released a deep breath; it felt like all the air drained from her as her body sagged like a falling accordion. That hope, however fleeting, had given her strength; it had given her something to do other than feeling helpless and wondering what terrible things were being done to the man she loved.

"What's going to happen to him, Aaron?" she asked, on the brink of tears. "The Russians, they know he's not one of theirs. What will they do to him?"

Aaron swallowed hard and averted his eyes from Sarah's. "I don't know," he said, quietly. "I really don't."

Sarah collapsed on the couch. She couldn't feel anything. She couldn't breathe. She couldn't even blink.

Slowly, Aaron knelt in front of her and tilted his head to catch her gaze. "Come stay with me," he said.

Sarah grimaced, disgusted, and immediately felt guilty for doing so. This wasn't a ploy for him to get close to her, something he'd done plenty of times. This was different. "I can't. I—And do what?"

"What will you do here?" Aaron asked. "It's not good for you to stay here alone and, quite frankly, I don't think it's safe, either."

The words sunk in, and Sarah knew he was right. Someone coming for her—maybe they'd be from the government, maybe it'd just be some raging psycho—was a real possibility, and Sarah would need a lot more than a softball bat to defend herself. Granted, Aaron was nowhere close to being bodyguard material, but at least he could offer her sanctuary until she figured out what she was going to do.

"Okay," she said, drawing a deep breath. "Let's get out of here."

Sarah packed a suitcase in record time, and when she came out of her bedroom, Aaron was at the door, texting someone. He looked up and, seeing Sarah approaching, fumbled to shove his phone back into his jacket pocket. Aaron's nervous reaction wasn't lost on Sarah.

"Who are you texting?" she asked.

"Huh?" Aaron blurted. "Just my folks. I was supposed to see them today, and they were wondering where I was."

Sarah nodded and tried to subdue what she assumed was paranoia.

Aaron took her suitcase, and they stood at the front door, shoulder to shoulder, bracing themselves for the assault that was awaiting them.

"You ready?" Aaron asked.

"No," Sarah replied.

"Well, can't turn back now," Aaron said as he shoved the front door open and placed his hand on Sarah's back to move her along. Maybe it was to keep them pushing through the sea of reporters they were about to face.

Or maybe, Sarah questioned, it was his way of getting her where he wanted her to be.

11

The plane touched down, and Mark awoke with a gasp. In the moment between waking and his eyes capturing the reality around him—a bitter moment—Mark thought he was waking up at home, in his bed. But then he remembered, and the feverish sequence of memories that came rushing back to his mind made him wince. He felt sick to his stomach, but the moment passed. He forced the moment to pass. Wallowing in his own misery wouldn't get him anywhere. It certainly wouldn't get him back home.

As far as the world was concerned, he was no longer Mark Strain, D.C. lobbyist, son of Joe and Lorraine Strain, husband to Sarah Conte, and expectant father. He was now Pyotr . . . whoever. And he was returning home to a place he'd never in his life even visited.

Mark was in Moscow.

After being whisked off the plane and forced into a photo op on the tarmac with his "fellow spies," Gregori, Mark's handler, shuffled him into a sedan—a vintage model that, intentionally or not, looked like it was straight out of a Sean Connery–era Bond movie—and had the driver whisk them away from the airport. Ania and Viktor stayed behind to take their places on a dais and meet the press and their adoring countrymen. They were heroes; Mark was something else.

"We've informed the press you were feeling sick and, regrettably, cannot participate in the warm welcome that's been arranged for you all," Gregori said as the sedan cruised slowly through Moscow. "I figure your inability to speak Russian might raise some eyebrows."

"You think?"

"How are you feeling?" Gregori asked. He sat across from Mark—the sedan's back seat had two benches that faced each other—and was leaning in to examine the bruises, bumps, and lacerations that traced a road map from where Mark was now and where this had all begun, back in D.C.

"As if you care," Mark said.

"Oh, but I do. We've sold you to the Russian people as a hero. A man who sacrificed much of his life to serve his country. It is in all of our interests to maintain your health and wellness and assure the people that sacrifice and dedication are indeed rewarded."

Mark shook his head at Gregori's assessment of his usefulness. He wasn't an idiot. Sure, they were protective of Mark *now*. Would they still be in three months? Six? When the press had turned their attention away from the returning spy heroes and Mark was no longer at the top of the public's mind, would it matter what happened to him? He could be disposed of at will, dumped in a shallow grave, and no one, not a single person in all of Russia, would realize he was gone.

Even with that knowledge racing through Mark's mind, he didn't have it in him to engage in another fight, even a verbal one. The adrenaline that had kept him going the past day and a half, along with the drugs Gregori had slipped him, had worn off. All that remained was a profound exhaustion that Mark honestly thought he'd never recover from. Every inch of his body felt sore to the touch and painful to move; even the act of shaking his head at Gregori's false assurances made him ache. He could only focus his attention on the strange world outside his window and take it all in. This would be his home until he either escaped or outlived his purpose—which would be the same day he was murdered and discarded.

Prior to this day, Mark's knowledge of Moscow's architecture began and ended with buildings like Saint Basil's Cathedral and the Kremlin. He thought the city would be a sprawling skyline of colorful onion domes and fortified complexes. And while those styles existed, Moscow proved to be a mishmash of several aesthetics, encompassing the glass-and-steel edifices that represented Russia's modernity as well the stout, utilitarian buildings that hinted at its oppressive past. Mark couldn't help but recognize how foreign it all felt to him. True, he'd traveled abroad numerous times, but he was an outsider—a tourist—in every trip he took; he was a visitor who, by definition, wasn't supposed to fit in. But now, he was being asked to look at everything around him with knowing eyes. This was, according to the narrative built around his identity, a place he knew and loved even though nothing could be further from the truth. Mark didn't know the look and feel of this place, didn't know the customs, he didn't even know more than five words of the language. Never in his life did he feel more disconnected from a place, and it worried him that, when the time came—*if* it came—he was going to need to navigate his way through it to get back home.

Roughly an hour after leaving the airport, the sedan stopped outside a skyscraper that shone with golden light against the darkening sky. The building itself looked like a giant throne with its central piece rising stories above its accompanying wings, which shot out like arms of the regal seat. The sedan pulled into the half-circle valet area just outside the lobby, and Mark's door was opened for him. He peered outside, noticing the immaculate glass doors that led into the building, and wondered what he and Gregori were doing there.

"Well?" Gregori prodded. "Are you just going to sit around?"

Mark took the hint and exited the car, figuring it was safe enough to do so. If they had stopped in the middle of an abandoned industrial lot, that would be one thing; Mark would know what to expect. But they were, as far as Mark could tell, in the heart of downtown Moscow, in front of a crowded hotel. He was safe—for the moment.

"Triumph Palace," Gregori said as he followed Mark out of the car. "One of our finest buildings, and the place you will call home."

Mark arched an eyebrow at Gregori. "You're really going all in with this returning hero bit, aren't you?"

Gregori shot Mark a disapproving frown. "Come," he said, leading Mark into the building. "Your unit is prepared."

The gold-plated elevator lifted Mark and Gregori to the Palace's twenty-third floor. With a muffled ding, the elevator slid open and Mark cautiously exited into a lobby. Mark was taken aback; in his mind, every floor of a hotel had doors lining both sides of the hallway, from one end to the next. But this was more like a penthouse. There was only one door—not including the emergency exits on the far sides of both ends of the lobby—and Gregori had already walked ahead of Mark and was using a key card to open it. Still concerned about what to expect, Mark followed Gregori, unable to disguise the exhaustion and soreness that hobbled his gait.

"Welcome to your quarters," Gregori said as Mark entered the lavish room.

Mark looked around, trying to stifle his awe but failing. He knew all about Russian excess—it was no different from the American brand, and in his work as a steward of the rich and powerful, Mark had encountered his share of excess—but he still couldn't help but be impressed by the riches on display. While the massive room did incorporate a modicum of modern simplicity, the flourishes felt like they were meant to provoke with their garishness. The wide-open design gave a clear view to much of the unit, and even with the most perfunctory glance as he strolled through the place, Mark could identify the top-of-the-line appliances in the kitchen, a priceless Pollock painting that hung on the wall opposite the dining room table, and an entertainment system in the living room that probably cost half of Mark's annual salary.

"Nice and homey," Gregori said, stating it as fact, not asking.

"Yeah," Mark said, "it totally mirrors the modest lifestyle I'm used to."

"We wish for you to be comfortable, that is all."

"What happens then?" Mark asked, unable to mask the bitterness in his voice. "You make me look like one of yours, then everyone forgets about me and . . . what? Suicide? I'm disappeared?"

Gregori smiled. "You seem tired. Maybe it's time you rested—on your own accord."

Without so much of a hint of feeling in his eyes—knowing what had been done to Mark's life, knowing what his future held—Gregori walked to Mark and handed him the room key. "Good luck, Mark Strain."

Mark accepted the key and, strangely, felt sad to see Gregori go; Gregori was his enemy, there was no doubt about it, but he was the only person in Russia that he knew.

"I'm not going to see you again, am I?" Mark asked just as Gregori was about to leave.

"Let's just say that if you do see me, it won't be a happy reunion," Gregori said, and then he left the room, leaving Mark alone.

Everything was silent. It was the first moment of peace Mark had experienced in what felt like days, maybe even weeks. He stood by the floor-to-ceiling glass doors that led to his patio, looking out onto the Moscow skyline. The city was vast and strange with its various buildings crowding the landscape all the way to the horizon. Mark became dizzy; the lights of the city blurred and twisted like he was looking at it through a kaleidoscope. Maybe it was the exhaustion, or maybe it was the realization of how far away he was from home, but Mark felt lower than he ever had in his life. He could just end the game right now, he thought, and he pulled on the sliding door's handle so he could get a clear look at the long way down. Mark tugged harder and harder, but it was no use: The door was sealed shut. They had even taken away his power to end the charade on his own terms.

Feeling light-headed, Mark walked to the bar and poured a glass of water from a bottle but stopped before he brought it to his mouth. Paranoia made him question if the bottle was sealed before he'd opened it—maybe it was poisoned, maybe it was filled with mind-controlling drugs. Mark had no idea, and he couldn't convince himself how pointless such a gesture would be. Why bring him all the way here, set him up in a posh apartment, then poison him? The logic, though, only applied to a world that made sense and, at the moment, Mark was living an existence that was primarily defined by how absurd it had become.

So, Mark paced. He fidgeted with the magazines on the coffee table—all in Russian—and searched the closets, his bedroom, and any other concealed space to ensure he was alone. When he was convinced no one was hiding, waiting to jump out and pull off the Kremlin's master plan of killing him by heart attack, Mark flipped on the TV. Beamed from an overhead projector onto a seventy-some-inch screen was the press conference welcoming home his fellow spies. Mark had no idea what was being said about them. Judging by the footage of adoring crowds and the happy looks on Ania's and Viktor's faces, he assumed everyone was sticking to the state-sponsored script of the brave spies returning home after a job well done. And for all Mark knew, maybe they had done their job. He just didn't give a shit.

Mark was ready to shut off the propaganda—he had his finger on the remote's power button, a moment away from shutting out the world, when the news network cut to different footage, footage that made Mark's heart descend into his guts:

Sarah.

The video recording was shaky, but clear enough for Mark to see his wife, his home, his *life* right there on the screen in front of him. He reached out, instinctually, wanting to touch it, to feel the fabric of his world and hold it close to him; but all his fingers met was the vinyl screen.

Sarah was pushing through a wall of reporters, trying to get away from their house. But to where? Mark wondered—and then he spotted *him*. Aaron, that little son of a bitch.

Mark knew jealousy was the least of his concerns, and he knew it was ludicrous to even question Sarah's faithfulness. But still. Mark was exhausted, beaten down, and still confounded by what in the hell was going on. And he was furious about all of it. Aaron moving in on his wife—his wife and his *child*—was the spark that ignited his rage.

He stormed to the front door, throwing it open and leaving it open behind him.

"Fuck this," Mark said as he stomped through the vestibule. "I'm out of here."

Mark jammed the down button next to the elevator. He jammed it again. And again. But nothing happened. It didn't light up, didn't respond to his touch. Mark gave the door a swift kick, then ran to the emergency exit at the west end of the room; it was locked. He darted to the east exit. Same result. Feeling helpless and trapped, Mark kicked and punched the exit, hoping someone, anyone, would hear him and come to his aid.

"HELP!" he screamed. "I WANT OUT! HELP ME!"

Over and over again, he screamed, punching and kicking until his voice went hoarse and his muscles burned and begged for him to stop.

But Mark couldn't give in. He *refused*.

He returned to his room, slamming the door shut this time. When it caught in the frame, Mark heard a clicking sound, barely perceptible over his labored breathing. He went back to the door and tried turning the knob, but it wouldn't budge; he tugged on the door, pushing it back and forth, but it refused to give. Mark was locked inside.

"Fine, you want to play games? Let's play."

With the ferocity of a feral, starving beast released from its cage, Mark attacked the room. He tore fixtures off the wall, used the one knife he'd been provided with—a miniature paring knife—to slice through the couch cushions, emptying them of their contents, and flipped over whatever wasn't nailed down. He continued his rampage, panting uncontrollably, until he found what he was looking for: hidden within an orb-shaped sconce in the kitchen was a tiny oblong object, no bigger than a lapel pin, with a small wire coming from its rear. A camera.

Mark examined it, and he wondered just how many of these devices were planted all over his prison. It was a comfortable prison, he acknowledged, but a prison nonetheless. Forced to guess, Mark would say he was being monitored and watched in more ways than he could possibly fathom. But that didn't mean he'd stop trying to undermine every attempt that was being made to keep him under control.

He held the camera out, pointed it right at his face, and then smiled, taking a pleasure in his tiny victory.

"Fuck. You," he said into the lens, then he dropped the camera to the ground and smashed it with the heel of his shoe.

As he stood among the ruins of his trashed living quarters,

Mark decided, at last, that he'd had enough. He was locked inside, he didn't want to see one more second of the real spies and their shit-eating grins, and he couldn't even trust the food enough to eat it. Weary, starving, and feeling on the brink of losing his mind, Mark fell onto the bed, and he was asleep before a pair of guards entered his unit.

12

Something wasn't right.

Agent Richard O'Neal was hesitant to remove the final pieces of casework that had been tacked to the corkboard that hung on the back wall of his office. The photos, the telephone transcripts, the intercepted email messages—all the evidence it had taken his team nearly a year to compile had been unpinned and dropped into a box in the time it took for O'Neal to finish his morning coffee. All he had to do was tear off the few remaining pictures, send the box downstairs to be catalogued and logged into storage, and the case would officially be closed. Maybe he could even take a few unofficial personal days; though he'd dozed on the flights to and from Vienna, O'Neal couldn't even remember his last good night of sleep, and even the strongest coffee in the world couldn't stop his brain from feeling like pancake batter. Maybe that was why he was having this moment of hesitation, these feelings of doubt: He was delirious from exhaustion. Considering this, O'Neal ran his hand over his face—pulling down the skin beneath his weary eyes—and sighed deeply. It was a plausible explanation, there was no doubt, but O'Neal didn't buy it. He could fool his superiors and colleagues, he could even fool Mark Strain. The one person O'Neal couldn't fool was himself.

O'Neal had been working counterespionage for decades, and he liked to think he was an expert. He didn't allow himself much praise, but deep down he knew that he was good at only two things: making French toast for his daughters every other Saturday morning and chasing down spies. As O'Neal stared at the few remaining pictures on his board—all of Mark—he couldn't help but recall all the times he found himself questioning how the hell an American-born D.C. lobbyist with a criminal record as clean as his own grandmother's rap sheet fit into a Russian spy cell. Because in O'Neal's opinion—which no one asked for, he understood—Mark's role didn't make a lick of sense.

Sure, the package was tight. O'Neal and his team had caught Mark meeting with Ania, who was no doubt a Russian spy, and they'd captured enough information to know how diligently Mark fought for Verge—an international private security company that secured much of its startup capital from Sergei Vishny, a Russian billionaire. There was nothing wrong with being dedicated to your job, but Mark's level of commitment was more than intense. It was suspicious.

Still, there were holes. O'Neal had put in a fact-finding request to see what could be learned from Mark's semester studying in Russia. What he got back from Duke and the abroad sponsor program was threadbare, and that was putting it mildly. O'Neal could overlook an incomplete snapshot; after all, Mark traveled there in 2001, before every move a person made was tracked by the internet. What troubled O'Neal more was a transcript he'd found on his own—a transcript that had Mark completing courses at Duke at the very same time he was supposed to be in another country. The transcript mysteriously disappeared from Duke's databases a day later.

There was also the matter of smaller details, and that's where O'Neal was convinced a case was made. Every so often he'd be fed reports from other agencies, reports detailing Mark's clandestine communications with his handler, of Mark receiving transmissions—presumably from the Kremlin—instructing him how to proceed with his work involving Verge. But O'Neal never witnessed these details firsthand. He saw Ania perform plenty of acts of espionage. Plenty. But Mark? Not a single thing.

O'Neal removed a picture from the board: Mark and his wife, Sarah, strolling through the National Mall on a sunny afternoon. O'Neal had taken this series of photos himself and remembered the day clearly. The Mall was a convenient place for intelligence agents to make contact, typically picking up, or making, a drop. The crowds allowed for furtive movements and quick passes of information from a handler's hand to an agent's. When O'Neal followed Mark there, he expected—hoped, even—to catch Mark in the act. To do *something* that unequivocally pegged him as a spy. But unless Mark was *really* good and O'Neal missed whatever he'd done, not a damn thing went down that day. The only thing O'Neal saw was a young husband and wife enjoying a beautiful afternoon, same as the hundreds of other people who were doing the exact same thing.

Shit, O'Neal thought as his face screwed into a grimace.

An interrogation would have been nice. Maybe even a trial—those usually helped separate fact from fiction. *But who needs due process?* O'Neal bitterly questioned. Orders from the commander-in-chief himself were clear: Round up the Russians, ship them the hell out, and get a few of our own agents back in return. A show of force was in order, a message telling the public that the United States wouldn't abide Russian agents on its soil. That we were standing strong against any Russian saboteur who threatened to compromise the fabric of our society. In a sense, O'Neal understood that need; he didn't like trashing a year's worth of work in the process, nor was he enjoying the feeling growing in the pit of his stomach that something was amiss with Mark Strain. Combine O'Neal's lack of surefire evidence with Mark's bizarre—and, if he was being honest, convincing—behavior, and one might begin thinking that a mistake had been made.

O'Neal tossed the picture into the box and strode down the hall to his chief's office. He wasn't about to voice any of his concerns—if this operation ended up going pear-shaped, the last thing O'Neal wanted was to be on the hook for knowing something was wrong and not doing something about it, even if it was impossible for him to do so—but he did want to get a feel for where his boss stood on all this. Having read O'Neal's case file, it was possible the chief had some questions. Or maybe, if O'Neal's paranoia was founded, he was responsible for feeding false information. O'Neal had learned the hard way, when it came to intelligence agents, you never took anything for granted. Motives were amorphous, loyalty was nearly impossible, and duplicity was everywhere. That's just how the game was played.

With a soft rap on Lewis's door frame, O'Neal got the chief's attention.

Lewis raised his head and fixed his gaze over the glasses that rested on the bridge of his nose to look at O'Neal. His eyes were bleary from the small type of the briefing he'd been reading, and while he may not have meant to, he released an agitated sigh at the sight of O'Neal.

"Got a second, Chief?"

"No," Lewis said, dipping his head back to the briefing. "Go home."

O'Neal and Lewis had been partners a lifetime ago. At least that's how it felt. At the time, both O'Neal and Lewis were on track to move steadily up the chain; not a meteoric rise, but a steady, upward trajectory. But then came O'Neal's divorce, and with it a year of his life spinning out of control. Feuding with Lindsay over money, over their relationship, and over the kids took a heavy toll on him, and by the time he got his head straightened out again, he looked around only to realize that his peers, like Lewis, had all taken the next step up without him. He was left behind, and there was no catching up.

"Come on, just give me a minute," O'Neal said, entering Lewis's office as he kept his tone casual. "I'm curious to hear your thoughts about the operation."

"Thoughts?" Lewis said with a twitchy smile. "Thinking is beyond my pay grade. We were ordered to do something, and we did it successfully. Now, it's on to the next thing."

"I know, I know. It was just so . . . unusual. Being there on the runway, making a spy exchange with the Russians. Felt like one of the stories the old-timers used to tell us back when we were still rookies."

Lewis's shoulders sagged and a soft grumble sounded in his throat—the tell that he was thinking, despite his claims to the contrary.

"Listen, Rich," Lewis began, "I know you spent a lot of time working these people. All the intel gathering, the surveillance . . . it's a lot. And I know you hoped for better results for all that work. We all did. You know how it goes sometimes. It's not ideal, but you just have to accept it for what it is and move on."

O'Neal nodded his agreement. He had no other choice.

"Have you slept since Vienna?" Lewis asked.

"I closed my eyes during your presentation this morning."

Time had inserted a wedge between O'Neal and Lewis, burying their partnership, and friendship, beneath a mound of sand. Every now and then, though, a reminder of what they once meant to each other crept over both their lives. Lewis smiled at O'Neal, right before telling him to get his ass home.

O'Neal knew his boss was right. He was exhausted. His body ached and he could hardly even think straight. Maybe a few hours of sleep would help him clear his thoughts and put aside whatever doubts he was having over Mark Strain.

"You're the boss," O'Neal said, and he left Lewis's office, heading right for the front door.

The morning sunshine blinded O'Neal. When his eyesight adjusted, the first thing he spotted was a pair of black SUVs parked on both sides of his modest Audi, which looked like a tricycle in comparison. O'Neal knew whoever was in those vehicles were waiting for him, and he knew he couldn't run. He didn't have to. This sort of dramatic confrontation between intelligence agencies was almost protocol. Someone wanted to talk to him about the swap, and they weren't waiting to take a meeting.

So, O'Neal would play along. Maybe he could sleep on the ride to wherever they were going to take him.

"You're not going to chew up my entire day, are you?" O'Neal asked a man in a black suit who popped out of the driver's-side door as he approached.

"Ask her," the driver said, nodding to the back.

A young woman stepped out of the rear passenger side. She was on the phone and, as she exited, she held a finger up; apparently, she'd be ready to begin the abduction in a minute.

During that time, O'Neal studied the woman. She was very young, that stuck out most. And she dressed well—like a corporate executive or something. The way she spoke was unusual; she rattled off words fast and with a sharp, commanding tone. It all meant one thing: This was no intelligence agent. Which made O'Neal wonder what the hell was going on.

"Richard O'Neal?" the woman asked as she lowered the phone from her ear.

O'Neal scoffed. "You tell me. You're doing the abduction here; I'm not going to do your homework for you."

The woman smiled. "I'd hardly call this an abduction, Agent O'Neal. The man I work for would like to talk to you. In fact, a few people are looking to share a few words, and I'm here to help everyone get what they want."

"Is that so? And what do I want?" O'Neal said, strolling toward the woman.

"From what I can tell? To be able to do your job and be left alone."

"Very observant, Miss . . . ," O'Neal probed.

"Lang. Kelly Lang. And thank you."

"I'm sure you've already realized this, Miss Lang, but it's pretty evident that what I want directly conflicts with what the people you work for want."

"Call me Kelly," she replied. "And you're right, but we promise to make the meeting brief, and you may find the topic of discussion intriguing."

O'Neal looked at his car and groaned; he was so close to getting home, but he knew whoever wanted to talk to him wouldn't leave him be until they were satisfied. Better to get it out of the way now, O'Neal decided.

"Just let me sleep on the way so I can at least try to be coherent when we arrive. Okay?" he said, walking toward the back seat of Kelly's car.

Kelly turned her attention to her phone, studying something, then turned back to O'Neal as he was getting in the car. "If you fall asleep immediately, you will be able to get exactly forty-two minutes of rest."

"Terrific," he said, and he took his seat.

By the time the SUV was turning into traffic out of the parking lot, O'Neal was fast asleep.

O'Neal woke to the SUV jostling him as it swayed from one side to the other on a gravel road. O'Neal squinted his eyes open, unhappy about returning to the waking world, and looked out the window. There, his view was consumed by trees—oak and spruce, in particular—and the sunlight positioned nearly over-head was scattering in individual beams. He was in tranquil sur-roundings, which meant only one thing: This was Virginia.

Not that anyone was trying to hide it—he had fallen asleep willingly, and no one had put a hood over his head while he was out. At least whoever was sequestering him for this meeting wasn't making a big show of it, which was a relief.

O'Neal looked over at Kelly, who was furiously texting with uncanny speed; if O'Neal attempted to punch text messages into his phone half as fast, the intended target would receive nothing but gibberish or a sequence of words strung together by autocor-rect.

"Four minutes," Kelly said, her eyes glued to the phone.

O'Neal didn't bother to break her trance, deciding to instead drop back in his seat and take in the view. He stretched open his mouth, feeling its dryness, and Kelly kicked the console between them.

"In here," she said.

Sure enough, O'Neal opened the console and found water in-side. He gulped an entire bottle down in two swallows.

The SUV pulled into the roundabout of a private estate, pushed back deep in the woods. The residence was a massive cabin. O'Neal was reminded of the Overlook Hotel, only this was a lot smaller and maybe even less inviting. Wordlessly, the driver led O'Neal and Kelly through the cabin's front doors, where they were greeted by a stunning vestibule. A fire pit crackled at its center, and O'Neal stepped toward it, only to have the guard shuffle him along to a room on his right side. No time for sight-seeing, O'Neal realized.

The guard pulled open the room's sliding doors, and O'Neal immediately understood just how much deep shit he was in.

When he stepped inside the room—a two-floor study, lined

from floor to ceiling with built-in bookcases and a gold-plated winding staircase providing access between floors—O'Neal had to blink twice, hard, to process what he was seeing. He'd been in plenty of situations where he was grilled by his superiors, questioned and undermined by diplomats, but he was never cornered by people like this: Senator Archibald Dudek and General Philip Hodges, together, and neither looked particularly happy.

For the life of him, O'Neal couldn't fathom what tied these two together, and for the second time in the same day, he found himself wondering what the hell was going on.

Neither said a word as O'Neal entered. Then a third man, one O'Neal hadn't noticed, stepped from around a bookcase, his arm extended as he approached O'Neal.

"Thanks so much for making it," the man said, vigorously shaking O'Neal's hand. "It's a real pleasure to meet you. I'm Jamal Trask, NSA. This is—"

"I know who they are," O'Neal said, cutting off Trask's effusive and strangely kind greeting. "What do you want from me?"

"We want to know why you failed to do your *job*, Agent O'Neal," Dudek asked, swirling a drink in his hands.

"Excuse me?" O'Neal said, struggling to unclench his jaw and follow the example—be pleasant—Trask was setting.

"You had an enemy of the state in your grasp, son," Dudek said, then paused to take a drink. "And you let him slip right through your fingers and return to his commie friends in good ol' Mother Russia."

"I followed orders," O'Neal spat. "If you have a problem with how things went down, take it up with the commander-in-chief."

"Let's—let's slow down a minute, here," Hodges said, stepping in. "Agent O'Neal, did you have an opportunity to interrogate Strain before he was sent back to Russia? Were you perhaps able to ascertain the depths of his knowledge?"

"That, if I may add," Trask said, "is what we find most disconcerting. We don't know what Mark—or Pyotr, whatever he's calling himself—knows. And all that knowledge he possesses—we just shipped it to Russia."

O'Neal pinched the bridge of his nose; he felt like a vise was squeezing his brain. "Of all the people in the ring, Mark was the one we knew least about. I don't know what he knows, and I don't know why I wasn't allowed to interrogate him. I was instructed to pick him up, play bad cop, and get him to Vienna. And that's what I did."

The room was silent. Dudek poured another drink while Hodges paced, contemplating. O'Neal had heard he was a thoughtful person, and not just by a soldier's standards.

"Might I ask," Trask said, "why wasn't the NSA looped in on this? It seems like an ideal situation for knowledge-sharing to occur."

"Until the order to move came down, I wasn't anywhere close to breaking up this ring," O'Neal said. "I was particularly interested in Ania and seeing how I could get her to help me snag an even bigger fish. I wasn't in a position to share anything of value, is what I'm saying. Not yet."

The sound of a whiskey bottle coming down hard turned everyone's attention to Dudek. "Well, son, your negligence made a very dangerous man even more dangerous. Well done."

O'Neal studied the room and couldn't stop himself from wanting to know how someone who seemed so innocuous made two very powerful people so tense. Mark was either getting to be more interesting or more of a nuisance; he'd decide which after this meeting was over.

"Who *is* Mark Strain?" O'Neal finally asked. "Because I've been working this ring he's allegedly involved in—"

"*Allegedly?!*" Dudek bellowed.

"I've been working this ring for a year," O'Neal continued, "and I have no idea what this man was up to."

"Are you not listening?" Dudek fired. "He's a damn menace is what he is!"

"He potentially holds many secrets, secrets that can cause harm to important American people," Hodges said. "Put those secrets in the hands of the Russians, and there's no telling how they'll be used."

O'Neal took a breath, calming himself down even though he wanted to crack Dudek's whiskey glass over his head. That would do him no good, though. Because if Mark did possess valued secrets and knowledge that compromised the safety of the United States, and he used it to light up the American media and give Russian intelligence agents—or worse, state-sponsored hackers—a strategic advantage, O'Neal's career would be over. Forget executive orders; O'Neal knew he'd fry for letting that knowledge escape his attention and fall into the hands of the enemy.

"I understand your concern, General Hodges," O'Neal said, "and know that I'll do everything in my power to find out what Mark was up to, what he knew and how he knew it, in as little time as possible."

"You do that," Dudek scoffed.

Before O'Neal could sling a barb back at Dudek, Trask was shuffling him out the door.

"Listen, I know how this goes," Trask said, pulling him aside once they were out of the room. "Anything you can provide on Mark, believe me, would be highly valued."

O'Neal sighed. "I don't see anything. I know he was lobbying hard for Verge, and Hodges just signed off on a security contract with them. Verge has ties to a Russian billionaire, Sergei Vishny, but nothing connected him to Mark, and I couldn't even see any motive for Vishny to be involved in Verge other than pure profit. From what I saw, they're an upstanding company."

"Well, they're good until they're not, right?" Trask asked.

O'Neal looked up to the ceiling, which spiraled into a cylindrical shape as it ascended higher than it looked even from the outside. "None of this is making any sense."

Trask clasped his shoulder. "Keep working on it. I'll be in touch."

O'Neal took his attention off the dizzying ceiling; by the time he looked back down, Trask was sliding the doors to the study shut. O'Neal was closed out.

When he stepped outside, the driver was waiting outside the SUV.

"Back to your car?" he asked.

"No, take me to Disney World," O'Neal snapped. "Yeah, my car. Get me the hell away from this place."

O'Neal had felt like he was being used when orders from up high forced him to ship Mark and the rest to Russia, and now he felt like he was being played by Hodges and Dudek. He didn't like either, and it fueled his determination to figure out the mystery behind Mark Strain before this whole thing blew up in his face.

Inside the study, Dudek finished off the bottle of whiskey and wasted no time broaching the topic on everyone's mind.

"Mark Strain needs to be eliminated," he said. "We all know it."

"Now that he's back on his own playing field, it's a significant risk," Trask said. "Are we certain it's worth it?"

"Within the span of twelve hours, he blackmailed Senator Dudek, broke into the Pentagon, and coerced me into signing a security contract," Hodges said, his voice as even as it would be if he was reciting his grocery list. "It's doubtless that he's a threat to our national security. I don't see any other choice for handling him."

"What about the software contract?" Trask asked. "Should we consider getting that killed?"

"Hell no," Dudek immediately replied. "That deal is signed, sealed, and delivered. We go back on it now and that's admitting we made a multimillion-dollar mistake with Uncle Sam's money. No, we won't be doing *that*. Hodges and me, we'll make sure the Pentagon's IT department keeps a close eye on it. Could be nothing wrong with the software, for all we know. And if there is, we'll just throw one of those eggheads under the bus and let *them* take the blame."

"Agreed," Hodges added. "It's best our recent encounters with Strain stay hidden."

Trask took a deep, resigned breath and looked at Dudek. Dudek smiled playfully. "Aw hell, son, you know where my vote goes."

"Then there's nothing else to discuss," Trask said, and with that, he walked out of the room and into the lobby. Dudek and Hodges didn't want to be around for what he had to do next.

Inside the vestibule, Trask dialed a number that wasn't programmed in his phone. It was committed to memory, as that was the safest way to keep it secret.

The phone rang once, twice, three times, and Trask started to get antsy. Maybe she was already on a job; maybe it was the middle of the night wherever she was. But this wasn't a call Trask liked to make more than once. He called, burned his phone, and that was the end of it.

Finally, the other line picked up. She answered with a cool "Yes?" and let Trask do the talking. It was their way.

"A new assignment's come up. Delicate, but simple. An easy target. One no one will miss. We want fast, not neat. Collateral damage is of no concern."

"Understood. Send the details through my channels," she said. "It'll be taken care of."

Trask already had the dossier prepared: One Mark Strain, living in Russia under the name Pyotr Dvanisch, was to be eliminated immediately.

"Be on the lookout," Trask said. "You'll have all the information you need within the hour."

13

Mark awoke to what he thought was the sound of a shotgun cocking in the other room. His body burst up in bed. The fear of being gunned down was as palpable as the sheen of sweat that'd accumulated on his body over the course of his dreamless slumber.

Without making a sound, Mark touched his feet to the ground. He stood silent for a moment, listening for footsteps stalking toward him. He was convinced he could hear the careful gait of an intruder coming his way, taking meticulous steps over the cold marble floor—with a shotgun poised in his steady grasp. Mark had to shake off the fear that clouded his mind, though, and focus on reality. And when he did that, there was only silence. Mark didn't hear a thing except his own heartbeat pumping in his ears.

Still, Mark didn't believe what his ears were telling him. He felt a presence near him, surrounding him, collapsing on him. He didn't care what his senses told him; after all, if there was one thing recent events had taught him, it was that there was no telling what awaited around the next corner—figuratively and literally. Owing to that, he'd never, ever take anything—especially his own personal safety—for granted again. With that in mind, he scanned the bedroom for a weapon, anything he could use to defend himself. Moving on the balls of his feet, Mark glided to the fireplace on the opposite end of the bedroom and wrapped his fingers around the fire iron. He pulled it off the rack and held the stout weapon parallel to his chest. Mark had no combat training, though. If there was an assassin coming for him, armed with a shotgun, Mark had no delusions about his chances for survival. Even if he could stealthily maneuver to get the jump on his would-be killer, he had a fireplace poker. Against a shotgun. Any attempt to conjure a strategy was pointless, so Mark didn't even bother.

"AAAAAAHHHH!" Mark screamed as he charged out of his bedroom, brandishing the fire iron.

His battle cry, though, quickly petered out. No one was in the living room, or the kitchen, or any of the bathrooms. Mark shook out curtains, checked closets, even looked inside the fridge—no one was in the apartment except him. Wiping away the sweat that had collected on his forehead, Mark came to terms with the assurance that he wasn't about to be killed.

At least not this morning.

As he walked back to his room, Mark noticed—by the sheer luck of a fortuitous sidelong glance—that the dead bolt on his front door had been released. Mark eyed the narrow sliver of space between the front door and where the dead bolt adjoined on the door's frame. A narrow sliver to freedom.

Cautiously, Mark cracked open the door and peered out to the lobby beyond. The space was empty, just as it had been the day before. There were no guards posted outside his door, no one on hand to keep him confined to his quarters. Whatever lockdown protocol his outburst the night before had provoked had been lifted, and that gave Mark however much more space to plan and execute his escape. Busting out of this prison was just like closing a deal: You study the details, learn your opponent inside and out, and find your opening. One step at a time. First, Mark put aside anything he was thinking or feeling—all the worries about Sarah, the anxiety over how daunting it was going to be to get out of the hotel, let alone Russia—and focused on his process for success like a Zen mantra. He calmed his mind, acknowledging panic would get him nowhere but dead. Whoever was behind the nightmare Mark was trapped in, they had taken a lot from him—but he was still alive. And no one had stripped him of his determination, his sheer force of will, which had been his greatest ally his entire life. One step at a time, Mark reminded himself.

One step at a time.

Surprises, Mark learned in his years dealing with fragile clients in volatile situations, were to be expected. Still, surprise didn't quite cover Mark's reaction when he called for the elevator, and the button acknowledged his request to be taken down. He took a nervous step back and considered scurrying back to his apartment. There was no telling, he realized, where the elevator was going to take him or, worse still, who would be waiting inside. But Mark knew nothing waited in that apartment other than despair and possibly death. No, the way out was ahead. Forward, always forward. His only choice was to follow whatever paths were presented to him and refuse to rest until he found the one weakness, the one blind spot, that he could expose for all it was worth.

As the elevator dinged on its arrival, Mark hugged the adjacent wall; he heard the doors glide smoothly open and, seeing no one come out, he ducked his head around the edge of the wall just enough to peek inside the car. It was empty.

"All right," Mark said, drawing a deep breath. "Let's see where you go."

Inside the elevator, the light indicating what Mark assumed was the lobby—it was all in Russian—was already lit. Mark pressed every other button, twice, but none of them worked. His destination had been selected for him.

A brief, smooth ride took Mark down to the lobby, which he barely remembered passing through the day before. It was like he'd been in a trance before and was now seeing his dreamlike visions unfold before his waking eyes. He recognized the golden accents, the leather furniture, and the well-postured staff moving briskly throughout the room, but only now, with a more attentive mind, could he really take it all in. Mark was already looking for a place to run toward—an exit that wasn't the front doors—when a meaty hand clasped his shoulder. Mark turned to find he was staring directly into a man's chest; he had to angle his head upward to look at the man in his eyes.

"Hello, Pyotr," the man said. "I am Oleg, your personal body-guard and assistant. And this"—Oleg gestured to a man stand-ing behind him—"is my partner, Alex."

Oleg's shoulders were remarkably broad; the strength that they boasted already had Mark on edge. Never had he felt so physically dominated by another man, and Mark could already tell what an obstacle the burly Russian would be. Picking up on Mark's twinge of despair, Oleg smiled through a well-groomed beard; his cold, unblinking eyes warned Mark that he was not to be trifled with. Still, Mark detected the strands of gray that crept into Oleg's beard and hair. He had to have been an older FSB agent—he'd be on the elderly end of the CIA or FBI, there was no doubt—and maybe he'd lost a step over the years. Maybe that was why he'd been slapped with being a glorified babysitter for the American fraud. Mark was a good judge of character, and he could tell—in just a single glance—that Oleg was more than mus-cle. To make it as long as he had, he must have had guile, great instincts, and undying loyalty. Mark knew not to underestimate him for a second.

Alex, meanwhile, stood uneasily behind Oleg. He awaited orders. Compared to Oleg, Alex was practically a baby. He was dwarfed by his superior, and not just physically. There was something about their posture—Oleg, tall and strong; Alex, slouched and hunched—that made it abundantly clear who was the superior in this relationship. With his pomade hairstyle and the innocent youthfulness that pooled in his eyes, Alex clearly was the charmer of the two, but that didn't change the fact that Oleg owned him.

Maybe, Mark mused, their contrast was something he could use against them. He was sure to pocket that idea for later consideration.

"Where would you like to go today?" Oleg asked after Mark failed to respond to his introduction.

"Home would be nice," Mark snapped.

Oleg's smile widened. "But you *are* home."

Mark grimaced. "Right, right. Well, you know, it's been so long since I've been in my native country. Why don't you show me around, catch me up on everything I've missed?"

"A sight-seeing tour sounds most appropriate," Oleg agreed. "Alex will get the car, and we will meet you in the front."

Alex nodded dutifully and was off, walking with a hurried step toward the front doors. Mark continued to study the lobby, following the staff as they went about their routines. There had to be a service entrance, some way to breach the building's inner workings. Mark had worked as a server in a couple hotel restaurants during and even after college, and he knew hidden behind the hotel's walls was usually a labyrinth of storage closets, machinery rooms, kitchens, and whatever else supported the business's continuous operation. If Mark could get lost in that labyrinth, maybe he could find an exit that wasn't covered in cameras and prying eyes. Mark made a mental note of everything he observed, and as he continued to scan the bustling area, he felt Oleg's eyes on him. The man hardly even blinked. Mark tried not to let on that he noticed Oleg's watchful eye, but he found it difficult not to be distracted by the Russian agent's intense glare.

His gaze bore into Mark, and being a practiced judge of character, it didn't take him long to understand just how seriously Oleg took his job.

"Damn it," Mark grumbled to himself. He knew he was being monitored, knew he was being imprisoned. What he didn't know—or expect—was having a stone-cold FSB agent on his ass the entire time.

Escape was going to be even more difficult than he thought.

It took Mark two weeks to earn even the slightest bit of Oleg's trust. Alex was just Oleg's chauffeur and gopher. It was Oleg calling the shots—all the places they went, the amount of time they stayed, the routes they took to and from everywhere. Mark literally couldn't take a leak without Oleg hovering over his shoulder. And that was in the two rare instances Oleg let him out of the car.

Those first fourteen days, Mark was under house and car arrest. Sure, they visited tons of historic Russian landmarks, and Mark learned all about them from the confines of the back seat of an Audi A8. He saw the grand tower of the Kolomenskoye estate, he witnessed snow falling on the Kremlin's golden domes, and he felt an unusual awe at the splendor of the Red Square as the lights turned on to counter the setting sun. They cruised by the childhood homes of historical figures and rolled through the downtown nightlife scene. Lunch was eaten every day at noon sharp; Oleg picked a location, and Alex dutifully ran inside to snag their orders. And while he was gone, Oleg turned and stared at Mark, wordlessly.

"This is the most awkward thing I've ever experienced in my life," Mark said on the third day.

Thankfully, Alex was a surprisingly effective—and enthusiastic—tour guide, narrating the history of his country with genuine pride and passion. Sometimes he managed to wrangle Oleg into the conversation, though the big, weird Russian interjected into Alex's narration only when a historical detail or fact needed correcting.

At the end of each day, without another word spoken between them, Oleg escorted Mark back to his apartment. And why would Oleg speak to Mark? He was just biding his time until word came down for him to deliver a bullet into the back of Mark's head. That's all Mark could think about on their silent elevator rides up to the apartment. Would this be the day Oleg plastered his brains on the carpet outside his room's front door?

For fourteen arduous days, the routine remained static. The door to Mark's apartment would unlock at 9:00 A.M., and no matter what time Mark arrived in the lobby, whether 9:03 in the morning or 2:27 in the afternoon, Oleg and Alex were waiting for him. Without fail.

But on the fifteenth day, things changed. Oleg loosened the reins, and Mark took advantage.

"Where would you like to go today?" Oleg asked when Mark stepped out of the elevator and into the Palace's lobby. It had taken every ounce of Mark's willpower to drag his body out of the apartment; he didn't want to hear Alex extol the splendor of another Russian administrative building, and he certainly didn't want to drive by the Kremlin for the millionth time. But as bleak as the prospect of cruising through Moscow under the eyes of his future killers was, staying locked in his room, alone with his thoughts, was even more depressing.

"I could not give a shit," Mark answered. "How about the gulag? Can Alex find fun things to say about the gulag?"

Oleg snickered. "Due to your obedient behavior, I've been instructed to allow you the privilege of leaving the automobile today. Now," Oleg said, straightening—his momentary smile had left him feeling too at ease, apparently. "Where would you like to go?"

Leniency was the last thing Mark had expected, and he never even considered life beyond his apartment and the Audi. But now, he was being given back a modicum of the freedom that'd been taken from him. And he had no idea what to do with it.

"I—I have no idea," Mark stammered. "Are there options?"

"Moscow," Oleg grumbled. "We stay in Moscow. We can visit our Museum of Modern Art. It is enjoyable, I'm told."

Mark groaned. "Hell no. I've been cooped up for two weeks, and you want to take me to a museum? I thought I was being given a reward, not more punishment."

Oleg nodded. "I share your feelings on museums."

"I want to eat in a restaurant. Like, a good restaurant. The *best*."

"You will have to ask Alex. I do not dine out."

Alex knew exactly the place, a steakhouse that he admitted he'd never be able to get into without the power of a celebrity by his side. At first, Mark had no idea what Alex meant, then he remembered that he wasn't Mark, he was Pyotr, master spy. He wasn't as enthused by his celebrity status as Alex was, but he let the conflicting feelings pass. If he was going to be saddled with this fictional life, he might as well make the most of it. For now.

With a heavy foot, Alex practically raced to the steakhouse, drumming his thumbs on the steering wheel the entire time. Oleg cautioned him to slow down, but they were already pulling up to the restaurant's valet stand, nearly skidding to a halt. Oleg growled his disapproval, and Alex mumbled something in Russian. An apology, Mark assumed. Apparently, not every FSB agent possessed Oleg's superhuman self-discipline.

Inside, the maître d' greeted Alex and Oleg with the kind of disregard Mark had come to expect in an exclusive establishment. But then, he saw Mark. Just a whiff of Mark's fame turned his attitude on a dime, and without hesitation, he led Mark, Oleg, and Alex to a table, chirping effusively in Mark's ear. Mark didn't understand, but the tone told him everything he needed to know. He smiled and nodded, realizing that the maître d' was parading him through the entire restaurant, showing him off like a prized poodle in a dog show. All eyes jumped from their meals and drinks straight to Mark and followed him on his tour around the room; he could hear the whispers and murmurs growing, and he knew every word was about him. While the attention gave him no pleasure, it did give him an idea. Maybe, Mark began to consider, he could use this attention to his advantage.

Before Mark could settle into his seat—with Oleg and Alex positioned close at his sides—a waiter swooped to the table with a robust sampler platter balanced on his right hand: beef and fish tartare, roasted vegetables, salmon, and a loaf of rye bread. He slid the platter onto the center of the table and then cheerfully said something before disappearing as quickly as he arrived.

"Drinks," Alex interpreted. "He said he'll be back with drinks."

"*Nyet*," Oleg said. Mark needed no interpretation.

Before the waiter could return with drinks Oleg had forbidden, Mark was tugged on his shoulder. He startled a little, unnerved by actual human contact, but he turned to see an elderly couple at his side, all smiles, holding up a camera and beckoning him into a photo op. Oleg grabbed Mark by his wrist, firmly, as Mark tried to get up from his seat.

"Oh, come on," Mark said with a smirk. "They just want to meet their national hero. That's what I am, right?"

Mark greeted the couple with a toothy smile, pumping each of their hands before throwing his arms around both their shoulders and pulling them into a perfect photo.

As the couple scurried away, Mark scanned the room. He saw people with their phones out, snapping photos. He saw people with eager expressions on their faces.

This was exactly what he wanted.

Mark beckoned them all in, gesturing people from all around

the room to come close. What they just saw, Mark making that couple's day, he was ready to do for everyone in the room. Mark was open for business.

"What are you *doing*?" Oleg growled into Mark's ear. He had his hand wrapped around Mark's bicep, squeezing it like a balloon he was trying to pop. Mark wasn't fazed.

"I'm a people person," Mark chirped. "This is what I do."

Before Oleg could say another word, he was separated from Mark by the fan club crowding around their spy hero. Mark shook every hand shoved in front of him and kept his mouth shut. He nodded and smiled, but he didn't expose his total inability to speak their language. All the while, he eyed Oleg and Alex, paying special attention to the space growing between them. Mark began to backpedal as he smiled and shook hands, inching his way toward the door. Oleg and Alex were out of sight, and Mark was a breath away from racing out the front door when someone grabbed him from behind and halted his escape attempt.

"You'll never get away," a woman's voice whispered in his ear in a thick Russian accent.

Mark turned and caught a brief glimpse of the woman before she ordered him to turn back around. Whoever she was, she was disguised in a black hat, big sunglasses, and a scarf that wrapped around her neck and covered her chin and jawline.

"Oh yeah? And who the hell are you?" Mark asked.

"A friend trying to help. Don't do anything foolish—I can get you *out*."

Mark's breath caught in his throat and he felt his body buckling in on itself. Mark had no shortage of determination and willpower; like he used to tell Sarah, his greatest strength was that he was too stupid to know when to quit. What Mark didn't have was hope. It had been squeezed out of him little by little during his captivity in Russia. Mark would never stop trying to get away from his captors, but he had no illusions about the futility of his efforts. He was just a man in a cell, pounding his head against the concrete wall. Eventually, something would break, and it wouldn't be the wall. But now, now he had this soft whisper in his ear, this one word. *Out*. The slightest opening, that's all Mark needed—it was all he ever needed. Hope came racing back into Mark's life so strong that it almost knocked him over.

"What? How?" Mark asked, breathlessly. "And who are you?"

Mark felt the hold on his arm release, but when he turned around the woman was gone. With a frenzied glance, he searched the room, and by the time he spotted the mystery woman, she was ducking out the front door.

The crowd behind him beckoned, but when Mark turned around, Oleg was standing on his toes. Rage burned in his eyes. Alex stood at his side, and his expression nearly equaled Oleg's in its fury.

"We are leaving. *Now*," Oleg commanded.

Before Mark could say a word, Oleg and Alex were using their bodies' momentum to push him out the front door. Mark stumbled backward, nearly tripping over his own two feet. The crowd watched him go, all of them sharing the same disappointed and confused expression on their faces. But Mark didn't care. All he could think about was the daylight he saw in front of him—the tiniest sliver of light poking through the end of a very dark tunnel. And Mark was ready to drive straight through it.

But first, there was hell to pay.

The moment Mark stepped outside, he was propelled forward with so much force that had it not been for the sleek sports car parked outside the restaurant, he would have gone flying into traffic. His body crashed into the car, hard, slamming the passenger door shut just as it was opening. Before Mark could even push himself upright, a hand grabbed his head and shoved it onto the car's roof. The right side of Mark's face was plastered against the cold metal, and when he tried to resist, he felt his left arm curve at an unnatural angle behind his back. Through a clenched jaw, he howled in pain.

"Do you think this is a game we're playing?" Oleg snarled into his ear. "Just because I can't kill you—not yet—doesn't mean that I can't make your final days very, very uncomfortable."

With that, Oleg wrenched Mark's arm farther back, twisting his elbow to its breaking point. Just a little more torque, Mark knew, and it would snap.

"Do not fuck with me, Mark Strain," Oleg said. "I will *break* you. Do you understand?"

"Yes," Mark panted, the searing pain in his arm nearly rendering him unconscious.

"I can't hear you," Oleg whispered, his acidic words laced with sadistic glee.

"YES!" Mark screamed.

"Very well," Oleg said, and released his hold. Mark dropped to the ground and cradled his searing arm. He had disliked Oleg from the moment they had met, this joyless, morose, hulking Russian who made Mark's bleak existence all the more dire. When he figured out Oleg would be the one to turn out his lights, Mark started to hate him. But now—now, Mark wanted Oleg dead. And he wanted to kill the sadistic bastard with his own two hands.

"Pick him up," Oleg ordered Alex as a valet pulled the Audi to the curb. "He's pathetic."

Alex, with what was the gentlest of care in comparison to Oleg's manhandling, helped Mark to his feet and into the back seat of the car. The door shut behind him, and Mark fought off the urge to lie down until the agonizing pain subsided. But he refused. He wouldn't give Oleg the pleasure of thinking he'd hurt him.

Alex pulled the car away from the curb and they drove down Sadovaya Street—a six-lane artery that cut through Moscow—

in silence. All the while, Mark considered what the mysterious woman had said to him, how she had a way to break him out of this prison. But how? And, more important, when? Mark's life was subject to the longevity of a timer that had been fixed the moment he set foot in Russia. He didn't know when it would expire, but he did have a feeling that after today's episode, it would be ticking away at a more rapid clip. The woman had to have been following him; it couldn't be a coincidence that she happened to be at that restaurant. Maybe he needed to take the first step, and she'd see him through his escape. She warned him not to do anything stupid, which is what the restaurant stunt was. But he couldn't just sit on his thumbs and wait—wait to be rescued, wait to be killed. That wasn't Mark's way.

But without warning, Mark's thoughts on making his escape came to a sudden, abrupt end. And they were snuffed out by a sudden feeling of sharp pressure that came piercing out of his shoulder. His body jolted forward and, in his disorientation, Mark thought he was experiencing a lingering effect of Oleg's manhandling. But then he saw the blood. Dark crimson stained his shirt, and he felt more blood dripping over the contour of his chest. Pressure turned into pain—scalding pain.

Mark's heart started to race. His breathing became short and labored as the entire world went nearly silent. Though faint, Mark could hear the delicate sound of glass cracking and the air being split right above his head. To Mark, the noise sounded like a bottle rocket streaking across the car before it penetrated its target. It wasn't until he looked up and saw Alex's blood and brain matter splattered all over both the windshield and the side of Oleg's face did he realize what was happening:

They were under attack.

14

For a moment, Mark's life shifted into slow motion as he pieced together everything around him. His hand, which had been gripping the pain in his shoulder, was soaked in blood; the car was swerving out of control; Alex's brains were sprayed everywhere; and Oleg, trying to grip the steering wheel, was turned back toward Mark and screaming at him. He was mouthing words right at Mark, but he couldn't hear a syllable that was being yelled in his direction. Mark was in shock, and it wasn't until he closed his eyes and reopened them after a long pause that the world came rushing back to his senses.

"GET DOWN!" Oleg was shouting over and over as Mark regained his clarity. "GET! DOWN!"

Mark snapped back to life and did as he was told, but his attention was diverted when the Audi smashed through the barrier dividing the directions of travel on Sadovaya Street; the car leapt into oncoming traffic, and Mark saw, through the bloodstained windshield, a semi-truck barreling right in the Audi's path. The truck blared its horn, and Oleg jabbed the wheel, slicing them out of the truck's way—just barely—but the sudden movement shot the car into the path of a coupe driving in the middle lane; the coupe T-boned the Audi, catching it on the passenger-side quarter panel. Mark's head whiplashed, smashing against the window with such force that a spider web splintered in the glass, cracking out from the point of impact. Cars honked, tires screeched, and Oleg bellowed something in Russian. The bodyguard tried to steer them away from danger, but he struggled to maneuver around Alex's slumped corpse; within seconds, Mark felt the Audi suffer two more collisions that sent the car spinning counterclockwise then clockwise again. Mark looked up just as they jumped a curb and was unnerved by the sound of metal scraping against concrete—the tires, Mark assumed, had been blown out, leaving nothing but the rims, and they howled from the undercarriage. Oleg shoved Alex's body aside and spun the wheel to the right, but the mangled car wouldn't respond. Propelled forward by the collisions that'd driven them off the road, the Audi smashed headfirst into a metal light pole that, finally, brought it to a stop. It was the last thing Mark remembered before blacking out.

"Wake up!" a voice called through the darkness. "Wake up, damn you! We have to move!"

Mark's brain fluttered back to consciousness as the voice continued to scream at him to awaken. He opened his eyes and was looking at the world through a wall of red fog; everything was hazy and distorted like it was very far away and coated in thick crimson. It took Mark a second to realize he was bleeding from his head, and it was his own blood that obscured his vision. Mark wiped it away from his eyes, and when he peeled his head from the window, he felt tiny shards of glass dig into the flesh around his temple. More blood trickled from the dozens of tiny cuts along his scalp and face, and Mark couldn't stop his head from swimming. Mark felt weak in a way he'd never experienced before, and he wondered how much blood he'd lost, not only from the lacerations in his head but also, more important, the gunshot wound in his shoulder. He just needed to sleep. Even as a voice was yelling for him to "get up"; all he wanted to do was lie down and rest. That's all he needed, just a little bit of sleep . . .

But the voice wouldn't let him. As Mark's eyes fluttered in his head and he let his mind drift away, he felt a giant mitt grab his arm—the one that didn't have a bullet in it, thankfully—and yank him through the back seat and out of the car. Mark screamed in pain, but when he looked up, through clear eyes at last, he knew resistance was pointless. Oleg had him tight in his grasp, and there was no getting free of his overwhelming strength.

"But, Alex . . . ," Mark offered, forgetting that the other bodyguard was dead.

"Fuck Alex," Oleg snapped. "He talked too much. Now move." Mark realized that Oleg, too, had a stream of blood coursing down the side of his face.

Oleg spun Mark to the sidewalk and ordered him to stay down. The fog lifted from Mark's head, giving him clear eyes to watch Oleg train his pistol straight ahead and scan every inch of space around them both. The area was crowded with pedestrians who screamed as they ran—terrified, their heads protectively ducked down—away from the bloodied madman wielding a gun. Oleg was barking in Russian into his Bluetooth, demanding, Mark assumed, backup. While Mark was pained even by the idea of moving his body, he realized that while Oleg was keeping a vigilant eye on their surroundings—watching for the gunman, wherever he was—he was keeping less of an eye on Mark. If there ever was an opening for him to make a run for it, this was it. Though bloodied, shot, and disoriented, Mark still didn't lose sight of the one and only thing that he had in his life, the thing that got him out of bed in the morning:

Home.

With his right hand—his left was immobile, hanging lifelessly from his shoulder socket—Mark mustered whatever strength he had and pushed his fragile body off the sidewalk. He rose, shakily, off the concrete, noticing the blood that was pooled on the ground beneath him. It was a lot—Mark was no doctor, but he knew he was losing blood at a concerning rate. The horrifying sight, and the realization it brought, was almost enough to drop him back down. Pushing himself would only make things worse, Mark reasoned, and Oleg's emergency call should bring help soon enough. But Mark refused to give in; he'd rather be dead than captive, and if this was the only chance he was ever going to get, he had to seize it. He squeezed his eyes shut and forgot about the blood; he forgot about the bullet in his arm and the glass in his head. *Think about Sarah. Think about holding her again. Feeling our baby kick inside her belly.*

It was all the motivation he needed.

Mark got to his feet, uneasily at first, but he found his balance. He stumbled in the direction most people were heading, thinking his best bet was to try and get lost in the crowd. He couldn't blend, not in his condition, but he just needed to be unseen enough to get out of Oleg's sight. Free of the bodyguard's oppressive eye, Mark would then worry about getting help and staying alive. But right now, he had to get away.

Every step Mark took was fraught with pain that shot throughout his entire body, but those same steps also brought him closer to escape. People stared at him, disgust and horror in their eyes, but Mark didn't care. He pushed his body forward, shuffling ahead with a hobbled gait as his lifeless arm acted like a weight tied to his body and pulling him down; he gritted his teeth, fighting off unconsciousness, as he felt the path to freedom open ahead of him.

But then he felt the dull pain of something blunt smashing the back of his head; he heard the horrified screams of onlookers, and before he knew it, Mark was on the ground again.

Oleg flipped Mark on his back, taking no care for his wounded shoulder, and before Mark could spit a bloody wad of mucus in his face—which was what he intended to do—Oleg pressed his pistol into the glass that was already buried into the flesh at his temple. Mark groaned in agony.

"You are not going *anywhere*," Oleg said in a low, maniacal tone. "And you will not die on my watch unless I'm the one who puts the bullet in you."

"Kill me," Mark wheezed. "Just do it already."

Oleg grinned a bloody grin. "Your life isn't yours to take. It's *ours*. You live until it's no longer necessary. Understand?"

Mark tightened his jaw, considered spitting his bloody phlegm after all, but couldn't find the strength to do so. He was beaten.

"Now stay down and—"

Suddenly, Oleg's words were interrupted by the sound of a car's tires squealing as they raced around the corner.

"Keep your head down if you want to live," were the last words Oleg said before he rose to his feet and ran back to the street.

Mark, wanting—*needing*—to know what was going on, raised himself upright enough to watch what was happening. Someone had shot him, someone had killed Alex, and now that person was making another pass. Mark knew there was no way he'd identify the assassin; still, it was worth getting a good look, for future reference.

An unmarked gray Renault raced down the street, quickly closing the gap between it and Mark. Oleg, though, was ready for the encounter. The moment the car got close enough, Oleg fired shot after shot. The explosive sound of bullets erupting from the gun's chamber rattled throughout the entire area; Mark heard people in the crowd scream, and he saw their frenzy hit a fever pitch. Behind him, the crowd pushed and pulled at one another, cursing—that was the one bit of Russian Mark did understand—as they fought for their lives.

Oleg continued to shoot at the Renault, but whoever sat behind the wheel was undeterred. Two bullets caught the windshield, leaving two massive holes in the glass's center. Before Oleg could perfect his aim, the car swerved laterally with the curved road, exposing its passenger side to Oleg's barrage. He continued to fire, and Mark saw three bullets pierce the fender; Oleg must have been aiming for the rear passenger tire. If only out of the instinct to survive, Mark found himself cheering for Oleg, hoping he would either stop the assassin or, better yet, find a way to direct one of his bullets into the assassin's head. But Oleg and the assassin, Mark realized, were one and the same; after all, sooner or later, it would be Oleg trying to kill him and not this assassin.

The assassin sped past Oleg, who had emptied his ammunition and was drawing only hollow clicks from each pull of his trigger. For just a split second, Mark saw inside the assassin's Renault, just as the passenger window, which was open, aligned with Mark's view. Mark couldn't see the face of his would-be killer, though. All he saw was a tangle of long blond hair swirling in the car's cross breeze. As if in slow motion, Mark watched as the hair blew out of the assassin's face, exposing delicate features made harder by a scar that ran over the assassin's left eye. Mark studied her face, knowing he'd never forget it. But his reverie was broken when he caught sight of something else: the assassin's gun. And it was trained directly on Mark.

Mark heard the pistol fire—a muffled shot in comparison to the hand cannon Oleg wielded—and thought he was done for.

But instead, Mark heard a scream. A horrible, painful scream that he'd never forget.

A woman, around the same age as Mark, dropped to the ground no more than five feet from him. Mark wanted to scream. The woman lay on her side, peacefully still; her lifeless eyes stared into Mark's, and though he knew she was gone, he couldn't stop himself from stumbling toward her. He didn't even know why he felt compelled to get to her, he just knew that it was something essential for him to do. Through the pain it caused him, Mark lifted the woman's body and cradled it; he didn't want her to be dead, to have been gunned down so senselessly with a bullet meant for him. He kept his eyes locked on hers, blue and absent, hoping beyond hope that she'd blink. But she didn't. Mark began to cry furious, devastated tears right before he felt a hand grip his right arm from behind. Mark knew by the strength and size of the grasp that it was Oleg, but he didn't care; he resisted the bodyguard's hold, yanking his arm back with whatever strength he could muster, but Oleg wouldn't let him go. He pulled Mark back, hard, and Mark tumbled into his body; Oleg greeted his ward with a forearm pressed against Mark's throat.

"Get your hands off of me!" Mark yelled. "We have to help her! We have to—"

"You should have kept your head *down*," Oleg whispered.

Mark's body sagged as he felt the weight of the woman's death press down on him. But then he remembered who he was, why he was here, and he grew even angrier.

"Fuck you!" he screamed, thrashing his entire body in Oleg's unyielding grip. "I'm not supposed to be here—*this isn't my life!*"

Oleg pulled Mark back and turned him around; waiting at the curb, Mark saw, was an ambulance flanked by three unmarked black sedans. Five men in suits, each holding a gun in their hand, anticipated Mark's arrival.

When they got close enough, Oleg yelled to the nearest agent, and that man holstered his gun and approached Mark. He tried to grab Mark's legs, but when he got close enough, Mark delivered a kick square in the agent's jaw. His head cracked back, and he nearly fell off his feet. He bounced back and punched Mark in his abdomen. Mark retched in pain, feeling like he was going to vomit. By the time he returned to his senses, the agent had Mark by his feet and, with Oleg, was lifting him inside the ambulance. They strapped Mark to the gurney, effortlessly subduing the little fight Mark had left to offer. The adrenaline had worn off, and pain filled its absence. But it was pain that meant nothing when compared to the guilt Mark felt as he thought of the look in that woman's eyes as she lay dead on the ground. Mark was certain he'd meet a similar violent end soon enough—unless he did something about it.

"You'll never stop me," Mark said, staring right into Oleg's eyes as he drifted into unconsciousness. "I'm going home."

"You will try," Oleg said.

Mark was out cold before he could respond.

15

Mark woke up panting and shaking, the memories of the shoot-out playing over and over in his nightmares. He didn't know how long he'd been out for, but his mind wasn't focused on piecing together where he was or how long he'd been there. Even in his waking state, Mark couldn't shake the terrible, violent images that'd been scored into his mind. He kept seeing the look in that woman's eyes as she died right in front of him. Her pupils seemed to dim as the life fled from her being. The memory haunted Mark, and the guilt pushed a cold shudder throughout his chest as he struggled to hold back tears. This woman died because of him, because of this lunacy he was caught up in, and there was nothing he could to assuage that tragedy. She was a real person, and now she was gone. Mark tried to remind himself that everything he was tangled in wasn't his fault. He didn't ask to be a pawn in this game of international intrigue. He didn't ask to be framed as a spy. That was the absolute truth, but in the cold recesses of his mind—those places that whispered the things to you that you didn't want to hear as you lay in the dark, trying to sleep—he knew that bullet was meant for him. And right now, Mark wished he would have been the one to have caught it and not that poor woman. He'd leave examining his tacit desire to die to another day—his psyche had endured enough trauma for the time being.

Even as the images of the woman being shot faded, Mark still couldn't help but recall everything that'd happened. In his mind, he saw Alex's body slumped over the steering wheel. His blood and brains splattered everywhere. He saw the blood oozing from his own shoulder, he saw his head crash into the window and the glass slice up his flesh. He saw Oleg shooting at the assassin's car and, again, he saw the pistol glint before firing off one shot. And that shot landed square in an innocent woman's chest. Over and over that memory played, with slight variations from one rendition to the next. The worst version was when Mark's attention stayed on the crowd as everyone scrambled to get away. Mark isolated the woman, running in a panic though she didn't know what she was running from. Then came the shot—only it didn't originate from the assassin's car. It came from Mark. He looked down, and in his trembling hand was the smoking gun.

Mark calmed himself. The guilt was raw, and it was real, and he'd use it as fuel for revenge against the people who'd exiled him in Russia and senselessly took an innocent person's life. They'd get what was coming to them—Mark was certain of that.

When Mark opened his eyes, he realized he was in a hospital room. He'd figured as much, given all the injuries he'd sustained and the fact that he was still alive. With an apprehensive glance, Mark looked at his left shoulder, fearing that he'd find a still-open wound or infection settling in. The punishment for his defiance, perhaps. But that wasn't the case. His shoulder had been stitched and bandaged; Mark tried moving it, and while it wasn't as if he'd never been shot, his range of motion wasn't all that bad. The Russians had patched him up nicely. There was even a bandage around his head, which Mark wasted no time unspooling. He reached for a mirror that rested on his bedside table and examined the work the doctors had done. Small butterfly bandages covered the side of his face, marking the countless places where glass had clawed under his skin, and a few stitches ran under his hairline just above his forehead. Mark was looking beat up, but he had survived a shootout—an attempt on his life—and was on the road to recovery.

And that was good enough for him to get to work.

He had no doubt that there was at least one security guard outside his door. Mark had to hope it was just one; one he could handle. But if it was two guards out there . . . two could overpower him. Two could call for backup. But one, Mark would take care of.

Silently—so he didn't alert whoever was outside his door—Mark searched the room for a weapon. Anything solid that he could knock somebody out cold with was all he wanted. But there was nothing. The monitors connected to the needles protruding from the back of his hand were too heavy and unwieldy to be used as weapons, and the room was stripped bare of anything else. Not even a visitor's chair had been left behind.

While Mark would have preferred a weapon to clobber his enemy with, he wasn't deterred; a blunt object would have been nice, but not having one only meant he'd have to get creative with his clobbering.

Pressing his ear to the door, Mark listened. It'd be better if no one was around for what he was about to attempt. He didn't need any unwanted guest, even if it was just a nurse or doctor, getting in the way of his jailbreak. This was between him and whoever was keeping him locked inside this room.

When the time was right—a few voices passed, but they seemed to have moved on—Mark took hold of the monitor he'd been wheeling around with him. He turned off the lights, positioned himself against the wall next to the door, and pushed over the monitor. It clattered against the floor, loud enough for the entire wing to hear.

Within seconds, the door to his room clicked open, and Mark saw a gun poke through the small opening. A deep voice sighed.

"Still trying to ice skate uphill, yes?" the voice taunted. Mark recognized that tenor and cadence immediately:

Oleg.

Mark had been afraid, nearly trembling at the idea of fighting an armed guard—armed and trained in self-defense—for his life. At the sound of Oleg's voice, he should have felt his fear escalate to terror. Oleg was physically superior to Mark, and he was in much better condition than Mark—after all, Oleg hadn't been shot or sliced up in the very recent past. Oleg was simply more capable; he probably knew more fighting techniques than Mark could even understand let alone hope to match. Still, Mark didn't feel terror.

Mark felt rage.

His heartbeat racing, Mark barreled forward, smashing a kick against the door. It slammed against Oleg's body, causing the bulky agent to groan in pain. Oleg stumbled back against the frame; his gun fell from his grip and skittered across the floor. Mark grabbed hold of the door and smashed it against Oleg again, and again, and again. He heard ribs crack as another hit from the door nearly dropped Oleg off his feet, but the bodyguard stayed upright. And the next time Mark tried to slam the door on him, he was ready. Oleg grabbed the edge of the door with both hands and, using his overwhelming strength, pushed it back against Mark. The force whipped Mark around and against the wall, and suddenly he was on the defensive.

Oleg came charging like a rodeo bull. Mark leapt out of his path without a second to spare; Oleg smashed a fist into the wall where he had been standing, crushing the plaster. Before Oleg could twist into another attack, Mark landed a punch into his broken ribs. Oleg grunted as Mark rolled away from him. Oleg had strength and power; Oleg had training. But Mark was quicker, more athletic, and most of all, he had a hell of a lot more to fight for.

Mark slammed the door shut, snuffing out the room's light. It was no advantage for him to fight in the dark, but anything that could diminish Oleg's proficiency was a benefit, Mark figured.

"I'm going to crush your skull with my bare hands," Oleg snarled.

He was carving a curved path around the room's edge; at least, that's what Mark assumed based on how Oleg's voice carried. Mark took slow, silent steps backward; he didn't have much time, and he knew it. There was no way he'd survive a hand-to-hand fight against Oleg. The Russian agent would make good on his threat, and that would be after he delivered Mark a severe beating.

Mark took another step back, and as he felt the heel of his foot press down on the fallen monitor, he had an idea.

"It's only a matter of time, Mark. I can hear you breathing. I can feel your fear. Come out now, and I'll make this easy on you."

Mark grabbed hold of the monitor, and before he made a sound that gave away his position, he chucked it like a spear into the remaining monitors behind his bed. The collision set off a chain of screeching metal and breaking glass, and it grabbed Oleg's attention. Mark heard him stalk forward—methodical, not charging like a wild animal this time. In his mind, he had his prey cornered, and he was going in for the kill.

But that wasn't the case.

As Oleg stomped right past him, Mark wrapped a wire—taken off the monitor he'd chucked—taut between his two hands. Mark heard Oleg's heavy footsteps as he strode by him, and Mark knew it was now or never. He sprung up from his crouched position, rising right behind the huge man. Oleg may have heard something, might have sensed Mark's presence behind him, but he wasn't fast enough.

Mark wrapped the wire around Oleg's throat and pulled it tight with all his strength. The pressure made Oleg gag, and he started to buck wildly, trying to break free of Mark's hold. He thrashed and threw his body forward, trying to flip Mark over; Mark, though, held strong, pulling with enough force to prevent being thrown to the floor. He wouldn't release his hold on Oleg; he *refused* to die in a Russian hospital.

Oleg drove his body backward, slamming Mark against the wall. Mark's spine pounded hard against the flat surface, and Oleg continued to drive him back again and again. But each time, his strength diminished; Oleg was fading. Mark could feel the air trying to escape the man's lungs, could feel his body slacken. Soon, Oleg was stumbling, swinging his arms wildly, hopelessly, at a person he couldn't reach. A person who was suffocating the life out of him.

Mark dedicated everything he had and tightened the wire's torque. His wounded shoulder felt like it was ablaze as he increased the pressure to Oleg's throat. The Russian agent dropped to his knees and tried to gasp for air one last time before he crashed face-first onto the floor. Mark could feel the fight end in an instant, but part of him was afraid that his crafty enemy was playing possum. He continued to pull on the wire, and even when he felt certain Oleg was dead, Mark still held his grip tight. Moments passed, and Oleg didn't move. Mark suppressed a cathartic scream and then, finally, he slackened his grip on the wire and rolled, breathlessly, off Oleg. He wanted to take a moment to catch his breath, to calm the twisted exhilaration racing through his system, to process the fact that he'd just murdered a man. In self-defense, that was without question, but he still had ended someone's life.

Mark was thankful he didn't have time to consider the moral implications of what he'd done. Time wasn't his ally. People would be checking on Mark soon and possibly looking for Oleg, and he needed to be gone by the time anyone came knocking.

First, Mark needed clothes. Although Oleg was much larger than Mark, he'd have to take what he could get. Mark flipped on the room's lights and stripped Oleg of his khaki pants, sweater, and boots, and put them all on. Oleg had an extra ammo clip in his pocket, a cell phone, and 6,000 rubles in a money clip. Not much, but it would have to do.

When Mark picked up the gun from the ground, he felt something—a presence in the room, like eyes on him. He turned around, expecting to see another agent, but instead he saw a nurse standing in the doorway. Her eyes were wide, and they darted from Mark, holding a gun, to the nearly nude man passed out on the floor, then back to Mark.

"No, no, no," Mark said, softly pleading. "It's not what you—"

Even if she could understand Mark's English, it wouldn't have mattered. The nurse screamed in horror and ran out of the room.

"Shit," Mark muttered.

Hoping he could get out ahead of reinforcements, Mark rushed from the room. It was the wrong move. Jogging down the hall were two FSB agents followed by a hospital security guard. Their guns were already drawn, and they yelled for Mark to drop his weapon. But that wasn't going to happen. He hadn't bested Oleg just to wind up right back in confinement. Assuming, of course, that was even an option. He'd just killed one of his enemy's own, and he was pretty certain they wouldn't look kindly on that. So, he bucked the agents' orders, raised his gun, and popped off two shots. Mark fired them high, knowing they would hit the ceiling, but they served their purpose: The agents and the guard dropped to the floor and took cover behind the nurses' kiosk.

Mark had to think fast. Behind him was a dead end, nothing but a window looking out onto Moscow's skyline at night. But judging by the perspective, it dawned on Mark that he wasn't that far off the ground. Maybe just a few floors up.

One of the agents craned his head around the kiosk, but

before he could say anything, Mark fired another shot. He then rushed to the end of the hall and looked down—it was a straight shot to the ground, and while a fall from that height likely wouldn't kill him, it would definitely break some of his bones. Possibly many. That would throw a serious wrench in his escape plans. But, there was good news: Off to the right side—just visible from Mark's perspective—was the hospital's entrance, and at the entrance was a canopy that covered the lobby's front doors. It was a narrow space, but if Mark could hit that canopy, he just might make the drop without shattering both his legs.

It was worth a shot if only because it was the only shot he had.

Mark raced back into his room, firing off another warning round in case the agents had any ideas. They didn't, but the security guard did.

He yelled something in Russian, then turned from around the gurney he'd ducked behind and opened fire. Mark dove back into his room, hearing a bullet ricochet off the door frame. He slammed the door shut and fired three shots into the window, shattering the glass and clearing the way for his escape.

And then he hesitated. He was about to jump out a window, and the ground below wasn't that close. He *assumed* he'd land without injury—or at least serious injury—but Mark knew it was a serious—and potentially painful—risk.

The agents were coming, though. He could hear them running toward his room, yelling at the security guard—reprimanding him for his stupidity, Mark bet—as they approached. There was no time to let fear get the best of him.

Mark ran to the window and looked down; he was directly above the canopy, which looked about a million miles away.

Sarah, Mark thought. *Our baby.*

He climbed over the ledge and closed his eyes. Right when the agents and the guard entered the room, he dropped.

The fall was over in the blink of an eye. Mark crashed onto the canopy, landing on his feet and then collapsing into a roll as his legs buckled beneath him. It was a clumsy roll; the momentum of his fall carried him faster than he could control, nearly throwing him over the side of the canvas platform. But Mark stopped himself just in time, gripping the roof's edge.

Mark took a quick moment to kiss the canopy, then he released his grip and dropped to the ground below. And just like that, for the first time in weeks, he was free. No guards were hovering around him, no cameras were monitoring every move he made. He was *free*.

Or so he thought.

The sound of a gun cocking clicked behind him. It was a sound Mark was getting used to hearing.

"Turn around, slowly, with your hands up," a voice said.

But Mark wasn't about to go back to following orders, and he wasn't going to even entertain the prospect of being dragged back to the Triumph Palace. Mark turned—that part he obeyed. But he turned with his gun held in front of his chest; he was ready to shoot or get shot, anything other than surrender.

But he hesitated, and he was relieved that he did. Because standing behind him was a person he never thought he'd see again:

Alice.

16

Or Ania. Whatever her name was. Mark never dreamed he'd see her again, yet there she was, standing right in front of him with a gun trained on his face.

"You've got to be shitting me," Mark said, maintaining his gun's steady aim on her belly.

"Listen, we don't have a lot of time, so you need to put your gun down and listen," Ania said, putting on her American "Alice" accent.

"Listen to you? Listen to *you*?" Mark growled. "No—no, I don't think so. You listen to me when I say I want you to get away from me—right *now*."

Ania twisted her head to look back at the hospital's entrance. Mark followed her line of sight and saw that a crowd was starting to gather. He and Ania were tucked away in a dark corner far enough away to go unnoticed, but Mark couldn't stay there forever. He had to run.

"You have no money, no identification, and you don't speak the language. How long do you think you'll last?" Ania asked.

"I'll take my chances," Mark said, backing away. "Now get away from me. You stabbed me in the back once, I won't let you do it again."

"I told you I could get you out," Ania said, following Mark. "I told you that, and I meant it."

Mark stopped. "In the restaurant—that was you?"

"There's a lot you don't know, a lot you don't understand," Ania said, her face softening. "Come with me—I can get you home. You know I'm the only chance you have."

Mark studied her while keeping one eye on the crowd forming around the hospital's entrance. Time was running out, and Mark knew that Ania was right. He had no plan. Running. That's all he had, and that wasn't a plan. That was a verb. And even if he did run, it wouldn't be long before a search party came after him. Dogs. Checkpoints. Armed officers. Whoever was behind this whole plot Mark was trapped in the middle of wouldn't let him escape so easily. They'd find him, and they'd kill him. At least Ania was offering him a chance. He thought she was full of shit, but if by some miracle she was telling the truth—well, it beat certain death, which is what he'd find trying to make it on his own.

"Mark, I'm leaving," Ania warned. "Come with me, now or never."

Ania lowered her gun, and Mark inhaled a deep breath.

"One condition," he said.

Ania's lips tightened as she suppressed her agitation. "We *really* have to get moving."

"Take me to the U.S. embassy."

"The what?!" Ania erupted. "Are you insane?"

"If you want me to trust you," Mark coolly said, "then you'll take me there."

"They'll kill you, Mark. You're a traitor. They. Will. Kill you."

"The embassy," he insisted

"Okay," Ania begrudgingly acquiesced. "But don't say I didn't warn you."

* * *

Ania's car—a boxy, rusted sedan—was parked in a loading zone around the side of the hospital's curved façade. They entered the car wordlessly, and both of them did their best to close their door without making a sound. It was superstitious in a way, like a catcher not talking to his pitcher in the middle of a no-hitter. Only the stakes here were a little higher. They didn't want to act confident that they'd gotten away because even as Ania turned over the engine, they weren't out of the woods just yet. Quietly, Ania told Mark exactly that, but he didn't believe her.

He changed his mind, though, when bullets started ricocheting off the sedan's body.

"This shit again?!" Fueled by the memories of the shootout on Sadovaya Street, Mark plunged his head below the dashboard. He wanted to dig a hole down there, somehow, and never come out. But that wasn't going to happen. Ania buried the gas pedal and peeled away, throwing Mark out of his cubbyhole and back against the car's seat.

"Good idea to waste time arguing about going to the embassy!" Ania yelled as she rocketed the car onto a busy street, whipping the vehicle around the cars that were in her way.

"Really?!" Mark shot back. "This whole thing is on *me*? You're really going to make a case of *that*?"

Ania didn't offer anything in response. She played no small role in framing Mark as a Russian spy, and she knew how her past actions directly contributed to his current predicament. As she struggled to think of something thoughtful to say in her defense, she was saved by the bell—the bell, in this case, being a bullet that drilled the driver's-side mirror.

"Go, go, go!" Mark yelled, but his urging for Ania to continue what she was already doing only succeeded in turning her already sour expression darker.

"What do you think I've been doing?!" she said as she whipped the car around a clunky station wagon and threaded the needle between two other cars before jumping across two lanes of traffic. It was a nice maneuver, but whoever was in pursuit wasn't so easily shaken. Mark heard the hollow sound of metal being pierced—the trunk, he assumed, as it was barraged by a trio of bullets. Daring to catch a glimpse of whoever was trying to kill him *this* time, Mark poked his head above the seat. Visibility was low in the night's darkness, and the sheen pouring off the many headlights only obscured Mark's vision further. But then he saw it: a black sedan jackknifing through traffic, hot in pursuit.

"Damn it," Mark snarled as he ducked his head back down. He pulled his gun out from the back of his pants. "They're gaining on us."

"And what do you think you're going to do?" Ania asked, her words punctuated by another series of bullets penetrating the car.

"I'm going to shoot *back*," Mark replied.

Mark opened his window and angled himself out. Their pursuers were directly behind them and getting close.

He fired off three quick shots, and the car swerved and twisted when Mark's bullets blasted its exterior. It was satisfying to give whoever was after them a taste of their own medicine, so when the car righted itself, Mark shot at it again. The enemy sedan jerked to its right, colliding with an SUV that'd been driving alongside it. The car spun out of control and another car, one that'd been driving behind the sedan, smashed into it midspin. Whoever was chasing Mark and Ania careened out of control; Mark had effectively taken them off the playing field.

He shot Ania a smile that hardly captured a modicum of how proud he was of himself.

"Don't get cocky," Ania warned, unimpressed. "There'll be more."

"Great," Mark said, putting the gun to his side as he pulled out the phone he'd taken off Oleg. "Another cheery forecast."

Ania's gaze practically burned a hole right through Mark. "Where did you get that?" she asked. "And what do you think you're going to do with it?"

"Order a pizza," Mark snapped as he studied the foreign keypad. It was an ancient model flip phone, not entirely surprising considering it had been Oleg's. "What do you care?"

"Oh, I don't know," Ania said. "Maybe I'm concerned about you making a stupid phone call to your wife, which will undoubtedly be traced."

"I'm calling Sarah, and you're just going to have to deal with it."

"I don't care about your wife, I care about you getting us caught."

Mark started punching Sarah's cell phone number into the phone. At least that's what he hoped he was doing. "I haven't spoken to my wife—my *pregnant* wife, in weeks. I need to talk to her. I need to warn her."

Ania shot him a dark look. "Have you figured out what'll happen to her once word gets out that you broke free?"

Mark countered Ania's stern expression with one of his own. One that said she couldn't stop him from reaching out to his wife even if she tried. "I don't know exactly what'll happen to her, but I know it won't be good. That's why I need to do whatever I can to get her to safety," he said.

Ania exhaled sharply and yanked the phone out of Mark's hands. "You're doing it all wrong," she said as she keyed in a series of numbers. "I had Sarah's cell memorized for work."

Ania tossed the phone to Mark and then turned her attention back to the road. "Just hit the button with the little green phone on it, and make your call fast. When you're done, toss it out the window."

Mark took a moment before he finished dialing to catch his breath. He felt like an uncertain teen checking his hair in the rearview mirror before picking up his date. He knew Sarah would be by his side, always. But what did she make of every-thing that'd happened? What had they told her about him? She wouldn't buy it, Mark was confident in that; but maybe every-thing she was fed—from intelligence agents, from know-nothing talking heads—would be enough to make her look at him in a new way. Maybe it would be enough to reconsider what she made of him.

For his own sanity, Mark had to shove those thoughts out of his mind. He gripped the phone tight, ready to make the call. Outside his window, the lights of Moscow at night raced by in a haze. At once, Mark felt drunk, exhausted, and disoriented. This, as Sarah would say, had been a day. Or was it days? Mark had no idea how long he'd been in the hospital—how much time sepa-rated him from when he'd been shot, smashed in a car wreck, and beaten up by Oleg—but it wasn't enough for him to recu-perate. He had healed well enough; he could function, but the damage he'd suffered was still with him, and it would be for a long time. For now though, pain would have to be a motivator. Pain would have to be what helped keep him going, not what broke him down. There'd be no rest and relaxation, there'd be no pause. Mark could collapse when his feet were firmly planted back on American soil.

Mark turned his attention back to the clunky cell phone. He punched the key as instructed by Ania and began to pray that Sarah picked up.

"Come on, come on," he murmured, phone to his ear. "Pick up, Sarah, please pick up."

The phone rang. Three times, then four. Mark panicked. Leav-ing a message, he supposed, would get the job done. He'd be able to convey the essential information—that he was innocent, that he was free, that he was coming home—he needed to tell Sarah, but that wasn't enough. He wanted to hear her voice; he *needed* to.

Her voice would get him through whatever else was ahead, whatever separated him from his wife and unborn child.

Mark's grip on the phone slackened with the fifth ring, and he
felt a wave of despair and sadness crash into him. He was tired—
so tired—but he could endure more fighting, more running, more
of anything that was thrown at him. What he couldn't take,
though, was the idea that something had happened to Sarah. That
the Americans, the Russians, or whatever bastards were behind
everything had gotten to her, too.

But then, the phone clicked.

"Hello?" came Sarah's voice, soft and apprehensive, through
the other end of the line.

"Oh my god—*Sarah*." Mark heaved a pent-up sigh, and he
emptied so much of himself that his body nearly collapsed on
itself like a Murphy bed folding into a wall. He pressed the phone
to his ear, ensuring he could hear every sound, every syllable,
that came through the receiver. "Where are you? Are you okay?"

"Am I okay? Mark, what's happening to you? The news, the
government, they—they . . ."

Mark could hear the tears Sarah was fighting to hold back and
felt conflicting emotions well within him. He wanted to comfort
Sarah, he wanted to allay all of her concerns and tell her everything would be all right; but, at the same time, he wanted to find
the people responsible for filling his wife with such profound
worry and rip their throats out.

"Sarah, honey, you have to believe me. You *have* to know that
I'm telling you the absolute truth . . . *none* of the things they're
saying about me are true. I'm not a spy. I haven't betrayed anything or anyone. I have no idea why this is happening."

"I never doubted that for a second, Mark," Sarah replied without hesitation, and now Mark was the one fighting back tears.

"Listen—I'm coming home. Okay? They had me, but I got out,

and now I'm coming home. But Sarah, with me out of custody, they're going to come for you. I have no doubt they'll try to use you as leverage to get to me. You need to hide, you need to disappear."

"Disappear?" Sarah asked, incredulous. "I—Why? To where?"

"It doesn't matter—anywhere you can't be found or traced. Anywhere that—"

Before Mark could utter another word, he was thrown forward, propelled off his seat by the momentum created as something smashed into the back of the car. The impact nearly sent him crashing face-first into the windshield.

Mark turned to find another black sedan—same model as the one that had been chasing them before—on their tail. Its grill was smashed from being used as a battering ram, and it was speeding toward Ania's car again. The sedan smashed into the rear end once more, and their car rattled and swerved with the impact.

"Damn it," Ania hollered, "they're going to be all over us."

"I'm sorry," Mark admitted. "I shouldn't have called, I should have—"

Ania shook her head. "No, there's no way they got us through the phone that fast. They're just following our trail, and soon enough they're going to have every nearby agent on our asses."

"What do we do now?" Mark asked as Ania swerved between cars, trying to stay separated from the sedan that was somewhere behind them.

"Now? Now we *have* to get to the embassy. Whoever these agents are, they wouldn't dare come after us and risk causing an international incident. We'll just have to hope the Americans don't shoot us on the spot."

Mark turned his attention back to the phone. He wanted to implore Sarah, one last time, to stay hidden, to not do anything reckless. He knew his wife, knew that she'd do anything to protect the people she cared about. Mark could only hope she had better sense than to get involved in the mess he was in.

But all the things he wanted to tell her would be left unsaid. The phone was smashed and nearly broken in half. It was beyond repair, dead and gone. Mark could only hope that Sarah caught enough of what he'd said and would act accordingly.

"I love you," he whispered to the busted phone that he cradled in his lap.

"You're sweet," Ania said, "but not my type."

Mark looked at Ania, and she winked at him. But when she turned her attention back to the road, her playfulness disappeared.

"Hang on to something!" Ania yelled, and Mark quickly did as he was told. He grabbed onto the passenger door's handle with one hand and gripped the seat cushion with his other. Even braced, Mark was still jolted forward, again, as Ania's car was nailed from behind. This time, the battering car must have gained some momentum because it felt like a garbage truck had smashed into them; Mark's body whiplashed forward so hard that his head smashed into the dashboard.

Mark came up bloody, crimson running out of his nose and over his mouth.

The sedan came in for another strike, but this time it sliced into the car's rear quarter panel. The car began to skid, but Ania held the wheel tight and prevented them from spinning out of control.

"How long until we get to the embassy?" Mark asked as he shoved a fresh ammo clip into his gun.

"Two minutes," Ania said. "We just have to hold out for a little bit longer."

Mark cocked back the hammer on his pistol as he watched the sedan roll up to his window.

"Get us to that embassy's front door," Mark said. "I don't care what it takes."

As the sedan pulled up next to Ania's car, Mark fired. He aimed for the tires, but his shots ended up in the sedan's wheel well. Still, it was good enough to keep the sedan at a distance—until the driver's-side window opened and an automatic rifle came poking out.

"GET DOWN!" Mark shouted just as a rat-a-tat-tat sound filled the air and a hail of bullets shredded Ania's car. Mark dove to the seat, pulling Ania's head down with him. He squeezed his eyes shut, but he could hear the automatic rifle belch bullet after bullet, each one pounding the car's exterior and erupting the windows; cubes of glass rained on Mark's head, and for a moment, he was convinced this barrage would never end. He thought the bullets would just keep coming and coming until he was dead.

But a pause did come. The automatic rifle, Mark assumed, must have needed a reload. Ania used the small window proficiently. Having miraculously guided the car through traffic, Ania was now prepared to strike back. The second the onslaught stopped, she sprang up, gun in hand. She fired three determined shots across their car and into the enemy sedan. Each shot landed squarely into the gunman's chest. He slumped over, onto the sedan's driver, causing the car to swerve off the road.

Mark looked at Ania. Like him, she was covered in glass and had a number of tiny cuts all over her face and body.

"Nice shooting," Mark said, impressed.

"It's all in the training," she replied. "I'll get you our instructional manual."

Mark looked at Ania, who smiled. It was the nicest moment—just that small bit of warmth directed his way—that Mark had experienced since arriving to Russia.

And then the car began to spin across the road.

Mark was thrown against the passenger door, fortunate that his would-be assailant had shot out all the glass. If he hadn't, it would have been Mark's head shattering the passenger-side window. Mark angled himself to check on Ania, who seemed to be doing just fine. She was gripping the wheel and fighting hard for control, but it was no use; a tire had been shot out, and when Mark considered everything else that had to be wrong with it, he knew their ride was hardly in condition to run a soapbox derby, let alone escape a squad of Russian agents. Ania must have realized the same thing, because she stopped fighting for control and, instead, worked on easing the car to a stop. It wasn't easy. The car was powered by so much momentum, and as far as Mark could tell, the brakes were hardly responding to Ania's pumping foot. The steering wheel bucked in her grip as the car jumped the sidewalk; Ania twisted and turned around fleeing civilians and brought the car to the safest stop possible, crashing it into the brick façade adjacent to a crowded bar.

Mark hadn't even finished huffing a breath before Ania grabbed his arm and started pulling him toward the driver's-side door.

"Run!" she ordered. "The embassy is straight ahead. Run, do *not* let them catch you."

Mark followed. He darted from the car right behind Ania, doing his best to hobble along at her pace. A few steps was all Mark needed to push past his body's resistance and straighten out his gait. He was especially motivated by the sound of Russian agents yelling from somewhere in the background, hot in pursuit. Mark expected them to open fire at any moment, but Ania was right: Their proximity to the embassy kept them from such an extreme means of capturing their quarry. Their reluctance to cause an international incident brought about a change in Mark. Instead of fear and despair, he could feel a renewed sense of hope coursing in his veins. He was going to make it to the U.S. embassy; he was going to unravel this nightmare.

Mark turned around once and spotted a black SUV idling halfway down the block, like an invisible barrier was keeping it in place. A team of Russian agents waited idly by the vehicle, and Mark knew they weren't going anywhere. Not yet. Like Ania, they must have known Mark's odds of finding any kind of amnesty from the embassy were practically nonexistent. Mark shared the same analysis. And once Mark was shoved off American soil, the agents would be right back on him, and he'd have nowhere to go. But Mark was nothing if not capable of talking his way out of impossible situations, so he wasn't ready to sign his own death warrant just yet. The power to convince people was his greatest asset. All he needed was someone—a diplomat, a high-ranking military official, even the janitor, it didn't matter— to listen. Someone to at least entertain the idea of Mark's innocence, especially since it meant that the real spy was still at large in the United States. The Russians had fooled the U.S. intelligence community, and Mark had to get them to understand not only the mistake that'd been made but also the implications it had for the country's safety.

The embassy stretched across nearly half a city block, fortified by an exterior of tan and white bricks. Upward-pointing lights gave the windows a warm glow, but they also made the building look like an American hotel. The building radiated familiarity, and it filled Mark with a sense of relief and comfort. He hadn't felt either since this ordeal began.

The center of the embassy opened to a brick-paved square just in front of its entrance but pushed back from the street. Mark slowed his pace as he entered the square and approached a barricade that was manned by armed guards dressed head to toe in black tactical uniforms, like they were part of a SWAT team. Even more armed guards, Mark noticed, prowled the square's grounds, which felt smaller and smaller with every assault rifle Mark laid his eyes on.

"Are you sure this is a good idea?" Ania whispered into his ear as they approached.

"Not entirely," Mark replied. "But it's our only chance."

"*Your* chance. I was never going to come into the embassy with you—I'm a *spy*, Mark."

"Look, if we can get our foot in the front door, we can cut a deal. I prove my innocence, with your help, and you can offer valuable information for immunity. What do you think?"

"I think you've watched too many spy movies."

Mark cautiously approached the barricade. He knew he looked terrible—a wound had reopened on his head during the crash, and blood was caked in his hair; his clothes were too big, and his face was saturated with his own sweat. But it wasn't like he'd had the option to clean up, so he'd have to work his magic beaten and bruised.

Halfway through the square, Mark heard a gun's safety being released. He slowed his steps and studied the guards that stood alert all around him. Their eyes were on him. Mark knew— even before the guard blocking the barricade yelled for him to "halt!"—what had happened:

He'd been identified.

More safeties were clicked off and guns were lifted, their crosshairs trained on Mark's head. He froze and raised his hands. So much for his hope to have a reasonable conversation.

"Please, you have to listen to me," Mark said, enunciating each word clearly. "There's been a mistake, a terrible mistake. I need *help*."

"There's no mistake, Strain," the guard positioned at the barricade said. "As a traitor to the United States, you've been stripped of your citizenship. You are an enemy and no longer welcome on American soil.

"You and your friend, both of you—get out. *Now.*"

Mark took a hesitant step forward. "I'm innocent. I swear—I *swear*—I am *not* a spy. I was framed, and the real spy is still—"

The barricade guard raised his rifle and caught Mark in his sights. "Not one more step," he ordered.

Mark couldn't have been squeezed tighter if he was in a vise. He had a half-dozen automatic rifles pointed at his face; he had Russian agents at his back, just waiting for him to get booted out of the embassy. And Mark knew he wouldn't be returned to the comfortable life in a posh apartment that he'd been treated to; there'd be no museum tours, no cruising the city, no upscale dining. He had crossed a Rubicon the moment he killed Oleg, and that meant there'd be a reckoning upon his return. Knowing the impermanence of his value, Mark had no desire to know what the consequences for his actions would be, what terrible retribution would be inflicted on him for what he had done.

But Mark couldn't go forward, either. He could beg the embassy guards. He could plead, he could explain, he could cry for their mercy. It wouldn't matter. There was nothing he could do to get one foot past the barricade; Mark was a traitor, a man guilty of the ultimate crime against his nation, and not a single United States citizen—something Mark no longer was, on paper—owed him the time of day. At best, they owed Mark one thing: a bullet. And if Mark did anything to provoke the guards further, he was certain they'd be happy to zero out that balance.

The guard at the barricade spoke something into the radio strapped to his right shoulder, then walked forward. "I hope you realize how serious my order is," he said, standing over Mark. "I'll explain it to you one more time: You are an enemy combatant standing on American soil. If you do not evacuate the premises, we will be forced to act."

Ania tugged at Mark, drawing him back. "Come on, they're not going to listen to you."

"I just need a chance," he contested, holding his ground. "If someone would just listen to me, I could—"

"Mark," Ania said as she gently turned his face to hers, "they'll kill you. They'll kill both of us."

Mark turned to face the guards. They hadn't moved; all of them still had their guns at the ready, just waiting for a reason to fire.

Mark began to backpedal, taking the smallest of steps toward the entrance. "You're making a mistake," he said. "One day, the truth will come out, and you'll regret what you did here." He turned and looked at the haunting chiaroscuro of the crowded street behind him, the dim streetlights casting only the faintest of illumination on the faces of passersby who paid no mind to Mark or the embassy. The courtyard's entrance was like a dark, open mouth waiting to swallow him whole. And that's exactly what would happen if the Russians recaptured him. He'd be swallowed, absorbed, and never heard from again.

Plan A—convincing the U.S. embassy to hear his case—was a dud. And Plan B—turning back to the Russians—wasn't a plan at all. What Mark needed, and fast, was Plan C. But this is what Mark did. In life, in his work, Mark excelled at thinking on the fly and creating his own opportunities. Mark wasn't going to let the Russians take him and Ania and have their way with them, and he certainly wasn't going to be gunned down by his own country. That's not how this night was going to play out. So, Mark improvised.

"Help me!" he yelled, the decibel of his voice as it pierced the still night air, surprising even himself.

Ania grabbed Mark by the crux of his elbow and yanked him a step back. "Are you crazy?" she asked.

"Probably," Mark replied. "But I'd rather be crazy and alive than sane and dead."

Mark screamed again. He looked over his shoulder; a few people—young people, presumably out for a night at the nearby clubs—took notice of his yelling and were reluctantly inching closer. It was exactly what Mark wanted.

"What are you doing?" the guard asked, agitation lacing his words.

Mark knew panic and stress—he lived and breathed them both nearly every day—and he knew how to control them both. But what he'd considered to be life and death situations in his past life as a lobbyist was nothing compared to what he was going through now. Appropriately, Mark couldn't pull off the same measure of composure under fire. The embassy guards at his front and the Russian agents at his rear, Mark wasn't in control; in fact, he was scared out of his mind, and he had to fight back against his own growing anxiety before it suffocated him.

"Hey!" the guard barked. "What. Are. You. *Doing?*"

Alex and Oleg weren't exactly ambassadors to Mark, but they did leave him with one valuable nugget: a protocol in the event things went bad. Enemies were everywhere, Oleg had grimly remarked on one of their drives around Moscow, and you never knew who might strike, or why or when. It just so happened that Oleg was paranoid for good reason. But in the mania of their car being shot at and batted around a busy Moscow street like a pinball, Mark was too disoriented—his brains scrambled—to put the one thing Oleg had taught him to use.

How to call for help.

"*Pogomi mne!*" he yelled, his calls directed at the growing crowd of onlookers at the mouth of the embassy's courtyard. "*Pogomi mne!*"

Mark took Ania's hand and staggered toward the street, shooting glances between the guards and the gathering crowd.

At the very least, no one could put a bullet in Mark with this many eyes on him. A couple of the onlookers had already whipped out their phones and were recording the scene. Which was good, but he needed more—and it only took a moment to get what he was looking for.

A young woman, shimmering in a sequin party dress, pointed at him and Ania, and though she was speaking in Russian to her friend, Mark knew what had happened: She'd recognized them.

Word was spreading among the crowd. This was Pyotr and Ania, their national heroes, and they were being accosted by those filthy Americans.

The crowd started to yell. It was unintelligible to Mark, but he got the gist. He could see their facial expressions, disgusted and indignant. They were sticking up for one of their own; they were spitting in the faces of the capitalist American pigs.

And, best of all, they were causing a distraction.

"Are you sure you're not a spy?" Ania whispered into Mark's ear right before she began yelling to the crowd and gesturing at the embassy, riling everyone up even more.

More people clumped in the crowd, and they were starting to encroach on the embassy's grounds. Their yells grew angrier. More phones were out, ready to capture any evidence of wrongdoing. Mark and Ania continued to back out, hands up, watching a sneer grow on the barricade guard's face.

"Get out of here," he snarled. "Go join your damn comrades."

Mark did as he was told, falling into the crowd at his back—his supporters, his protectors. But as he drifted out of the embassy, something caught his eye. Something that made his blood run cold.

Directly above the embassy's entrance—a lone ornate door with an intricate pattern carved into gilded wood—was a small balcony that hung just a few feet out from the building itself. One of the French doors leading from the building swung open, and out into the night, directly beneath one of the spotlights that cast the façade in a dull glow, stepped a woman with flowing blond hair and a scar over her left eye.

The woman from the car on Sadovaya Street. The assassin.

Mark felt his chest cave. Disbelief and rage bottlenecked in his throat as Mark struggled to make sense of the inconceivable truth that was staring him right in his face:

The assassin was an American.

The Americans wanted Mark dead.

Mark had to flee. He had to get as far away as possible from the embassy guards he'd thoroughly pissed off and the killer whose job was to see him dead. The crowd continued to push him back, out of the embassy, and he moved in a daze, like he was being carried along without any movement of his own. He stared at the assassin, straight into her impassive eyes, which looked at Mark—*through* Mark—like he was nothing. She had made herself visible just to taunt him, to reinforce, in the coldest way possible, that he had no sanctuary. He was a dead man no matter where he went.

Mark stumbled out of the courtyard, separating himself from the protective mass that had once felt like a shield to him but was more like a tomb now. He turned his attention to where the Russian agents' SUV was parked. As if following the script of a nightmare, Mark spotted the agents immediately. They were out of their car already, heading right for Mark and Ania. Pursuing them. Stalking them.

Ania spotted it, too. She tugged at his arm, leading him away from both the embassy and the agents.

"Come on!" Ania yelled. "There's a train station across the street—it's our only way out of here."

This time, when Mark screamed *"Pogomi mne!"* he didn't have to fake his fear. He didn't have to manufacture a sense of frenzy. Both were clawing at his insides like a feral animal trying to get out.

"Pogomi mne!" he bellowed again, stabbing a finger at the agents, who were closing in fast.

The crowd surrounding Mark, worked into a patriotic frenzy, interpreted their hero's cue exactly as it was intended. *Save me,* Mark pleaded. *There are more enemies I need protection from.*

Obediently, the crowd directed their attention, and their fervor, at the agents. They marched to cut them off. Mark saw the agents' faces shift from sadistic anticipation as they picked up their pursuit to confusion when the people they assumed were their allies turned on them. The last thing Mark saw was the crowd swarming the agents, smothering them physically and vocally. They screamed the agents down, neutralizing them. Mark didn't know how long it could last, and he didn't care to find out.

Following Ania's lead, Mark darted into the traffic crisscrossing the street, almost getting plastered by a speeding Bimmer the second he stepped off the curb. He didn't have time for caution. His window for escape was narrow, and it was the only window he'd get. The Russians wanted him dead. The Americans wanted him dead. His only shot was to disappear and pray he could find a way out before either side got to him.

Car horns blared from both directions as Mark and Ania weaved through traffic. He heard screeching tires when an SUV swerved out of his way, but he hardly paid it any notice. All that mattered was getting on the train. Barrikadnaya Station was straight ahead, no more than thirty yards away. Mark recognized the massive relief carved into the entrance—three workers intertwined with one another, representing events from the Revolution of 1905—and he knew that just beyond the station's double doors were trains. Trains that would take him far away from where he was right now, and that's all he wanted.

Mark and Ania raced through the square leading to the entrance. His heart thumped in his chest and sweat rolled down his forehead as his furious sprinting combined with raw fear to accelerate his entire body into overdrive. Without breaking stride, Mark whipped his head over his shoulder to see if they were being pursued. He scanned the lane between them and the embassy, but the assassin was nowhere in sight. It was little comfort, though, as Mark assumed that she was skilled enough to elude Mark's perfunctory glance. She could be anywhere, Mark thought with a shiver, and the first sign of her presence would likely be his termination.

With another quick turn, Mark looked for the agents. They were shoving and pushing people out of their path, shedding Mark's protectors. Mark met their cold eyes just as they broke free of the crowd and took off in a full sprint after him.

He turned back around and bowled into a couple right in front of him. They all tumbled to the ground, but Mark wasted no time getting back to his feet. Ania helped him off the cold ground and muttered what sounded like an apology to the couple. The man, a beefy linebacker type with a flattop haircut to suit his build, yelled after Mark, but he didn't care what was being said. He ran, pumping his legs harder than he ever had in his life; he felt every muscle below his waist burn, every ligament stretch to what felt like the point of shredding.

Inside Barrikadnaya Station, Mark and Ania were stymied by the throng of people clogging the space between the entryway and the escalators descending to the underground tunnels.

"Damn it," Ania grumbled. "We don't have time for this."

"Come on," Mark said, taking Ania's hand. "We'll just have to be a little rude."

Mark cut a serpentine path through the crowd and onto the escalator, nudging and shoving past people and squeezing by others. Finally, the escalator emptied them out to a tunnel lit by overhead fluorescent lighting that shone off the multicolored marble tiles lining the walls. Just a few feet ahead of him, the tunnel forked.

"Where to?" Mark asked.

"Out, away from the city. This way," Ania said, pulling him toward the tunnel on the left. Mark followed her, slicing between the people peppered between the artful walls. Sprinting the entire way, they reached the end of the tunnel, and Mark cursed. Sure enough, there was a train waiting at the platform, and it seemed ready to depart. But, as Mark's mom liked to say to the point of annoying overusage, there were no free rides. The train was no exception. A line of turnstiles bisected the platform, separating Mark from the train. They'd need a pass to get through, but there was no ticketing booth in sight. Mark had seen just one since entering the station, and it was upstairs.

"Damn. *It*," Mark growled.

"I never take the train," Ania said, apologetically. "They have cars that take me everywhere now."

"Okay, okay—think," Mark said to himself. He surveyed the scene. Every system had a weakness, a design flaw of some kind. It was just a matter of finding it.

The turnstiles were airtight: Passengers scanned their transit cards, and the thick plastic partitions that separated the two sides of the platform opened, letting people through before whooshing shut again. The turnstiles ran from the wall on one side to the wall on the other, interrupted only by a narrow service kiosk. There was no maintenance access in the tunnel that Mark could see, which meant the only possible directions were ahead through the turnstiles or back the way they came.

Error, though, came in all shapes and sizes. Mark knew this, and he also knew that his favorite flavor of error was the human variety. It's practically what his career had been built on. As skilled as he was at capitalizing on someone's wants and desires, he was as equally skilled at identifying weaknesses and exploiting them. Granted, Mark was much happier to be bribing, flattering, and gifting people into submission instead of blackmailing them. But

Mark always justified his maneuvers by contending that you walk through the doors that are opened for you. And the grimy station agent that was out of his kiosk trying to make time with a pretty young commuter was just the door he needed.

The agent was doubtless distracted, and Mark considered leaping the turnstiles and hoping his attention was diverted enough not to notice. But he needed better assurance, and he'd be damned if he wound up back with the FSB because some sloppy station agent who looked like he hadn't bathed in weeks busted him trying to get a free train ride.

"I've got it," Mark told Ania. "I hope you're okay with some minor theft."

"I should be able to live with myself. What are you going to do?"

"Just . . . be ready."

Mark hurried toward the agent and the girl caught in his snare, his eyes locked downward on the broken phone in his left hand. Acting the role of the oblivious commuter too busy fiddling with his phone to pay attention to the world around him wasn't difficult to pull off. And that's when he made his calculated move, bumping straight into the back of the young woman, toppling her right into the agent. Mark cringed at what he'd done; however gross the agent was to him, he had to be about ten times grosser to the woman.

As she fell into the agent, Mark kept walking, hardly breaking his stride. He turned, shrugging apologetically, but didn't slow for a moment. The agent, Mark took full notice, was practically having a conniption fit, awkwardly trying to help the woman regain her balance and his own at the same time. Profoundly distracted, he didn't even flinch when Mark and Ania hurried to the nearest turnstile and glided over the partition.

They were in.

They hurried onto the nearest train; all the seats had already been taken, but Mark didn't care. He didn't need to sit, didn't need to know where he was going. His time in Russia had wound him tighter than the strings on a violin, and he finally had a moment to exhale. To not feel the pressure of the surveillance watching his every move, of Oleg breathing down his neck, of someone coming in the middle of the night to deliver a bullet straight into his head. He was regaining control, and control was everything to Mark. He could do a lot with a little—like get out of Russia, prove his innocence, and reunite with Sarah.

An automated voice crackled through the overhead intercom, and Mark prayed it was announcing the train's departure. His gut knew better.

"That's bad news, isn't it?" he asked Ania.

"They say there's work being done on the track ahead. But they *always* say that."

"How long?"

Ania shook her head. "Hopefully not long."

Mark glanced over his shoulder through the still-open doors. He let his eyes scan every inch of the station, capturing the hustle and bustle of commuters fishing for their transit cards and pushing through the turnstiles. He was about to turn away from the crowd, from the idea that he was still being pursued, when his burgeoning hope was snuffed out by the sight of one of the agents racing toward the station. Mark whipped his head back around and hugged the wall. Ania pressed closer to him, also doing her best to stay out of view.

Unless Mark did something.

Mark poked his head out again; the agent was searching, frantically, but he was alone. He and his partner must have split up at the fork, Mark assumed. That was good—one less enemy to deal with.

Inside the train, another announcement was made; the commuters chattered in response, and while Mark couldn't understand what they were saying, he recognized the relieved tone.

"We're about to depart," Ania said. "Maybe our friend won't get on."

Mark espied the agent as he pushed through the turnstiles on the far end of the station, parallel to the train car behind Mark's. Mark seethed. He was never one for moaning about catching breaks; luck, he believed, was nothing more than perseverance plus presence. You had to work harder than the person next to you, and you had to stick around long enough for your number to be called. Still, while Mark wasn't about to renege on his perspective, the hurdles being thrown in his path—the unending hurdles—were getting ridiculous.

"He made it through the turnstiles," Mark grumbled. "He's coming."

"If we can just make it to the next station, we can get off and—"

"No," Mark said. "I can't let him on this train—it's too much of a risk."

Shuffling, squeezing, and elbowing, Mark pushed through the crowded train car, drawing his fair share of groans and angry glares. Through the windows that lined the train car, he saw the agent head toward the adjacent car. Mark shoved harder and reached the rear exit; he lowered his shoulder into the metal door and crossed from his car to the next, again hurrying his way through the crowd. He pushed his way forward, focused on the agent who was approaching fast. Mark, though, was a step ahead, and when he finally purged himself from the sea of bodies cramming one end of the train car to the other, he found himself face-to-face with the agent. Mark was ready for the confrontation; the agent was not.

Mark drove his forehead into the agent's nose; the blow sent him tumbling back and nearly knocked him off his feet. Blood erupted from the agent's nostrils, and Mark used his disorientation to deliver another blow, driving a hard kick straight into his gut; the agent doubled over, and Mark shifted all his weight and strength to grab the agent by his shoulders and spin him away from the train and into the wall. His head smacked against the tile and he dropped to the ground, unconscious.

Mark stepped back, secure on the train, just as the doors slid closed in front of him. He turned to find every set of eyes attached to him, every jaw agape.

"No ticket," Mark said, knowing no one would understand what he was saying or the reference, and as the train rumbled to life and pulled away from the station, everyone went back to eyeing their phones, talking to friends, and focusing on wherever they were going. Mark rejoined Ania, who had followed him into the rear car. She nodded approvingly.

"You're full of surprises, Mark Strain," she said. "I like it."

"Let's not pop the champagne yet—we still have a long way to go."

Mark and Ania agreed that word of what happened would reach someone—train authorities, police, the FSB, who knows, and they'd be pursued once again. But by the time they got to this train, they'd be long gone. Mark and Ania would get off at the next stop, they'd switch from one train to the next with no discernible pattern until, finally, they vanished.

17

Sarah wanted to believe she was paranoid.

Riding the Metro, her fist clenched around the standing rail, Sarah couldn't stop searching the morning rush-hour crowd for eyes watching her. Or for eyes suspiciously not watching her. Armed men breaking into her home and abducting her husband by force had shaken Sarah to her core. The memory played over and over in her mind, each iteration feeling more violent, more intrusive into her life even weeks after the fact. Aaron had set her up in his guest bedroom, yet there were nights when Sarah would startle awake to the sound of a creaking floorboard or the hissing furnace, and her mind would fool her into thinking she was back home, in bed with Mark, in the moments before the agents came and took him away. She'd feel the anticipation of the moment strangle her throat and collapse her chest; she couldn't breathe, couldn't move, couldn't do anything but wait for the terrible thing to happen. But then she realized that she was living a memory. Mark was gone, and she was alone. The anxiety would pass as Sarah lay in bed, staring at the ceiling. She managed to keep herself together during the day, chewing at her waking hours by talking to friends, going on walks, and binging whatever show the internet told her was worth the investment. Work decided it was best she took a "temporary personal leave," though she knew it was anything but temporary. They wouldn't dare trust the lives of their patients to a woman whose husband had betrayed the country. At best, that meant Sarah had been living in oblivion the entire time Mark's treachery took place right under her nose; at worst, she was complicit with his traitorous operation. Either way, the hospital wanted nothing to do with her. That left Sarah with more hours to fill, more time to consider what had happened and what in the hell she was going to do next. And most days, despite the trauma she knew was a wound inside her that wouldn't heal, she got along well enough. In time, she'd move back in with her parents. She'd have her and Mark's baby; she'd love it and do anything in the world to keep it safe. If that meant moving to Canada, if that meant changing her name and starting her life over in the middle of nowhere, then that's what she'd do.

But then came Mark's call and his warning that she was in danger. Even in her most secure moments since Mark's abduction, Sarah knew it wasn't over. She couldn't just walk away from being a Russian spy's wife without facing a reckoning of her own. Sarah now lived in a world where federal agents could kick down her door at any moment and take away everything she knew and loved, and that fear—palpable and paralyzing—was only the tip of the iceberg. Because if it wasn't a federal agent that came after her, maybe it'd be a lone psychopath—furiously "patriotic"— looking to do his part to make America great and safe. Or maybe the Russians would come calling, looking to tie up loose ends. Or who knew what else.

The train rattled to its Union Station stop, and the doors sighed open. Most of the passengers departed, and Sarah shuffled along with them. In Sarah's mind, they were all watching her. Even if they weren't looking at her, they were still seeing. She wanted to believe that it was all in her head. But since Mark's warning, she couldn't help but feel that at least one person in the crowds she clung to—Sarah had made it a point not to go any place she'd be isolated—had their eyes on her. Paranoia, she thought, was defined by deep concerns over things that weren't true; that being the case, Sarah couldn't be paranoid. This was real. Someone, whether near or far, was watching her.

While keeping an attentive eye on any pursuers—though she did figure that anyone following her would likely be worthy of the job and, therefore, able to easily avoid detection—Sarah hurried through Lower Senate Park, the crisp chill in the air nipping at her exposed neck. When she came to the Russell Building, she wondered what kind of trouble security would give her getting into the building. Assuming they'd let her in at all.

Crossing Massachusetts Avenue, Sarah passed under the limestone columns that ran along the building's exterior, a showy display of its Beaux Arts design. Inside, she was met with little resistance, almost as if she was expected. The most suspicion cast on her was when the guard monitoring the lobby asked why Sarah was meeting with Senator Schmidt, and Sarah sniped, "For a chat about privacy invasion." The remark raised an eyebrow on the guard's face, an expression less of agitation, which was what Sarah had expected, and more like she was impressed. The guard probably didn't get much attitude as the front line of defense for U.S. senators' offices—both the gravity of her position and her bodybuilder physique, Sarah assumed, commanded a lot of obedience. Still, despite Sarah's short fuse, the guard let Sarah continue on her way.

Sarah tried to temper her expectations, reminding herself that even as a U.S. senator, there was only so much Dale was capable of. He could just as soon pluck Mark from Russia and drop him back in his home country as he could leap to the moon. Sarah knew he wouldn't even have access to the intelligence that led to Mark's abduction and deportation. But she had to start somewhere, and even if Dale ended up being someone who shared

Sarah's grief, fury, and confusion, that might be enough. While Dale would never assume to know Sarah's trauma—he was too tactful for that—she knew he must be suffering in his own way. He was Mark's friend, and in the absence of a real father figure in his life, Dale was often called on to fill that role. And like Sarah, Mark was torn from Dale's life without warning or explanation. The time to grieve over what had happened was over, Sarah decided. Now it was time to do something about it.

After being ushered into Dale's office by his plucky assistant—Sarah always marveled how everyone who worked directly for the government was either twenty or fifty—Dale greeted Sarah with a gentle hug that felt like the way someone embraces you at a funeral.

"I'm so sorry this is happening," Dale said as he pulled out of the hug but still held Sarah by her shoulders. "How are you holding up?"

Sarah eyed Dale. His words sounded forced, his posture stiff. It was the way he performed when Sarah watched him on C-SPAN; like he was staging his actions. It made Sarah feel guilty, in a way; it wasn't like she was close with Dale, and odds are he didn't quite know how to deal with the baggage she brought to his doorstep. While friendly, generous, and always kind, Dale wasn't the most expressive person. Even with Mark, he kept much of his life close to his chest. Mark contended that Dale had no private life. He was married to his job, and the pride he took in serving his country as a senator was about as romantic as the man got. Which might be true, yet Sarah couldn't shake the feeling that she was making Dale uncomfortable, for whatever reason, and she was already starting to regret this visit.

"Excuse the mess but please, sit down. Make yourself comfortable," Dale urged as he stepped behind his desk. "Can I get you anything to drink?"

So lost in her thoughts, Sarah hadn't noticed that Dale's office was cluttered with moving boxes. His bookshelf was bare, and his picture frames were gone from the wall.

"Are you . . . moving?" Sarah asked.

Dale took a deep breath. "I had meant to tell you and Mark before . . . everything. But, I'm retiring. The news is actually set to break this afternoon."

Sara furrowed her brow. She couldn't imagine Dale as anything but a senator, and she wasn't sure if he could, either. "Should I congratulate you?"

Dale chuckled. "Maybe? I don't know. I've been at this for so damn long, and I think it's time to go and do something else. I can be one of those old farts who fishes all day down in Florida."

"It just seems so abrupt," Sarah said, wishing she hadn't.

There was an awkward silence, which Dale finally broke: "So, how about that drink. Coffee? A shot of bourbon?"

"No, no," Sarah said, forcing a smile. "Especially not the latter."

Dale winced. "I am so sorry. Now *I'm* the one wondering if it's okay to congratulate *you*. Is that appropriate?"

Sarah sighed. "I can hardly make sense of my life right now; etiquette is the least of my problems."

"Understood," Dale said. "In that case, congratulations. Despite this . . . whatever this is, it's still a good thing. And you're going to be a wonderful mother."

Sarah nodded, fighting back tears, unable to think of a single thing to say.

Thankfully, Dale took the initiative, simply and bluntly.

"We should talk about it," Dale said. "That's why you're here, and I'm glad you're here. I've been waiting for you to come, in fact. I wanted to reach out, but I also wanted to give you the space you needed."

"I just can't wrap my head around how this could happen," Sarah said. Much to her growing frustration, that was Sarah's starting and ending point whenever she tried to make sense of Mark's abduction: absolute confusion. It was beyond her understanding to make any sense of how Mark could be mistaken as a spy, how he got snatched from their home like a murderer on the run, and how he could be shipped off to another country without so much as a hearing.

Dale took a deep breath and shook his head, expressing more anger than confusion.

"With what this country has become, not a single thing surprises me. Not anymore," he said. "You've got citizens, actual U.S. citizens, being thrown out of the country or denied entry. People separated from their families, people afraid to leave. And then Mark, arrested and shipped out without anyone even having time to say 'due process.'"

"Well, why *didn't* he get a lawyer and a trial, a chance to prove his innocence? This whole thing, every bit of it . . . I feel like I'm losing my mind."

"I've tried to find out anything I could, but no one's talking about his case. A lot of people in this town are tight-lipped already about everything concerning Russia—you bring up Russian espionage, and they run the other direction. Whatever Mark was involved in, it had to have rattled the cages of some people way up the food chain. That's the only way he could get pushed through the system and shoved into the Russians' hands that quickly."

Sarah narrowed her glance at Dale. His tone was clinical, like he was reading the autopsy of someone he didn't even know. Her visceral core told her to scream her disgust in his face, but she kept a level head and allowed Dale a small benefit of doubt. Sarah knew, especially from her experience as a nurse, that everyone coped with trauma and loss in their own way; maybe detachment was Dale's mechanism.

Even so, Sarah had to establish a few fundamental truths that, prior to walking into Dale's office, she assumed they shared. Particularly, that Mark was innocent.

"What do you mean 'whatever Mark was involved in'?" Sarah carefully asked. "You know he's not guilty, right? Everything about him and his ties to Russia, it's all lies. Every word of it."

Dale sighed in a patronizing way, and he gazed at Sarah with sadness in his eyes. He seemed to be lamenting Sarah's naïveté more than Mark's deportation. It made her want to take Dale's phone receiver from its cradle and smack him in the face with it.

"Listen. I know that, of everyone closest to Mark, this pill is toughest for you to swallow. What I'm going to say to you, I say only because I hope, in the long run, that it helps.

"You have to understand that the United States doesn't make a habit of arresting its own citizens for treason and kicking them out of the country. There has to be *something* there for this to happen. Now, that isn't to say Mark is the Russian James Bond, the way the press is making him out to be. I'm not saying that. It guts me to confess this out loud, Sarah, I swear it does—but given what's happened with Mark, it's unfathomable that intelligence agents got this completely wrong. That Mark is totally innocent."

The air rushed out of Sarah's lungs. She gripped the arm of her chair and leaned forward, twisting her right ear toward Dale as if her problem was a physical one. Because her ears, they couldn't have heard what she thought they did. Dale believing in Mark's guilt—that was *impossible*.

"I'm sorry," Sarah said. "What are you saying?"

"Just think about it. This town, the business we're in, it's a house of cards and the walls are fortified with duplicity. Who knows? Maybe in the course of one of his deals, Mark got mixed up with the wrong people and . . . I don't know. Maybe he got involved in something that spiraled out of his control. Maybe he was a puppet for some bad people, and he didn't even realize it. There's no telling what happened, there just isn't."

"Which is exactly why he deserves a trial," Sarah said, clawing at the chair's arm. "A trial that will prove Mark's innocence to the entire world."

"And I'm trying to get him that trial. I'm doing everything I can to help Mark. But I'm not going to tell you everything's going to be okay, Sarah. I don't know if that's true, and I've been in this business too long to know that there's never this much smoke without at least a spark of fire. I've learned the hard way that trust doesn't come easy, and it isn't absolute." Dale paused and narrowed his glance at Sarah. "But you already know that, don't you? Because if you did trust me, the first thing you'd want to talk about would be Mark escaping."

Sarah tried to keep a poker face, but she couldn't help flinching. Dale was right; the more he talked, the harder it was to trust him. In minutes, he had become like any other politician, exposing a flippancy toward his relationship with Mark the second it became inconvenient. She could already see Dale on the news, downplaying what he meant to Mark and what Mark meant to him, selling him out with platitudes and rehearsed statements. And this game Dale was playing—like her, he was withholding the news of Mark's escape—made her uneasy. She got the impression that Dale's intention wasn't to exonerate Mark at all costs. He had a cost, and it was the tarnishing of his political career.

"Don't be so surprised," Dale said. "I've been using every resource I have to keep close eyes and ears on Mark. I know all about his escape, and I know you two have been in contact. If you know where he is, where he's heading . . . Sarah, you *need* to tell me."

Inhaling a deep breath, Sarah steeled herself. This wasn't right. None of this was right, and she was too smart to allow herself to be used as a pawn in whatever game was being played all around her.

"And if I tell you—you'll bring him home?" Sarah asked, but she already knew the answer.

"I can't do that. It's not in my power. But at least if he's in custody, he'll be relatively safe while I work on a way to get him out of there. On the streets of Moscow, though? He's on his own, and there's no telling who will get their hands on him and what they'll do."

"But why? Why do the Russians even want him? They obviously know he's not their spy, which makes it hard for me to believe that they're invested in his well-being."

Dale leaned back in his seat. "That's an interesting question. Why *would* the Russians want Mark? If he wasn't one of theirs, in some capacity, they would have never taken him in. They wouldn't be going along with this charade. But they did take him. And they're playing along—which makes you wonder if it really is a charade after all."

"You can believe that if you want, if it helps you feel better, but I know the truth," Sarah said as she stood up and moved toward the door. Gutted hollow, she felt like an apparition floating through the room. She hadn't hoped for comfort from Dale, but commiseration would have been helpful. What she got was something different, and not only was it unexpected, it was also unnerving. Mark was out there running for his life, and the one person who could help was more inclined to devote his energy to convincing himself of Mark's guilt rather than working tirelessly to prove his innocence.

"Where is he, Sarah?" Dale said. "Tell me, and I can help. You're doing him no favors by keeping things from me."

"Mark's innocent. Find out how this happened, find out how we can get him back home, and then we'll talk. But no one's getting close to Mark, at least not through me, without proving that they're going to make this thing right."

"You might be waiting a long time," Dale said, but just as

Sarah was about to open the door to his office, Dale raised a hand for her to stop. He put his pointer finger to his mouth, urging her to remain quiet, then started scribbling something on his notepad.

"Cooperating with me," Dale continued, "is the only way to get Mark to safety. We both want the same thing, Sarah—to ensure, first and foremost, that nothing bad happens to Mark."

Dale silently tore the sheet from its pad and walked, taking cautious, quiet steps, to Sarah.

"We can agree on that, right?" Dale asked.

Sarah raised an eyebrow and suspiciously considered the slip of paper Dale was handing her.

"Right?" he said again, motioning for her to respond.

"Right," Sarah agreed, taking the sheet from Dale's hand. As instructed by his written message, she read a line of text, verbatim. "But I don't know where he is. I'd tell you if I did."

Dale took a deep breath as Sarah continued to read:

Apologies for everything I've said. There're ears everywhere. Talk to Mark's assistant, get her to dig into his deals. There has to be something. Find it, then bring it to me. No one else.

"We're on the same team," Dale said as he opened the door to his office, ushering Sarah out. "One way or another, we'll get to the bottom of this. Together."

Sarah took one last look at Dale, who gave her a conspiratorial nod. Then the door closed, and Sarah was left with nothing but questions. Who would be spying on a U.S. senator? What did Dale know that he couldn't say? Why was it necessary for him to act like he was doubtful of Mark's innocence? *Was* it an act?

As thoughts rattled through her mind, a terrifying realization kept popping up in her head, from the elevator back to the subway:

Whatever she and Mark were caught up in, it was way bigger than she had ever imagined.

18

Snow fluttered softly from the sky. Thick, chunky flakes had all but covered the dingy Russian landscape in a coat of pure white. Mark watched it tumble through the illumination cast by a nearby streetlight, feeling a tinge of guilt for enjoying the comfort of a warm hotel while the man who paid for it might still be unconscious in the parking lot of a desolate convenience store, his body being covered in a blanket of snow.

Just two hours ago, Mark and Ania were staking out said convenience store, looking for the right person to mug. Ania had convinced him it was necessary, seeing that they had no money, no car, and no place to stay—and in the event she'd been identified as his accomplice, she couldn't risk using any of her credit cards and leading the FSB to their location.

The convenience store was the one business open on a street crowded with buildings that were either closed for the night or closed for good. Much of the exteriors were covered in graffiti, an eclectic blend of colors brightening the monochromatic aesthetic of the neighborhood, which resembled more of a futuristic prison than a community. Hovering above the stout row of spray-painted buildings were residential towers made of drab, thick concrete that looked capable of enduring a war. Mark had no idea what part of Russia he was in, but he knew it wasn't good. That's why he figured it would be wise to be selective about who they robbed at gunpoint. People around here probably weren't pushovers.

Unsurprisingly, even though it was an island among desolation, the store attracted very few customers in the dead of a cold, snowy night. A few people arrived on foot, which was of no use to Mark and Ania. They needed wheels, first and foremost, and Mark knew that poking his mug out in public was a bad idea. Trains, buses, taxis—none of it would do. Avoiding recognition, either as a beloved national treasure or a man on the run, was priority number one. But if Mark was going to get the hell out of Russia—with Ania's help, supposedly—he needed a few essentials.

Crouched behind a van that'd been stripped of its tires, shivering in the cold night, Mark waited for a proper victim to arrive. A few cars came and left, but none of them were right. Even if they worked together, Ania and Mark knew it was unwise to try and jack a car full of people and risk failing. And unlike Ania, Mark couldn't live with himself if he stole an old man's ride, and he certainly didn't want to try to take a car off the guy in jeans and a tank top, tattooed from his neck down, built like a brick wall, and probably immune to intimidation. They had no choice but to wait, even as the night got colder and colder. He was exhausted, famished, his body bruised, beaten, and sore all over. Mark knew that if they didn't get what they needed soon, he might pass out.

Finally, the perfect mark arrived. A rusty sedan rattled into the parking lot, pulling into a spot parallel to the entrance—placing it outside the store clerk's field of vision. A middle-aged man got out of the car, and as he headed into the store, Mark hurried into position. He waited along the store's brick wall, and when the man came out, Mark, riddled with guilt, acted. Even though it was a mugging, Mark wanted to handle it delicately.

Politely, even. But he couldn't risk things going wrong; he couldn't wait for another opportunity to get what he needed to survive.

The man, focused on the pack of cigarettes he was trying to open, didn't even notice Mark step out of the shadows.

"Hey," Mark said, his voice hoarse. "Hey, you."

The man turned to face Mark, a look of agitation on his face. Mark was supposed to move behind him and smack him on the back of the head with his gun. That's what he and Ania had agreed to when Mark insisted that he do the mugging. He still didn't trust Ania, and he didn't want her killing anyone because, as far as Mark knew, that's just how she operated. Still, this plan never involved Mark talking, especially since no one would understand him.

"Give me your keys," Mark ordered, but the man continued to just stand there, confused and not comprehending. "I said give me your keys," Mark repeated, this time pushing his gun in the man's face. This drew a response, but not what Mark had hoped for. The man was getting pissed, not scared. Which meant this was not at all going as Mark expected.

The man stepped toward Mark, and Mark stepped back. Suddenly, his mind went to Oleg, seeing him dead on the floor of the hospital, and he began to envision the possibility of having to kill this man, too. The thought nearly made him wretch.

"Just give me your damn keys," Mark said, but the man wouldn't listen. He kept walking toward Mark, and Mark kept taking steps back until he was nearly pressed against the convenience store.

The possibility of having to shoot this man became more and more real with every step, causing his hand—and the gun it held—to tremble.

"I—I don't want to hurt you, I—"

Mark's stuttered pleas were cut off by the sound of a muffled impact, like someone punching a bag of sand. The man dropped to the ground and landed with a thud, and when Mark looked up he saw Ania, gun in hand, standing where the man had been.

"What the hell was *that*?" she scolded.

"Nothing, I just . . . I didn't want to hurt the guy."

"You didn't want to hurt him? Well, boo-fucking-hoo, Mark. Listen, you're fighting for your life, and putting my life on the line, so if we agree on how something's going to be done, you do it to the letter. You got it?"

Mark just stared at her.

"Earth to Mark. Do you understand me?"

Finally, Mark managed to nod his acquiescence. Ania inhaled a sharp breath—she was doubtless frustrated by how this situation had spiraled out of hand. Downward spiraling, though, was Mark's normal.

"All right," Ania groaned. "Pick his pockets clean and let's get out of here."

Mark did as he was told, relieving the man of his car keys, his cell phone, the money in his wallet, and his license. Ivan Popov. Mark would have to repay him, provided he lived long enough to do so.

Mark dragged the man to the sidewalk, not wanting him to get run over by a car while unconscious, and whispered an apology into his ear. He joined Ania in their new car and drove off into the quiet night. Thirty minutes later they were warm inside a hotel room, and Mark had his first respite in what felt like years. As he thought about the man's body being covered by a layer of snow, Mark tried to refocus his mind on what was important: He needed ideas, he needed a *plan*.

Exhaustion, though, took hold of him. Body and mind, Mark was spent. Beyond spent. And try as he might, he couldn't push himself any further. Couldn't conjure the magical solution that would alleviate the many, many obstacles in front of him. Mark shut the drapes to his room's window, bolted the door, and collapsed on the rock-hard chair. He looked at Ania, who was asleep on the bed, and he slipped into slumber before he could count to three.

Mark awoke late in the morning, throat raw, head pounding, and body aching from head to toe. He was dehydrated, starving, and bruised in places he didn't even know could bruise. But all those problems were silenced when he realized Ania was gone.

She'd sold him out. This was an elaborate ruse and the FSB was going to bust down his door any second, and Ania would lead the charge, a hero once more.

Those were Mark's immediate and only thoughts as he paced the room, cursing Ania for betraying him and himself even more for trusting her. Mark was so blinded by his frenzy that he failed to see the note Ania had left for him. But there it was, a small handwritten message on the foot of the bed. Mark read it, and his panic quickly gave way to embarrassment. Ania had gone to get food and supplies, and she hadn't wanted to wake him. She'd be back soon.

Mark sat on the edge of the bed. His body was trembling, his heart racing. If he couldn't control the situation he was in, he at least needed to get control of himself. He knew it was a long shot for him to survive this ordeal, and the odds of him making it out of Russia and getting back home—an exonerated man— were even slimmer. But Mark never liked being told the odds. And the fact was, he had no alternative other than to get out or die trying. If he couldn't make it home to Sarah and their baby, he might as well be dead. So until either one of the two happened— his return or his termination—he'd face whatever came his way with a level head. It was the only way through.

But just like his lobbying work, success could only come one step at a time. First, he needed to get as much of his strength back as possible. He had to replenish.

Sticking his mouth under the bathroom's faucet and lapping up metallic-tasting water like a dog helped diminish his thirst. With water dripping from his chin, Mark stripped off his clothes—Oleg's clothes—and started the shower. Even with the temperature valve buried on the hot side, the water struggled to reach lukewarm. But Mark didn't care. What mattered was rinsing everything—the blood, sweat, and dirt—off his body and feeling as revived as possible.

As he let the water run over him—every inch of his body sensitive to the touch—Mark considered his options. It was a brief train of thought because he really didn't have any options. At least not yet. Without identification, he couldn't clear Russia's borders in his car—assuming the junker he had acquired could make it that far—couldn't buy a train ticket, and he certainly couldn't get on a plane. He hoped Ania had enough pull to secure him a counterfeit ID so he could at least try to make it out of the country. That had to be the starting point: Get out of Russia.

Mark turned off the shower and wrapped a towel around his waist. He dug into his pants pocket and retrieved the phone he'd taken off Ivan Popov at the convenience store. Like Oleg's phone, it was another bulky model outdated by about a thousand years. He dialed Sarah's number, wanting to get in another call before Ania returned, but all he got was a dial tone and a message spoken in Russian. Mark guessed that international calling wasn't available on this prehistoric relic.

Though he was yet to shake off his sluggishness—Mark needed more rest and a whole lot of food—he still had enough energy to jump to attention and ready himself to fight when he heard the front door click open. Mark's instinct wasn't to run, it wasn't to hide; Mark was ready to brawl with whoever dared come after him.

But he couldn't even imagine the shades of red his face turned when Ania walked through the door and caught him dressed in nothing but a snug-fitting towel, poised to take on an army of attackers.

"Well, good morning to you, too," Ania said as she closed the door behind her.

"Sorry, I just thought—"

"That someone was going to come in here and try to kill you? I'd say that's a reasonable expectation. Here," Ania said, tossing him a grocery bag. "I got you some new clothes. As much as I like to see you parading around in a towel clearly cut for children, I figure it's better for you to be comfortable."

"Thanks," Mark said, suddenly feeling very aware of his mostly naked body. He backed into the bathroom and got dressed. Ania had chosen his size perfectly and supplied him with new briefs, jeans, and a thick sweater. The little bit of normalcy—having clothes that fit him—went a long way to putting him at ease.

Still, Mark had questions. While he was grateful for Ania's help, he harbored some real skepticism as to why she had jumped back into his life. Why take the risk? What did she have to gain? Her aid was a gift horse Mark was hesitant to look in the mouth, but he had to know: What could possibly motivate her to risk her neck to help him through what was very likely a suicide mission?

When Mark stepped back into their diminutive room—it was just large enough to hold a queen-sized bed, an armchair, a small table with two folding chairs, and a heating/air conditioner unit that ran beneath the window looking out onto the parking lot—Ania was laying out breakfast: a bag of bagels, lox, and a couple of apples.

"The money we took last night didn't go far, but we can always get more," she said. "Assuming you don't talk your way out of a perfectly good mugging."

Mark gave a halfhearted laugh, and Ania stopped what she was doing. She glanced over at him with a put-on look of worry on her face. "Uh-oh," she said. "Someone's about to get serious."

"No, no," Mark said, trying his best not to sound serious. "I just . . . I've been wondering—"

"You want to know why I'd risk my ass to save you. Right?"

Mark rubbed the back of his neck. "Well . . . yes."

"Because you don't trust me?" Ania asked, the sting of Mark's perceived slight creeping into her tone.

"What? No—I mean, yeah, at first I didn't trust you. But I trust you now."

"Okay," Ania shrugged, "then what's there to talk about? I'm saving your life. Let's just leave it at that."

Maybe Mark didn't know Ania, but he did know Alice. And while their relationship had been a ruse, there had to be *some* truth in it. Like when Alice told Mark about the brother she'd lost at a young age, how that had motivated her to get into medicine. Sure, the medicine part of that claim was a total lie, but the hurt of having lost a sibling, Mark knew was real. Just like he knew that there was something to whatever was driving Ania to help Mark, and it was genuine. Regardless of what it was, Mark didn't like the idea of Ania shouldering it on her own.

"You can talk to me, you know," Mark said, taking a step toward Ania as she turned away. "Before all of this, we . . . we were friends."

"No. You're wrong. I'm not allowed to have friends, or family, or . . . anything!" Ania's voice rose to a yell, and with an effortless swipe of her arm she flung a folding chair clean across the room. "They took me from my home—my mom and dad—when I was just a girl. The government took me from the only life I knew so I could train to become . . . whatever it is that I am."

For a moment, Ania looked so small to Mark. She *was* small, standing only five and a half feet tall, but she carried herself

198 • Michael Moreci

much larger. And in her diminished size, Mark saw Sarah in her. He saw his delicate wife, and it made him want to reach out and hold her and have the piece of him that was missing filled just a little bit. He knew, though, how wrong that was—wrong to touch Ania, wrong to assuage his heartache with anything less than the real thing.

"I'm—I'm sorry," Mark softly said.

"You really want to know about me?" Ania asked as she took an aggressive step toward him. "Do you?"

"I do."

Ania scoffed at him. "That brother I told you about? He wasn't my brother, he was my friend. The only one I had at the academy, and he died in what they called a 'training accident.' More like he was pushed too hard and decided to get out the only way he could. He was just a kid, we both were, and nobody cared that he was dead. Nobody but me. And that's when I learned that I was disposable, that I wasn't a human being in their eyes. I was just a tool that the agency could replace at any time. I wanted to leave, I wanted to disappear and never look back. But my parents—they'd kill my parents if I ever tried to run away, and I knew they weren't bluffing.

"So I stayed. I stayed for my mom and dad, so they could be safe. I trained and eventually convinced myself that what I was doing was noble and good, that I'd be making a difference. It was the only thing that got me through.

"And after all that, you know what my first assignment was?"

Mark shook his head, and Ania lifted her stony gaze to meet his. "You," she said. "And what was the point?" Ania questioned. "Everything I sacrificed, everything I endured, it was all in the service of ruining the life of an innocent, good man. Ruining his wife, ruining the life of his child before it's even born. The only thing that had kept me going was the threadbare belief that I'd be able to make a difference, that I'd be able to help people. But no, instead I was instructed to deceive you. And for what? So some oligarch filth could get even richer."

Mark brought his fingers to his temples. Suddenly, the room was spinning. "Wait wait wait," he said. "What oligarch? What are you talking about?"

"That's what this is, Mark—at least, in part. Sergei Vishny is one of the wealthiest men in Russia, and he is a silent principal in Verge. The foundation of my mission was to ensure that the Verge deal went through and that Vishny got paid."

Mark had to sit down and catch his breath. "I didn't . . . I had no idea. I thought Verge was a typical Silicon Valley startup that hit it big. Not one that's financed by the damn Russians—no offense."

"Hardly anybody knows. Some people say that Vishny has a hand in half the world's tech companies, but no one is certain. He's completely reclusive. No one has laid eyes on him in over five years. It's like he doesn't even exist."

"Hold on," Mark said as he sprang to his feet and started to pace. "This can't just be about some oligarch's money, because I would have pursued this deal whether I was being framed as a Russian spy or not."

"You catch on quick," Ania said as a sly smile spread across her face. "They sold us the line about national duty, which was basically a nice way of telling us to shut our mouths and not ask questions."

"Something else is going on here," Mark said, turning his attention to the window. The pieces of this mystery floated in his mind—the Verge deal, his own role as a diversion to protect the identity of Russia's real mole, and now the oligarch—but he was nowhere close to understanding how they fit together.

"You're right about that, something *is* going on. Something's wrong with all of this. And if you're wondering what my stake in all this is, it's finding out why I was used. I want to know what is worth giving up my family, I want to know what is worth my friend's life.

"I want to know the truth."

Mark listened, but his attention was diverted from Ania's determined words to the parking lot. He had noticed something weird: cars. Not that it was unusual for a hotel to have occupants, but last night, the lot was empty. Even Mark's stolen car, per Ania's order, was parked on a side street. That way, if it was reported stolen and found, whoever found it wouldn't necessarily think to search the hotel for the thieves. But now there were three cars in the parking lot. All newer-looking, which was suspicious considering that the hotel was a dump. Mark tried to convince himself that he was being paranoid. But then a man stepped out of one of the cars—a man dressed in a black-and-white suit, exactly like Oleg.

It was the FSB. Those bastards had tracked him down. Panic and anger wrapped barbed wire around Mark's chest.

"They're here," Mark said, his stunned voice sounding like it was coming from a thousand miles away.

"What?!" Ania said as she raced to the window. "That's impossible—how? How could they find us?"

Mark knew, but he didn't want to say a word about calling Sarah while Ania was out. He realized, too late, that her line must have been subject to tracking, and the call—though it technically didn't even go through—was enough to lead the FSB to his and Ania's location. With no small amount of burning shame, Mark confessed.

"You're lucky I don't have time to kick your ass," she snarled. Ania stomped to the bed and took her spare bullet clip out from underneath her pillow. "They're going to bust in here any second. We have to be ready."

"Wait . . . we're not running?"

"We'll never make it. Never. The only chance we have is to catch them off guard."

Mark raised an eyebrow. "They're here for us. I think the element of surprise is long gone."

"No," Ania corrected. "They're here for *you*. There's a chance they don't know you and I are together. There's no telling if anyone identified me at the embassy last night, and even if they did, information doesn't travel quickly, or efficiently, in the agency."

"So what am I supposed to do?" Mark asked, failing to catch on to Ania's plan.

"Nothing. Stay here, and let them break that front door off its hinges. When they storm you, I'll storm them."

"I'm bait."

"Uh-huh," Ania said, stepping into the bathroom. "Now be ready to act surprised when they bust in here. And then be ready to help me kick the shit out of everyone in our path."

Mark thought he should prepare himself somehow. As he stood alone in a Russian hotel room, he thought there might be a way to steel himself for the barrage of enemies he was about to face. Not only was his hope wildly impractical, but also he had no time. Moments after Ania disappeared into the bathroom, Mark heard the cheap wooden door frame burst into splinters as the door itself was battered off its hinges. Four agents rushed into the room led by automatic rifles; Mark leapt off the bed and shot his hands in the air, offering no resistance. The closest guard grabbed Mark hard by his neck, turned him around, and shoved him against the wall. A violent frisking followed, but the agent only got through Mark's legs when he was interrupted by the sound of one of his fellow agents screaming behind him.

Mark turned to find one agent unconscious and on the floor and another caught in Ania's grasp; she had him by his shoulders and was driving her knee into his torso, over and over. The agent tried to kick his leg out at Ania, but she was too fast. She blocked his leg with a kick of her own, driving the sole of her foot into his knee. Mark heard something crack, followed by the agent's scream.

Ania used the close quarters to her advantage. The agent nearest Ania tried to aim his gun for a clean shot at her, but she swung the agent in her grasp against his rifle, causing his shots to go wild. She then bashed her forehead against the nose of the agent she was holding, and Mark heard another crack. The agent went down on his knees, and Ania finished him with a round-house kick to the face.

The agent who had pinned Mark took a step toward Ania, but Mark kicked him square in his back and sent him tumbling against the far wall. By the time he turned, Mark was on him; he delivered a series of short punches into his abdomen, and when the agent tried to drive his fist down on Mark's head, Mark spun out of his way and used the agent's forward momentum to trip him onto the ground. Mark heard his head thump against the floor, and as he tried to get up, woozily, Mark delivered a kick to the agent's face, knocking him out cold. He looked up to see Ania holding the last remaining agent by his shirt, his body limp in her grasp. She delivered two fierce punches to his face, then dropped him to the floor.

Ania grabbed two of the rifles, tossing one to Mark.

"Now we have machine guns," he said as he tightened his grasp on the weapon. "You know, *Die Hard*?"

"I know," Ania said. "I just don't care. We're not out of the woods yet."

Mark studied the rifle, which was lighter than he'd expected something of such killing magnitude to weigh. He was unde-cided if that made him more or less comfortable.

"We don't want a gunfight," Ania continued. "Not only are we outnumbered, but these guys are armored. They'll pin us down and, if I had to guess, execute us on the spot. I think we should—"

Her words were cut short by a tinny sound that carried into

their room as something was thrown through the erupted door frame. For just the briefest moment, Mark saw a thin gray canister bounce across the floor, and in that moment, he was certain he was dead.

The canister erupted in a flash of white light—so bright, so intense that Mark felt like he could taste it—that knocked Mark off his feet and burned out the pupils in his eyes. Accompanying the burst of light was a sharp explosive bang that not only felt like it had burst Mark's eardrums, but it was so strong that it was like a punch buried into his guts. He was left blinded and deafened, writhing on the ground, nauseous, afraid he'd never see or hear the world around him again.

Mark still had his sense of touch, though, and he certainly felt the pair of hands tear him off the ground and slam him onto the bed. Sound was starting to return, and he heard voices above the ringing in ears: men yelling in Russian, and a woman—Ania, he believed—yelling in return. Mark's arms were twisted behind his back, and his wrists were squeezed together at his waist. Mark considered resisting, but just as he started to fight he felt a knee press hard against his spine. He screamed in pain, his voice sounding far away, and then he felt hard, cold metal slam over his left wrist. Handcuffs. Mark struggled, trying to pull his right arm free from the overpowering grasp that held him in place. Then he remembered: his pistol. The agent had been lazy, maybe arrogant, and didn't think to frisk Mark. The gun was tucked into the back of his pants; he felt it there, pressing against his lower back. Mark didn't need to pull his arm out, he just needed to push it down. And that's what he did.

His movement caught the agent off guard, and Mark was given the freedom he needed to reach his gun. He grasped it, wrapped his finger around the trigger, and fired. One shot, then another, then another. At the third shot, he felt the pressure on his body release, and he felt his attacker slump to the ground.

Mark rolled off the bed and held the gun out in front of him, hoping it would at least make anyone hesitate to come near him. His vision was returning, but all he saw around him were blurry oblong shapes cast against a haze of white. Instinct told him to shoot the shapes, but he couldn't risk one of them being Ania.

Four figures remained, three tall and one short—but just as Mark assessed the situation, the shortest figure sprang up and knocked one of the others to the ground. Mark heard another body, followed by the sound of a voice calling out to him. It sounded like Ania, but he couldn't make out what she was saying. The shape he assumed was her melded with one of the others—attacking an agent, Mark figured—as the last remaining shape raced closer to Mark. The voice called out louder and louder. Mark strained to make out the words, was desperate to know what he was supposed to do.

Just as the shape crowded his entire vision, the voice came through. Not crystal clear, but clear enough.

"Shoot!" Ania was screaming. "SHOOT!"

Mark did exactly as he was told, firing four bullets that riddled the shape in front of him, blasting what Mark now understood to be an FSB agent right off his feet.

As he gasped for air—the intensity of these life-or-death situations never got easier—Mark felt a hand grasp at the handcuff dangling from his wrist. He jumped at the touch before realizing it was Ania, unlocking him. She pulled him toward the door, yelling for him to run.

Mark followed, his vision and hearing returning incrementally as they darted out of the room, down the hall, and down the stairs. When they reached the bottom of the stairs, Ania shoved Mark to the ground, pushing him down by his head, and fired off at least six bullets from her pistol.

"Okay, let's move!" she yelled, pulling Mark back up to his feet.

"How . . . ," Mark fumbled, "how are you not blinded?"

"Training," Ania snapped, dragging Mark along. "Now come on."

Mark's senses were nearly restored by the time they got back to the car. Ania threw it into drive and peeled away from the curb, leaving the hotel and the FSB behind.

"What now?" Mark asked as Ania sped onto the expressway.

"Now?" Ania replied, sucking in a deep breath. "There's no choice what we do now. We go on the offensive."

19

Sarah had never seen the Lincoln Memorial so quiet. Most days, the place was teeming with tourists, school buses loaded with children on field trips, and agitated locals trying to get to work through the daily throng of visitors. But at 10:00 P.M.—on a night where a brisk winter wind whipped off the reflecting pool and took ten degrees off the already below-average temperature—the memorial was a ghost town. Jenna had to know that, Sarah assumed, and that must have been why she chose this place, at this time, for their meeting.

But she was late. Thirty-two minutes late, and Sarah was ready to leave. She dug her hands deeper into her pockets and buried more of her face into her coat, trying to escape the cold like a turtle crawling into its shell. Sarah had no idea what she was even hoping to achieve. Whatever this cloak-and-dagger game was, it was well out of her league. Bugged senator offices, clandestine messages, late-night meetings—she was a nurse, not a counterintelligence agent. Still, she'd have to fake it, or at least maneuver her way through well enough to get proof of Mark's innocence. That's all that mattered. And if getting it meant pursuing this unusual path, she'd take it to its very end and beyond.

Sarah checked her phone again. It was almost quarter to eleven; Jenna wasn't going to show. When Sarah spoke to her on the phone, Jenna didn't give the impression that she was enthusiastic about helping. Or even talking about Mark at all. Which Sarah understood. The revelation of Mark's treason—his wrongful accusation—left a blast radius that affected a lot of lives, and Sarah was certain things hadn't been easy for Jenna since. She knew, though, that Jenna and Mark were close; they were similar in a lot of ways, and of all the assistants Mark went through—and they changed faster than socks, sometimes—he respected none more than Jenna, and he had made that point very clear to her. Sarah hoped Jenna hadn't lost sight of the person she once knew, and if she had even a sliver of doubt over what happened to Mark, she'd do what she could to help. But as more and more minutes ticked off the clock, she realized it wasn't going to happen. She was back to square one.

As she walked the length of the reflecting pool, her head covered by her down coat's oversized hood, Sarah couldn't help feeling like she was being followed. Through the padding of her down hood, she heard footsteps following at a fast pace behind her. Sarah sped up, and the footsteps hastened as well. Under normal circumstances, Sarah would be terrified. Here she was, being pursued by . . . who? A government agent? A Russian assassin? Someone else entirely? Regardless of who it was, Sarah was tired of the games. She was tired of feeling like danger lurked everywhere she went. If someone wanted to come after her, she wasn't going to run.

Sarah was ready to fight.

With her right hand balled into a fist, she pivoted in midstep and turned; she cocked her arm all the way back, ready to put her free one-week trial of Krav Maga to use.

"What the hell?!" Jenna yelped, nearly jumping out of her skin.

"Jesus, Jenna!" Sarah said, clutching her chest. She felt like her insides had leapt into her throat, and now her heart was working double-time to shove them all back down. "You scared the shit out of me!"

"I scared *you*? I've been calling your name. Maybe if your head wasn't being smothered by your hood, you could hear a little better."

"Well, I heard you following me, so I caught that. Where have you been? We were supposed to meet an hour ago."

"Yeah, sorry about that," Jenna said. "I had to make sure no one else was following you."

"Following me? You mean you've been here, watching me, the entire time?"

"I've been on you since you left that guy's house you're staying at. The good news is that you're clean—no one, as far as I can tell, is tailing you."

"I've been freezing my ass off out here!" Sarah yelled.

"I said I was sorry," Jenna replied, and Sarah could hear Mark in her curtness. He didn't like mincing words when he had something important to say, either.

Sarah focused. Jenna must have found something worthwhile, otherwise she wouldn't be taking such precautionary measures. What mattered to Sarah was what Jenna had found, and how deep she was willing to go down the rabbit hole. Sarah didn't have an easy sell on her hands, but if she could get Jenna to come this far, maybe she could get her to go a little further. Depending on what Jenna had discovered, the pursuit of Mark's innocence might ruffle a lot of feathers along the way.

"You found something, right?" Sarah asked, not even trying to hide the eagerness in her voice.

Jenna let out a long breath, a dramatic gesture. "I called in some big favors. I dug in places I shouldn't have been digging. But, yeah—I think I found something."

Sarah eyed the manila file folder that Jenna pulled from her shoulder bag; she'd hoped for a chunky dossier detailing all the bastards behind Mark's framing. Instead, just a plain manila folder.

"That's it?"

"What were you expecting?" Jenna asked sardonically. "You think I'm going to pull out a wall map exposing a giant conspiracy?"

"No," Sarah responded. *Though that would have been nice*, she thought.

"Just check this out," Jenna said, opening the folder. The first sheet revealed what looked like a holdings report, as far as Sarah could tell. "Look, Mark's most recent deal—the Pentagon cyber security? He was working on behalf of Verge. That's something we all know. But Verge is a huge multinational company. It's massive. So what do you do when you want to get to the bottom of something?"

Sarah and Jenna's eyes met, and they shared a smile. "Follow the money," Sarah said.

"Exactly."

Jenna flipped to the next sheet, which revealed a blurry photo of a plump middle-aged man in a V-neck shirt. His beard extended so far down his neck and his chest hair so far up that they joined as one. It looked like he was wearing a shag rug Snuggie.

"Which brings us to this guy here," Jenna continued. "Sergei Vishny, one of the wealthiest men in Russia. An oligarch, through and through. He thickens the plot," Jenna said, flipping over to another holdings report.

It didn't take Sarah long to recognize the point of interest. There, highlighted in bright yellow marker, was Sergei Vishny's name. The Russian oligarch was one of Verge's money players.

"Son of a *bitch*," Sarah spat.

"Now, let's not make any leaps, not yet. Guys like Vishny, they have their hands in *everything*. He might not even know he has an investment in Verge. Not in detail, at least."

"But a Russian invested in an American security firm? Especially with how things are between Russia and the U.S.?"

Jenna waved Sarah off. "You know how these guys are: Why

worry about international security when there's money to be made? Thinking that, I played devil's advocate. Let's just assume his investment is benign. It's just another thing he's making money off of, he doesn't care what it is, and Verge is taking money where they can get it. Business as usual for everyone. This is where the line of inquiry gets interesting."

"Interesting good or interesting bad?" Sarah asked, anxious.

Jenna pursed her lips and nodded her head from side to side. "A little bit of both. It's bad because nothing I found supplies us with a clear-cut exoneration for Mark. There's nothing for us to go public with. But it's good because it gives us a whole lot of questions that need to be answered. And those questions will bring us closer, I *think,* to whatever the hell is going on here."

"Okay," Sarah said, drawing a deep breath. "What are we looking at?"

"First of all, this Vishny prick. If this information becomes public, it's a smoking gun for Mark's guilt. It looks like Mark is colluding with a Russian oligarch. Although, get this: Allegedly, no one has laid eyes on Vishny in, like, years. He's agoraphobic or something. Which is weird, right? A twenty-eight-year-old billionaire who sits at home all day? That's fishy, to say the least. Like, who is this guy?"

Sarah shrugged, expressing her disinterest. "One mystery at a time."

"Okay, okay, here's the thing: As Mark's assistant, I have that man up my ass—figuratively—twenty-four/seven. I find it hard to believe—no, I find it *impossible* for him to carry on a clandestine relationship with this Vishny guy—who supposedly doesn't talk to *anyone*—without me knowing it. Before all this happened, I could tell you where Mark was at any time of any day. Always. So if I didn't know, and you didn't know, Mark would need a clone running around to make this work. Unfortunately, our word means zilch.

THE THROWAWAY · 211

"Also, Verge isn't Mark's only account Vishny was invested in. He's in on several, but it's totally weird. Because he had his hands in stuff that didn't make sense for him to be in. Remember that nutrition company Mark worked for, trying to get their healthy food into Virginia schools? Vishny was an investor there. And not only that, by cross-referencing dates, I found out he didn't become an investor until *after* Mark was hired. A detail most people would miss."

"Damn," Sarah said. "You're good."

"No shit. Anyway, I take this to mean only one thing: Someone has been setting Mark up for a long time, and Vishny was a means to create a trail linking them together. If there had ever been a proper investigation into Mark, for whatever reason, this would have popped up. An easy link between Mark and Vishny, but it makes *zero* sense."

Sarah shook her head, trying to absorb all this information and, more importantly, figure out what to do with it. "Okay, okay . . . someone's been working to tighten the case against Mark. After everything that's happened, that's not surprising. The question is, what do we do, knowing that?"

"For starters, we find out how the information was leaked. If there's one thing more valuable than money, it's information. And it's not like Mark's clients were public knowledge. Whoever framed Mark has to be someone close enough to know what he was up to and then share that information."

"Yeah, but who?" Sarah asked. "It's not me, not you. Who else is there?"

"No clue. A friend? A rival? Someone at the firm? Someone we don't even know? I mean, we could guess suspects all night long. But let's put that aside for now. Because there's one other thing: the software."

"The Verge software? Isn't that just another company Vishny threw money at to help frame Mark?"

Jenna started to talk, then she stopped. She scanned the area across the pool, where a trio of teenagers had gathered. "Let's walk."

Sarah nodded and followed, even though she thought Jenna was being a little overcautious.

They walked the length of the reflecting pool, toward the Washington Monument. Ground-level bulbs illuminated it in a shimmering gold that, in turn, cascaded off the water's surface. Sarah remained quiet as they walked, waiting for Jenna to resume their talk whenever she felt comfortable.

They reached the edge of the pool where just a few people lingered, all out of earshot.

"I'm not sure if you know this," Jenna said, "but Mark didn't want to take the Verge contract. It was a little out of his league, and he knew it. But Verge? They would *not* take no for an answer. They persisted. They pestered. They offered a shit ton of money and kept raising it until Mark agreed to work for them. The question is: Why? Mark's good, but he's by no means the only persistent lobbyist in town. And getting to your question, was Verge just another company Vishny was invested in? No. No it was not."

Sarah cocked an eyebrow at Jenna. "What do you mean?"

"I mean," Jenna said, drawing near Sarah and lowering her voice, "that of all the companies that linked Mark to Vishny, Verge is the only one he was invested in *prior* to Mark's involvement. If we're going to go ahead and call this thing a conspiracy, then, to me, this is its centerpiece."

A strange feeling shivered through Sarah, starting in her throat and going all the way to her toes. It was fear, she recognized. Whatever was going on, it had depth. It had scope that extended well beyond Mark. His safe return would always be Sarah's priority, but now it seemed like the Russians were at work infiltrating the United States defense system, and Mark was just a cog in a much larger plot.

"Jesus," Sarah whispered. "What the hell is going on?"

Jenna shook her head, and Sarah could tell she was at a loss. "I have no clue. Not yet. But in the short time I've had, I've asked around a little about the contract, and *no one* wants to talk about it. People in Hodges's office, Dudek's aides—they hear anything about the software or Mark and they stick their fingers in their ears and run the other direction. Something is happening here."

Information, theories, and suspicions swirled in Sarah's mind, all vying for attention. Sarah had no doubt Jenna was right: Something was doubtless happening. But it was like looking at an overcast day through frosted glass. The world was familiar but blurred enough to be deceptive, to remain unclear. Still, she couldn't shake the feeling that if she shifted her perspective, she'd gain the focus necessary to see things clearly. Jenna had given her plenty to think about, but what stuck in her mind most was the chilling truth that whoever set Mark up was close to him and, that being the case, close to her as well. She considered that, considered Vishny and what he seemed to be after—

And then it hit her.

"God. *Damn*. It," she spat, her anger roaring so intensely within her that she felt light-headed.

Jenna recoiled at the ferocity of Sarah's words. "Uh—what?"

"Listen, I need you to do me a favor," Sarah said as she backed away from Jenna. "Keep digging—find out anything you can about Vishny and whatever ties he has. Pull the bastard out of whatever hole he's hiding in if you have to."

"And what are you going to do?" Jenna shot back, mystified.

"I'm going to have a little chat with a *friend* of mine," Sarah said. "And when I say 'chat,' I mean I'm going to kick his ass."

20

Dr. Maximilian Steele.

The persona was born of a lark, but a well-intentioned one. On their third anniversary, Mark and Sarah assumed fake identities and met at a hotel bar, pretending to not know each other. It was meant to be a sexy tryst, but it ended up being more of a gag as neither Mark nor Sarah could keep a straight face as they tried to connect using their fake, and ridiculous, identities. Mark never imagined Dr. Steele would return to their lives, yet he was grateful the good doctor was in. He just never imagined he'd be needed under such circumstances.

Mark worked at the only English-language keyboard at the internet café, keeping his head down to avoid being identified. The café's individual computer banks were open, but the bulky monitor—a decade old, at least—did an adequate job giving Mark something to hide behind. But, seeing that the café was occupied only by an elderly couple and a group of loud, obnoxious teens, Mark was confident he could fade into the background and not be bothered.

While Mark knew Sarah's phone was being monitored, he had no idea how thoroughly her online activity was being watched. Neither did Ania, and while it took a lot of convincing, she eventually gave Mark permission to reach out. Despite Ania's hardened exterior, Mark knew she understood the lengths he was compelled to go to in order to protect Sarah. She had done the same to protect her parents, and that softened her to Mark's relentless need to do whatever he could to ensure his wife's safety.

Contacting Sarah via email was a waste of time. Mark's message would surely be intercepted, traced, and discarded. Same went with social media, he assumed. But whoever was watching Sarah's Facebook, they were waiting for Mark to reach out.

Not Maximilian Steele.

Using pictures found from a Google image search—of beach parties, to give Maximilian the appearance of a man who enjoyed a life of leisure and make him seem less like a spambot—Mark constructed a profile for Maximilian that looked as convincing as possible. He liked a bunch of fan pages, wrote a "Hello, I'm new to Facebook!" post, and even tried to friend a few people from the high school that Maximilian had not actually attended. But Sarah had. Sure enough, a handful of the grads from the class of '02 accepted his request, and Maximilian was well on his way to being unsuspicious.

With Maximilian's life established, Mark reached out to Sarah, sending her a friend request and a note via Messenger. The note was the key; Mark could only hope that Sarah not only read it, but also remembered who Maximilian was and deciphered Mark's real message. He wrote:

"Sarah! I finally broke down and joined the Facebook. I've been abroad for so long, and I'm still here, stationed overseas. Not by choice. My work has a way of putting me in unusual situations. Anyway, how are you? Please let me know how you're doing. Are you okay? I'm good, safe and sound for the time being. I'd love to reconnect with you, so feel free to contact me here whenever you can. We can share all our latest news, which is what Facebook is for, right?"

Mark leaned back in his chair and ran his fingers through his hair. He exhaled sharply as his eyes stayed glued to the monitor, praying that a message popped up sooner rather than later. Staying more than a few minutes would be a mistake. If whoever was monitoring Sarah's account flagged his message and identified its point of origin, it would be a dead giveaway. Mark would be swarmed by FSB goons in a matter of minutes, and he wasn't sure he had another escape in him.

Anxiety gnawed at Mark. As long he kept running and fighting, he didn't have to think. About Sarah. About the baby. About what was going to happen to them now that Mark was on the loose. Would someone use Sarah to get to him? Would they hurt her—or worse?

But then salvation arrived.

The little blue-headed dialog box popped up, and there was Sarah. Mark almost collapsed to the ground, and he hadn't even read a word. Sarah was safe. She was okay. That, first and foremost, was all he needed. Mark gathered himself and read the screen.

"Maximilian! What a strange surprise. It's so good to hear from you. I'm doing well, safe and sound, like you. But these are very unusual times with everything happening in the world. You never know what could happen. But in this moment, I'm perfectly ok. Life has been unusual lately. I'm helping a friend with a research project, pretty much as a hobby. We've been able to discover some really interesting things, things that I think will interest you. It could really change things for the better. Did I mention I was pregnant? Here, let me show you a picture—my first ultrasound!"

Mark's bottom jaw slowly separated from the top, and Mark raised his hand to cover his mouth. His heart jumped in his chest, and he could already feel the tears running out of the corners of his eyes. There, that tiny image, that was his child. His *child*. And it needed Mark. It needed its father, and Mark needed it, too. Though he tried, Mark couldn't stop himself from sobbing. Tears of love and fear and rage poured from him. This baby, it was out there in the world, however many miles away, and Mark already loved it. And at the same time, he hated whoever was keeping him apart from his life, his real life. He pounded his palm against the monitor, not thinking about the attention it drew.

Regardless of the attention—and both the teens and the elderly couple were staring at the blubbering, angry man at this point—Mark knew he couldn't stay in this location much longer. Not when FSB agents could very well be on their way. He wrote back, doing his best to withhold his emotions:

"You have no idea how touched I am to see this photo. You must be thrilled, and I know things will only get better. I have to run, but if you ever need to be in touch, this is the best way to get ahold of me. I'd like to hear more about your research project, when we have time. Like I said, I'm abroad still, but I plan on being back home soon. I'm working on it. Until then, please be safe."

Removing himself from the computer was like severing a limb. He wanted to write how much he loved her, how he was doing everything in his power to get home. But if he wanted to see her again, Mark had to be smart. He had to be cautious, more than cautious. He had to make every decision like his life depended on it.

Mark logged off and wiped out the browsing history, leaving a clean computer behind.

Just as Mark was walking out, Ania was walking in. She'd gone down the street to grab them some food and, according to her, "do some research."

"Hey," Mark said, accepting the sandwich Ania handed him, "you find anything?"

Ania nodded. "We have to work our way up the ladder to get to the bottom of all this: why you were framed, what the connection to Vishny is, who's pulling all the strings—and why."

"I get the feeling you know the rungs to climb."

"I do," Ania admitted. She reached around Mark and grabbed the remote control off the clerk's counter. The clerk started to complain, but Ania said something in Russian that shut him up. "Check this out," she said, and surfed through the TV channels until she found the one she was looking for.

Broadcast on the screen was a red carpet event, sort of like the Oscars. Nothing of what he was looking at—men and women dressed up in designer clothing, parading for paparazzi—stood out as meaningful to Mark. It was just wealthy jerks being worshiped, same as they were in the United States.

"What am I looking for here?" Mark asked.

"An old acquaintance," Ania said. "This gala, celebrating the anniversary of the government-funded station you're watching—I was supposed to attend. Another public appearance for the national hero."

"Sorry you had to miss it," Mark sardonically replied.

"It's better that I did," Ania said with a sly smile. "Because in my absence, they have to send my backup."

"Look," Ania said, directing Mark's attention to the screen.

There, Mark saw a hefty, bald-headed man scowling for the cameras.

Viktor.

"I'll be damned," Mark said.

"Want to climb up the ladder?" Ania asked. "Here's a crucial rung. Viktor's relentless and ruthless, and I have little doubt he's used both qualities to wedge himself deeper into the FSB since we've gotten back. People like him, believe it or not. They trust him—which means they tell him things."

"Yeah, I got the sense that being stationed in the U.S. as a glorified babysitter wasn't his dream assignment."

"He wouldn't stop complaining about the mission, and I'm willing to bet someone like him was let in on the truth. If only to shut him up, but most likely to bring him into whatever inner circle is at work here."

Mark nodded. In theory, it was simple enough: get to Viktor, and somehow persuade him to spill what he knew.

"I'm guessing you have a plan to get information from him?" Mark asked.

"The only way you get information out of anyone: We're going to have to beat it out of him."

21

All O'Neal had were dots. The product of his clandestine investigation, laid out on his kitchen table, was nothing but dots that didn't connect. And he tried. In different ways and from different angles, O'Neal tried to do what his mentor—Gil Pak, long retired to Florida—had taught him to do: Create a narrative. Evidence was important, as was the psychology of your criminal. But putting it all together in a story? That was the key. Stories gave evidence and psychology life; stories strung everything together and answered the vital questions of how and why. In truth, evidence could be misleading and a diagnosis of another human's mind wasn't foolproof. Pak insisted that O'Neal take a step back during any investigation and see for himself how the case made sense as a narrative.

In the case of Mark Strain, it was impossible to manufacture a story, no matter how hard he tried, that made a lick of sense.

O'Neal paced around the evidence he'd collected, no longer conjuring ways to piece everything together in order to prove Mark's guilt. Instead, despite all the suggestions that he move on from this particular case, O'Neal was doing something entirely unexpected.

He was trying to prove Mark's innocence.

"God damn it, Strain," O'Neal grumbled under his breath as he sipped on his third cup of coffee. It was almost two in the morning, but he couldn't sleep. The dots called to him, pecking away at his analytical brain and eroding any chance for him to rest.

For the umpteenth time, O'Neal went over his discoveries, tirelessly trying to piece everything together into a whole that made sense. Of course, that meant shrugging off his disbelief at this entire situation. He had never been fully comfortable with the way Mark was scooped up and shipped out of the country without anyone so much as whispering the words "habeas corpus." And now? Now he was baffled. And suspicious. And angry. Assuming Mark was innocent, someone had not only framed him to take the fall, but also had used O'Neal to make it happen. The seasoned agent didn't like that one bit. But O'Neal knew his feelings weren't the real thing at stake here; it was a potentially innocent man's life, and whoever manufactured the conditions that made Mark look guilty enough to be stuffed into an airplane and exiled to Russia had to wield considerable power. Which meant O'Neal had to tread carefully.

He again considered what he knew, studying all those dots through an assumption that Mark was innocent. First, there was Sergei Vishny, the mysterious oligarch. In and of itself, that was a damning connection. But how were they connected, really? O'Neal had discovered the business ties between them, but also learned that Vishny had invested in Mark's accounts after the fact. Four times Vishny got financially involved with Mark's clients after Mark took them on. Most investigators these days, eager to close cases, would look at that connection and see a smoking gun. They'd go no further. But O'Neal needed his narrative. If Mark and Vishny were co-conspirators, or even if Mark was in a compromised position with Vishny and unwillingly doing his bidding, O'Neal needed their connection to be more profound than a paper trail.

But there was nothing that linked Mark to Vishny on a personal level. Those dots just floated out there, unable to connect. So O'Neal went broader. How did Mark connect to Russia, in general? Becoming an operative for a foreign country—and a traitor to your own—was no small matter. O'Neal had encountered individuals who'd been flipped, and in each case the person had undergone a form of indoctrination. Brainwashing. They were defamiliarized from the world they knew—stripped of their identity, more or less—and re-created into a new person. And these people were usually social exiles to begin with, people with no friends, no family, nothing to keep them grounded in reality. Mark had a wife, a baby on the way, a mom in Minnesota who he called regularly. Indoctrinating someone like that wasn't easy. And Mark had never even been to Russia. His phone and email records, a perfunctory search had shown, revealed no suspicious contacts. O'Neal was willing to take that with a grain of salt. If Mark was a spy, he would know to be more cautious than to use his personal accounts for his operative communications.

That meant Mark would need to make clandestine contact. Well, both his personal and work computers—now property of the U.S. government—showed no encrypted accounts, no shadow log-ins. O'Neal studied what the tech eggheads had given him, and while he didn't understand all of it, he was smart enough to get the gist.

There was nothing hidden in either computer.

O'Neal even followed up on Ania, Mark's coffee-shop buddy and alleged co-conspirator. He had the photos that showed them together at Starbucks. Plenty of photos. But not a single snapshot, not one report, showed Mark and Ania passing anything between them other than a newspaper—a newspaper that Mark had purchased at Starbucks and, again, there was no photographic evidence of him loading anything into the Health and Science section. A file, an external drive, anything. They never even leaned in for a sneaky chat. O'Neal had gone to the Starbucks and interrogated the workers who covered the early morning shifts. Their take? Just a couple of flirting regulars, something they saw all the time.

O'Neal groaned.

"Strain, you're either the most cautious spy of all time, or this is all bullshit."

And bullshit, O'Neal concluded, was what all of these dots reeked of. The question, then, was who was responsible for spreading this bullshit all over Mark's life.

The noose that tightened around Mark's neck, apparently without him even knowing it, cut off his air right as that cyber defense contract he'd been working on closed. That's when Mark's case—though O'Neal was loathe to use the word "case" to describe what had been constructed against Mark—came to a head. O'Neal flipped through the documents he had on the contract itself; something about firewalls, mainframes, and a bunch of other tech jargon he couldn't even pretend to comprehend. Data didn't build stories, though. People did. Assuming Vishny was a smoke screen, whoever was in on Mark's frame job must have been involved in this contract. It's what they had to have been after, and once secured, they tied up their loose ends. And that meant discarding Mark.

O'Neal studied the players. The people at Verge were worth a look; a multinational security firm was always worth putting under a microscope for one reason or another. But, again, the question came down to connecting Verge to Mark. Because if Vishny being peppered throughout Mark's career was any indication of a frame-up, then this plot had been going on for years. That's too long and uncertain of a game for Verge to play for one contract. Especially when contracts in D.C. came and went like farts in the wind, O'Neal mused.

That left him with unnerving options for who was responsible for setting Mark up. Because whoever had played Mark and the FBI like a fiddle, they were still out there.

The real traitor was still at large.

If O'Neal had been cautious with this private, unauthorized investigation of his before, he was being downright paranoid now. Because the people closest to this contract weren't men you trifled with, whether they were spies or not. General Hodges and Senator Dudek were two D.C. players who'd been kicking around the American political scene since there was an actual declared war—a cold one, but still—against the Russians. Through wars, shifting political control, cultural upheavals, scandals, and more, they had endured. That kind of temerity was not for the faint of heart, O'Neal thoroughly understood, and neither Hodges nor Dudek had survived this long without accruing a whole lot of power. Enough to squash the career of one FBI agent like a bug under their shoe, O'Neal was certain of that.

Either Hodges or Dudek could be reasonable paths to pursue—after all, if O'Neal had learned one thing about powerful people, it was that they constantly craved power. Even if the pursuit meant the deepest of betrayals. Power was a drug, and like any drug, addicts would do anything for their fix. But while Hodges and Dudek were the official committee appointees who decided on this cyber security contract, O'Neal discovered a third player, buried deep in the contract logs, one who worked as a consultant to the decision-making process. It struck O'Neal as strange, having someone involved without being officially involved.

It was almost like they didn't want anyone knowing about their influence.

O'Neal picked up his cell phone. Even at this hour, he had to tell someone, and he knew Lewis was a light sleeper. He'd be pissed, but he'd come around once he heard what O'Neal had to say.

But O'Neal was interrupted by the sound of something crashing just outside his house.

There was a momentary lapse as O'Neal's brain pulled away from the puzzle laid out in front of him and toward the unnerving intrusion that had undermined his domestic solitude. It was by no accident that O'Neal's home was located at the end of a rural Virginia road with nothing but sloping woods trailing off from the end of his property line. His ex-wife called him paranoid, and his colleagues had their share of inside jokes about O'Neal's need for seclusion. But with over twenty years' experience acting, at times, as the eyes and ears of the government, O'Neal learned to never discount the value of privacy. That's why he lived in the woods, why he scanned for bugs weekly, and why, when a sound shredded his quietude and 2:00 A.M., O'Neal immediately jumped to high alert. It could be raccoons rifling through his trash again—or it could be something else entirely.

Treading cautiously over his creaky hardwood floor, O'Neal made his way to the living room, which is not only where he thought the sound came from but also where his hunting rifle was stored. His standard issue pistol was upstairs, on his nightstand. Where he always kept it while he slept.

The living room was dark. Darker than usual. A dim exterior floodlight, set on a timer, ran from dusk until dawn; its glow cast dim illumination in the room, enough to give it shape. But now, the room was completely black. Someone had knocked out the light.

O'Neal crept closer to the window looking out to the light; beneath that same window was a chest, one that housed his loaded rifle. O'Neal knew exactly which steps to take, not only to avoid the room's furniture, but also to best avoid the creakiest floorboards. Still, every step he took was exaggerated by the silence around him. The floor sighed and moaned despite O'Neal's precise movement.

As O'Neal drew closer to the window, he felt a draft. A lazy, chilly breeze. The window came into focus in greater detail.

O'Neal was only a few steps away when he noticed that the window was open. From the inside.

He rushed forward, flinging open the wooden chest and plunging his hand inside. But the rifle was gone.

In that moment, where he caught himself gasping in fear, O'Neal realized how meticulously he'd been set up. Before he could turn to act on his realization, O'Neal was grabbed from behind. A forearm and elbow wrapped around his throat. It wasn't that impressive of a lock, but the hold wasn't important.

It was just a slight diversion for the knife that followed, driving into O'Neal's side.

O'Neal roared in pain and anguish. He tried to break free of the hold, but whoever was behind him pulled him in tight and then stabbed him again. And again. And again.

O'Neal dropped to his knees. He slapped his right hand over his many wounds, knowing how futile the gesture was. A crimson pool was already forming beneath him, and he could only watch it increase with each passing second. O'Neal tried to choke a cry for help out of his throat, but when he opened his mouth to speak, all that came out was blood. And as much as his body tried to convince him how nice it would be to sleep, O'Neal's mind kept it alert longer than he should have. In death as in life, O'Neal was driven by questions, and as he bled out in the living room of his own home, he couldn't help but wonder "Why." Why had this happened to him? To Mark?

O'Neal collapsed, his body corkscrewing as it dropped onto the hardwood floor. He looked up, and before his eyes closed for good, he saw a man. O'Neal had no doubt that his killer had been sent by the third man in the Hodges-Dudek committee.

Suddenly, all the dots circling around Mark Strain connected. O'Neal had sent a patsy to Russia, while the real spy was still out there, and he had help. He wanted to say something to his fellow agent, Banks, as he stood above him, a bloody knife in one hand and a ski mask in the other. But he couldn't get any words to come out.

O'Neal could only hope that someone else was able to make the connection he had made—and survive long enough to do something about it.

22

The golden sheen of the Hotel National's ballroom glimmered like the inside of a necklace's pendant. Mark made an apparition of himself, floating the room's periphery in a stolen server's jacket that fit snugly over his clothes. The jacket, luckily, zippered up to his neck with a collar that clasped over his Adam's apple, concealing at least part of the wear and tear he'd endured the past few days. He couldn't do much about the rest of his appearance—the bruise pasted to his cheek, the blood pooled in the corner of his left eye, the lacerations running along his hairline, or the swollen gashes protruding from his knuckles. His pugilistic mien was reason enough to keep hidden; the notoriety associated with his face, and the unwanted attention it would bring, was only further motivation to remain separated from the ritzy gala that occupied the entirety of the ballroom's massive space. Mark clung, instead, to the shadows, stalking his prey with sidelong glances, relishing his opportunity to pounce.

Viktor sulked around the room, engaging in conversation only when he was dragged into one. Mark watched—looking without looking—his every move. Viktor made a quick exit when roped into a chat with an inebriated group of what Mark guessed to be politicians. The disdain on Viktor's face shone like a neon light in the middle of a pitch-black forest. He sidestepped away, a sneer on his face, and checked his watch for the umpteenth time.

There must have been a threshold he had to hit before he was able to leave, and he was determined to watch every minute tick by.

Later, Viktor showed at least some sign of life when speaking with a decorated military man; he probably had something to gain by behaving like a human being, either that or he genuinely respected the man he was talking to—who, Mark would guess, was a lifelong serviceman. On one hand, Mark had a weird kind of respect for Viktor's complete disdain for putting on appearances. Mark had made a career of doing just that, and he'd never found it particularly enjoyable. There was something to be said about someone who refused to play the game, Mark supposed. But on the other hand—well, Mark wanted to use his other hand to strangle Viktor into submission. But Mark had to keep his emotions in check, suppressing the anger he felt at Viktor and everyone like him, people who didn't bat an eye at ruining innocent lives to serve their twisted purposes. Viktor, Mark reminded himself, was a means to an end. A link on a chain, and nothing more.

The question of where that chain led had been dominating Mark's thoughts. Mark liked to think he was skilled at looking at the world from a myriad of different angles. It's what gave him his power over people and situations; he understood, thoroughly, what made everything tick. If you knew what people wanted, you could confidently predict what they'd do. But what did the Russians want with Mark? He studied the question from every angle imaginable, but whenever Mark attempted to answer that nagging question he only came up with one answer:

Not a damn thing.

Mark didn't possess a shred of valuable information; he had no ties to powerful people, people who could be negotiated against for his exoneration; he clearly wasn't a Russian sympathizer. Mark was worthless, and he knew it. He'd known it ever since his first conversation with Gregori. What mattered now was discovering the real angle being played. Because in any negotiation—and that's all relationships were, negotiations, even between countries—you only attribute value to something that's worthless to create a distraction. To protect something *else*. Mark was a smoke screen, and he was determined to know what he was being used to cover.

As Mark narrowed his glare on Viktor, he felt his body temperature rising. He followed Viktor's path to the other side of the room, toward the ballroom doors, and had to remind himself of Viktor's value. But the more he thought about the position he was in, having been manipulated into a charade that existed to obfuscate some hidden truth, the more furious he became at being cast as an expendable pawn. A pawn whose life had been indiscriminately destroyed.

Mark carved a path through the room, keeping his eyes firmly locked on Viktor. An older man with an arrogant smirk on his face—probably some hideously wealthy oligarch—grabbed Mark by his elbow as he passed and said something he didn't understand. Even with the language barrier, the words sounded condescending and rude, and it was clear he was ordering something from the server he saw in front of him. Mark pulled the man's fingers off his body, twisting them hard, and shoved him out of his path. The surrounding crowd turned their attention to the scene and a murmur grew, but Mark didn't care. He felt capable of fighting his way through the entire room if that's what it took to reach his target.

Mark quickened his pace as Viktor cut through a thick crowd in front of the doors and disappeared beyond. Mark reached into his pocket, retrieving a cell phone Ania had purchased at what looked like the Russian equivalent of a currency exchange. She paid cash, buying a phone for herself as well, and had them both activated on the spot. No one asked for their names, and Ania didn't offer them. The phone, Ania instructed Mark, was to keep her updated on Viktor's movements. Mark had yet to use it—there had been nothing to report—but he shot her a quick text as he followed Viktor to the ballroom's double doors.

V is on move, Mark tapped into the phone. *Leaving ballroom.*

Mark hurried into the lobby and scanned the area, panicked that Viktor had possibly darted to the hotel's exit. More gala attendees were mulling around, and Mark couldn't spot his quarry. He dashed around the room, searching, his anxiety growing with each passing second that Viktor remained out of sight. If he had somehow made it out of the building, he'd be long gone, and Mark and Ania would have lost their one real chance to rip this conspiracy to pieces.

Then, out of the corner of his eye, Mark caught a flash of a lumbering figure. He turned and saw Viktor, bottlenecked by people as he headed toward the bathroom.

"Lobby bathroom," Mark texted, hoping Ania was already on her way. "Now."

Waiting for Ania and cornering Viktor together was the best approach. Mark knew that. But Mark wasn't feeling measured or pragmatic. Or levelheaded. He eased into the men's bathroom, pulling his gun out of the back of his pants.

The heavy bathroom door opened with a creak. Viktor didn't even look up, too busy relieving himself in one of the urinals that ran in a row along the left side of the room. No other urinal was occupied, and the stall doors were all wide open. Mark and Viktor were alone, which was exactly what he'd hoped for.

He walked toward Viktor, eyeing him out of his periphery as he tightened his grip on the gun. He was right behind Viktor when he heard him zipper up.

That's when he whipped his gun out from behind his back and cocked the hammer—the sound of it clicking into place made sharper by the room's emptiness.

"Don't. Fucking. Move," Mark said, breathlessly. Anger, fear, and anticipation pounded in his head; life was unsustainable with the stakes so high, with never knowing what was going to happen next. But Mark thought of those stakes, thought of Sarah and their baby, and it helped ward off how exhausted and overwhelmed he felt. *Home,* he reminded himself, as he trained a gun on the back of the head of a relative stranger. *I have to get back home.*

Even though Mark had ordered Viktor not to move, the Russian slowly twisted his head around so he could see over his shoulder. A patronizing smile spread across his face when he spotted Mark, then the smile turned into a snarl.

"The American nobody—Mark Strain."

"Turn around," Mark ordered. "I will shoot you, I swear to God I will."

Viktor did as he was told, but his condescending tone remained intact. "No, you will not. I heard that you had escaped, and now you must be here because you need something from me. Yes?"

"Good for you, you're capable of deductive reasoning. I do want something from you, that's right. And if you don't give it to me, then I *will* shoot you. I don't have a damn thing to lose."

Viktor grunted. "And who said I have something that can help you?"

Right on cue, the door squealed and Ania entered the bathroom. Both Mark and Viktor turned and watched her, and they both saw her snap the dead bolt shut once the door closed behind her.

"I told you to wait for me so we can do this together," Ania scolded.

"Aaaaahhh," Viktor said before Mark could explain himself to Ania. "The rogue spy. Now I see what's happening here."

"Viktor, you can speak when you're spoken to," Ania said as she pulled out her gun and held it down at her hip.

"She put you up to this," Viktor said to Mark, not asking, but stating.

"Why me?" Mark asked, ignoring Viktor. "Why was I framed? What's really being hidden?"

"She's using you, American," Viktor said, a hint of mirth in his tone. "Whatever she told you, it is a *lie*."

"I'm warning you," Ania spat, training her gun on Viktor.

"Or you'll shoot? And draw all that attention to yourselves? No, I don't think you will."

"Answer my question!" Mark yelled. "Who's behind all this? Why did they pick me?"

"American, do you want to know why Ania is really helping you? What she really wants?"

Ania took an aggressive step forward, pushing her gun toward Viktor, her tone subdued but furious. "Shut your mouth, Viktor. I'm warning you."

"You think she is helping you, but no, no," Viktor said, mocking both Mark and Ania. "She has a mission of her own. A *revenge* mission."

"Ania?" Mark asked. His eyes darted to her face, which was red and constricted, like she was enduring an excruciating pain.

"Ania always needed her role to have meaning, to have some kind of grand, noble purpose. But what was it we had to do? Frame some American so rich Russians could get richer? She hated every minute of it, even more than me. Isn't that right, Ania?"

Ania didn't say a word. Mark could see her out of the corner of his eye, seething. She looked ready to put a bullet right through Viktor's forehead.

"We did what we were instructed. Made you look like a Russian spy, and then we returned home. But that is where trouble began for Ania. She learned that her parents—the only reason she stayed with the service—died in a boating accident while she was away. And no one told her."

"God damn you, Viktor," Ania said, her voice cracking as she tried to maintain her fury while fighting off grief.

"And now, now she is angry," Viktor said. "Angry for being forced into this life. Angry that she was thousands of miles away while her parents were being lowered into the ground. I know this woman. She wants payback. Payback for whoever put her in the United States. Payback for whoever is benefitting from what we did to you.

"You're being used, Mark Strain."

Mark looked at Ania, whose eyes were on Viktor. He didn't even have to ask the question, he knew by the look on her face: Every word Viktor had said was true.

And in that moment of realization—that moment of distraction—Viktor made his move.

With lightning-quick speed, he whipped around and punched Mark's gun out of his hand, sending it skating across the bathroom floor. He grabbed him by his jacket and turned him around, putting Mark between himself and Ania, blocking any clear shot she had. Mark grabbed Viktor's arms and tried to break his hold, but his grasp was too strong. Before he knew it, Viktor was racing forward, using Mark's body as a shield against Ania.

She tried to spin out of the way, but Viktor anticipated her move. He twisted Mark's body and threw him forward, sending him spinning into Ania. They both tumbled to the ground, and Viktor was on them fast. He kicked Ania's gun out of her grasp just as she was whipping it in his direction. Mark recognized that he and Ania were both weaponless, and it felt like they were outnumbered, too.

Mark rolled off Ania's body just as Viktor stomped his foot down at her; she spun out of the way, and his foot smashed against the floor, splintering the tile. Ania, in a crouched position, kicked out Viktor's knee and leapt into an uppercut that sent the man tumbling backward. She tried to follow her strike with a kick to his midsection, but Viktor recovered too quickly, and he caught Ania's foot before it reached him. Using his tremendous strength, he whipped Ania around and sent her flying into the outer wall of the row of stalls. She landed on the ground, hard, and didn't move.

"I'm going to kill you," Viktor said, his voice as even as it would be if he were telling someone he was going to take them to lunch.

As Viktor kept his attention on Ania, stalking toward her like an animal about to pounce its hobbled prey, Mark charged at him. He drove Viktor back into a urinal, and Mark felt the man's spine pound into a metal pipe sticking out from the flushing valve.

Viktor screamed in pain, and Mark continued his assault by driving a series of punches into Viktor's stomach.

Viktor, though, was quick to recover. He grabbed Mark by his shoulders and drove his knee into Mark's midsection so hard that it felt like Mark was going to cough up his kidneys. Viktor lowered an elbow into the back of Mark's head, and he saw stars right before Viktor sent him sailing toward the other side of the room; there, he crashed into a mirror, shattering it to pieces. His right arm immediately gushed blood.

Mark felt his vision darkening as he came close to losing consciousness. Viktor must have counted him out, because as Mark's vision came back into focus he saw the man bending down, about to grab Mark's gun. Just as he was about to lace his fingers around the butt, Ania rushed forward and delivered a perfect kick right into Viktor's head, drilling it against the wall. The blow dented the wall, and Viktor looked ready to collapse when Ania grabbed his head and, unsatisfied by the damage she'd already done, smashed it again and again and again.

"WHY?" Ania screamed as she assaulted her former partner. "Why were we there? Who put us there?!"

With the fourth blow of Viktor's head against the wall, which was crumbling into powder, Ania relented. She let Viktor drop to the ground, and Mark was certain he was dead. Ania, though, wasn't done. She straddled Viktor, pinning him down at his shoulders.

"Tell me now, Viktor, and I'll let you live. What was that mission really all about? Tell me."

Viktor gargled, choking on his own blood. Ania didn't care.

"Talk," Ania demanded.

Viktor's voice came out distant and disoriented. It was almost like someone else was talking. Mark crawled his way forward, positioning himself to hear the words as clearly as possible.

"The oligarch . . . Vishny," Viktor hazily said. "He's dead."

"So. *What?*" Ania screeched.

"He's been dead . . . dead for years. Gregori. . . . it's all Gregori. Him and his man in the U.S., they have been using . . . using Vishny's identity for profit for years, and no one knows. And now . . . and now . . ."

Ania shook Viktor's head, keeping him conscious. "And now what?"

"Their biggest plan. They made . . . millions . . . and the software . . . the software . . ."

Viktor was fading, barely holding on.

"That's all this was—money?!" she screamed in Viktor's face. "That's what I gave my life for?!"

"Not yet you haven't," Viktor grumbled.

Mark, so focused on Viktor's confession, hadn't noticed. Ania, focused on her grief and rage, certainly hadn't, either. But at some point, Viktor had managed to grab Mark's gun. He found the strength to raise his arm just high enough to blast a bullet into Ania's side.

The sound of the gun firing ripped through the bathroom, echoing off the walls—and the inside of Mark's head—like they were in an underground cavern. Slowly, Ania's body slumped off

Viktor's, and the huge Russian spy, somehow, started pulling himself off the floor.

"NO!" Mark screamed as he saw Ania's unmoving body. He rushed toward Viktor, grabbing hold of his hand and pushing it toward the ceiling just as he fired off another bullet. Mark tried to overpower Viktor by driving him back against the wall, but even in his weakened state he was still a powerhouse. Viktor, yelling in pain and rage, lifted his leg and kicked Mark just below his sternum. The blow sent Mark tumbling backward, and just as he planted his feet, Viktor was there to plow his fist into Mark's face. The blow felt like it shattered Mark's cheek, and it spun him around and down.

"I told you I'd kill you both, you stupid American dog," Viktor said. Mark could feel the barrel of the gun right at the back of his head. His life was about to end by way of a bullet ripping through his skull, and it would have ended if he hadn't realized that his hand was bleeding. Mark looked down and saw that his left palm had been cut by a shard of glass from the mirror. And the shard was still in his grasp.

"Good-bye, Mark Strain," Viktor said, but before he could pull the trigger, Mark sprang to his feet and plunged the dagger of glass directly into Viktor's throat.

Blood erupted from the wound, and Viktor started to gag. He dropped the gun and, in a daze, covered his throat with both hands. But it was no use. Viktor was bleeding out, rapidly, and there was nothing he could do but fall to his knees and then the floor. His body convulsed once, twice, and then he was dead.

Mark rushed to Ania. He propped her up and brushed her hair from her eyes.

"No, no, no," Mark whispered as he desperately tried to think of some way to save Ania, who, despite everything, he thought of as his friend. "Please, Ania, *please*. Talk to me. Tell me how to make this okay."

Ania opened her eyes, but just barely. "I'm sorry, Mark," she gasped, barely audible. "I wanted . . . wanted to help you. I swear. I . . ."

"I know, I know," Mark assured her. He looked at her side and saw that her shirt was covered in blood; a puddle of crimson had pooled on the ground next to her. Mark knew she didn't have much time, but he had to try.

He pulled his phone from his pocket and thought to call 911, but he didn't know who to dial for an emergency in Russia.

"Ania, who do I call? How do I get help?"

"Go," Ania murmured. "It's too late . . . for me."

Hot tears ran down Mark's face, and they ran down hers as well. "I can't leave you, Ania. I *can't*."

"They're coming . . . be here . . . soon," she said, and groaned in pain. "Go. Get Gregori for me. For us *both*."

Mark nodded and wiped away his tears. "I promise, Ania. I *promise*."

She closed her eyes, and Mark was certain she would never reopen them.

He twisted the dead bolt and threw open the door. People were gathered around the bathroom, and when they caught sight of Mark, their expressions shifted from curiosity to terror. Mark paid them no mind, running straight through them all, rushing for the lobby's exit.

23

Of all the skills the assassin had learned over the years, the most valuable had to be her ability to effectively infiltrate the minds of her targets. It was one thing to follow the bread crumbs every target left leading to their whereabouts, it was another thing altogether to understand *why* they were going there.

The assassin considered this as she sat in her car, across the street from the Hotel National. Tracking Mark here was easy enough. It was just a matter of knowing what Mark wanted, and that was obvious: a reunion with his wife, Sarah. A noble pursuit, but wanting things made you vulnerable. Always. They made you predictable, they made you sloppy. And Mark was no exception.

The assassin was certain that no official agency would be monitoring Sarah's social media accounts. They didn't have the acuteness of mind to think outside the box and consider Facebook and Twitter viable means of communication. But the assassin knew better. When Mark sent Sarah a thinly coded message using an obviously fake name, the assassin was there, watching their conversation in real time. Tracking the origin point of Mark's communication came within a minute's time, and the assassin was at the internet café thirty minutes later. She knew Mark would be long gone, but that wasn't important. She was closing the gap between herself and Mark; and the sooner she could discover where Mark was going next, the sooner she could become his shadow. And that's when her real work would begin.

A security camera at the internet café was just one of those lucky breaks, and the assassin was grateful for the help now and then. Positioned in the rear corner of the café, it overlooked the entire cramped space—which meant it undoubtedly captured Mark's brief visit. The café's clerk tried to get tough with the assassin, refusing her permission to see the closed-circuit footage, but a couple of broken fingers changed his mind. The assassin didn't know what she was looking for, but she had conditioned herself to be thorough in all things; chance wasn't a game she liked to play in this business.

She was pleasantly surprised that her tenacity paid off. On the black-and-white footage, the assassin watched as Mark met his accomplice—Ania, the Russian spy gone rogue—at the front door. They discussed something, and then Ania directed his attention to the television.

The assassin zoomed in on the screen, the image it projected getting grainier with each magnification. Before it turned into a pixilated smear, she deciphered it, and she knew exactly why it had caught Mark's eye: It was Ania's comrade, Viktor, being photographed at an event at the Hotel National. And it was live.

The assassin had no doubt where Mark had rushed to next.

Sirens were already blaring by the time the assassin arrived. She parked at a safe distance from the hotel and switched on her police scanner. When she heard that a man and a woman had been murdered in the men's restroom, the assassin speculated on the possibilities. At first, she figured Viktor had killed both Mark and Ania when they had tried to get the jump on him, wanting what, the assassin couldn't say. But Mark had survived. He was, to say the least, one of her more unusual targets. But what had he wanted from Viktor? That detail—and others like

THE THROWAWAY · 241

it—gnawed at her. She didn't like messy jobs. And she didn't like being misled by her employers, either.

None of this assignment sat well with her. She could understand the Americans wanting Mark dead. If the official line was true—and the more the assassin pursued and watched Mark, the more she doubted the validity of that allegation—Mark was a spy who could possess dangerous or damning information. It made sense to ship him out and silence him, permanently, far from domestic shores. But if that was accurate, if Mark was a Russian spy, why would the Russians also want him dead? The assassin had no tolerance for being manipulated and lied to; it was bad for business, bad for her reputation, and dangerous for everyone involved. Particularly herself. While she never demanded full disclosure from her clients, she also didn't appreciate being thrust into volatile situations. And this situation, which now likely included at least two dead Russian spies, was getting more and more volatile by the minute.

As the flashing blue lights of the emergency vehicles surrounding the Hotel National cast a dizzying display over the entire scene, the assassin tried to understand Mark's purpose. He couldn't have come here just to murder Viktor. It was hasty and sloppy, and he'd gain nothing but quenching some primal thirst for revenge. No, that couldn't be it. As evidenced by Mark's desperate pleas outside the American embassy, he was a man on the run. A man searching for something that was simpler than revenge.

Mark wanted the truth—and so did the assassin.

The assassin reached into her pocket, pulling out her vibrating phone. The caller's number was blocked, as expected, but the assassin knew who it was.

"Yes?" the assassin asked as she put the phone to her ear.

"Why is the job not complete?"

"I'm pursuing the target now," she replied. "This case requires . . . more delicacy than expected."

"We don't take well to excuses, I'll remind you."

"And I don't take well to being lied to," the assassin snapped back.

There was a moment of silence. She didn't need to say anything else; she wasn't the one who was trying to deliver a message of urgency, and if her client didn't like the way she did business, that was just too bad.

"You listen to *me*, woman," a voice said—a new voice, one with a Texas twang. "We hired you for a purpose, and your job isn't to question the delicacies of said purpose. Your job is to produce results or get flayed alive. Understood?"

The assassin took a deep breath. She could have reminded this man what, exactly, her profession was, and how easily she could train her crosshairs on whoever was on the other end of this conversation. But she had no interest in trading threats. Instead, she allowed herself a few more deep, calming breaths, said she'd be in touch, and then she ended the call.

Somebody on the American side, she concluded, had fucked up. And they were desperate to clean up the mess. A mess the Russians had no use for.

Mark was caught in the middle of this international spat, one the assassin couldn't determine the size or shape of. And she didn't need to. Only Mark was relevant. Mark and what he wanted: answers. A way to exonerate himself.

The area just outside the hotel was crammed with police, emergency responders, and hotel staff. Everyone was trying to look useful, which reduced them to idle mulling, occasionally directing onlookers away from the scene. The assassin wasn't focused on them, nor was she even looking for Mark. She already knew where he was; she had spotted him parked across the street from the hotel within ten minutes of her arrival. Mark was watching—he was waiting. The assassin did the same, trying to survey the world through his eyes. Whatever he'd wanted from Viktor he must not have gotten it. If he had, odds are that Viktor wouldn't be dead, and Mark certainly wouldn't be lingering around the scene of the crime. So, Mark had to go higher up the ladder to get what he wanted.

Gregori Dayenko.

After an hour of waiting, the cagey FSB agent—a Cold War relic whom the assassin knew only by reputation—spun out of the Hotel National's revolving door, a cigarette dangling from his lips. The hotel was undoubtedly a no-smoking venue, but Gregori wasn't the type of man who obeyed frivolous rules. He was practically a legend of Russian espionage, and that went a long way in this country.

He shuffled away, not responding to a single person who spoke to him. He seemed to be in a daze, as far as the assassin could tell. Losing his own spies—although it had to have happened to him numerous times over the years—wasn't likely something the old man took lightly.

He shuffled away from the scene, past the sirens, past the onlookers and the blockade, and into the passenger side of an enormous black SUV parked just a few cars ahead of the assassin's. He had a driver, who most likely doubled as security. And there was probably at least one more guard in the back. After a few long moments, Gregori's car started and U-turned away from the hotel. As expected, Mark followed right on his tail.

And the assassin, careful to keep some distance between them, pursued them both.

24

Sarah wished she had a gun.

Under normal circumstances, she would never feel threatened by Aaron. But these weren't normal circumstances. Everything Jenna had shared, it was like watching a canvas get painted right before Sarah's eyes. Brushstroke by brushstroke, the image began to take shape, moving from abstraction to something discernible. Something Sarah didn't have to work to interpret. And it told her something loud and clear: Whoever set Mark up had to be someone close to him, and the plot against her husband was executed in exact accordance with the software contract he'd been brokering with the Pentagon.

Suddenly, Aaron seemed like less of a friend and more a threat. His motivations to bring her into his home less to protect her and more to keep a watchful eye on her. After all, who else knew what to do with this security software? And who was close enough to Mark to feed Vishny information that would position him to look like a Russian spy?

Sarah was on to Aaron, and as she charged the front steps leading to his house, she knew he had no idea that she'd put these pieces together. Or that she was going to confront him.

She jammed the key into the front door's dead bolt, feeling the indignation of what it meant—a means not to let her in, but to keep her locked up. As she swung the front door open, she spotted Aaron immediately, pacing the living room with his iPad in his hands.

"Sarah," he said. "Where've you been?"

Sarah didn't bother answering. She didn't say a single word. Instead, she rushed Aaron and threw a right hook across his face. The blow, which he wasn't braced for in the least, knocked the iPad out of his hands and sent him falling backward.

"What the fu—" Aaron yelled, cupping his right jaw. Before he could finish, Sarah was on him, delivering her knee into his midsection and forcing the air out of his lungs. Even as Aaron heaved, Sarah didn't relent. She grabbed hold of his sweatshirt with both hands and shoved him forward, sending him head over heels over the back of the couch. He crashed to the ground, smacking his head on the coffee table.

Sarah catapulted over the couch, reaching into her pocket to remove her pepper spray as she did. Aaron, struggling to get to his feet and catch his breath, wasn't close to matching Sarah's speed or her determination. Driving her knees into his shoulders, she pinned him to the ground and aimed the pepper spray directly at his face.

"Talk," she demanded.

"I . . . I . . . ," Aaron gasped. "I . . . can't . . ."

Sarah moved the canister closer to his eyes. "Find a way."

Aaron swallowed three deep breaths, enough for him to get a few words out. "What the hell . . . why are you beating me up?"

"I know what you *did*, Aaron. I know you helped frame Mark to look like a Russian spy, and I know you have some sort of involvement with that dirty software he helped sell to the Pentagon."

In the blink of an eye, Aaron's face leapt from confusion to utter bafflement. He blinked hard and rattled his head from side to side; it took his mouth a few efforts—stops and starts, tripping over unintelligible garble—to even get a response out. "WHAT?!" Aaron yelled, after all the effort.

If this was an act, Sarah thought, it was a damn convincing one.

"You're the only one who's close enough to keep tabs on Mark and feed it to the Russians, and you have clear ties to whatever this software is and getting it implemented."

"Sarah, I have no idea who you've been talking to, or what you're talking about right now, but I had nothing to do with what happened to Mark. *Nothing.*"

"Bull*shit,*" Sarah spat.

"Wait, just . . . wait. The software—what about it? What does that have to do with me?"

"Whoever set Mark up, they were using him to get the software contract closed. I don't know why, but the software is vital to this whole thing, and you fed Mark crucial information that helped close his deal. You're on the Pentagon IT team—you're telling me you had nothing to do with that?"

Aaron remained frozen beneath Sarah, even though he could have shoved her hundred-pound frame off his body with relative ease. The frenzy of her physical assault had assuaged, and she noticed the beads of sweat forming along Aaron's hairline and running off the side of his face. His eyes were frozen on her, unblinking, and Sarah could see that he was scared. Not nervous, not anxious to talk his way out of being busted, but scared. She wasn't ready to withdraw the physical threat she held over him, but Sarah's certainty of Aaron's guilt began to flag. Guilty people were afraid of being caught; Aaron was clearly afraid of being hit again.

"Sarah . . . I just implement the software and keep it running. I have no say, *none,* in what we use or the scope in which we use it. I mean, occasionally they'll ask my opinion, but it's not like anyone actually listens to me. I'm just an IT nerd."

Sarah dug her knees into Aaron's shoulder, and he grimaced in pain. She believed him, but she didn't want to—Aaron was the key, she had been certain, to free Mark. But now it was seeming less and less likely that was the case.

"What about Vishny?" Sarah pressed, just to cover all her bases. "You have no relationship with him at all?"

Aaron's face twisted in full-on bafflement. "Sergei Vishny?" he asked, confused. "That's . . . weird."

"Don't test my patience, Aaron," Sarah warned, driving her weight into Aaron once more. "Weird how?"

"Okay, okay," Aaron yelped. "Sergei Vishny . . . he's rich. Crazy rich. You know that, I'm sure. What you probably don't know is Vishny got his start in the underground tech world. He was, like, the best Russian hacker, and he earned his fortune by developing spyware software and apps that blew everything else out of the water."

"So what?"

"Well, after Vishny left the underground a different Vishny emerged. Or was created. That's what a bunch of people say. There was a moment where the Vishny everyone knew—this weird, reclusive, innovative anarchist—disappeared. Like, poof. He was just *gone*. And then this new Vishny emerged. And people have speculated that the real Vishny is gone, bumped off by his own government.

"These days, Russian hackers use the name Vishny for their work. If someone stole everyone's personal information from, like, a video game server, 'Vishny' would take the credit. Or when the Ukraine government was hacked, 'Vishny' claimed responsibility. Basically, Vishny is the calling card for Russian hacking. It might be one person, it might be a group of people, it might even be the Russian government. No one knows. It's like Anonymous, but not as obvious."

"So the real Vishny, he hasn't made a comeback?"

"Not that anyone knows."

"Aaron, if you're lying—"

"I *swear*, Sarah," Aaron pleaded. "I swear."

With a small amount of reluctance—Sarah harbored suspicions against everyone, and Aaron was no exception—she pulled the pepper spray away from Aaron's face and stood up, releasing him from her hold. "Sorry about beating you up," she murmured.

Aaron dusted himself off and dabbed his finger over his cheek, checking the gash Sarah's ring had made against his skin. "I wouldn't say you beat me up—it was more a sucker punch, and a couple lucky knee shots to my stomach."

"I also knocked you over the couch," Sarah added.

"All right," Aaron said, waving Sarah away as she stepped close to help examine his cut. "Let's drop it while I still have a shred of dignity left."

He fell onto the couch and exhaled sharply. "So, you mentioned that Pentagon software—I haven't told you, but we've been having *nothing* but problems ever since launching that new program. That's why I've been working so late every night."

"The software is bad, Aaron," Sarah said, sitting on the coffee table across from him and catching his gaze. "Someone has been setting Mark up for a long time, using Vishny . . . whatever . . . to make it look like he had ties to Russia. From what I can tell, Mark wasn't only being framed as a traitor, he was being manipulated into getting this software contract closed. Somebody—probably the Russians, if I had to guess—were hell-bent on Mark making that deal."

Aaron's face went flush. "If that's the case . . . shit. Then what does that software actually do? I mean, if someone is planting some kind of virus or spyware into the heart of the Pentagon, that could be, like, apocalyptic."

"That's why we have to get to the bottom of this and stop whoever's behind it."

Aaron snickered. "Sure, an IT drone and a nurse are going to unravel an international conspiracy. And how would you suggest we do that?"

There was a long moment of silence as Sarah processed Aaron's point. They were standing on the shores of deep, dark water, and neither of them were equipped to navigate their way to the other side. Or get there before someone shoved their faces beneath the waves and held them under until they stopped moving. Still, Sarah couldn't stop. For Mark, for their baby. She couldn't stop until Mark was free or their unknown enemies broke her. And this was *not* her breaking point. Not even close.

"How do we learn what this software does, what it's really doing?" Sarah asked.

"I'd have to hack my way into its root operations. And I can only do that from the Pentagon's central mainframe. Which is restricted from me and especially from you. I guess we just break our way in, hack it, and find what we're looking for."

Sarah nodded, resolved. "Okay."

"Okay? Okay . . . what?" Aaron said, an eyebrow cocked in Sarah's direction. "Breaking into the Pentagon mainframe, that . . . that was a joke. We can't *really* do that."

"Aaron, my husband's life is at stake. The safety of this entire country might be at stake. We can't *not* do this."

"Sure we can. We just need to tell someone else what you've found out."

"Aaron, we have nowhere to turn." Sarah stood up from the coffee table and began pacing the room. "I can't go anywhere with what I know because no one will ever, ever believe me. I'm the wife of a spy, as far as anyone is concerned. And you can't bring this to anyone because it looks like a crazy conspiracy theory."

"It sorta is."

"And," Sarah continued, ignoring Aaron, "if anyone asks how

you found this stuff out, the road leads right back to me. We have to do this, Aaron. We have to *find* a way to do this."

Aaron exhaled, fanning his lips as he did. He was caving, Sarah saw it in his eyes. "I mentioned the part where I'm just an IT nerd, right?"

"Well," Sarah said, grasping Aaron's hand and helping him to his feet, "we'll just have to make do with what we have. Now come on, we need a plan."

25

Though Mark was learning—quickly—how to survive in extreme circumstances, he was far from being an actual spy. Still, some tactics were obvious. Like, when you're following someone, stay a few car lengths behind them to avoid detection. That insight came to mind after a few blocks of riding on Gregori's tailpipe, anxiously waiting for him to get to where he was going.

Wherever Gregori was going, though, it wasn't in Moscow. And that filled Mark with a profound sense of unease. Leaving the Hotel National, he pursued the oversized SUV—oversized and reinforced with blacked-out windows, like the military-grade cousin of an Escalade—down streets and landmarks he'd become familiar with thanks to his field trips with Oleg and Alex. Mark had a strong internal compass, and that helped him acclimate to new places in a short amount of time. Within days, Mark had begun deciphering how Moscow functioned. Ultimately, it was a major city like so many others—its streets had their own rhythm, the architecture its own character. There were tourist traps and insulated wealth, wasteful sprawl and islands of poverty. Mark would never claim that he knew Moscow completely, but he was at least achieving literacy. The more the SUV drove, however, all those things Mark had acquainted himself with were becoming less and less part of the fabric of his surroundings. Ornate buildings, ripe with history, gave way to uniform concrete housing edifices; those edifices gave way to industrial lots and belching smokestacks. And, soon, all the vestiges of Moscow, shed piece by piece, were gone, replaced by a flat landscape barely visible against the night's darkness.

Snow started to fall and Mark drove on, thinking of Ania. His only ally; his only *friend*. And he'd left her, dead, on the floor of a bathroom. He couldn't shake the image of her dying in his arms, and he didn't want to. Her life had been ruined by machinations beyond her control, the same as Mark's. Ania's existence was destroyed for no reason other than greed. Greed and power. He'd made a promise to her, to get Gregori. To make him pay for what he'd done to both of them, and damn it, he was going to make good on his word.

Mark couldn't even guess where he was, and he was even more clueless about where he was heading. Each mile he traveled took him farther away from the hard-fought confidence he'd accrued, not only by becoming acquainted with the city that held him captive, but also by preventing it from killing him. That was gone, leaving Mark with only the dim taillights of the SUV he pursued long into the night. He'd turned his own headlights off when twisting around a bend and out of the SUV's rearview scope, making the darkness ahead even more sharply pronounced. Mark, kept alert by adrenaline, maintained a white-knuckle grip on the wheel and reminded himself that out of darkness comes light. Clarity. And Mark would wrench clarity straight from Gregori's mouth if that's what it took. He hadn't come this far to be denied the light that'd been snuffed out the moment Agent O'Neal wrapped a sack over his head and took him away from everything he knew and loved.

After two long, uncertain hours of driving, the SUV took a slow right turn, disappearing into a tree-lined road. Mark, cruising on the fumes of an empty gas tank, drove past the turn without even slowing. He glanced down the unpaved road just in time to see the SUV swallowed by the snow-covered trees, their branches bowed downward and resembling an expectant maw. Taking precaution to keep his distance, Mark drove a safe measure before pulling off to the side of the road. He took a moment, standing at the cusp of the wintry forest ahead of him. He didn't know what to think or what to expect, but it was probably better that way. Maybe he'd descend into those woods and encounter Gregori's sanctuary, maybe he'd find an FSB stronghold. Mark had no way of knowing, and it wouldn't matter if he did. This was the chance to get some payback and possibly even take back his freedom and his life. As he stepped into the wilderness, the few inches of untouched snow crunching as it packed beneath his feet, Mark knew that everything was on the line. All roads bottlenecked here, and the other side only offered two scenarios: He'd walk away a free man or he'd dragged away a dead one.

It was one or the other.

From the bottom of a recessed slope that led away from the solitary cabin deep in the woods, Mark watched. Two guards armed with automatic rifles slung across their shoulders roamed the front of the cabin, pacing and re-pacing the tracks they left in the snow. As far as Mark could tell, this was the only security on hand. The cabin, diminutive and shielded by nothing other than its knotted-wood exterior, was no base of operations. It was clearly a getaway home that, at the moment, was acting as Gregori's safe house. And if Mark had to guess, Gregori was hiding from him, whether he knew it or not. The murder of two of his spies— one of whom had turned coats against him—drove Gregori off the grid, and not even seclusion was good enough. Gregori needed guards. He needed protection. Which meant one thing:

Gregori was spooked.

That was good, Mark reasoned. He wanted Gregori rattled

and off his game. He wanted him to feel like his life was at risk. And it was a life, judging by Gregori's run-and-hide response to Viktor's death, that Gregori didn't want to have taken from him. He'd respond just fine, Mark considered, to having a gun shoved in his face.

Mark moved low and slow, crouching as he followed a crescent-shaped path that flanked his way toward the rear of the cabin. He hugged the bank of a frozen lake that demarcated a separation between the trees; through the fog that hung low over the icy surface, Mark could only catch a glimpse of the grove on the opposite bank, the bare trees resembling elongated specters hovering in space.

Positioned behind the cabin so the guards surveying the acreage ahead couldn't see him, Mark tread cautious steps toward the back door. Every footfall, to Mark's ears, was like a record needle scratching across the surface of spinning vinyl; every step he took, every twig hidden beneath the snow that he snapped, was amplified to an unbearable pitch. Even as the crisp air of the breaking dawn breathed its frigid tendrils down Mark's back, beads of sweat still formed at his neck and rolled down the length of his spine. His hand, twitching over the butt of the gun, trembled as the nervous unease coalesced within Mark's body. Fear, though, could be a revelatory experience. When Sarah told him that she was pregnant, one of the many emotions that flooded Mark's brain was fear, right alongside happiness, excitement, and awe. Fear clouded Mark's vision of his future as a father like a splash of ink dropped into a glass of water, spreading until the glass was robbed of its transparency. Mark figured he'd be afraid during labor, afraid the first night they all came home from the hospital and were alone with this brand-new human life. Feeling such palpable fear that those days—and many more like them— were coming, and all because of something that was the size of a jelly bean, alarmed Mark. But, strangely, he had been okay with that. He had been okay with having his life turned upside down and seeing what happened. As Mark treaded toward the cabin, he realized how little concern he harbored for the armed guards that were no more than a shout away. What really scared Mark was missing all those changes that would come with the birth of his child. If he didn't win this encounter with Gregori, he'd never even know what life as a father was like. The more Mark thought about being robbed of that experience, the more his determination to outsmart Gregori grew. His entire life—however much of it was left—would be shaped by what Mark could pry from Gregori. Extracting information would not, Mark was certain, be easy.

Mark came to the back door, a fortified wooden slab that'd been warped by the effects of time. Though disjointed, it still hung snugly in the frame, protecting the interior from the elements, hungry animals, and intruders. Steadying his hand, Mark gripped the dented metal doorknob and gave it the slightest twist.

It clicked.

Mark continued the knob's clockwise spin, enough to pop the catch away from the stop. Mark slowly pushed the door open, allowing just a few inches of space. Enough for him to squeeze his way through.

He reminded himself to breathe.

Inside the cabin, he held a steady, unmoving pose. Ahead of him was a narrow hallway leading into the cabin's central artery. Three open doorways lined each side of the wall. Mark trained his gun straight ahead, his gaze unblinking, as he waited for someone to respond to his entrance. Being forced to fire a single bullet would spell trouble with the patrolling guards, but trouble was an upgrade compared to being gunned down by Gregori before he even had a chance to ask him a question. He waited, unmoving, for a long, anxious stretch. But no one came.

One foot in front of the other, each barely leaving the ground to minimize impact, Mark crept down the hall. Leading with his gun, he twisted into the first open doorway—an empty bathroom. Mark breathed the smallest sigh of relief then turned his attention back to the hallway. It seemed to stretch and deepen before his eyes. Another step forward; the subtle sound of his footsteps shuffling across the floor became drowned out by the rising treble of his heart thumping in his ears. Mark corkscrewed into the second room, which was crammed with nothing but boxes and plastic containers, dusty and smelling like they hadn't been touched in a long, long time. One room remained, and Mark began to wonder if, somehow, Gregori had known Mark was pursuing him, and he was lying in wait. Mark could very well be walking into a trap. Gregori might be old, but he was seasoned, smart, and he probably didn't make many mistakes. It was entirely conceivable—likely, even—that the spymaster had spotted Mark's car in pursuit, and now he was just waiting for Mark to fall right into his hands. Mark hugged the wall adjacent to the third and final door's frame, ready for anything. But just as he was about to twist his body to confront whatever was inside, Mark spotted something:

Gregori. Seated in the far corner of the living room, his back to Mark.

Mark waited for the old spy to respond to his presence, to whip around with a loaded gun in his hand or somehow alert the guards stationed just on the other side of the room's northern wall. But he didn't. Gregori, occupied by the computer that rested on the desk in front of him, had no idea Mark was there.

Terror washed over Mark. The man who held Mark's future in the palm of his hand was sitting fifteen feet away; Mark had never known higher stakes in his entire life.

Mark approached, his thoughts occupied by how he'd draw Gregori's attention. Maybe something simple like calling his name; maybe something more dramatic, like pressing the barrel of his gun into the back of Gregori's bare neck. But then, a floorboard creaked. It squealed and sighed beneath Mark's right foot, loud enough—in Mark's mind—to be heard back in Moscow. Gregori froze. Mid-typing, he stopped his fingers exactly where they were and his body went rigid. Unblinking, Mark watched, waiting for him to do something. To somehow turn the tables. But Gregori had no play to make. No dramatic maneuver that would give him the upper hand. His body rigid as a slab of wood, he did the only thing he could: Slowly, Gregori raised both his arms to the sky. He said nothing.

"Turn around," Mark said, his voice sounding like a worn-out record crackling against the quiet of the moment.

Gregori swiveled his chair around. His impassive face revealed nothing.

Mark took a step closer and pushed his gun forward, sure to call attention to its presence. "Why?" Mark asked. "Why did you do this to *me*?"

Gregori sighed. "You *are* a persistent one. You should be in a shallow grave by now. But here you are."

"Sorry to disappoint," Mark snarled.

"I ran a counterterrorism program a few years ago in Paris," Gregori said, his voice gruff. "We pinpointed our target to a small hotel just outside the city, and I ordered a team to move on the location. Shoot to kill, as you Americans say.

"My men went in, and the intel was good. But there was a maid, doing her rounds later than she normally did. Unfortunately, the maid became a casualty."

"And that's what I am," Mark sneered, "some casualty to a greater good?"

"To us, yes."

Mark took another step forward and cocked the hammer. "Bull. *Shit*."

Gregori eyed the gun then darted his eyes to Mark, studying him. He opened his mouth to speak, but Mark didn't give him the chance.

"Your life or mine. I'm not compromising on getting what I want—just ask Viktor."

Gregori nodded, chewing the inside of his mouth; Mark could almost hear the gears churning inside his mind, examining every angle, every path that would lead him out of this situation. But Mark knew the upper hand was his, and nothing could change that. While he never meant to kill Viktor, he wouldn't hesitate to unload all the bullets he had into Gregori's chest. This situation was binary: Mark wanted one thing from Gregori, and Gregori was a dead man if he didn't provide it.

"What good will it do you?" Gregori asked. "The Americans, they branded you a traitor, sent an assassin to murder you. Do you really think you can go back?"

"That's for me to worry about. Now tell me why—tell me how this happened. My patience is in short supply."

Gregori stood and, reflexively, Mark took a step back. "You are *nothing*, Mark Strain. You know that as well as I do. But we positioned you to look like you were *something*. Like you were a spy. A traitor."

Mark shook his head and exhaled sharply. "We both know that. Nothing about that is news. What I need to know is why you picked me—and how I can clear my name with the *truth*."

"The FBI was getting close to discovering a well-placed agent of ours, so we fed them a fake. We fed them you. We activated Ania and Viktor, making them look like they answered to you, like you were the ringleader of a cell of Russian spies. But everything, all of it—it was just a charade to keep our asset safe and, more important, hidden. And it worked."

Mark studied Gregori's face, paying close attention to the cadence of his words. Both his expressions and inflections were emotionless. He didn't reveal a thing he didn't want to. Still, Mark knew there was more. He hadn't come this far to be told what he'd already figured out for himself.

"Who's Sergei Vishny? Who is he really?" Mark asked. For the first time, Gregori's face twitched.

"What do you know about Sergei Vishny?" Gregori asked, his lip upturning into a snarl.

"I know he doesn't exist. Not anymore. My guess? You tracked him down, killed him, and assumed his identity. You used his name to invest in contracts that you and your partner could control—like the Verge deal. Now tell me who it is. Who's your American partner?"

Gregori smiled, sardonically. "You are gifted at exceeding expectations. But you'll never be entrusted with the identity of one of our most prized agents."

"Because I'll know who it is," Mark said.

As Mark processed the situation, Gregori began pacing a tight counterclockwise circle. Mark followed, staying across from him at all times. He knew time was running out.

"Who is it?" Mark asked as he and Gregori continued their mirrored paces. Only now, he trained the gun right on Gregori. He was done playing games. "I'm not going to ask you again."

Gregori stopped pacing, and his smile widened. "Like I said, you exceed expectations. Which is impressive, but it also makes you a nuisance.

"But the trouble you've caused—it ends. Now."

Mark, a flutter of panic rising within him, stayed focused on Gregori and saw his eyes—almost imperceptibly—dart off to the side. Mark turned, and he realized he was positioned, thanks to Gregori's maneuvering, directly in front of the cabin's lone window. Mark's heart jumped. Through the warped and clouded glass, he spotted one of the guards a split second before he lit the cabin up in a hail of gunfire.

Mark dove for the floor a second after Gregori, barely avoiding the bullets that shredded the room. The window's glass shattered and wood splintered and erupted as the gunfire was unleashed, seemingly without discretion, from outside the cabin. Mark screamed as he covered his head, a scream of fear and frustration. One last bit of information—the identity of the real spy—was all he needed to get everything back that'd been taken from him. And with Gregori on his stomach just a few feet away from him, he couldn't be any closer to it.

Mark had to think fast. He only had a few precious moments before the guards rushed the cabin, and given the circumstances, he had no way of making Gregori talk in that time. But then it dawned on him—maybe he didn't need Gregori to talk at all.

The second there was a break in the onslaught, Mark leapt to his feet and ran across the room. He grabbed Gregori's laptop—which was untouched by the assault—and slammed it shut. As he turned to leave, he was met by Gregori, who was charging right at him. Grabbing the computer, he instantly knew, was the best thing he could have done.

Mark responded quickly, sidestepping Gregori and pulling him into a choke hold with a nearly effortless movement. Gregori was old, old and slow, and Mark's sharpened reflexes gave him an overpowering advantage.

"You'll never get out of here alive," Gregori spat.

Over the man's shoulder, Mark saw the knob on the front door twist. "We'll see about that," Mark said, and shoved Gregori forward. Timed perfectly, the old spy stumbled toward the door just as it opened. The last thing Mark saw before he turned to run was Gregori's body flailing like it was a marionette as it was riddled with bullets.

Mark charged down the hall, throwing his weight into the back door so it burst open without him having to so much as stutter in his frantic pace. The guard yelled something in Russian, and Mark knew he and his partner would be in pursuit.

Dawn was encroaching, and Mark could feel the increasing warmth in the air. As he ran forward, his feet kicking up the thick snow with every step, Mark knew that every direction led to the same place.

The frozen lake.

He reached the glistening white shore and paused. There was no telling the integrity of the lake's surface, particularly if it could hold his weight or not. But a quick glance over his shoulder, seeing the guards closing in on his position, smothered his fears of plunging into fatally cold waters.

Mark stepped onto the lake like walking onto a tightrope. With every step he took, he entered into the thick fog that hovered over the surface. Murmurs chased him, the hushed tones of the guards as they took the same steps over deadly terrain. Mark looked back, but couldn't see beyond the fog staring him in the face. The guards were there, pursuing, but their whereabouts were as uncertain as the lake's opposite shore.

Suddenly, the sound of bullets erupted, tearing through the air. Mark nearly dropped to the ice but thought better of it. The guards had to be spraying, hoping to get lucky, and for the sake of his survival, Mark had to assume, sooner or later, they would. Aiming the gun over his shoulder, Mark fired off a few rounds of his own—not with the expectation that he'd hit anyone, but he knew he couldn't let the guards get comfortable.

It only took him two pulls of his trigger to realize the mistake he'd made:

He'd given his position away.

For a few breathless moments, Mark walked slower than ever while his eyes scanned the impenetrable fog around him. He considered making a run for the shore, but he hardly had time to bring the thought to conclusion. A pair of arms reached through the mist—Mark spotted them just out of the corner of his eye—and grabbed him, hard, around his neck and chest. Mark gasped, but his voice was hardly an audible pitch as it squeezed out of his constricted throat.

The guard tightened his grip. Mark's efforts to squirm his way free were futile, and as the guard called out in Russian—signaling for his partner, no doubt—Mark knew he had to do something. Gripping Gregori's laptop tight, he brought his gun around to his side, trying to aim it; the guard responded by squeezing Mark's throat even harder and used his other hand to knock the gun out of Mark's hand. He heard the gun skitter across the ice as it disappeared into the fog.

The guard called again, and Mark remembered what separated him from his captor. What separated him from anyone he encountered:

Mark had nothing to lose; he'd rather die than be taken back alive.

That's when he started stomping his feet on the ice.

Nothing happened on his first few attempts, but by the fourth stomp, Mark felt the ice begin to crack. He heard the splintering of the frozen water, and he continued to stomp. Harder. Faster. The guard tightened his grip around Mark and began throttling him, admonishing him in Russian. Ordering him to stop, Mark guessed, but he didn't care. He continued to pound his feet against the ice, and the guard's yells were soon silenced when the icy surface collapsed beneath them both.

They plunged into the water, water so cold it was painful to the touch. As Mark fell, he reached out with both arms and managed to catch an unbroken chunk of ice in front of him; the computer smashed to the ice nearby, and Mark could only pray it hadn't broken. The real estate he snagged was enough to hold him above the surface from the waist up, but he was sinking fast. During the fall, the guard had lost his grip on Mark's chest but somehow managed to grab onto Mark's legs. He could feel the guard gripping him around his knees, desperately trying to claw his way up. Mark could only imagine how unbearable it was to be submerged in the deadly water, but he didn't care; he kicked his legs as much as he could against the guard's weight, trying to break himself free. The guard refused to relent.

As he kept his legs moving, Mark worked on pulling himself out of the water. His body was too heavy, though, with the weight of the guard tied to him like an anchor. Mark managed to throw a few inches of his frozen lower torso out of the water only to be pulled back down as the guard thrashed against his own creeping death. Mark's grip on the ice nearly failed; the ice itself, buckling under the pressure of Mark's and the guard's combined weight, was ready to give. Mark felt the strain throughout his body, the pain of his lower half intensifying the longer it was submerged in the water. And just when he felt he couldn't carry both his weight and the guard's, Mark felt lighter. The guard, finally, let go. For a moment, Mark envisioned what it would be like to be trapped beneath the surface, the cold and the darkness overwhelming him until, finally, his body simply quit. In his final moments, all the world would go black before, lifeless, he drifted to the lake's depths, never to be found again.

As Mark pulled his body back onto the ice, inch by excruciating inch, he all at once felt release. Mark stumbled back to his feet. His legs struggled to support his weight, and his joints were stiff and weak. He knew it would be impossible for him to get anywhere fast. But that limitation worked in direct opposition with his most immediate necessity, which was to get the hell off the lake. The other guard would be on him any moment, and he was in no condition to offer any resistance.

Mark grabbed Gregori's laptop and trudged forward. His legs felt like they were on the brink of giving out with every step he fought to take. Gunfire sounded, the bullets cracking through the air all around him. Mark dove to the frozen surface, feeling it give below his weight. More bullets screamed overhead, and

Mark lay flat on his belly, covering his head with his hands. This guard had learned from his partner; trying to capture Mark was a mistake that wouldn't be made twice.

There was a pause in the assault. Mark swiveled his head around, but as expected, saw nothing. The only way out was forward, and Mark had to keep moving. Military-crawling, he pulled his frozen bottom extremities across the ice. He only made it a few paces when he saw a shadowy shape straight ahead of him. His gun. Mark hurried, fiercely dragging his body toward the weapon. Behind him, he heard ragged breathing and footsteps. Approaching fast.

He had no fight in him; he could barely move from the waist down. He got lucky once, a stroke of luck that almost buried him beneath a ceiling of ice. He couldn't expect to have fortune smile on him twice. The gun was his only chance.

Forgetting his pain, denying his immobility, Mark planted his right foot onto the ice; his thigh burned with the strain, and the searing pain only doubled—Mark swore a muscle tore in half, somewhere in his leg—as he pushed off his foot, diving for the gun. The labored breathing was closing in on him, practically huffing in his ear. Mark reached out and grabbed the gun; it nearly fumbled out of his grip as the joints in his hands proved to be as stiff as his legs. But Mark gripped the handle, gripped it *tight*. He rolled onto his belly, firing the moment he was facing forward. He pulled the trigger again and again until all that was left was a dry clicking sound.

Mark saw nothing in front of him, heard nothing except the sound of his own shallow breathing. For a moment—brief and terrifying—Mark waited for the guard to pounce from the fog and deliver a single bullet right between his eyes. Freezing, lost in the middle of rural Russia with no idea how to get out, part of him wanted that. A small part, the part that was exhausted, the part that was in agonizing pain, the part that was beginning to lose hope. Mark resisted, propping his weight on his elbow as he tried to get up. If the guard was coming, and if this was where Mark made his last stand, he'd at least do it on his feet.

But Mark didn't have time to pull himself up. A shadow lumbered toward him, and he recoiled. But Mark noticed the shadow's stumbling gait, moving like a drunk lost in the night. The shadow materialized into the shape of a man, his features gaining clarity with each step he took until, finally, he was standing over Mark. Incrementally, Mark had been easing away from the guard, but then he noticed the absent, vacant look in the man's eyes. Though he had his automatic rifle strapped over his arm, his hands were pressed against his abdomen. Blood gushed over his fingers, pouring out of the gunshot wounds that'd pierced his stomach. The guard dropped down on all fours, his lips quivering as if to say something, then he collapsed onto his side. Mark remained still, staring into the man's lifeless eyes.

With no small amount of exertion and pain, Mark got to his feet. He grunted and grimaced with every small ounce of pressure applied to his lower half, but the alternative—doing nothing, staying put—was worse. He pried the automatic rifle off the guard's shoulder, slinging it over his own, tightened his grip on Gregori's laptop, and headed off toward the shore. Mark Strain disappeared into the fog.

When he stepped out of the woods, the road he found looked identical to the one he'd come in on, but he knew that couldn't be right. He'd traveled so far from Gregori's cabin, and in the opposite direction from which he'd come. This road wasn't the one he needed—the one where he'd find his car, assuming Russian agents hadn't already hauled it away. Mark had trudged his way through a dense forest chewed bare by the merciless teeth of winter, willing his body to stay upright and moving ahead. One step at a time, he forced himself to keep going.

Mark limped his way to the north, which he assumed was away from the cabin. If the FSB wasn't already on the scene, they would be soon, and they'd be scouring the area for him. There was little he could do if found, but he didn't have to make his enemy's job any easier by heading toward them. His only hope was to stumble upon some form of civilization—a gas station, a house, anything—or barring that, cross paths with a soul kind enough to pick up a hitchhiker who looked as beaten and bloodied as Mark knew he must. The odds of finding either, Mark recognized, were incredibly bad.

As he came to a sharp bend in the road, he thought to shuffle across the street where the roadside tree coverage was thicker; in the event of an FSB search party, Mark could at least dive into the brush and hope to go by undetected. But just as he was about to dash across the street, a black SUV skidded in front of his path, cutting him off in midstride.

Mark froze as the driver's-side door swung open, and a woman leapt out.

"Mark Strain," the assassin said as she took brisk, determined steps toward Mark. Mark shuffled back, but he was too slow to even try to escape. The assassin raised her gun and brought it down hard on Mark's head. "You're a dead man" were the last words Mark heard before his world went black.

PART THREE

26

Mark woke to sunlight shimmering in his eyes. It took a good amount of time for them to focus with the hazy daylight dancing across his pupils; it took just as much time for his thoughts to return to coherency. Mark squinted, bringing into view rows and rows of evergreens, painted white with snow. He lifted his groggy head and studied the world, covered in white, as he cruised past it. He closed his eyes; the motion of the passing landscape made him feel nauseous. In the darkness, images flashed before him in bits and pieces. Ania, dying in his arms. Being chased over the ice. Falling into the water. Freezing. Running—running for his life. Mark fought to remember, but it was like he was still looking at the world through the fog he'd just escaped. He strained his mind, trying to remember. He'd fought his way off the frozen lake; he'd reached the road. He could almost feel the bitter pain in the lower half of his body as he begged his legs to last long enough to get back to his car. But he hadn't made it. There was a car, and it sliced right in front of his path. The Russians? Mark pictured Gregori, but that wasn't right. This person was going to kill Mark, he heard her voice in his head. And then it came to him:

The assassin.

Mark's eyes shot open as his mind snapped back to focus. He sat upright and gasped, nearly choking on his own breath. He realized he was in a car, hurtling through the snow-hushed world. In another life, the landscape would have seemed idyllic, serene even. But not in this world. Mark slammed his finger down on the button that controlled the window, but the sheet of glass at his side didn't budge. His head swimming, Mark pressed the button again and again, harder and harder, desperate for air, but nothing happened.

"It's locked," a voice said, next to Mark. "You just need to breathe, Mark. Breathe."

In his panic, Mark hadn't even considered who was at his side, driving the car. But he knew. That voice was forever seared in his mind, the voice that told him he was a dead man.

Mark turned to face the assassin.

"What are you . . . ," Mark said, struggling to speak. He studied the woman, who had her eyes fixed on the road ahead. He should be dead. Or at the very least, he should be tied up until they reached the place where the assassin was going to kill him. "What the hell is going on?" Mark finally blurted out.

"I found you before the Russians did," the assassin said. "You'd be dead otherwise."

The assassin looked at Mark, and he swore she cracked a smile. "You're welcome."

Mark allowed himself a moment to digest . . . everything. And still, none of this made sense. He could have woken up with a set of horns growing out of his head and been less surprised. "But . . . why?" he asked. "Don't get me wrong, I appreciate it, but you've seemed pretty intent on killing me."

"Things change."

Mark nodded like he knew what the assassin was talking about. But he didn't. "Like, what kind of things?"

The assassin glared at Mark, studying him like he was a callus on the tip of her finger; the sooner she could remove him, the better. "Look, this isn't some charity case, all right? I was on the fence about killing you when I picked you up. And I would have but . . . damn it, you're good at causing problems for people, aren't you?"

"I excel at it."

The assassin grunted, and the car fell into uncomfortable silence. Mark—who took four hours to talk about three hours of his workday, Sarah often joked—wasn't any good at silence.

"So what was it?" Mark asked. "That changed your mind, I mean. Why didn't you kill me?"

The assassin pursed her lips and exhaled sharply. "You have two options in front of you, Mark. I don't know if you've noticed, but we're not in Russia anymore."

Butterflies fluttered in Mark's stomach, a feeling he couldn't remember having since he was a teenager. It was a feeling of pure joy, joy tinged with profound relief. Even when Sarah broke the news of her pregnancy, Mark still felt a hint of worry crowding the happiness inside of him. But this, this was different. He could have cried, but he figured the assassin wouldn't care for that kind of display. His reaction didn't matter, though. What mattered was that he was free.

He'd gotten out of Russia.

Mark studied the world outside his window with fresh eyes. Now, it did seem idyllic. It seemed peaceful, and Mark felt the same peace creeping deep into his heart. He had the urge to have the assassin pull the car over so he could get out and run. Run until he was out of breath, at which point he'd drop to his knees, feeling the cold ground beneath him, and laugh until he cried. But, again—tears. And catharsis probably wasn't on the assassin's agenda. So instead, Mark kept things strictly business.

"Where are we, then?"

"Finland. Nearly to the airport. You've been out for over twelve hours."

Mark remembered the condition he was in when the assassin had found him. Not only was he exhausted, but he was also likely frostbitten from his plunge into the frozen pond. The assassin had tended to him, he realized.

"My clothes," Mark said. "You got me out of those clothes."

"You were hypothermic," the assassin said, flatly. "I had to."

Mark was reminded of Ania, who had shown him similar kindness. Saved his life, in fact. Mark wanted her here with him; he wanted her to still be alive. He'd gotten her the revenge she'd craved, but it was no comfort for what'd happened to her. Mark's burst of elation slowly gave way to anger as he considered the lives ruined by these damn games. Games of power and greed that satisfied few and terrorized many. It reignited Mark's drive to make every single person responsible for what'd happened to him pay. Gregori's death was satisfying, particularly since it fulfilled the promise he'd made to Ania. But Mark's work wasn't complete. There were still loose ends.

"So, what now?" Mark asked. "We're going to the airport, but what happens when we get there?"

"I'm going to give you a fake ID, passport, and enough money to keep you going. You can take all those things and disappear. While you were unconscious, I took a photo of your bloodied face, almost blue from hypothermia, and I sent it to the people who assigned me this contract. In your condition, you made for a convincing corpse.

"I also shared that photo with certain Russian channels that are sure to spread the word throughout the intelligence community.

"What this means, Mark, is that the Americans think you're dead, and so do the Russians. You can disappear, and no one will ever even bother looking for you. Find a job that pays cash, live a quiet life. In time, you can find a way to send for your wife and child, assuming—"

"Assuming Sarah isn't murdered by someone from either side," Mark interrupted.

"It's still a possibility, yes," the assassin said. "Someone may want to close the circuit."

Mark closed his eyes and imagined. For a moment, he allowed himself to fantasize about a quiet life in a small town in Finland, living out his days in peace. After everything he'd endured, just the idea brought him so much comfort. He pictured Sarah and their baby making it there, somehow, and he could see how happy they all were.

But Mark knew it was impossible. His vision was a fantasy, and he hadn't come all this way to indulge in make-believe.

"Sorry," Mark replied. "But I can't do that."

The assassin shook her head and let out a quiet groan. "I figured as much."

Mark cocked an eye at the assassin. "How so?"

"You could have fled before, but you didn't. Instead, you went hunting. First Viktor, then Gregori. You want *revenge*."

Mark considered this, but his quest for revenge, since Gregori's death, had taken a nebulous shape in his mind. Someone in the United States had partnered with Gregori and, together, they used the persona of Sergei Vishny to secure various contracts and make untold millions. For some reason, Mark's work securing the Verge deal was their masterstroke, but he couldn't understand why. A major piece was missing: the identity of Gregori's partner. While Verge's contract was undoubtedly lucrative, that couldn't have been the only reason why Gregori and his mystery partner's scheme climaxed at this point. If Mark had to guess, based on what he knew of Vishny, they had already made millions. There was something else going on, and the danger that unanswered question was hiding made him shiver.

But the assassin knew. She knew what Mark didn't.

She had to, Mark reasoned. She must have discovered something that persuaded her of Mark's innocence and forced her to spare his life, defying her employers and putting herself at risk.

Then it came to him: Gregori's laptop.

"You know, you still haven't told me why you decided to let me live," Mark said.

The assassin craned her head toward Mark and met his gaze with a smile loaded with mischief and danger. "I haven't, have I?"

"You know who's behind all this. You cracked Gregori's computer?"

"You were smart to take it," the assassin replied. "The old spy wasn't as cautious with his laptop as he should've been. It took hardly any time at all to break through his security."

"I want to see it," Mark said, his voice telling the assassin that it wasn't a request. He had risked his life for the information stored in Gregori's hard drive, and it was his to consume.

"You can," the assassin assured Mark, "but ask yourself if that's something you really want. Just because you return home, that doesn't mean you have to make trouble for yourself. The shadows are a fine place to live, Mark. Believe me when I tell you that."

"I do, I believe you," Mark said, and he meant it. The assassin had saved his life, not only by deciding not to kill him, but also by ensuring that he didn't die from any number of causes: hypothermia, falling into the hands of the Russians, starvation in the wilderness. After escaping from Gregori's cabin, there were no shortage of ways Mark could have expired. And the assassin was helping him again, trying to nudge him down a more reasonable path. Mark got the sense it wasn't a path the assassin would take, either, but that didn't mean she failed to see the value in it, the same as Mark should. But he couldn't. Someone had played a role in Mark's death sentence, had violently torn him away from his wife, his career, and his home, and that someone had to pay. If not only for Mark's peace of mind, then for the danger this person posed to countless others. An enemy was out there, not only hidden but also positioned in a place of power. And Mark was the only person who could do something about it.

"If you believe me," the assassin offered, "then why don't you take the safer route?"

"Because of Dustin Wheeler," Mark said with a smile.

The assassin shrugged. "I have no idea who that is."

"Dustin Wheeler was a kid I knew in the sixth grade who got beat up pretty much every day. We walked the same route home from school, and this group of assholes from the year above us started following him home just so they could rough him up. I walked by a few times, acting like I didn't see anything. I just minded my own business. But then Dustin called out to me. He was . . . he was such a mess of a kid. He picked his nose, was terrible at sports, and he said the weirdest shit. We weren't friends, we hardly even knew each other. But here he was, begging me for help.

"I didn't even think about what to do next. I walked right over to the kid closest to me, turned him around by his shoulders, and landed a right hook across his stupid face. That little shit went down like he'd just been hit by Mike Tyson. It was amazing. What was less amazing was the three other kids who were still there. And they didn't like their buddy getting knocked out. So they turned away from Dustin and beat the shit out of me instead.

"Every day for the next week I stood up for Dustin, and every day I got beat up. I got a few shots in here and there, but nothing compared to what they gave me.

"But after a week, those kids stopped bothering Dustin. Maybe they lost interest, maybe they got busted by someone who saw what was going on. Personally, I like to think it was because they got tired of dealing with me. They had it easy beating up Dustin. He didn't resist, didn't threaten to tell on them. He just took his beating. But me, I made those punks work for it. I made it hard for them.

"So why don't I take the safe route? For one, I'm clearly too stupid. But also, damn it, I can't help but pick the *right* route. I'm a glutton for punishment that way."

The assassin was silent as a plane flew low overhead. Mark looked around and noticed that their rural surroundings had transformed without him even noticing. Just like that, a European city was now crowding Mark's vision. He was caught off guard, but the locale meant very little to him. As long as it wasn't Russia, Mark would happily embrace wherever he happened to be.

"You're going to make things harder for me, you know that, right?"

"I know," Mark admitted. "And if what I'm going to do, if it's going to cause real problems for you, I won't do it. The last thing I want is someone else dying because they tried to help me."

"I can take care of myself," she said. "I already collected the money for this job, and I know how to lay low. I'll just have to hope the people who hired me aren't more resourceful than they seem."

Mark sucked in a deep breath. With his sights set on a specific course of action, he was eager to discover what the assassin already knew. A sliver of him wanted to really make sure that he wasn't putting the assassin in danger, but he couldn't wait any longer. Mark needed to know what was on Gregori's laptop.

"So what was it?" Mark asked. "What did you find that was so compelling that you decided to save my life?"

The assassin eyed Mark, her tongue running along the inside of her cheek. After a moment, she nodded to the back seat. "Go ahead and take it," she said. "It's best you see it for yourself."

For a moment, Mark hesitated. He had imagined that seeking evidence in Gregori's computer meant sifting through bank records and emails, mundane work that would expose who the old spy was connected to. If Mark had to guess, the assassin wasn't one for theatrics; she wouldn't have him slog through Gregori's bank statements to get him to that point. No, Mark concluded, it wasn't a paper trail that the assassin discovered. It was something else entirely, and that made him nervous.

"Go ahead," the assassin urged. "It's waiting for you."

Slowly, Mark reached back and grabbed the laptop. He opened it, but the keyboard was in Russian.

"Just click the right mouse button to log on," the assassin said. "I removed the password protection."

Mark did as he was told, and the computer's home screen filled the monitor. In the center of the screen was a video window, all black with nothing but a white PLAY triangle in its center.

"Click it," the assassin instructed, and Mark did.

The nighttime video was grainy, but Mark saw enough to know that the recording was centered on Gregori, standing beneath what looked like an expressway overpass. He seemed to be waiting, impatiently, for someone to arrive. Gregori was anxious, pacing, checking his watch over and over, scanning the area all around him. He muttered something in Russian to the guard standing behind him, but the bulky guard said nothing. Gregori slammed his half-smoked cigarette to the ground, stomped it out, and was about to light another one when someone else arrived.

"You're late," Gregori grumbled, but the person he was talking to—a man—had his back positioned to the camera so Mark couldn't identify him.

The man apologized, and Mark swore he recognized the voice. It was familiar, but the ambient noise of the recording muffled and distorted it just enough so Mark couldn't hear it clearly.

From there, Gregori and the man launched into a banal exchange. It was brief, but it covered things Mark already knew, specifically the details of the money they were about to make and if Mark had been thoroughly positioned as the dummy spy. The man assured Gregori that an investigation had been mounted against the entire spy ring, centered on Mark, and they were all primed to be rounded up and shipped out with the pulling of a few strings. Gregori threatened that the man had better be sure—they couldn't afford any surprises. The man scoffed.

"And the software Verge will deliver to the Pentagon, you're certain that your team has it ready?" the man asked.

"I've had the very best Russian hackers thoroughly ensure the software will give us exactly what we want, and it will be installed without issue. No one will ever know it's there," Gregori said. "Not until it's too late."

"There's no second chances on this one, Gregori," the man said. "It has to be perfect, because if it isn't, everything we've done will have been for nothing."

"I wouldn't call becoming wealthy beyond our wildest imaginings 'nothing,' my friend."

"This isn't about money," the man stated sharply. "Not for me."

Gregori smiled. "I wish I shared your idealism, but I don't believe the system can change. Not even with this."

"I don't want it to change," the man said. "I want the system brought to its knees. I've had to suffer, for *years*, surrounded by so-called colleagues who had no interest in serving the public good, who had no interest in doing anything other than serving their wealthy masters and bringing our government grinding to a halt. It was an insult, working with these people who've morally bankrupted the principles of my nation. I want them to *know*. I want them to understand that their abuse of power is what made me do this. And they're going to pay the price because of it."

"They will pay," Gregori assured the man. "They will pay."

They shook hands. "I'll see you on the other side," the man said. "I look forward to disappearing."

"A new beginning awaits," Gregori said, and he released the man's grasp. The man turned, his face fully in the camera's focus, and Mark could only stare, his body trembling like the frozen lake's icy grip had returned, as the video ran for ten more seconds to its completion.

It was Dale.

"What the *fuck*?"

"Seems there's no honor amongst conspirators; I imagine the Russians recorded that chat as collateral, just in case," the assassin said. "The other man, the American. Do you know him?"

"I—I—yeah. I know him. His name's Dale, Dale Schmidt. He was my mentor . . . my friend. He did this to me? *Why?*"

Mark thought he'd feel rage the likes of which he'd never known when he learned who was behind his harrowing ordeal. That he'd be suffocated by his own anger and its accompanying need for revenge. But seeing Dale—who'd been like a father to Mark—revealed as the man who'd poured gasoline over his life and then tossed a struck match onto it, Mark could only feel sadness. Profound, terrible sadness. He couldn't accept this as true, and for a moment he allowed himself to wonder if maybe the assassin had set this whole thing up. Maybe she'd uploaded this doctored video to Gregori's laptop while Mark was passed out, and she was manipulating him into doing something on her behalf. But he was quick to debunk this theory, knowing how little sense it made. He stared at Gregori's monitor, the video frozen on a still image of Dale's face, and he knew this was real. Dale had chosen Mark to be his shield. Dale orchestrated everything that had happened—

Everything except for Mark's escape.

The assassin pulled the car over, stopping in front of what Mark assumed was the international terminal at the Helsinki airport. She dug a letter-sized envelope out of the console on her door and passed it to Mark.

"Passport," the assassin said. "You're Phil Young of Ohio. There's also money in there and a phone."

Mark accepted the envelope solemnly, like he was a courier being passed a message that would save the world. And to him, that's exactly what it was: a way to save his world.

"A flight to D.C. departs on American Airlines in two hours," the assassin continued. "Last I checked, there were still seats available."

Mark clutched his door, knowing this was his cue to leave, but he couldn't. The assassin had defied her employers—powerful people—and risked her own neck saving him from the Russians and smuggling him out of the country. And now she was providing him with the means to get home. It was impossible to express the proper amount of thankfulness for that level of kindness and generosity, but Mark knew he had to try.

"I—I still can't believe you did all this for me. You saved my life and put yourself in danger. And for a stranger. I don't know that there's any way I can ever repay you or thank you enough."

The assassin grimaced; Mark could tell he was making her uncomfortable with his candid display of gratitude, as mild as it was. "Just get an answer to your question," she said, staring straight ahead through her windshield.

"What question?"

"You want to know the why of it all, don't you? That's what's slicing a hole in the pit of your stomach: You want to know why this Dale set you up."

"Yeah," Mark said. "I do."

"You can ask him when you see him," the assassin said, then she tapped her finger on Gregori's laptop. "And you even have proof."

Mark shut the computer and looked over at the assassin. He knew it was time to go, just as he knew she didn't want to hear any more awkward expressions of gratitude.

"I promise you, he's going to answer every question I have to ask," Mark said, extending his hand out to the assassin. "And then he's going to pay."

The assassin shook Mark's hand, then nodded to the terminal. He opened the door, stepped out of the car, and watched the assassin's SUV drive away until it was out of sight.

Mark then turned toward the airport.

He had a plane to catch.

27

Sarah and Aaron's plans had leapt from ridiculous to absurd.

It dawned on Sarah how out of touch with reality they'd gotten when Aaron retrieved his iPad and pulled up a three-dimensional architectural schematic of the Pentagon. They were studying ventilation shafts that led to the central mainframe—the place Aaron needed to break into and hack if they were going to find out what the Verge software was hiding—trying to figure out an entry point. If they could enter the ventilation system in a place Aaron wasn't restricted to enter, they could tunnel their way through the building, unnoticed, and drop into the central mainframe. But even with the schematics, they had no idea where the ventilation shafts traveled. Which meant it was a stupid plan that would never work. And Sarah told Aaron as much.

Aaron groaned and flopped back on the rock-hard sofa in the hotel they were holed up in. Earlier that morning, Sarah had called Jenna from a pay phone and instructed her to find someplace safe and stay there. People were after all of them, and Sarah wouldn't be able to live with herself if Jenna or Aaron got hurt. But she knew none of them would be out of harm's way until this entire conspiracy was blown wide open.

"I just don't know," Aaron said, rubbing his forehead. "I mean, this is the Pentagon we're trying to break into. Security is kind of their thing."

Sarah understood Aaron's frustration; she felt it herself. Prior to them tossing around the idea of crawling through ventilation shafts undetected and hoping they'd magically wind up where they needed to be, and that they tripped no alarms in the process, their best idea was to start a fire near the central mainframe, evacuate the area, and sneak into the room during the chaos.

Sarah didn't even want to think about the bad ideas they'd conjured.

"I know, I know," Sarah said, pacing among the Chinese takeout boxes that littered the floor. "But there *has* to be a way."

"No," Aaron scoffed. "There doesn't have to be a way. It's not like we can just walk right in there."

Sarah stopped dead in her tracks. "That's it," she said. "That's exactly it."

"Um, what's it?"

"We've been wasting our time trying to think of these complicated ways to break into this mainframe room—ways neither one of us are capable of—when we just need to keep it simple: We'll just walk right in."

Aaron laughed. Sarah stared at him.

"Oh. You're serious."

Sarah thought of Mark, who was a master of doing things he wasn't supposed to and being places he didn't belong. And his method, as he had explained it to Sarah, was twofold: catch people off guard, and always act like you belong. That's all Sarah and Aaron needed to do. Simple as that, she thought, trying to convince herself.

"You can get us to the central mainframe's doors, right? Just not inside. Your security clearance can get us that far?"

"It can get *me* that far. Not the wife of Mark Strain."

"I guess that means I won't go as Sarah Strain," she said with a devious smile. "Which means we have work to do."

Aaron groaned. "I really, really wish I had run away when you started telling me about all this conspiracy business. Like, literally run. Away from you."

"Come on, think of all the Chinese we're getting to eat, guilt free, because of the sheer lunacy of this situation."

"I do love chow mein."

"That's the spirit," Sarah said, putting on her coat.

"Wait—where are you going?"

"I'm going to get hair dye and some cheap glasses," Sarah said. "My disguise."

"And what should I do—besides order more Chinese?"

Sarah stopped at the door and shot Aaron a cunning smile. She reveled in being on the path to outsmarting the bastards who'd tried to ruin her life. Payback was coming.

"You're a computer whiz," Sarah said. "Start working on making me fake IDs."

Sarah followed Mark's first rule of getting into places you're not supposed to get into:

Catch people off guard.

But this was the Pentagon, and that meant the standard for "off guard" was still more attentive than Sarah would have liked. The best chance they had at slipping into the mainframe was during the night shift, when security was reduced to one guard. Not only that, Aaron explained, but the day-shift guard, Melanie, also happened to specialize in IT systems. Which meant there was no bullshitting her. And bullshit was the nucleus of Sarah's plan. Because Mark's second rule was:

Act like you belong.

Aaron spent the day creating not only fake IDs for Sarah, but also an entire fictional persona. She was Erin Greene, an IT guru who'd been hired directly by the White House to conduct an independent study of the efficiency of all high-level security systems.

When Aaron explained this to the night-shift guard, Hank, the man twisted his head on its axis and stared blankly ahead. For a second, Sarah thought they were busted, that their bullshit had been detected already. But then she realized Hank was just confused.

"Wait . . . what?" he asked.

"It has to be in the daily logs," Aaron said, then cleared his throat for about the seventieth time. "Erin's been with my team all day, going through our processes, workflow, stuff like that. I'm her guide."

"But why is she here so late?" Hank asked as he searched the logs.

"Because I get paid for the contract's completion, not its duration," Sarah responded, her tone stiff and direct. It was the no-nonsense way Erin communicated.

Hank looked up from his computer screen and scanned Sarah with a suspicious eye. "Yeah, I'd do the same," he said, then he continued to study the logs until he got to the end. Of course, he didn't find the entry he'd been looking for. Because it didn't exist. "There's nothing here, and without official clearance, I can't let either of you in."

"Well, um, are you sure—" Aaron began to stammer, until Sarah interrupted.

"You heard Mr. Cutter here mention my job is to evaluate efficiency, correct?" Sarah asked. Erin didn't like having her time wasted, so her question was equal parts inquiry and accusation; because if Hank had heard Aaron, he wouldn't be gumming up the works.

"I did," Hank answered.

"And that my contract was executed by the White House—the director of Homeland Security, as a matter of fact."

"I got that as well," Hank admitted. Sarah could tell he was trying to maintain his posture, but she could hear the uncertainty creeping into his words. Hank didn't know what to do. But Sarah did. After all, this is where Sarah belonged.

"Then why are you contributing to your system's inefficiency? I examined your logs this morning, Hank. I found three irregularities from today alone, which is why it's no surprise my clearance is nowhere to be found."

"Let me just call," Hank said. He placed his hand on the phone's receiver, and Sarah took a step closer and placed her hand on Hank's. It stopped him immediately.

"Show some initiative, Hank," Sarah said in a cool, hushed tone. "That's what strong, successful people do."

"We won't be in there more than a few moments. What do you really think we're going to do?" Sarah took another step forward, nearly pressing her body against Hank's. She could feel him quiver.

"You won't be in there long?" he asked, then swallowed hard.

"We'll be gone before you know it," Sarah said, sending Hank a playful smile.

Hank sucked in a deep breath and allowed them inside. Sarah withheld a massive sigh of relief—which would have been out of character—until she and Aaron were safely inside.

"That was, like, some Jedi mind shit," Aaron said as they hurried away from the central mainframe's entrance. With the rush of the moment wearing off, Sarah felt like she was going to be sick.

"That was just the first step," Sarah said. "Now comes the hard part."

"Piece of cake," Aaron said, waving off Sarah's concerns. "Follow me."

The central mainframe was like a hedge maze, only with the shrubbery replaced by obsidian towers, about Sarah's height, that were dimly lit by the soft blue glow of their internal processors and motherboards and other computer stuff that Sarah didn't understand. But she didn't have to; that's what Aaron was there for. So, she followed Aaron through the dark space, unable to discern one row of towers from another, hoping he had something brilliant up his sleeve.

"You know what you're looking for, right?" she asked, keeping her voice hushed, just in case.

"Nah, I'm just playing it by ear."

"Aaron, now's not the time," Sarah scolded.

"Yes, of course I know what I'm looking for," Aaron admitted. "It's just a matter of what I'm able to accomplish when we get there."

Aaron led Sarah down a row like all the others, but he seemed to know what he was looking for. He counted off the towers one by one and, as they got closer to the center of this particular row, he started to peek inside. Each tower had a rectangular opening at eye level, and Aaron muttered to himself as he examined . . . something. Sarah was just anxious to get this done, and she didn't care much about the details.

"Ah, here it is," he said as he tapped the tower's thick metal shell. "This is the one—the gateway to the Verge software's core operations. If we're going to learn anything about what it's really up to, this is where we'll do it."

"And you can crack the code or . . . whatever's hidden in there?" Sarah asked, starting to pace.

Aaron shrugged and laughed nervously.

"Oh man," Sarah huffed.

Cautiously—and, more important, quietly—Aaron removed the tower's cover. Its interior revealed a series of crisscrossing wires, flashing bulbs, and myriad slots Sarah couldn't even venture to guess the purpose of. Aaron grabbed his laptop from his backpack and plugged it into one of the tower's outlets.

"So, yeah, in theory I should be able to swipe all the information stored inside this bad boy," he replied.

"What do you mean *in theory*?" Sarah asked, trying not to get fuming mad at Aaron. "Maybe you should have mentioned this detail, I don't know, *before* we broke into the Pentagon's computer mainframe?"

"I mean, look—it's not like I can just type in 'command, colon, show me secret nefarious program' and find what we need," Aaron said. "It's going to take time."

"How much time?"

"If I knew exactly what I was looking for and the route to get there? No time at all. If I'm blindly looking for a needle in the program's haystack? That could take days."

"And you are?"

"Closer to the former."

Sarah withdrew a long, worried breath. "Jesus, Aaron."

"Relax," he said, sitting down and positioning his computer on his lap. His eyes were fixated on the glowing screen in front of him. "I'm good at what I do. Remember that."

As Sarah wore out the floor beneath her feet, she removed her phone from her back pocket and started typing in a message.

"Please tell me you're not on any form of social media," Aaron said.

"Of course not. I'm texting Dale Schmidt—you know him, right? Mark's mentor, the politician?"

"Maybe," Aaron said, absently. "Politicians are all just politicians to me."

"Well, Dale's on our side. He's the one who put me on this trail, and he wanted me to contact him if I came across anything. Correct me if I'm wrong, but it seems like we're about to find ourselves a big something."

Aaron hummed, considering. "Maybe it's better if you didn't tell him anything. At least not yet."

"Look, Dale's one of the few people I can trust, and I kind of want someone else to know that we're in here. Just in case."

Aaron raised his head from the screen and let Sarah's reasoning sink in. "Right," he agreed. "When you put it that way."

Sarah danced her fingers over the screen, letting autocorrect do most of the work as she crafted a message to Dale. She had found something, the text read. Something with the software from Mark's deal with Verge. She was in the Pentagon's central mainframe with a friend, trying to find out what this software really did.

After firing off the message, Sarah's nerves went even tauter. She expected to hear back from Dale immediately. A confirmation. A reassurance that they'd make things right. But five minutes passed without a response, and Sarah worried that she'd made a terrible mistake revealing so much information through a text message. It was careless.

Ten minutes passed. Sarah's anxiety grew until she was not only pacing, but breathing like she'd just run a marathon.

"What, are you going into labor already?" Aaron asked. "Chill out—you're making me more nervous, and I was already on the cusp of fully freaking out *before* we did something that would land us in prison."

Sarah stopped. She knew getting herself so worked up wasn't helping anyone, and if there was one thing she needed right now—and for whatever was going to happen next—it was sharp wits and steely nerves. Looking back on where this all started, Sarah took stock of how far she'd come. She reminded herself that if she could endure some of the horrifying things she had witnessed and helped remedy as an ER nurse, she could withstand anything. And that's all this was: trauma that needed to be remedied. If she didn't freak out when assisting in the removal of a chunk of steel girder from a construction worker's abdomen, then she could keep her cool during this as well.

"Holy shit, I've found something," Aaron suddenly said. Sarah stood behind Aaron; she was ready.

"Found something what?" she asked.

"Um," Aaron stammered, "this is . . . this is bad."

"You're going to have to fill me in here, Aaron. What is it?"

"It's . . . it's everywhere," Aaron said, his eyes mesmerized on the screen in front of him. "Nobody would find this. Not until so much damage had been done. It's so eloquent, so . . . advanced."

Sarah considered slapping Aaron and ordering him to snap out of it, but she restrained herself. She'd give him one more chance to pull himself together without her assistance. "Aaron, if you don't get a grip and start explaining—"

Aaron turned to Sarah. His face couldn't be any more flushed if he'd just seen his own ghost. "Okay, okay," he said, getting ahold of himself. "See, this program, the one Verge sold Mark on, was supposed to be a new and totally advanced way to stop hackers from getting into the Pentagon. I mean, people try to break into our system all the time. All. The. Time. And from everything I've seen, Verge's software does exactly that. But there's something else."

Aaron ran his hands over his face, his fingers through his hair. Sarah saw beads of sweat collect at his temple and start to dribble down his cheek. Aaron had been nervous before, maybe even afraid. Now? Now he was unnerved.

"The software . . . what it does is cast a shadow," Aaron explained. "While its main programs run and function, hidden programs, embedded deep within the system and designed to spread, operate based on their own directives. It's insanely complicated, and even I don't totally understand how it works—but I understand what it *does*.

"The shadow program infiltrates and transmits. Meaning it's going to spread across everything. Everything protected within the Pentagon, this program will record, and then it'll send that information out."

"That . . . that would devastate the entire country," Sarah said, dumbfounded. She understood what Aaron was telling her; she just couldn't believe it.

"Sarah, we're talking classified military information, the names of deep cover agents and their locations, intel given to the U.S. from its allies. Everything. If that information was exposed and delivered into the wrong hands—and whoever is behind this program, they can't be the right hands—our country's entire defense matrix would be trashed. Countless lives would be in danger. The *entire world* would be in danger."

"But we can stop it, right?" Sarah asked, her resolve kicking into overdrive. Sarah hated the person who had framed Mark. Even through her own fury, she thought she understood that person, that he or she had used Mark because of their own greed or thirst for power. But this? This was the work of someone who wanted to watch the world burn. This was someone evil, and he or she had to be stopped. "We have to do something about this before it happens."

"Huh?" Aaron said, as if snapping out of hypnosis. "Sorry, I just . . . this is so much bigger than I ever imagined. But, yeah— the program isn't live. Not yet. We can stop it."

Sarah nodded and swallowed hard. She was about to instruct Aaron to pack up the computer so they could get the hell out of there, but her words turned into a breathless gasp.

Voices. Both Sarah and Aaron froze, listening to the murmurs clarify into whispers, whispers into muffled words. The voices were coming their way.

"Hide," Aaron whispered to Sarah, leading her down an adjacent row.

"Hide where? They know we're both here," Sarah protested. "They—"

"Just go," Aaron urged. "Try to escape, call for help. Just *go*."

Sarah looked at Aaron, reading his refusal to compromise. And she knew he wasn't being selfless; he wasn't saving her, he was charging her with saving them both. She ran down the row on the balls of her feet, careful to not make a sound. When she reached where the row ended in a T, she turned to head toward the exit. But then she heard a familiar voice. She exhaled her relief like a breath she'd been holding in for days. She'd panicked over nothing; it was just Dale.

In the sliver of time it took for Sarah to redirect her course back the way she came, she had thoroughly convinced herself that everything was going to be okay. They'd prevent this terrible plot from being executed, saving the country from an incalculable amount of mayhem and destruction. With Dale on her side and the Verge software nullified, combined with whatever else Jenna had discovered, surely they'd be able to exonerate Mark.

But when she turned and faced the long, deep row that led back to Aaron, all those feelings evaporated.

Sarah slowly crept forward, squinting to get a better look at what was ahead. Because it wasn't Dale at the end of the row, lumbering over a cowering Aaron, that much she was sure of. She hugged the side of the row, moving out of the light and into the shadows. She stalked closer and closer, one small step at a time, until the man came into view:

Banks. That was the man's name, the one who'd almost choked the life out of Mark when he was abducted from their home. She'd never forget Banks's name or his face, his look of maniacal joy as he watched Mark suffer.

"She's not here! Sarah's gone, she left!" Aaron yelled.

"Where did she go?" a voice asked. It was Dale, Sarah recognized. He was standing where she couldn't see, hidden from view. Sarah didn't know why Dale had come here and not texted her—or called—when she reached out to him, and she certainly didn't know why he was paired with Banks. But whatever the reason was, she knew it wasn't good.

Sarah realized she should run, she knew she should try to escape while she had the chance. But she couldn't. She had to know. Why was Dale here? In all the ways she'd known him—as Mark's mentor, his father figure, as someone she considered a friend—was it all just a lie? Her idea of who this person was had been completely wrong. This wasn't Dale, this was a complete stranger. A stranger was threatening her friend, trying to intimidate his way to what he wanted. Which, apparently, was Sarah.

"Don't make me ask again," Dale said, his voice laced with menace.

Sarah darted back to the end of the row, but instead of turning toward the exit, she headed in the opposite direction. She weaved down rows, cutting a path that would take her to the row on the opposite side of where she'd left Aaron. As she moved, unseen, behind the towers, she heard Aaron scream again.

"She's. Not. *HERE!*" he yelled, though his final syllable was cut short by the sound of a muffled impact, then something heavy crashing to the floor; Sarah knew Banks must have punched Aaron, and the blow had caused him to drop to the ground.

"The guard said two people came in, and no one's left," Dale said. "Care to try again?"

Sarah reached the tower adjacent to Aaron; she found enough of a gap before the next tower to peek in on the scene. She pressed her eye to the narrow slit just in time to see Banks press the bottom of his shoe against Aaron's face and push it into the floor, hard.

"Fuck. You," Aaron replied, and Sarah turned away from the slit and winced. She knew more pain was about to be inflicted on her friend.

Just as Aaron started to scream, Sarah's phone began to vibrate in her back pocket. She rushed to silence it, terrified Dale or Banks would hear it over Aaron's pain-wrought howls. When she yanked the phone from her pocket, quickly disconnecting the call, Sarah took a quick look at the screen. She knew, because of the extra digits, that it was of foreign origin.

Sarah panicked, convinced it was Mark. She felt, deep in her bones, that it was him. But she couldn't answer the call. She had to physically restrain herself from answering the call.

Putting the phone aside, Sarah turned her attention back to Aaron.

"What did you find?"

"I don't—" Aaron grunted as Banks applied more pressure to his neck. "I don't know what you're talking about. I'm a Pentagon programmer. I'm just performing maintenance."

Dale pursed his lips and shook his head ruefully. At his signal, Banks delivered a short, compact punch to Aaron's face.

"Tell us what you know!" Banks yelled, holding his fist above Aaron's face, letting him know it could be dropped on him again at any moment.

"Don't bother," Dale said, then motioned for Banks to pull Aaron up on his feet. "We don't have to play this game. I know what you know—but it doesn't matter. In about an hour, as I'm being honored with a lifetime achievement award from the DoD, the Verge software will go live. You know what happens then."

"Are you fucking crazy?!" Aaron yelled.

Dale smiled. A terrible, twisted smile. "I've never felt saner in my life."

Aaron shook his head, horrified, but he couldn't bring himself to say a word.

"Want me to get rid of him?" Banks asked without the slightest inflection in his voice. Killing Aaron was as pedestrian as doing his laundry, and it made a shiver run up Sarah's spine.

"There's not enough time to deal with a corpse and cleanup, and I need you here for the ceremony," Dale said. "There are holding cells, down in the basement. We'll store him there.

"But for now," Dale said as he viciously grabbed Aaron by his hair, "we have to smoke out Sarah."

"I told you she's not—" Aaron's words were cut short when Banks threw a punch into his side, doubling him over.

Sarah backed away from the tower, slowly, just as Banks pulled a straight razor out from his pocket. She couldn't witness what was about to happen next.

"Sarah," Dale called in a chilling, playful tone. "Don't make us do this to your friend. Just come out, and he won't get hurt. Now, Sarah."

Turmoil weighed her down. She tried to rationalize all the lives that were now in the palm of her hand against whatever agony awaited Aaron. The future of the country was relying on her ability to somehow make it out of this situation and share what she and Aaron knew before that knowledge, and their lives, were snuffed out for good.

She turned her thoughts away from Aaron and tried to conjure an idea—of where to run, where to hide. But even if Sarah could have somehow manifested an escape plan out of thin air, it wouldn't have mattered. Not after her phone's text message alert vibrated in her pocket, its muffled sound amplified by the room's silence.

Everything came to a halt. But then Sarah heard footsteps, heavy, hurrying down the row beside her. She was being pursued.

Being caught was an inevitability, but she had to take what she knew and pass it on, to someone, anyone. As she ran down the row, she took out her phone, and her heart stopped. She couldn't believe what she was seeing, but she had no time for disbelief. The message that had doomed her—it would also save her.

The message was from Mark.

"In D.C. Trying to find you. Where are you?"

Sarah attempted to breathe, but found it difficult. She zig-zagged between the rows, her feet slapping against the hard metal floor. She had to tell Mark what he needed to know, but there was so little time—time for Mark to save himself, to save her and Aaron, to save the country. She pressed her back against a tower, quickly crafted a reply.

You have to listen to me. It's Dale. He's behind everything. He framed you and the Verge software is bad. Has to be stopped. I'm in the Pentagon and he's going to catch me and take me to cells in the basement level. Mark you have to stop the software from going live. Whatever you do. I love you.

Just as Sarah pressed the SEND button, she felt her hair pulled back, hard, and her body following.

"There you are," Banks said.

They couldn't know Mark was back. It was the only thought that occupied Sarah's mind as Banks dragged her down the row of towers. Though instinct urged her to fight back, to do whatever she could in the desperate hope to break free, she knew nothing was more important than protecting Mark's return.

Sarah tripped over her own feet and dropped to the ground. As she fell, her hair still wrapped in Banks's fist, she slammed her phone against the floor. She heard the phone crunch as it met the ground, felt it shatter in her grasp. Banks didn't seem to notice or care. He pulled her back up, and as he turned, Sarah pushed the phone across the floor, sending it sliding beneath a tower. At the very least, she thought, she had kept Mark safe.

Dale shook his head at Sarah, as if everything that was happening was such a shame. She wanted to claw his eyes out.

"I'll be honest, Sarah," Dale said. "When we spoke in my office, I never dreamed you'd figure any of this out. But here we are."

"You're a pig," Sarah spat.

Dale shook his head, then looked at her with an expression of pitiful condescension. "You'll never know it, you'll never understand, but everything I've done, *all* of it, has been for the greater good."

"Mark trusted you, he believed in you."

"Knowing what's about to happen, from a certain point of view you could say I did Mark a favor."

Sarah lunged forward, but Banks got to her before she made it a half step in Dale's direction. He wrapped his arm around her shoulders and, as she fell back, she felt something hard jam into her back. She knew, instantly, that it was a gun.

"Take them both to the basement," Dale ordered Banks. "I'm going to celebrate my retirement by seeing the Verge program go live with my own two eyes.

"We'll take care of them later on, together. I want to personally make sure these loose ends are dealt with."

28

Mark hurried through the Pentagon's lobby, relieved to see his old friend, Private First Class Danny Rand, still working the overnight security shift. Danny wouldn't shoot him on sight.

Mark hoped.

Danny, however, didn't share Mark's enthusiasm over their reunion. Mark was halfway to the security barrier when Danny spotted him; he did a double take, nearly hard enough to give himself whiplash.

"Mark?!" Danny exclaimed. "Wha-what? How?"

"Hey man," Mark said, a smile on his face as he chewed the distance between them. "I know this seems strange, but it's totally fine. I can explain."

Danny stepped out from his station, his right hand hovering over the gun holstered at his waist. Not gripping it, not yet, but close enough.

"I need you to back off, Mark. Right now."

Mark almost felt bad. He knew the only reason Danny hesitated was because of his personal connection to Mark. It's much easier to shoot—or even arrest—someone you don't know. And Mark used that hesitation. Before Danny could decide what to do, Mark was nearly on top of him—close enough to discharge 35,000 volts of electricity into his side, shot out of the Taser Mark had concealed in the sleeve of his coat.

Danny's body corkscrewed in a fit of convulsions; Mark wrapped his arms around the unfortunate PFC and helped ease him to the ground. There was no telling if anyone would walk in the front door and spot a national traitor standing over the body of an unconscious serviceman, so Mark had to act fast. He pulled off Danny's jacket and used his identification badge to open the security barrier. Dragging the young man's body inside the small security station was no easy task, but Mark managed. He relieved Danny of his handcuffs and locked him by the wrists to one of the desk's immobile legs. The guard started to murmur, his eyes fluttering as he broke out of his forced slumber.

"I'm sorry, Danny," Mark said as he stuffed a cloth in his mouth and wrapped duct tape around his face and the back of his head to keep it in place. Mark used the money he had remaining after purchasing his flight to get prepared. Taser, tape, a sturdy backpack for Gregori's laptop, new clothes—he was as ready as he could hope to be. And now he had a gun, lifted out of Danny's holster.

All he needed, now, was to blend in.

With no amount of shame—Mark was well beyond that point—he stripped Danny of his well-pressed pants. "I guess it won't do either of us any good to apologize again. But believe it or not, I'm the good guy here."

Mark stepped out of the security station, dressed in the fatigues, equipped with full security clearance and a loaded Beretta. His time in Russia, Mark mused, had taught him *a lot*.

What it hadn't taught him, though, was where these underground cells were. For that, he'd have to use the skills he'd relied on in his previous life. Meaning, he'd have to bullshit. And he'd have to do it fast, before someone found Danny handcuffed in his skivvies.

Mark roamed the Pentagon, asking whoever he encountered about basement access. The best response he got was a laugh, like he was playing a prank. Everyone else arched an eyebrow at him and admitted they had no idea before moving right along. Mark's concern over finding this clandestine location grew with every puzzled expression, and he worried he'd soon be left with no other option but to run around the Pentagon, checking every door. Which might attract suspicion. He was on the cusp of giving up hope when he queried a grumpy sergeant who Mark could read as clear as day: He knew the basement existed, and he knew how to get there.

"Why do you ask, Private?" the sergeant tersely inquired.

"I've been asked to retrieve some materials from storage, Sergeant," Mark responded.

"I'm not sure I know of any basement level," the sergeant said, failing dismally at being coy. "Who sent you to find it?"

"General Hodges, Sergeant," Mark said. "I thought I knew what he meant when he asked me to retrieve his materials, but I was mistaken."

The sergeant grumbled. "What kind of materials, Private?"

"I'm afraid I'm unauthorized to say, Sergeant."

The sergeant eyed Mark suspiciously, but Mark knew his cover story was impossible to refute. No one wanted to obstruct Hodges, especially on something that seemed so trivial. "Take the east stairwell. There's a door at the very bottom of the stairs. Take that door to the basement."

"Thank you, Sergeant," Mark said with a grateful smile, then went on his way, fighting the impulse to sprint. He thought of nothing but Sarah as he hurried to the stairway, suppressing the impulse to fear the worst. At the moment, he didn't care about Dale or whatever the hell he was up to with the Verge software. There was only his wife and getting to her in time.

If he didn't save Sarah and their unborn child, all of this, everything he'd fought for, risked his life for, would have been for nothing.

* * *

Mark hugged the twisting rock wall that led down into the Pentagon's depths. His gun held tight in his hands, he proceeded with caution; for all he knew, Dale could have a militia waiting down there, ready to overthrow the government. A month ago, Mark would have laughed his ass off at the idea of Dale leading a revolution, or whatever it was that he was up to. Now? Nothing could shock Mark. Nothing was so outrageous that he'd discount it as a possibility. Whatever awaited Mark at the bottom of the stairwell, he was ready for it.

But, for the first time since he broke out of the Russian hospital—which felt like years ago—Mark wasn't confronted by one worst-case scenario after another. Instead, Mark found himself staring at what had kept him alive the entire time.

Sarah.

Mark bolted off the stairs, hurrying to the freestanding cell Sarah was confined in at the other side of the room.

"Mark?" Sarah said, incredulous. Then she said his name again, this time on the cusp of erupting into tears.

"Sarah," Mark softly said, repeating her name three, four times as he pushed his hands into the cell, caressing her face. Even as he overcame odd after impossible odd, Mark never thought he'd see his wife again. He never thought he'd touch her, hold her, feel the heat of her breath on his skin. Even in his most optimistic moments, he couldn't help but be convinced that his journey would end with him buried in a shallow grave. But here she was, and here he was. And nothing—*nothing*—would ever tear them apart again.

"*Mark*," a voice interrupted. "Mark!" Mark looked over Sarah's shoulder to see Aaron, of all people, backing into a corner of the cell. Mark hadn't even noticed him before, and now he couldn't focus on anything but the terrified look on his bloodied face.

Sarah pulled away from Mark, abruptly. Fear and dread erased all the joyful relief that had occupied her face just a moment ago as she screamed: "Mark, move!"

Before Mark could react to the warning, he felt a fist drive into his back, bringing him to his knees. The punch was followed with a knee to his face, and before Mark had even realized what was happening, he was writhing in pain on the floor.

"Well, if *this* isn't a surprise," came a voice above him. "Mark Strain, American spy."

He looked up to find a man—a muscular, seething man—standing over him.

"What, you don't recognize me?" the man asked. "Let me jog your memory."

Mark thought to reach for his gun, which he'd jammed into the back of his pants when he spotted Sarah. But the man was on top of him before he could move. He wrapped his hands around Mark's throat and squeezed, hard, like he was trying to pop Mark's head off his neck. Mark tried to gasp, but the best he could muster was a dry, painful heave. He was being killed—quickly, efficiently—and there wasn't a thing he could do about it.

"I was doing this to you when we first met. Remember? Me strangling the life out of you before I was so rudely interrupted?"

Mark's mind took him back to the morning of his abduction, when O'Neal and his team burst into his home. It came to him, almost like déjà vu. This man—Banks, Mark hazily recalled—with his hands squeezing Mark's throat, just like he was doing right now.

"No interruptions this time," Banks continued. "This time, you're all *mine*."

Darkness narrowed Mark's vision into a tunnel. Sarah and Aaron screamed incoherently to Mark, their voices starting to fade. Mark tried to shove Banks off him, but he was too powerful.

But then Mark remembered his Taser. Just before his lights went out for good, Mark had a vision of it in his pocket.

Mark reached into his jacket. His hand felt numb, and he had trouble gripping the Taser. His fingers kept slipping off the handle, unable to grasp it. On the verge of collapse, on the verge of the end of everything, Mark finally secured a firm enough hold on the weapon. There was no time to take it from his pocket, no time to aim. All Mark could do was pull the trigger.

The voltage tore through Mark's jacket and connected with Banks's abdomen. The Taser's jolt wasn't enough to knock Banks out like it had Danny, but the jolt didn't go unnoticed. Banks's grip on Mark's throat released, and after Mark inhaled three sharp, deep breaths, he pulled the top half of his body upright, meeting Banks face-to-face. His muscles still taut and uncontrollably shaking, Banks didn't offer any resistance as Mark pushed him away. Banks rolled stiffly on his side, and Mark crawled away.

Banks was already nearly on his feet by the time Mark's lungs recovered enough so he didn't feel like he was still being suffocated.

"You can't just die, can you?" Banks asked.

Mark knew he could never hope to hold his own in a fight against Banks. While he'd survived a lot to get to this point, Mark didn't for a second downplay the luck and help that kept him alive and moving. But here and now, there was no help to be found, and he'd be a fool to rely on luck.

Which meant Mark couldn't afford to mess around.

He jammed his hand into the back of his pants and came up with his gun. Banks froze in midstride, seeing the gun pointed at his chest. He smirked, even as Mark slammed back the hammer.

"And what do you think you're going to do with that?" Banks asked smugly.

"What I've learned to do, thanks to you and your boss."

In an instant, Banks's arrogance drained from his face. He

took a step toward Mark, about to charge at him, but it was too late. Mark pulled the trigger, and the force of the bullet reversed Banks's momentum. Banks was still upright, so Mark fired two more shots. Both hit the mark, and Banks was instantly on the ground.

Mark stood, ignoring the throbbing pain in his throat, and stepped cautiously toward Banks. He kept his gun trained on the dirty FBI agent, watching him with an unblinking eye. If Banks so much as twitched, Mark wouldn't hesitate to put another hole where one wasn't supposed to be.

But Banks wasn't doing anything other than writhing in pain. He had three bullets lodged in him, two in his thigh and one, as far as Mark could tell, in his kneecap.

"You're lucky I have a feeling your testimony might be valuable," Mark said. "Otherwise, I would have aimed higher."

"Go to hell," Banks spat.

"Where are the cell keys?" Mark asked, all business.

"I told you to go—" Banks began, but Mark had heard enough. He plunked his gun on Banks's head, knocking him out cold. "Always the hard way with you a-holes."

He searched Banks and found a pair of vintage keys in his pocket. He returned to the cell and opened the door, releasing Sarah and Aaron.

Sarah collapsed in Mark's arms, and he could feel her sobbing into his shoulder. She was seldom one for tears, but as Mark squeezed her closer to his body—as if he needed to feel her, all of her, to know that this was real—he felt the distinct warmth of tears forming in his eyes as well. Tears of relief, joy, and comfort. Every second of every day, since the moment he'd been abducted, had been wrought with either fear, pain, or anger. Mark hadn't had a moment of peace, and though he wasn't out of the woods yet, holding Sarah in his arms brought him closer to feeling like his life could make sense again.

"I never thought—I never thought we'd—"

"No," Sarah said, interrupting him. "I don't want to think about it. I just want this—just this."

Mark closed his eyes and sank into Sarah's shoulder. This was all he wanted, too. It was all he needed.

"Hey, uh . . . guys?" Aaron said. "I don't want to interrupt, but . . ."

Mark pulled away from Sarah and turned his attention to Aaron. He didn't want to let go of Sarah, not ever again, but he knew his work wasn't finished. Not yet.

"Dale," Mark said, finishing Aaron's thought.

Aaron nodded. "Yeah, he still has his finger on the button. So to speak. We have to do something about that."

"Did you know?" Sarah asked. "About Dale—did you know?"

Mark sighed, trying to shake off his disbelief. Even now, he struggled to wrap his head around whatever it was that Dale was up to. He believed it—he'd witnessed Dale's betrayal with his own two eyes—but the logic simply did not work. It betrayed everything he understood about how his world functioned.

"I knew he was the one who set me up," Mark said. "Him and an old-school Russian spy named Gregori have been scheming for a long time, using the alias of a dead oligarch to make millions in American contracts."

"Sergei Vishny?" Sarah questioned. "He's dead?"

"You know Vishny?" Mark said, taken aback.

"Yes, I know Vishny," Sarah huffed. "You think I've been sitting around while you've been gone?"

"No, not at all," Mark said, smiling. "Hell, you probably know more about all this than I do. Like about the Verge software. What did you mean in your message when you said that it's bad? What does it do?"

Sarah's expression sank. She shook her head and turned to Aaron. "Aaron, you understand this better than I do."

Aaron swallowed hard and explained. How the Verge software infiltrated the United States' deepest, most sensitive defense secrets. How it stole that information and disseminated it. Exposed it.

And that was just the beginning.

Mark nodded. He had only one question: "Where's Dale? You said he's here, being honored by the DoD. Where?"

"Close, I can take you there," Aaron replied. "The ceremony should be happening right now, and it's going to culminate with the launch of the Verge software."

Mark's mind was already piecing together a plan. "In that case, we're going to have to have this little ceremony culminate in a totally different way."

"That would be ideal," Aaron said. "But, like . . . how?"

"Easy," Mark said, "we just have to let everyone know that Dale's a spy."

Mark moved to lead them out of the basement, but Sarah stopped him. He could tell she was nervous; Mark, whose hands were steady as a rock, realized that he now took for granted how common this kind of high-stakes situation had become.

"Do you really think you can convince a room full of military and defense personnel of Dale's guilt—as he's being honored?" Sarah asked, trying to mask her doubt.

"I'm not going to convince anyone," Mark said with a smile. "Dale is."

29

The assembly hall was crowded with what looked like, from Mark's perspective, a collection of floating heads. He'd slipped into the back of the dimly lit room just as a reel highlighting Dale's career achievements began to roll. The attendees for Dale's momentous send-off were seated in high-backed chairs positioned in neat little rows. Everyone's attention was directed at a screen that hung just to the left of a stage that crowned the hall.

And seated on that stage was the guest of honor himself: Dale Schmidt. Mark spotted him watching the video with an expression of delighted satisfaction. It was an expression Mark couldn't wait to wipe off his former mentor's face.

Mark had to wait, though. He had a plan, and it was imperative he stick to it, regardless of how badly he wanted to rush the stage and deliver to Dale the ass-kicking he deserved. Mark fought back not only his impulse to attack the man who betrayed him but also the nausea the video elicited. To him, the footage felt more like propaganda and less a retrospective of a revered public servant. A clip of Dale being interviewed about the importance of supporting America's armed forces played across the screen, followed by congressmen and military leaders offering their praise and admiration for Dale's long-standing dedication and sacrifice. It made Mark's stomach churn. Dale was to them what he'd once been to Mark: a defender of American values, a sensible advocate for the country's military, and an ally to justice. But, more than that, Dale was his friend. Mark now knew it was all a lie. He had to bite down on his tongue and suppress the urge to act before it was time. He remained hidden in the back of the room while Dale—the man who'd laced a noose around Mark's neck as he plotted to sabotage his own country—sat on the stage, a satisfied look on his face as he watched a history of his own deceit. Everyone in the room was watching, engrossed. It was all leading to the very specific end Dale had meticulously arranged and, as far as he knew, everything was going according to plan.

But then the screen began to flicker.

For a moment, the audience respectfully maintained their attentive focus, acting like nothing had happened. The sound began to crackle, and Dale's trip down memory lane continued to break up until it cut out completely, leaving a white screen. Soft murmurs started to pass through the audience; Dale, on the stage, stood up and began to look around, searching for someone who could help.

Then, as abruptly as the footage stopped, it came back. Only it wasn't the movie that'd been specifically made to celebrate Dale's career before he rode off into the sunset.

Aaron was putting Gregori's laptop to use.

The video was a little grainy blown up to such a degree, but not enough to obscure what was being shown. Gregori—an infamous character most people in the room were very familiar with—waiting, impatiently, for something to happen. The guests looked at each other, puzzled, unsure if this was part of the program or something completely different. Even Dale, who doubtless had no clue that this exchange he'd had with Gregori was recorded, gazed around with a confused look on his face.

That look, though, quickly slipped from off his face when he saw himself enter the footage. His face wasn't visible yet, but Dale knew who he was looking at. Mark took immense satisfaction in watching Dale realize that he was on the cusp of being totally screwed.

The audience collectively gasped as Gregori and Dale detailed how framing Mark as a spy was going to make them rich. Mark could feel the unease build as the incriminating evidence continued to roll, and he knew it was only a matter of time before someone, in a room full of politicians and military leaders, acted. He just hoped they could wait until the big reveal. They had to, because the video wasn't going to stop playing. In the A/V room that controlled the assembly hall's projector, Sarah had Mark's gun gripped in her hand, directing it at the three A/V techs who oversaw the footage.

Dale wasn't about to idly wait for the spear that was racing toward him to bury its tip into his guts. Mark looked to the stage and saw Dale stand up from his seat, backing slowly away. His eyes shifted from the screen, where they'd been transfixed, to scan the crowd. Ensuring, Mark assumed, that no one was eyeing him as he made his getaway.

And that's when Dale spotted him—and then he took off.

Mark bolted after him. He darted around the stage and shoved an exit door open with his shoulder, following Dale's path. Behind him, Mark heard his favorite part of the video beginning to play, the part where Dale rationalizes his treason and reveals his face to the camera. And the entire audience. Mark wished he could be there to see all those jaws hit the floor, but he couldn't let Dale escape. Who knew what kind of connections he had with the Russians; with their aid, he might be able to disappear into the wind, and Mark would sooner throw himself in a gulag than let Dale dodge the reckoning he deserved.

The exit led Mark into a narrow stairwell; he poked his head over the side of the railing and was greeted by bullets flying at his head. Mark fell back and tumbled down a flight of stairs. The bullets had missed him, and Mark was grateful not only to come away with his life, but also to gain important knowledge: Dale had a gun. That tidbit would certainly color his pursuit.

Mark trampled down the remaining stairs, hugging the wall and trying to narrow the gap between himself and Dale. Dale had a good lead on him, and the time Mark lost recovering from his tumble down the stairs only helped to widen the distance between them.

Mark found every door on the way down locked until he reached the first floor. He kicked open that door and slid out, concerned Dale would be waiting next to it, ready to put a bullet in Mark's head.

When no shot was fired, Mark continued to race forward, though he didn't see Dale anywhere. He burst through the glass front doors, and the brisk night air hit him like a slap to the face. He frantically scanned the area, but he couldn't get his sights on Dale. He spun in circles, searching, gripped by the dread of what losing Dale would mean: Without him to face trial, or to at least deliver testimony, there was a chance Mark's conviction— or whatever it was—could still stand. He could still be branded a spy. After all he'd been through, Mark could see, with very little strain on his imagination, people claiming that the video showing Dale's guilt was inconclusive, or that it'd been doctored, or whatever. Dale, a U.S. senator, was a big fish; Mark was not. There'd be plenty of people invested in preserving the reputation of the entire government by denying the possibility that a member of Congress had turned coat. It would be a catastrophe, whereas keeping Mark on the hook, although possibly controversial, wouldn't tarnish the nation's soul.

As Mark tried to stop himself from fearing the worst, his attention was drawn ahead, to the sound of blaring car horns. He looked toward Washington Boulevard and couldn't believe his eyes:

Dale was zigzagging across the expressway, heading straight for Arlington National Cemetery.

Mark sprinted toward the boulevard and, with very little caution, raced into traffic. He knew if Dale got into the cemetery without Mark at least knowing which direction he was heading, he'd be gone. The grounds were too vast, and there were too many places to hide. Dale could lose Mark in an instant and be gone forever.

A horn blared and tires screeched as Mark made it across the first lane. Ahead of him, cars zoomed by, close enough for Mark to reach out and touch; he could feel their swift power as they passed, and it was terrifying. But Dale was already working his way through the opposite flow of traffic, so Mark didn't have time to waste. He sucked in a deep breath and exhaled it as he took off.

A car swerved behind Mark as he darted across the middle lane, and he could swear he felt it graze the back of his pants. His momentum kept him going, but the third and final lane was too tight with traffic to cross. Mark turned right, running with the cars that shot past him in a blur of glowing red taillights. He could hear their velocity, a rolling thunder that roared again and again with each car. Finally, Mark caught a break in the stream and threw his body across the final lane. He reached the barrier dividing the two sides of the street and gripped onto it. He couldn't believe there were still three more lanes to go.

Dale was just crossing the final lane of traffic, and that gave Mark little time to catch up. Which meant if he was reckless before, he'd have to be downright suicidal now.

Mark leapt over the barrier and hoped karma was on his side as he bolted into traffic. Just like before, but this time, there was no stopping.

He hurried across the first lane, ignoring an obnoxious horn blown in his direction, followed by a stream of obscenities. The second lane was clear, but barreling down the third lane was a semi-truck, and it was already howling at Mark. The horn sounded like a steamboat blaring in the dead of night, and Mark clearly understood its message: Don't even try it, idiot.

But Mark had no choice. He propelled his body forward, following his own momentum and pushing to move faster than he ever had in his life.

He thought he was dead. The semi's headlights engulfed Mark, blinding him as they did.

But Mark didn't break stride, even though he was convinced that his innards were about to erupt against the mass and force of the speeding semi. When he made it to the other side of Washington Boulevard, tumbling to the ground when he reached the shoulder, it was a shock. The rhythm of Mark's heartbeat lessened from terror to relief, and though he was panting, he peeled himself off the concrete. Dale was scaling the cemetery's wrought-iron fence, and Mark was on him, narrowing the distance between them as Dale struggled to push himself up and over.

Dale cleared the hurdle when Mark was only steps away, but just as Mark was about to jump up and grab hold of the fence, Dale turned and fired two bullets in his direction. His shots were wild, as Dale loosed both bullets with an awkward motion of his body. Still, it was enough to send Mark leaping off the fence, and it bought Dale some time.

Mark couldn't even venture to guess what Dale was thinking, if he was looking to kill his former protégé for self-preservation or if he simply craved seeing Mark dead out of spite. The last thing Mark could do confidently was predict what Dale wanted, and that made it impossible to predict what he was going to do.

Regardless of what Dale wanted, Mark knew he had to move carefully and quickly. He entered the cemetery facing a copse of cherry trees. Though seasonally stripped of their flowers, the trees were clustered far too densely for Mark's liking. He stepped past the first row of trees, knowing he was crossing a deadly Rubicon. Hiding somewhere amongst the trees, Dale was laying a trap for him. One of them, Mark was certain, wasn't going to leave this cemetery alive.

Mark did his best to search around every darkened crevice between and behind every tree before taking each step. He wished he had a gun, or even a jagged shard of broken glass. Anything he could use to defend himself. But he was back to where this whole thing started, stripped of everything but his guile. He listened for any kind of sound—maybe Dale's ragged breathing, or Dale snapping a twig as he maneuvered to spring his trap—that would break the night's silence. But there was nothing.

Until Mark heard a gun's hammer click behind him. Mark froze and closed his eyes. He wondered how much he'd feel of the bullet that was about to tear through the back of his head.

"Unbelievable," Dale said. "I knew you were a resourceful and relentless bastard, Mark, but *Jesus*. Escaping Russia? Making it back to the U.S.? That's no small feat. Too bad it all ends, right here, right now."

There were so many questions Mark wanted to ask. He knew pleading for his life was pointless, but deep down he didn't care why Dale had chosen to use him as a pawn in his plot. There was only one single thing Mark wanted to know:

"Why?"

"Excuse me?" Dale asked.

"Why did you do this?"

Dale laughed. "You think *I'm* the one trying to destroy the government? Let me explain something to you, Mark: I've been involved in politics since I was nineteen years old. And you know what I've seen over all these years?

"A backsliding into an apathetic, useless system of government, where men and women who are supposed to be the voice of the people will tell you, without an ounce of shame, that their top priority is to protect the interests of the moneyed elite who stuff their coffers.

"And when things don't go their way, what do they do? They threaten to shut it all down. It's their greatest dream—to get rid of tax regulations and safety regulations and environmental regulations so their corporate masters can run this country with no one to stop them. The barbarians are banging on the gate, Mark. Rome is burning. But no one wants to do a thing about it. No one except me.

"I've dedicated my *life* to this job. To this country. But I'm one of the few left who remember that this job used to be about building the government up so it could fulfill the fundamental role of serving the public. These spineless weasels—they want to tear it down? So be it. I was going to throw a nuclear bomb in the entire system and give them exactly what they want. And then, *then*, maybe they'd learn. Maybe they'd see the value in what it is we're supposed to be doing.

"Call me a traitor. Call me whatever you want, I don't care. Because I know that I was doing this, all of this, to save my country."

Mark shook his head. He pitied Dale, but he also felt a strange kind of empathy toward his former mentor. No one knew Dale's passion better than Mark, and as dangerous—and insane—as his reasoning was, Mark knew it was coming from a place of fierce love and loyalty. Dale did sacrifice his life for this job, that wasn't an exaggeration. Mark had seen him give so much of himself—sacrificing rest, relationships, his own well-being, and more—to the people he represented. To Dale, the job was a sacred vow. And Mark knew that having to live a life where he saw everyone betray that vow, so casually and so regularly, had to eat Dale up inside. To the point where he couldn't take it anymore.

The man who stood behind Mark, pointing a gun at his head,

he was the same man Mark had always known. Fundamentally. Dale had just been warped, twisted, and driven to ends he'd never imagined possible. Considering that, Mark understood one other thing: Dale wasn't a killer. He could scheme and plot, he could do terrible things that ruined lives, if it was all in the service of some greater good. And that was a far cry from pulling the trigger and killing a man—a man who'd once been close to him—in cold blood.

Mark counted on that logic as he whipped around, praying he was right.

And he was, partially. Mark spun on his heel and batted the gun away. Dale hesitated, just enough for the bullet to blast over Mark's head.

Mark screamed and charged Dale, forcing him back, hard, into a nearby tree. Dale groaned, and Mark used the moment of weakness to knock the gun from his hand.

Dale, though defeated, still had some fight left in him. Mark's wild swing had left him open, and Dale took advantage. He delivered a right cross to Mark's chin, following it with a couple of left-handed jabs that ended in a right hook. Mark fell back onto his knees, his head ringing.

"You never could just stay down, could you, Mark?" Dale said striding forward. "I had it all in the palm of my hand, and you *ruined it.*"

Dale drove an elbow into the back of Mark's head, and Mark collapsed into the dirty ground. Two kicks pounded Mark's ribs, then a third turned him over on his back.

"They'll never try me, Mark. The scandal it would cause—our country couldn't take it. Hell, our *president* couldn't take it. Not to mention I have dirt on nearly every single person who has the power to pursue legal action against me.

"But you?" Dale said as he dropped onto Mark's chest. He

drove his fist into Mark's face, and he could feel the bones in his nose shatter upon impact. "You'll be sent back to Russia. And what they'll do to you—you have no idea the cruelty and agony that awaits, you stubborn bastard."

Dale punched Mark again, and again, the second blow so hard that Dale had to shake out his fist. Mark's bloody head lolled to the side.

Through his blurred vision, Mark spotted a splintered tree branch on the ground, just past his reach. He stretched out his arm and could feel a sliver of its jagged end, though not enough for him to grab.

"Princeton boxing," Dale said as he closed his hand back into a fist. "And I still spar to this day."

Dale shifted his weight on Mark, and it was just enough for Mark to stretch out his hand the extra two inches he needed. As Dale was about to drill Mark with another combination of punches, Mark grabbed the branch and swung it across his body. It connected with Dale's face, sending him tumbling off Mark's chest.

All Mark could do was crawl away and hope clarity would soon return to his punch-drunk head. He was about to stand up and get ready for round two when he heard Dale charge after him.

Dale screamed as he attacked, and Mark had just enough time to sidestep his lunging body. They both fell to the ground, hard, and they simultaneously spotted metal glinting in the darkness in front of them:

The gun.

Mark and Dale sprang ahead, using each other's bodies for leverage to propel themselves forward. They scraped their way toward the gun and, as they did, Mark realized that Dale—who was in full control of his senses where Mark was not—was

316 • Michael Moreci

moving faster and would get to the gun before he could. Which meant Mark had to fall back on what had become his greatest asset the past few days: He had to think and adjust on the fly.

Dale grabbed the gun, but Mark was waiting for him. When Dale spun around, gun in hand, he was met by a fist that smashed directly into his face. The blow caught Dale off guard, and before he could get his bearings, Mark was already on top of him. Now, it was his turn.

Mark drilled his right fist into Dale's face, over and over, and he used his free hand to block Dale's attempts to bring the gun around. Mark buried his knuckles into Dale, thinking of the hell he'd gone through with each punch. His separation from Sarah. Having to kill Oleg, Viktor, Gregori, and the two other agents. Holding Ania in his arms as she died. All of it, every bit of anguish he'd stored inside, he released on Dale. He punched the man responsible for all of it until Dale stopped moving.

Still cautious, Mark grabbed the gun out of Dale's hand and then got to his feet. Just as he trained it on Dale's head, bloodied and battered, his mentor's eyes flickered open.

"Do it," he mumbled. "Kill me."

Mark had every reason to. Every justification. But he couldn't. Every life he took, even though they were taken in self-defense, made it feel like those souls were now clinging to his own, weighing it down. He didn't need another.

"No," Mark said, throwing the gun away from him. "I won't let you off the hook so easily."

Mark heard the sound of a dozen sets of boots swarm from every direction. He had a split second to see men in army fatigues, assault rifles at the ready, before he was tackled to the ground.

Mark remained silent, furiously so, as his face was shoved into the dirt and his hands were twisted behind his back.

And just like that, he was in handcuffs once again.

30

The sun's waning light shimmered off the ocean, sparking a kaleidoscope of color on its surface. There was no sound other than the lapping of waves on the white beach—and Mark's phone, vibrating on the table next to him. It had been ringing all day, and Mark was considering chucking the damn thing into the ocean. But he knew he'd just get another phone, and they'd get that number as well. It was best to answer and just be done with it.

"Hello?" Mark said groggily, as if he was just waking up. He wasn't; he was just that relaxed.

"Mark Strain," the voice on the other line said. "I imagine, right now, you're staring at waves crashing against a tropical beach. Am I right?"

"You are, Senator Griffin," Mark admitted. "That's exactly what I'm doing."

Everyone knew about Mark's settlement from Uncle Sam, which was as excessive as it was swift. Shipping off an innocent man in the dead of night without so much as giving him a phone call—let alone a lawyer and a trial—was costly, and it was one check Mark was happy to cash. After settling with Mark—and hinting they were not only making amends but also, hopefully, buying his silence, meaning there'd be no tell-all book in the years to come—the government did what it did best: It got in its own way. The Feds launched a probe and members of Congress delivered strong words about terrorism and Russian interference in democracy, but Mark knew it wouldn't go anywhere. In his own twisted way, Dale had been right. It probably gave him a lot to think about as he awaited trial in whatever federal penitentiary he'd been locked away in.

Mark got up from his seat. The hot sand burned his feet for the first few steps he took toward the water, but he got used to the heat by the time he was halfway there.

"Listen, I'm going to be blunt," Griffin said. "My team needs you. *I* need you."

Mark laughed. "Me? Okay, I'll bite. You need me for what?"

"I'm making a run at the White House in the next cycle, Mark. And I want you part of my team. You're determined, you're smart, and let's be honest, you're a God damn American hero."

"That's very flattering," Mark said as he stood on the edge of the beach, right where the ocean met the sand.

"My aim isn't to flatter, it's to recruit," Griffin said. "I know you, Mark. A man with your talents and drive, this is the role you deserve. This is the big time—I'm offering you everything you could ever want."

Mark turned his head; a wide, satisfied smile ran across his face. Sarah, standing next to him, returned his smile. She brought Mark close and placed his hand over her bare belly, which was beginning to show her pregnancy.

"I'm sorry," Mark said, "but I already have everything I want."

Mark threw the phone into the sand behind him and moved closer to Sarah. He wrapped his arms around her and placed his head over her shoulder. Together, they stood at the edge of the beach, the ocean's water dancing over their feet, watching the sun set.

ACKNOWLEDGMENTS

Every time I sit down to write my acknowledgments, I realize how incredibly lucky I am to be able to write books, and I get more and more grateful. I'm so lucky to do this, and have so much gratitude to the people who help make it possible.

In the case of *The Throwaway*, I owe a debt of gratitude to Phil Westren and Alex Tse, who trusted me to tell their story. Brendan Deneen, my amazing editor (who is also one heck of a writer), gave me the opportunity of a lifetime. Thank you all for bringing me into Mark Strain's world.

My agent, Jason Yarn, is never far from heart (or my in-box). Thank you, as always, for your dedication and guidance, both of which are invaluable.

My family, miraculously, has shown me so much patience through the ups and downs of writing a book and being a writer; I love you all, and the best world I create is the one we get to make together.

And, of course, you the reader. Thank you for taking this journey with me!